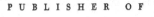

Alfred · A

PUBLISHER OF

Dear Reader,

Leila Mottley exploded onto the scene with her debut novel, *Nightcrawling*. An Oprah's Book Club pick and instant *New York Times* bestseller, the book received magnificent acclaim and international awards attention. The fact that Leila wrote the manuscript between the ages of sixteen and seventeen boggles the mind. But the real testament to her talent is the novel itself: electric and alive and achingly true.

That Leila has already returned with a new novel—one that surpasses even the impossibly high bar she set for herself with *Nightcrawling*—is further evidence of her outsize talent.

*The Girls Who Grew Big* is brimming with life. Leila has given us not just one voice but three: Simone, Adela, and Emory each leap off the page in inimitable, fierce, and joyous ways. I doubt you will ever look at teenage mothers—or the Florida panhandle—the same way again. This piercing, uplifting portrait of love and friendship will leave your heart full.

It is a privilege to reintroduce you to one of the most unique, fearless writers of our moment. To quote Kiese Laymon, who said it perfectly: Get ready. Or don't. It doesn't matter. Leila Mottley is here.

Yours,

Diana Tejerina Miller
VP, Executive Editor

# Praise for Leila Mottley's
## NIGHTCRAWLING (2022)

A Best Book of the Year:
*The New Yorker, The Washington Post, Los Angeles Times,
San Francisco Chronicle, Time,* NPR, Minneapolis *Star Tribune*

Winner for First Fiction at the California Book Awards • Winner for Fiction at the Northern California Book Awards • Finalist Lambda Literary Award • Finalist Hurston/Wright Legacy Award • Longlisted Booker Prize • Longlisted Center for Fiction First Novel Prize • Longlisted PEN/Hemingway Award for Debut Novel

"Dazzling and electrifying. . . . A spellbinding story and a
*Catcher in the Rye* for a new generation."
—Booker Prize Judges 2022

"Revelatory. . . . My god—that voice."
—Ron Charles, *The Washington Post*

"Searing. . . . An intimate portrait of a young Black woman
searching for autonomy and fulfillment."
—*The New Yorker*

"A fierce, lyrical debut novel. . . . Essential to understanding how
maddeningly elusive justice can be. . . . Mottley channels the natural prose
of everyday life, the way people and cities breathe and spit and shiver.
It is unflinching writing, the kind that soothes even as it strikes."
—Cassandra Landry, *San Francisco Chronicle*

"Mottley writes with a lyrical abandon."
—Lauren Christensen, *The New York Times Book Review*

"*Nightcrawling* marks the dazzling arrival of a young writer with a
voice and vision you won't easily get out of your head."
—Kit Fan, *The Guardian*

"Leila Mottley has an extraordinary gift. She writes with the humility and sparkle
of a child, but with the skill and deft touch of a wizened, seasoned storyteller."
—James McBride, author of *The Heaven & Earth Grocery Store*

"Mottley accesses the feelings one sometimes has while reading Dickens, the breathless sense that some massive unfairness is being inflicted on a good and innocent person. . . . [The] book finds its buoyant humanity."
—Sam Sacks, *The Wall Street Journal*

"*Nightcrawling* blew my mind and my heart. . . . A scorching, layered, incredibly readable book that takes seriously the task of readerly provocation on every page. . . . Get ready. Or don't. It doesn't matter. Leila Mottley is here."
—Kiese Laymon, *Poets & Writers*

"*Nightcrawling* bursts at the seams of every page and swallows you whole."
—Tommy Orange, author of *There There*

"Mottley's writing is electric and stylish, which makes her subject matter especially chilling."
—Kate Dwyer, *Teen Vogue*

"So compelling that one cannot put it down. . . . Through Kiara, Mottley gives voice to countless Black women and girls who remain invisible, vulnerable, and dehumanized by a system that deems them disposable. . . . We need Kiara's story, but more importantly, we need young writers like Leila Mottley."
—Karen M. Thomas, *Liber*

"Incendiary. . . . The captivating, distinctively voiced Kiara is a young Black American who can shoot hoops and skateboard, but her literary antecedents are Zola's Thérèse Raquin, Victor Hugo's Fantine, and Elizabeth Gaskell's Ruth."
—Patricia Nicol, *The Sunday Times* (London)

"Hard-hitting but never heavy-handed."
—*The Economist*

"With its powerful poetry and courageous, unsparing vision, *Nightcrawling* is more than just a magnificent debut novel. It is a bid, by this prodigiously gifted young writer, to heal a broken world."
—Ruth Ozeki, author of *The Book of Form and Emptiness*

# MARKETING & PUBLICITY CAMPAIGN

- Online Consumer Advertising Targeting Top Literary, News, and Lifestyle Sites
- Extensive Influencer Outreach
- Major Social Media Campaign
- Early Reader Review Campaign, including Goodreads and NetGalley
- Book Club Outreach with Reading Group Guide Available
- Backlist Campaign, including Giveaways
- Library Marketing Campaign
- Academic Marketing Campaign
- National Media Appearances, including NPR
- Newspaper and Magazine Features
- National Review Attention
- Most Anticipated Book Lists
- Women's Magazine Coverage
- Black Interest Media Coverage
- Extensive Podcast Outreach
- Author Events

# The Girls Who Grew Big

## A Novel

## by Leila Mottley

ALFRED A. KNOPF  PUBLISHER, NEW YORK

■ ON SALE: 24 JUNE 2025
■ U.S.A.: $28.00 ■ PAGES: 352

FOR MORE INFORMATION OR TO INTERVIEW THE AUTHOR
Tricia Cave, tcave@penguinrandomhouse.com, 212-782-8604
Micah Kelsey, mkelsey@penguinrandomhouse.com, 212-782-9000

# THE GIRLS WHO
# GREW BIG

# THE GIRLS WHO
# GREW BIG

## LEILA MOTTLEY

ALFRED A. KNOPF
New York
2025

www.aaknopf.com

Knopf, Borzoi Books, and the colophon are registered trademarks
of Penguin Random House LLC.

Library of Congress Cataloging-in-Publication Data [TK]
ISBN: 978-0-593-80112-3 (hardcover)
ISBN: 978-0-593-80113-0 (ebook)
ISBN: 978-1-52471285-3 (open market)

Jacket photograph by TK
Jacket design by TK

Manufactured in the United States of America
First Edition

*I reintroduced myself to myself, this time*
*a mother. After which, nothing was ever the same.*

—Camille Dungy, "Trophic Cascade"

# THE GIRLS WHO
# GREW BIG

# SIMONE

NOBODY EVER WARNS you about the placenta. Like, you spend days seizing and stretching open to get some shoulders out your coochie and then the baby, or babies in my case, are writhing in your arms, and you realize it's not even over. You've still gotta push out this pulsing purple heart bigger than your man's head—and my man had a big-ass head—and find a way to cut the cords.

I guess if you're in the hospital, then maybe somebody hands you a fancy pair of scissors to cut them or mentions the placenta in between the choke of contractions to get that second baby out, but I gave birth set up in the bed of my boyfriend's red pickup truck, so I wouldn't know. I'd tell you I did it that way 'cause I couldn't afford the hospital without no insurance, which was true, but really I just didn't want people looking at me funny like, girl what are you doing having a baby with this gangly man who keeps telling us to call him Tooth? I knew how it looked. I was sixteen. He was twenty-two.

But really, at the time, I didn't think it mattered any more than the birthmark on my ankle and so I didn't wanna have to explain to some nurse as I chewed ice that I love him, have to say, *They my babies, I wanted them, I want them,* even though at that point I don't think I knew what I wanted or who I loved or how I ended up in the back of a pickup truck in Florida giving birth at thirty-six weeks.

At least in the truck, no questions was asked. Except, why didn't nobody tell me about the placenta? I thought it would come out with the rest of that fluid, but nope, I had to do all the work while Tooth just stared at me, repulsed.

The twins was still attached to the fleshy heat of my body, slippery and smaller than one of his shoes, and I'd passed them to Tooth when I felt the faint cramps begin and knew I had to push one more time, maybe twice 'cause I'd been told there was two placentas up in there. But now Tooth was tryna give the babies back like they wasn't half him, holding them out to me like grocery bags with the handles torn off.

"Should we go to the hospital?" Tooth asked, trying not to look between my thighs even though I saw his eyes drift there and shoot back up, his lashes fluttering in disgust.

I didn't respond, mid-push, and then one soft big placenta slipped right out, two cords dangling from it, and I glared up at Tooth. "You think after all that, I'm about to go to the hospital now? No."

I didn't care none about the mess or the fact we ain't known what we was doing, 'cause all those months of torment—when I'd been stretched out like an old sock by a big foot, expelled from the only family I'd known, whispered about among the throngs of a town high on contempt—was suddenly worth something. My babies.

I was exhausted, but I knew I couldn't rest yet. "We have to cut the cords."

"I think I got my pocketknife," Tooth said.

He reached into his back pocket and pulled out the dirtiest pocketknife you'd ever seen, popped the blade and it was all crusted in dried brown blood, shed fur from some long-dead animal, and Lord knows how many fishes' yellowed intestines.

"Where do I cut it?" he asked.

I looked at him. He stared back.

"Are you fucking with me? You can't cut 'em with that," I said.

"Why?"

I gawked. "It's *dirty*."

"So is that thing," he said, nodding to my placenta.

"That thing fed your children for nine months. I'm not cuttin' nothing with that."

"Then what you gonna do?"

I looked around again, like I was gonna find some spare scissors among the pooling fluid, and then I looked back at the placenta, and I knew. This was the moment I became a mother, when I was the only person in the world that knew what needed to be done to keep my babies safe, to excavate myself just to feed them.

"I'll bite it," I said.

Tooth's face twisted up like I'd just said I was gonna eat my own shit. "The fuck you talkin' 'bout? I'll go find another knife, just stay here and—"

Before he could do nothing, I had one cord in my mouth and I was gnawing. It didn't take much work before my teeth found each other and then I tied it and moved to the next cord and my teeth ripped through that too. I expected them to be chewy, dense, but they felt like nothing but pasta before it's cooked through. And then it was done, both cords severed.

The babies now fed on breast and body, each of their little mouths searching my skin for nipple. My girl found it first, and she was lucky 'cause my right breast had been leaking for days and was ready for her, far more full than the left one, so when she latched, the yellowish liquid came out thick and spilled right into her mouth. My boy kept searching but he was stuck around my heart, and he turned his head and opened his mouth wide and let out a roar. With a new fever, he continued until he found his life source and I helped get it in his small mouth.

I gazed down at my children, amazed, both of them latched to my titties and feeding, then I turned to look at my now-cut cords, still and white, and finally back to Tooth. I was grinning. His mouth was warped with loathing but I didn't care none. I shoved him with my foot.

"Look! They so perfect. Ain't they so perfect?"

He tilted his head, tried to shake the repulsion from his face, pocketknife still in hand, and sighed. "Yeah. They perfect."

• • •

To tell you the truth, I didn't know much of nothing back then, sitting in that pickup truck staring at my placenta. How could I? Not 'cause I was young, but 'cause I was new. Like my newborn babies, skin so soft it seemed like they could tear open at any moment, I was just a fragile thing in a sharp world, like every other girl is before they meet themselves, before they meet their child and know what it means to give.

I already know y'all will take any chance you get to say we don't know what we talking about, I've seen all the *Teen Mom* shows, but that's not what I'm saying. All those shows get made just to give y'all some white girls to laugh at, pity, and say they should've known better, but really maybe you should've known better than to believe a camera is a mirror or an ocean is a pool or a mother is anything but a mother. You won't know till you know, and now I do.

So that's gonna make it even harder for you to understand why, four and a half years after I gave birth in the back of a pickup truck, I found myself squatting in the ocean pissing on another stick.

I'll put it this way: teen moms, like Florida, are the country's favorite scapegoat. Your favorite niece got addicted to fentanyl and is living with her boyfriend's grandpa? At least she's not a teen mom. You got laid off and have to move back to your parent's house in Colorado? At least it's not the hellhole they call Florida. Your daughter's a lesbian? But she's not pregnant! Got hate-crimed? But it'd be worse in Florida!

I'm from Florida and I was sixteen when I had my kids, so take it from me, it's not a golden walk down a yellow brick road or nothing. But we don't exist to calm your woes that at least your shitty life could be shittier. I love my kids. I spend my days rolled out in the sun in a little town called Padua Beach and I wouldn't have it no other way. Or maybe I would, but wouldn't we all? Grass is always greener. Ocean looks so much bluer from far away.

They say that in Florida, you go north and you get South, the Panhandle being the most South you could get in the Sunshine State. Padua Beach being one of those towns on the Panhandle coast nobody bothers to stop in on their way to the only thing that warrants a trip down to Florida: spring break and retirement.

Us Girls didn't think about ourselves like that, though.

Sure, our accents slung themselves into the room 'fore we even made it through the door and we ain't needed more than one trash bag to stuff all the clothes we owned in, but that wasn't all we was. We was more than South, more than Florida, more than sea. Don't be foolish, thinkin' Padua Beach was just some coastal blip on the way somewhere bigger and better. We big on our own. And the Girls and me only made it bigger.

The Girls began the way all things do: in the seething foam of a wave spitting us to shore. Me first, then each of the Girls following. One after the other, cast off by the venom of a town built on *y'all being good now?* and *babies havin' babies,* said in the rasp of a loud whisper and one polite little shake of the head. We found each other from our singular aloneness, made family out of a truck bed and the milky delight of watching our babies grow through the fog of distant shame.

I wasn't the first one, that's for sure. Young girls been having babies as long as there was babies to have. Meaning, forever. Not even a hundred years ago, nobody woulda batted an eye at me and my children, but things had changed. Somewhere along the walk of history, somebody decided we was a transgression to all things good and pure, and ever since then, despite the fact there's less of us now than there was a decade ago, politicians and pastors and regular folk always talkin' 'bout preventing teen pregnancy and poverty and sin, all in the same boastful breath. As though that's all we was. As though the pace our skin stretched and spotted defined our motherhood.

But before we were an us, before we merged into one glorious sea, we were just our own sad drops of water in a cavernous basin of thirst. And I was the very first pellet of water, or at least that's how it felt.

What the town would inevitably call a gang of teen moms who lost our way started as the day I needed to wash my panties. I won't go into detail or nothing, I'm still my momma's daughter after all, but those first six months of motherhood had turned my coochie into a swampland. I grew up in a house on top of some cinder blocks most people would call a trailer so I was used to cleaning some clothes without a washer or dryer.

All I had now was the dune lake. It was a miracle, the way stream and sea connected in one big crater of water. Mostly fresh water until some storm came along and rearranged its molecules with the flood, but the lake knew how to clean itself, emptied out into the Gulf and welcomed us back, to splash and fish and fling into her shallows.

I drove out to the dune lake on a Sunday morning, thinking most folks would be at church, and parked the truck a few feet from where the cypress tree bowed to the ground, worshipping the earth it came from. The babies slept on a blanket in the truck bed, face-to-face, while I crouched in the lake washing all their clothes and burp cloths.

Once the twins' clothes was hung up to dry, I switched to washing my panties. I was tryna get a stain outta my only white pair of panties, the rest already on the clothesline, when I felt the familiar quake of footsteps. I turned, ready to grab the babies and start the engine going, leave my clothes there if I had to, but instead of a ranger or a man, it was a girl.

I knew her. I knew everyone in this town. Lucille Calder. She was still wearing her church clothes, her dress just past her knees, her shoes flat as the Florida terrain.

I could tell she was hesitant to get any closer to me. With what she'd prob'ly heard about me, I couldn't blame her. I was an example of who she shouldn't become, and any girl who had some sense would run at the sight of me.

I pulled out my phone and saw the time. "Service ain't even over."

Lucille glanced out at the water and that's when I saw she'd been crying.

"Can . . . Can I tell you a secret?" she whimpered.

This is how all family's created. Confession. A yearning to release. Somewhere to place your shame and have it wrapped up, coddled, and cradled like an infant who don't have words yet to explain all the ways the world haunts them.

"You seen my panties, so can't be much worse than that." We both laughed. A Padua Beach lady could show her swimsuit bottoms, ass cheeks rippling and all, but the minute you get a flash of a polka-dot granny panty, she might as well be a whore.

Lucille took a breath. "I'm pregnant."

Those words would become so familiar to me they sounded like church bells echoing inside me long after they stopped ringing. Lucille was the first in a long line of Girls to join me, shaming the town for shaming us with nothing but our smiles and our shimmies.

They'd all go back and forth, spending nights with parents, boyfriends, cousins, and then in the back of my red truck, where we all found solace, took turns holding each other's children, and washed our panties together under the crude sun that loved us. I taught them how to rid a child of gas, how to fish a pebble from their mouths, how to cure mastitis. They taught me family could be something tender and loud and boundless.

This was how the Girls began.

Now, at almost twenty-one (I'd be counting down the days, 'cept nobody cards here), we'd cycled through over fifteen Girls. That August before everything changed, it was me, Emory, Tori, Crystal, April, and Jamilah. I liked these ones, 'specially Crystal 'cause she was older and had some more sense than the rest of them. And, of course, Emory, being my little brother's new baby mama, was family.

I pulled the pregnancy test from the back pocket of my shorts, the box at the bottom of some trash can behind the Tom Thumb gas station on the very edge of Padua Beach. I looked at it and all I could think was, *This shit can't be happening again.* I didn't have no excuses this time. I knew it all, the way all these other Girls thought they did up until they really learned.

I'm not saying I don't love my babies or that I'm not happy with my life or that some of the Girls ain't wanted to have another kid after their first. I get why they would.

But not me. The Girls were the something I lived for, and Luck and Lion were my biggest hope, watching them get older and start saying shit more profound than anything I ever thought in my life. Really, I didn't have a purpose till they showed up and, a lot of the time, I think they saved my life.

But another one? Another one would ruin it.

A new baby would set me back five years and, more than that, it meant I might be too tired to keep trying to give my children something beyond Padua Beach.

Not to mention, another baby would tie me to Tooth. I knew I was already stuck with him, after the twins, but it would be different if we had another. It wouldn't just be a mistake no more.

He'd think I was his forever, just when I was starting to think I might not want to be.

So that's why, when I shook the pregnancy test dry, pulled up my shorts, and turned to look at it in the glare of the moon, I felt like I had when I realized I'd have to birth the placenta; aching with dread, 'cause I already knew what it was gonna say.

The lines showed magenta. Pregnant.

I was twenty. He was twenty-seven. Maybe that sounds just about the same to y'all, but to me, everything was different. And that was before the new Girl showed up, before the storm that would be the next nine months, before everything changed. But maybe it already had.

# FIRST TRIMESTER

OUR WHOLE LIVES, *all we'd been was blurs. Flashes in a story that was always about somebody else. So it's only right we tell you this in parts, give you our stories as variegated as the moss we lay our backs on in the sacred moments we get to sleep. We rotate, ripple, revolve, so you can't know one of us without knowing all of us, love one of us without loving the metal scrape of the truck we found, gave, claimed life inside.*

*Judge us if you want, but first you have to witness us contort and expand. First you have to watch us become. Then, when you have seen the war we wrestled just to be here, the lives we created out of the void of this place, you can decide whether you want to talk to us about how we were too young, too ravenous, too susceptible to grief. But we bet, once you look out across the water we drank from, you'll decide we were exactly what we always said we'd be. Girls. Mothers. Big, small, endless. But first, we were this:*

*Nothing, and then the itchings of a new thing grasping for life. We sense the presence before our bodies register it as a cell worth multiplying. Dry heaving, nausea, a burning heart begins, pulling us in like a foaming wave before spitting us out onto the shore, convincing us it had never meant to hurt, that the water was a friend and our bodies were in fact our own, only to suck us in again. Breasts that had not yet caused an aching in the shoulder blades that most of our mothers knew well soon swell, areolas doubling in size, and us Girls touch them tenderly in the heat of night, like bruised fruit.*

*Somewhere in these first thirteen weeks, each of us will pause—perhaps in the middle of solving for the area of an isosceles triangle in geometry class or scooping mashed potatoes onto plates in our mothers' kitchens or mid-fuck in the twin bed of a boy we aren't sure we like, when we have to cup our titties just to keep them from throbbing as he thrusts—and we will realize what is taking place inside us. Will know, with an undeniable certainty, that we are sharing our bodies with this foreign thing, that it is—in this very moment—expanding.*

# ADELA

I WASN'T FROM this town and, frankly, I didn't want to be here. What sixteen-year-old girl wants to live out her golden years in a poor beach town in Florida, of all places, sharing a shack with her grandmother?

I certainly didn't, and I knew Dad would say *Adela, these are the consequences of your actions* in this taut voice that was just a veil for what he really sounded like. Southern. Black. Florida. He'd always described Padua Beach as the last stop on a trip to hell, a wasteland of reckless men and guns. Dad described it as though there was nothing but polluted water and rednecks in all of the small town. The forgotten Panhandle of Florida that was better off remaining forgotten.

I guess it was the perfect punishment for my *situation*. That's what they called it. Mom and Dad decided they would stay back in our Indianapolis suburb, with the country club men still pleased to grab a drink, the other mothers thrilled to discuss how a blond beauty like Mom found herself with . . . Dad. Their reputations intact. My actions, well, consequated.

You'd think I'd started drug dealing or burned down a building with the way they talked about it. Unthinkable, unforgivable, unfortunate. But really, I was just pregnant. And, honestly, sitting in the backseat of my noni's car, looking out the window at a place I'd never wanted to be, I didn't think I deserved this, pregnant or not.

Sure, it was pretty. At least the trees were, wrapping around each other, making arches of Spanish moss that looked like open mouths, only to turn into a stretch of reaching pines. But then Noni took a left off the highway, away from the ocean, and suddenly we were on a strip of gravel and dirt and all these men in sagging sweatpants and wife-beaters slouched across the street without waiting for our car to stop.

I'd never seen so many other Black people in my life, not ones like these. They were gritty, and I was embarrassed to admit I was afraid of them. I knew I was part of them in some ways, but also not at all, and it made me feel small and out of place.

Another turn and I watched two women slink toward a porch with their stomachs hanging out, a piece of someone's tracks sweeping in the breeze like a tumbleweed. I wondered if it was one of those Girls' hair.

We passed the Girls on the way into town and, the moment I saw them, I knew they were ruthless. It was the way their lips spread wide to show gap teeth and tonsils enlarged in the heat of the air they'd fed on long before I arrived. Their hips already the shelved slopes mine were becoming, children running around and clinging to their shins even as each Girl placed hands to the inside of her thighs and popped her hips. Left, right, left, right. Faster and faster until the jiggle of their inner thighs matched the beat coming from the stereo inside the truck.

The Girls knew how to run wild and, at first, I, like most of this town, feared them. Children mothering children and never apologizing for it, the country's shame clear as the gloss of the babies' eyes staring up as they suckled on their mothers' breasts. I feared the Girls until the day I realized I was becoming one of them, that every week my skin was stretching me closer to the way they let loose. The pregnancy showed itself eventually and the Girls rubbed off on me like sand on wet feet, so I could not be rid of them.

But in the beginning, when I first caught a glimpse of them from the backseat of my grandmother's neon-orange Civic, I thought they were crazy.

Noni, insistent that I was still too young to sit in the passenger seat, flashed me a look over her shoulder, pointed to them dancing in the empty parking lot of the Baptist church, and said, "Those them Girls. Stay away from 'em."

"Who are they?" I asked.

She shook her head. "They what you gonna be if you don't got some sense. Droppin' outta school, running around with whatever boys would have 'em, popping out ten babies before they even hit eighteen. Ain't right."

And when I looked back at them, hanging from that red pickup truck, taking videos of each other with their old Samsungs like it was 2012, I saw it: the ones who pressed a hand below their stomachs, cradling them as if to relieve the weight. Others spoon-feeding blubber-cheeked children something from a jar held in the crook of their elbows. Another with a toddler on her shoulders allowing her the freedom of her limbs to swing in sync with the beat. All of them pregnant or recently birthed. All of them with the same youthful ripple in their cheeks.

I wanted to ask Noni if I wasn't already like them, but I knew what she'd say. I couldn't be like them; I was destined for something; I was so much more. After all, I would have said the same thing back then. Back before I knew the Girls.

◆ ◆ ◆

Panhandle Florida was a landscape of green and sky, unrelenting thick heat that made my throat feel soggy from the moment I stepped outside the car, hugging my duffel bag to my stomach, trying to see past the live oak leaves obscuring the house from sight. All I could see was a red door, which didn't surprise me. Noni loved anything that screamed.

"You comin' inside?" Noni asked, already pushing past the tree branches, holding them above her like a doorway for me to duck my head beneath. I rushed to follow, and behind the curtain of leaves, the house was in full sight.

It was low to the ground, a slight A-frame that seemed to want to collapse at its small peak. So few windows, shingles missing from the roof, a dog door that had been nailed shut. It was nothing I imagined, and I wished there was at least some kind of charm to it, but it was just fading beige paint and a bright red door, pillars that seemed to do nothing to hold the house up framing the barely there porch.

I thought it would be more spread out from all the other houses, would have been easier that way, to do what I had come here to do: hole up in whatever room Noni gave me, speak to no one, find a pool to practice in, and wait until I could give birth and go back home, leave with as much speed and downturned eyes as I had arrived. Maybe the child would even come early and let me off the hook before my seventeenth birthday.

It had only taken a week since my parents found out about the pregnancy before they'd arranged everything with Noni and put me on a plane so I didn't miss any more school, since Florida's school year started earlier. All because Violet DeFleur couldn't stand that I had a better freestyle time than she did. She knew I was going to be the best swimmer in the country, maybe even the world, and she was going to find herself in a state school dorm room watching me win gold in the 2028 Olympics.

She wouldn't admit that she snitched on me, not even when I confronted her the day before Dad drove me to the airport and left me there, but only the other girls on the swim team could have gotten into my locker and found the tests, told Coach, who called my parents in and ruined eight years of training in one day. Either that or Coach knew I hadn't gotten my period when I said I had and figured out the reason why.

Either way, I knew the minute Coach told my parents, my life was basically over. Mom and Dad met at a Christian college in Indiana and about the only things they had in common were their faith and me. I heard them fighting in their room the night after they found out, and Dad said the word *terminate,* which made Mom scream like her tongue was on fire, and the next day they sat me down and told me I was leaving.

Now here I was, in Florida, not more than an hour from Alabama and Georgia, in the liver of the South, and I didn't have any choices. Or at least, I didn't think I did on the day I arrived. Before I knew the Girls, before Florida became a solace and a punishment all at once, I wouldn't have expected to end up where I did at the end of those months.

At the time, I thought the choice was simple. Get this baby out and go home. But I had at least seven months of Florida life to live, a life that would cause my choice to blur, flail, and falter, and I had no idea what was coming when I arrived at Noni's house that day.

She took my duffel bag from me, opened the door, and led me inside. I watched her sneak a glance at my stomach. I wondered if she was surprised to find nothing there, not even a hint of a slope. She didn't say anything, though, let me take in the summer storm stirring inside her house.

Noni had lived alone since my dad left two decades ago and her house showed it. Overflowing, as if she'd never bothered to donate or throw anything out, instead piling every newspaper, magazine, and bill she'd ever gotten on any available surface. She'd filled the house with antique lamps, ones with beads and gems and embroidered shades that, if she ever changed the lightbulbs, would have surely blinded us.

"I like to go on into Pensacola to the flea market sometimes," Noni said, gesturing with a brazen pride to the worn furniture, the quilts stitched out of what appeared to be old bandanas, the box television screen the only thing void of dust as we wove through the living room and down the hall.

Noni pointed to a door, said it was her room and I wasn't to go in there, ever, and then opened the door beside it that revealed stairs leading me down into a basement. Here, beside tubs and boxes of storage, she'd turned the sofa into a pull-out bed and put sheets on it already. Floral ones, suited for a granddaughter much younger than me, like she'd expected me a decade before and I never showed up. Not until now.

Noni set my duffel bag on the bed and turned to me, pulling me into her chest, rubbing the back of my neck with her other hand. For the first moment since she'd picked me up from the airport, she paused. "My grandbaby. You alright?"

I let myself relax into her sun-worn chest, scent a mix of eucalyptus and dust. I wanted to shake my head into her chest, tell her no, I wasn't. I wanted to sprint up the stairs, out of the house, take her car and drive it all the way back home. But I couldn't. I couldn't let her know how scared I was, how badly I wanted to undo what I'd done and return to my life.

Instead, I said, "I'm fine, Noni. Thank you for letting me stay with you. I know it's probably not ideal for you, especially once I start, like, showing." I pulled away from her and went to my duffel bag, fished out a tank top and shorts to replace my sweatpants so I could change and go back outside, go anywhere. I had already sweated my roots limp and Noni's house smelled like cinnamon and age, and the only thing I could think about was how these missed months of training would ruin me.

Noni understood I wasn't going to confess to her, seemed to respect that and headed back toward the stairs, but before she climbed them, she turned to me and said, "I'm not embarrassed of you, Adela. For the longest time, I thought you and your daddy was embarrassed of me. Still do."

I looked over my shoulder, caught the sight of Noni's skirt hem flutter as she disappeared upstairs. I felt instantly ashamed to have said what I said to her in the car, when we drove past a group of people standing in front of a McDonald's, eating out of paper bags and cackling. *I could never live like that.*

I knew from the moment I said it that I'd done something wrong. Noni had been going on about how my dad used to love to go fishing out on the Gulf when he was a kid and the moment I said it, she quieted. Didn't respond or cajole me or tell me who those people were and which ones were distantly related to us, which I'd soon learn she'd say of just about anyone we saw in town.

After another few minutes of complete silence, Noni said, "The woman in the wheelchair's name is Carol and we have dinner after church together every Sunday. The man with the long beard, that's Lawrence and he's my daddy's stepson, so he's kinda like my brother, and we get each other somethin' for Christmas every year. And that restaurant"—I couldn't believe she called McDonald's a restaurant— "that restaurant is my favorite place to get some lunch while I'm at work if I'm lucky enough to have a little extra time and money."

"Dad sends you money every month," I said. "If you needed to buy lunch, I'm sure you could afford something healthier."

"Healthy? Baby, life ain't all about whole grains and calories. I see how you treat yoself, tryna get ready for all your little swim competitions, making sure you all lean, and I respect that, I do. But don't you go around thinking you better than us 'cause you'd rather eat some lettuce than something that fills you up, something your body knows as well as it knows the womb it came from. I promise your body don't know the difference between a french fry and a baked potato."

I hadn't gotten a chance to find a way to respond, to tell Noni that my body was an instrument of my sport, and it was important I feed it certain things. At least it had been important. Now I wasn't sure. I wasn't even sure my body was mine anymore. But before I could consider any of it, we rolled past the Baptist church parking lot and saw the Girls and all other thoughts flew out of my mind, leaving only them and that red truck.

So much had changed in a few short weeks.

I had been simply sixteen, about to begin my junior year of high school, succeeding in all definitions of the term. And now I was a thing to be hidden. Forgotten. At least I would get to go back, at least I would get to return as though I'd gone on a year abroad, looking tanner and older and ready for my senior year. The Girls would have nothing to return to but that truck and the McDonald's they all seemed to love so much, tearing up a french fry with their acrylics and plopping it into a child's gummy mouth.

I pulled the tank top away from the sweat collected beneath my breasts and climbed the stairs, found Noni at the dining room table hunched over a sewing machine.

"I'm going on a walk," I told her.

"If you take a right at the highway and walk a mile, you'll find the closest beach. Ain't very nice this time of year, but you prob'ly won't get bit by no snakes there neither." Noni lifted a hand and tucked a piece of her pearl-white hair behind her ear. "You be back for dinner in two hours. Time I feed you right," she said, not lifting her eyes from the fabric.

◆ ◆ ◆

I walked along the gravel road that was Noni's nameless street. I kept looking for a sign that would tell me what it was called, give me any marker to find my way back, but there were no signs away from the main highway in Padua Beach and every street looked the same. House after house held up by tilting cinder blocks, obscured by a mass of overgrown weeds and trees that threatened to consume.

I knew somewhere around here there was a bayou, one marked by bald cypress trees and a few lone boats on the other side of the water, but I couldn't see it from here. I couldn't see anything but what was right in front of me, these small houses and ground dusted in red dirt.

At the fork, I turned left, up to the main road. On the corner of the highway, in front of what looked like a dead trailer park we'd passed on the way in, a group of guys stood around a grill on the other side of the fence sipping beer. They grinned at me, looked me up and down as I passed.

After about twenty minutes of sweating myself into a damp droop on the edge of the highway, I saw sand. I'd never seen anything like it, the sand making mountains Noni said they called dunes and what had been trees on both sides of the highway turned into a tunnel of sand and weeds. Later I would learn there was a parking lot and an entrance onto the beach, but all I saw that first time was the dunes, and so I started to climb them. My feet lost their grip inside the sand, my hands turned ashy, and it took me ten minutes to climb to the top, but once I got there, I saw it.

The water.

Ocean not just in front of me but to all my sides, stretched out so it almost blended with the sky on the horizon. Clear but somehow murky. Even from far away, I could feel the sting of salt on my feet, the soft caress of warm water against my ankles. It was nothing I could have imagined before, not in the movies, not in books, not from descriptions of my friends' Hawaiian vacations. The real thing was grandiose, endless, pure. A magnificent green blurring into nothing, where sight could no longer comprehend her reach.

Sixteen and I'd never seen the ocean. I'd lived in artificial waters my whole life, thought I knew what it meant to absorb. To look out into blue and feel known. But as I slid down the dune onto the beach and began walking across it, my ankles aching, I was aware of how wrong I'd been.

A pool made you feel invincible, but an ocean did the opposite. It reminded you what a fragile thing you were, how every cell that made you up was nothing in comparison to the waves that could take you down as quickly as a bullet shot through your softest skin. And walking on the beach, that white sand fine as powder and squeaky, I felt, for the first time, how this small thing inside me could consume my whole being. How, in a matter of months, I would have nothing to hide behind.

I just wanted to touch the water.

I stepped into the first edges of it, surprised by its warmth, by how green it was, with some kind of algae floating around in it. After touching it, I needed to feel more, so I kept walking. Shins, knees, thighs, the water lapping at my skin, my fingertips grazing it, and as I breathed the sea in, I heard the sounds of them laughing, music booming.

I turned away from the water to see the Girls across the beach, up in that red truck again, and it seemed like there were even more of them than there had been when we drove into town this afternoon, toddlers crouched in the sand. I thought I could see one of them looking straight at me, but I couldn't make her face out, not before the wave came up on me and threatened to take me under.

# EMORY

I SAW ADELA FIRST. Out there, in the water. From the moment I caught sight of her, I knew it was only a matter of time before she was gone. Still, I wanted to know her. Needed to know her. It was like what Grammy said about our family. *We were always meant to end up here, Emmy, and you know why? 'Cause hundreds of years ago, some pirate ship sunk and spilled treasures all over the bottom of our sea and now the water shines emerald green for us and if that don't make us treasures too, I don't know what does. So even when we havin' a hard time, you just remember the world gon' send you some treasures when you need it most, even if it takes hundreds of years to see 'em shine.*

Adela was my treasure. Even before I knew what she would do to me, to us. Kai was only a few weeks old when I saw Adela for the first time, standing by the water. She was too close to the waves. Thigh-deep and turned away from them and that's how I knew she wasn't from here. Wasn't one of us. That's how I knew it would swallow her.

I'd never known someone not from the Emerald Coast. Well, that's not true. The summer before high school, Pawpaw sent me to go work on my uncle's farm in Georgia and I met folks out there, but they weren't much different from us. Same gamey mouths. Same curling toenails. Back then I thought maybe I'd own a farm one day. Thought I'd tend to the land, learn how to hunt, maybe build a giant house for Grammy and Pawpaw like the one we used to have. Before

Pawpaw got laid off and we moved into my auntie's house on the other side of the highway.

But now I wasn't sure that was ever gonna happen. Prob'ly wasn't. The thing was, I'd gotten pregnant at seventeen. I'd planned it, it was my choice, and, lately, I'd been thinking it was my mistake. I'd been his mom for three weeks and I would've done just about anything to reverse it. That makes me sound like an ungrateful bitch. I'm not. I just had a lot to lose and I always thought a baby'd give way more than it took.

I liked babies and I wanted to be his mom and then I was his mom and now I wanted all the other things and nobody told me you couldn't have all those other things just 'cause you had to carry a little alien around with you. And maybe that means I'm stupid, but I think it just means everybody else was lying about how great it was and they tricked me into thinking it would be something it wasn't and now I had to suffer 'cause of all those old mom's lies.

Plus, Grammy and Pawpaw had barely spoken to me in the three weeks since Kai was born. 'Specially Pawpaw, who refused to be seen with my baby inside or outside the house, and I even heard him tell Grammy that she wasn't supposed to help me neither, said if I wanted help I should have thought about that before I let that Black boy knock me up. Said this wasn't no town where you could just be out here mixing with the wrong kind of people.

The wrong kind of people. Funny, I thought. It was the only time in my life I'd ever heard Pawpaw talk about us like we were the right kind of people. Usually, he was always going on about the rich folks and the tourists who stayed down in the fancier beach towns, how they didn't care about people like us. But "us" didn't include my baby or his daddy or the Girls. And if "us" didn't include all of them, I didn't see how it could include me either.

The thing was, I'd always wanted a baby. Up until I had one. Most things are like that, though, but I didn't know it back then. Time moves fast as a coyote going after a hare.

When I was pregnant, things were good. Hell, I woulda told you I'd do it again and again. I'd spent those thirty-seven weeks Kai was inside me dreaming of his golden curls and green eyes and small dimpled hand wrapped around my finger. His coos as I held him on my hip and walked us along the shore. His pride as he stood, somewhere around five years old, two front teeth missing from his grin, at my college graduation.

I liked to picture later too, at Kai's high school graduation. I was hoping I'd still be pretty as a pepper, my skin without dips or wrinkles, hair still thick and dyed a seamless bleach blond as I stood beside him, towering over me in cap and gown, saying *This my ma* when people asked him if I was his half sister or his girlfriend.

It was gonna be a dream of a life. Like the one Ma had meant to give me when I was born. Before my daddy broke her heart. Before she got into some shady shit in Jacksonville and passed me off to Grammy and Pawpaw. I was gonna give my son a good life. We were gonna be happy as two pigs rollin' in the mud.

But then Kai was born. He wasn't anything like I'd pictured. Nearly as brown as his daddy, Jayden, and he was colicky and distrustful of the world. In the few weeks he'd been alive, everything I'd dreamed had faded with my stretch marks, gone almost translucent.

Now Grammy was giving me a talking-to as I leaked milk all over the kitchen, having lost my bra and shirt somewhere between the bedroom and the shower, somewhere between last night and this morning.

"You think I'm gonna help you feed him? What you gonna do when I'm not there, hmm? What you think I'm here for, to hold your little hand after you gone on and acted like some kinda whore for nine months, sleepin' with all these boys instead of doin' what you gotta do and marry the boy who done got you pregnant. But that boy don't wanna marry you, do he? And it's good too, 'cause you know your Pawpaw's not about to have him up in his house. So you want help, you go on and ask all your little boyfriends."

"Grammy, please."

I'd been crying since I woke up from another one of Kai's short bursts of sleep, trying to figure out how to get Kai to nurse. Since he was born, he refused to hook his mouth onto my nipple, so I'd been switching off trying to breastfeed and pumping, milk piling up in the freezer.

But then, a few days ago, my pump broke. And now my breasts were so full they'd turned rock-hard and begun to leak when he cried, which was all the time.

I pleaded with Grammy. "I wouldn't ask y'all for help if I didn't need it and it's not like I can call Ma, so if you could just buy me a new pump or teach me how to get him to latch, then I could—"

"Teach you?" Grammy scoffed, throwing a rag down onto the floor and using her foot to wipe up the milk. She was late for her second job at the Walmart one town over and I knew she'd hold it over me, but I didn't know what else to do. She looked up at me, smacking her gum between her thin teeth. "I am teachin' you, hon. I'm teachin' you to not go around openin' your legs to any colored boy who walks by."

"Grammy! You're not supposed to say that anymore. Just 'cause Jay's African American don't mean he's not a good dad." In fact, Jay was such a good dad it made me angry, how the first time he held Kai, he took his neck into the web of his hand with ease, like it just came naturally to him. "I just need a little help so I know how to nurse Kai for when I go back to school and I gotta come home and feed him real quick at lunchtime."

"School? Emory, how you gonna raise a child and go to school at the same time? Who gonna be stayin' with him?"

"I thought maybe you could . . ."

Grammy's eyes flared wide and I stopped myself.

Grammy shook her head. "And don't be asking me to get you nothing else either. Insurance only covered one pump and I'm not buying you another. Not my fault you broke it."

I nodded. The school year had already started but I made a deal with the dean that I could do the first few weeks online. It was September and I had to go back next week. "I guess I'll figure it out," I said.

"You a mother now. You don't got no choice." With that, Grammy left the rag on the floor and my tits still dripping and grabbed the keys from the table, slamming the screen door shut on the way out, waking Kai up from his first two-hour nap in his whole life.

◆ ◆ ◆

You have to understand, we're not what you think. If you're thinking me and the Girls are some kind of ratchet group of reckless teen moms, you clearly haven't ever had to learn how to massage gas out of a baby's stomach before you learned the basic laws of physics.

And if you think I don't make sense with all of them just 'cause I'm white, you wouldn't believe what happens when a girl these days gets knocked up. Suddenly, it's the most important thing about you. Suddenly, you don't have green eyes or a two-bedroom shack on Willow Street or straight A's in Biology. You are nothing but a young mother.

Besides, Padua Beach is full of all kinds of people. I could walk two minutes and be on a street full of African Americans, another minute and I'd be standing in a Filipino's driveway. We coexist here. There's even a couple of other mixed babies, but Pawpaw and Grammy don't understand that 'cause they're from a different time. A time when Jay and I couldn't hold hands on the same beach. A time when plenty of girls got pregnant younger than me and no one batted an eye, as long as you were married.

But it's not like that anymore. Now folks aren't shocked when we show up with swollen stomachs, they're disgusted. They think we're stealing their welfare and ruining the image of God. They think we shouldn't have been so stupid.

The smartest thing any of us did was join the Girls. I didn't intend to, said up until I was about thirty weeks along I would never be one of them, but then I began to feel it: the eyes shifting along the circumference of my stomach, whispers that traveled from church ladies to high school hallways, boys who no longer sought me out at the beach parties but found me in an empty room at school, asking if fucking would hurt the baby.

Nobody got it. I was used to that, though. I'd spent my whole life baking under a cruel sun, and even when I felt crisp, I still knew how to suck water from damp places beyond sight. I was from Florida, after all. I could survive any summer, pretend like I was made for this harsh heat. But things changed quick.

In the weeks when the pregnancy embedded and became real, one degree of heat tipped the scale and, suddenly, I couldn't handle the sun I was birthed beneath. I was downright dying. Felt like a tropical plant gasping for life in a drought, and I looked around and saw everybody else thriving, their leaves reaching for the sun like a toddler's outstretched hand, but I was choking.

I was tired of feeling like I was hanging in the trenches of hell with the devil. That's when I really started to pay attention to the Girls. They were boiling and burdened by the same air, but they'd found ways to irrigate, to stretch and assemble their own life source. They knew how to survive when you could no longer pretend you were perfect. The sun was theirs, the glory they glowed beneath.

When I first approached Simone, Jayden's sister and their leader, she took me on a ride in the truck that altered everything I knew. For the first time in months, or maybe ever, I belonged somewhere.

I hadn't seen them since I had Kai, though. The newborn daze kept me captive. Besides, Pawpaw said the Girls weren't allowed around the house. And, until today, I hadn't been able to bring myself to leave. But now Kai wasn't giving me much of a choice.

I'd been trying to get Kai to latch right since the day he was born, but even when I got him on my tit, I wasn't sure he was getting anything from it. It'd take an hour to feed him from my nipple and when I finally pulled him off, they still felt full. That was okay, though, because I had plenty of milk in the freezer and more coming every day. But with my pump broken and my tits swollen, I had to get him to eat or I was pretty sure they'd burst, so I went searching for my nursing bra and some shorts and wrapped Kai in his blanket, off to find the Girls.

• • •

Simone's always been the easiest one to find. Hard to miss her with those swinging blond braids that don't match her real hair at all and how she's always climbing up onto the top of the truck cab, standing and dancing until her twins start trying to climb up there too. I used to think she was crazy. Still do, but I love it now.

It's like when you're a kid and you go to the zoo, you think all the animals are happy as can be up in their cages. But when you go back, older, you start to see the glaze of those chimpanzees' eyes, the twitch of the gorilla's neck, and it makes you wanna climb into the cage and set them all free. Padua was full of caged monkeys, but Simone wasn't like that. She was free.

I found the Girls parked in the church parking lot off the main road. Took me twenty minutes of walking around town to all their favorite places to park, my thighs gone slick with sweat at first and now bumpy in red chafe. When I walked up, they hollered. Simone jumped down from the truck and strutted to me.

"Girl, you lookin' like a goddamn mayhaw bush, all red in the face and shit." Simone cackled and then reached out for Kai, her acrylics careful not to puncture the back of his soft neck as I handed him over. "Let me see my nephew. Hi baby, your mama takin' good care of you? She leavin' you with your wack-ass great-grandmama?" Simone cooed, and if I wasn't so tired I might have protested that no matter what she thought about her, she was still talking about my grammy.

April and Jamilah came up next, each with the other's baby on her hip. They were the youngest in the group, fourteen and fifteen, and ever since they'd met hadn't left each other's side, always making out in the truck bed when they thought the rest of us were asleep. I wasn't judging or anything, but it wasn't natural. They had kids and baby daddies and all they were focused on was sucking each other's faces. We'd all silently and collectively decided not to discuss it, to let them go on like it was some secret love when really it was as clear as the pines peaking in the distance.

"He's beautiful," Jamilah said, widening her eyes at Kai's face, as though he could see her pupils. He barely opened his eyes, except for right before he started crying. Sometimes I thought he was dumb. I didn't tell anybody, but it's true.

"Yeah," I said. "He won't eat, though. I've been pumping, but whenever I try to nurse he just cries and now my pump broke and my tits feel like they're about to explode and I don't know what else to do."

Simone stuck a fingernail into Kai's mouth and lifted his top lip, found his tongue, and moved it around. "He don't got no tongue tie. What's the problem?"

"I don't know." I was about to start crying again, but the twins came up and started pulling at my shorts and asking me to let them braid my hair 'cause it was so soft and straight. I didn't want them to start asking what was wrong and have to say everything.

Simone understood, nodded at the twins. "Go on and find the Goldfish in the glove compartment." The twins did as their mother said, running toward the truck, and Simone turned to me. "Take that bra off and let's get this baby some titty."

I followed Simone to the truck bed and she had me perch on the back, breasts drooping heavier than I'd ever felt them, leaking again. She handed Kai to me, upright, eye to eye.

"Make sure he's stomach to stomach with you, and you hold his head up with your thumb."

I did what Simone said and positioned Kai so I was really looking at his face, and he blinked his eyes open just for a moment, all
those lines like cobwebs around his pretty black eyes, and his mouth
moved just a little, like he was smacking those small lips, and, for the
first time since he was born, I thought he actually looked kind of
cute.

"See his hands?" Simone asked. I looked at his balled-up fists
squirming on his chest. "If he makin' fists, it mean he wanna fight
'cause he hungry. When he full, he won't make no fists."

I tried to think back to a time in the past few days when his hands
were open and could barely remember a single moment, maybe only
after he took a bottle. There was nothing worse than knowing he'd
been laying there most of the day, hungry, and I hadn't even known.
I just thought he was a skinny baby, that he didn't like the way milk
tasted, that he had colic.

"Okay, so now you gonna squeeze your titty and touch your nipple to the spot between his nose and mouth and then he gonna yawn
and that's your chance to stick it in his mouth. Try to get as much in
there as possible, above his tongue, and it should feel like a vacuum,
kinda. And then it might hurt for just a minute, but once he start
sucking you won't feel much more than a little tugging at your nipple, like when a guy be sucking on your titties. But not my brother."

Simone's lips squirmed at the thought. I laughed, remembering
back to when Jayden used to do that. Back when I was delusional
enough to think we were something, that the baby would bring us
close. I took a breath and went through the steps Simone told me.
For this moment, she felt like a sister. Squeeze, touch to his cupid's
bow, place nipple above tongue.

Just like that, I felt something I hadn't felt before. Like pricks
running through me and then this little fucker just suckling on my
nipple, like he'd known how to do it this whole time. Draining my
breast of all the milk that had nowhere to go before.

"It doesn't even hurt," I said, the relief cosmic.

"It's not supposed to hurt none, not more than your feet after a long day of walkin'. If they scabbin' and bleeding, something's wrong," Simone said. I'd thought the pain was just another punishment of motherhood. "Don't forget to switch him to the other one too. Look at you go, bitch. You joinin' the club."

I grinned up at her and I couldn't imagine a life without the Girls, without Simone. She'd done all this before and now here she was, twenty years old and helping me latch an infant onto my tit when she could've been anywhere else, could've married that man who got her pregnant five years ago and tried to do what so many of the Girls before us did. Reverse it all, cover her sin up in attempts to mother the way the whole town urged her to, while still whispering behind her back about what a fool she was to have ended up a mother at all. They wanted us to be anything but what we were.

There wasn't no way to satisfy the rest of the world, but the Girls didn't care whether I used cloth diapers or graduated or stayed with Kai's daddy. They lived on whims of want and need, nomadic and ravenous and naked in their hurt. We weren't nothing like what was expected of us, and, for the first time since my baby was born, I didn't feel like the sky was about to collapse on top of me.

Sitting in the truck, with Kai finally feeding, I wondered if Grammy was wrong. Maybe I could do everything I wanted. Maybe I could have it all.

April laid a blanket in the truck bed right below the sun umbrella they put up in the corner. I scooted back under it, Kai still furiously sucking on my nipple. A few of the Girls were napping with their children, but most were entertaining the kids however they could in the glaring heat or staring at me and waiting for me to talk.

"We haven't seen you in weeks and you're not even gonna tell us anything?" April asked after I'd been nursing Kai for a while.

"Don't have much to say," I told her, smoothing Kai's tuft of hair with my finger. It was always slightly matted with sweat, yet I never saw a drop roll down his furry forehead. Couldn't understand how he was hiding things from me already. How I would never really know all that was happening inside him.

"Where's your mans?" Tori asked, bouncing her son on her lap.

"I don't know. Ask Simone," I said. "Besides, y'all know Jay's not mine. He meets me outside the house to see Kai when Pawpaw's not around, but he's not allowed in my house and his family doesn't want me in his."

"My parents don't want me in they house either. Surprised they let Jayden stay, after what they did to me. When I talked to him, he seemed to think y'all was good," Simone said, each of the twins on one of her knees munching on stale Goldfish. "But if you want, I can tell him he best get rid of you while he still can."

"Fuck you," I said, but I wasn't mad.

I'd never had friends. Before the Girls, I hung around people that never gave much of a shit about me. Before that, it was just me and Grammy and Pawpaw. So Simone was more to me than just Jay's sister; she was my first real friend.

She was also the only person in the world who understood what Jayden was to me, how I had wanted him only when I couldn't have him, only for what I thought he would give me, and how, when I found out what he actually had to give, it was never enough. Simone understood he was family, like she was, but not the kind of family any of us wanted. He wanted me to be his confidante, his friend, his wife. I wanted him to be my escape. The problem was those two things were never meant to exist at once. And now I was finding out Kai was not the saving grace but the reality that had shaken us apart. Finally and forever.

Except it wasn't that simple. Jay texted me all day begging for time with Kai and, when I got lonely in the days stuck at home with a newborn, I'd respond. He'd show up in his white truck outside my house and swaddle Kai perfectly, comfort him like Jay was the shell

Kai grew within. Jay put him to sleep and kissed each of his temples, sang to him, and asked me a whole bunch of questions I wasn't prepared to answer about the color of Kai's shit and his cry patterns.

Then I'd take sleeping Kai from Jay's arms and set him on the dashboard and I'd scoot toward Jay on the truck bench, where I'd bend and give him a blow job until he came in my mouth. I liked it until the moment I swallowed, and then I wanted nothing more than to get away from him again.

That's how it went with us, over and over. I wanted him until he wanted me back. He wanted me and that made me want to run. We chased each other around this town, and we both ended up sorry for it.

Instead of telling the Girls all that, though, I said, "Y'all know it's more complicated than us being together or not. Besides, I have bigger dreams than Jay and his horny ass."

"Big dreams, huh? You gonna try breastfeeding upside down?" Simone pulled the braid one of her twins was trying to undo back and stuck it under her bikini top strap.

"No, I'm gonna graduate, class of 2024, as planned. And then I'm gonna go to college."

They all paused and looked at me. I don't think any of them had ever said the word *college* and definitely not after joining the Girls. Of course they didn't. It was dangerous to speak something so far from reach, to allow it to float through the air even if the possibility of it was moments from evaporating. Maybe already had. Even I had to admit the word felt funny on my tongue, like a stray piece of hair that was nearly impossible to find but could be felt in the choke of my throat.

But I was different. I knew I could do it. While the Girls wasted their days and nights dancing or doing nothing that wasn't for those kids, I was gonna live a big life. If I was being honest, I was just smarter than the rest of them. They probably knew it too, the whole town did, and as much as I loved spending time with them, I knew it wasn't my forever. I was gonna have more.

As they all stared at me, Crystal's daughter tried running across the truck bed but tripped on Jamilah's foot and face-planted. She didn't even cry, just stood up and started running again, until Crystal swooped her up right before her little legs ran themselves off the edge of the truck, and that's when she started crying. Not at the pain of falling but at the loss of the chance to do it again.

"College?" Jamilah looked at me like I was crazy. "You know how hard it is to raise a baby and be in high school? How you gonna go to college too?"

"Jamilah's right," Crystal said, finally getting her daughter to stop crying by pulling her shirt down and showing her her nipple. "I bet you won't even graduate high school."

"Yes, I will," I said. "I only have one year left and I've got good grades. Great, actually. Besides, if any of us are gonna go to college, it'll be me."

"So you think you're better than us?" April crossed her arms. "You're just like the rest of your family."

"No, I'm not," I retorted. "It's just, I got that scholarship last year for five hundred dollars toward tuition after writing that essay about beavers in the bayou, and my grammy took me on a road trip down to South Florida to see some colleges last summer, and Miss Luella from church says I have a lot of potential. Anyone ever told y'all you got potential?"

"No," Jamilah whispered. "But my cousins say I'm the smartest one in the family."

April cut in again. "I just don't understand why you're acting like you're better than us and you can't even feed your baby."

Grammy would've said not to throw stones when you live in a glass house if she saw me now, but I didn't care. I loved the Girls, but I wasn't about to let them dilute my chances of a respectable life. What

I was saying was the truth and they could insult me all they wanted, but that wouldn't change that I was going places and they were staying here, in this red truck, forever.

Simone pushed the twins off her and stood, climbing through the window of the cab and sliding into the driver's seat. She called into the back, "All y'all can keep fighting, but I don't give a shit if Em graduates or not, and she's my brother's baby mama, so I can't have y'all fucking with her. Now it's hot out here and the kids real hungry so hush up and let's go to the beach."

Without checking that we closed the truck bed or that the babies weren't about to start rolling, Simone revved the engine and pulled out of the parking lot, speeding to the beach, Kai's mouth still stuck to my left breast.

◆ ◆ ◆

I saw Adela the moment we pulled up on the beach, all the way onto the sand. She was impossible to miss. Not 'cause she was outstandingly pretty or 'cause her hair protruded from her scalp in a way no other African American girl down here dared to do. The thing about Adela that really got me was her shoulder blades.

I'd never seen someone with a back like hers, sculpted like she was made of clay. She held her shoulders down and back from her ears too, which made me think she looked kind of like she was staring up. Toward heaven or something. A girl like that, whose body looks like it could only exist created by the hands of another person, who held herself with an assuredness that told me she was of something else, it would have mesmerized anyone.

"Who's that?" I asked the Girls, but none of them heard me. They had turned the music up and started dancing again, laughing, and that's when Adela turned around.

She looked right at me. Even from this far away, I could tell she was meeting my eyes or at least the place on my forehead between them, and she turned her body even more so that mountain of a back, those dagger shoulder blades were facing the sea and her face was to me and that's when I saw the wave. It was a wave any surfer would've been envious of. A perfect curl. A turquoise that looked like dyed bathwater.

In a single moment, it wrapped itself around Adela and I thought she was going to disappear beneath it, wash away with the tide, but when the water pulled back as it always does, she was standing just the same. Looking at me. The only thing different was her hair, now limp and reaching her shoulders, water not inside it but sitting on top of it, the glint of each droplet shining in the sun's glare.

I watched her walk out of the water, slip on shoes laying on the dry sand, and make her way up the beach, where she started climbing the dune, until she was standing on the top of it facing the road, her back still strong, impenetrable. Her eyes still on me, until she lifted her feet and glided down the dune hill, out of sight.

I didn't know she was gonna be one of us when I saw her. I didn't know why I wanted to run after her or who she would be to me that first sighting, but I knew one thing.

Adela was important. A treasure that landed at the bottom of my sea the same day my baby learned how to feed, and who would become something to me in the same way he would. Slowly, slowly, morphing in front of my eyes until one day I looked at him and knew I loved him more than anything, until one day he was not a baby but a boy and then not a boy but a man. And by his side, by Adela's side, I would be so much more than I had been before.

I would be the sea itself.

# SIMONE

ELLING A MAN you pregnant with his child is like taking a bite of a tender peach. The only way to know if it's good is if you sink your teeth into it.

The first time I told Tooth I was pregnant, I didn't even know I was having twins yet, hadn't told no one else. I was scared shitless when I went to him, meeting where we always did in the back room of the bait shop where he worked, and before he unzipped his pants, I blurted it out. Dug my teeth in and waited for the taste.

I couldn't've been more shocked when he picked me up and spun me around, waiting for me to wrap my legs around his torso so he could squeeze my ass, whispering in my ear, "We gon' have a baby," and he didn't sound angry or disappointed or scared at all, so I laughed and said, "Yeah, we are," and that was that.

I was hoping everyone else would react the same way Tooth did, and that was my first mistake. You've prob'ly thought about how pissed you'd be if your baby came home from high school telling you she's pregnant, but imagine the other way around. A closed fist for a stomach, thinking about your momma looking you in your face and picturing all the dirty things you was doing. So I tried not to go in acting like I was making a death announcement.

Instead, when I told Momma and Pops, I had a big old grin on my face, trying to make my voice sound like all those women in the movies, high-pitched and exploding at the first syllable in *PREGnant.*

Momma slapped me across the face before I got the rest of the word out. Pops just shook his head and got up to throw my clothes into a trash bag and hand them to me.

"You not gon' embarrass me in my own house," he said, even as I sobbed on the fake grass mat outside the trailer all night, even as I begged him to let me back in the next morning, Jayden staring out the window at me at age thirteen, tears welled up in his eyes, but never standing to open the door. Never even getting to say goodbye to my little sisters, both of them six at the time, 'cause Momma told them not to talk to me.

At least this time telling Tooth, I didn't have so much to lose, but that didn't make me feel any less like gagging all over the McDonald's table as I waited for him, staring at my fries.

When he finally walked in, the urge to retch became even stronger, the way his cheekbones sloped and his eyes grazed over every other table even though I was the only one in the place. When he slid into the plastic booth across from me, all I could think about was how pretty he still was and then, as I looked closer at him, how age was starting to creep its way into his face.

Back when I was fifteen and he was twenty-one, I didn't know how old he was. I swear, you really couldn't tell. I just knew he was the pretty boy who worked at the bait shop and that every single girl in town would stop on by just to see if he was the marrying type. When we first met, I thought we looked like we was the same age, him and his baby face, but now I could see he was slowly wilting. Dusky patches growing beneath his eyes from staying up too late and forgetting to eat, skin dulling from that radiant buzz that made him look soft, suede. You had to look for it, but it was there. So I forced myself to look 'cause if I didn't fight to see his age, I would forget not to love him, and Lord knows how that worked for me before.

"Hey babygirl, where my kids at?" He took my fries, pulling them toward him, eating them three at a time.

"They with the Girls," I said. "Luck been askin' when you gon' teach her to surf like you said you would."

"She not even five, can't be surfing."

"Then you shouldn't've promised her," I said. It irked me, watching him munch on those grease-soaked potatoes, not having to deal with Luck sobbin' 'bout how he promised her, flailing on the ground and puffing up her lungs with more fury and air than I knew a little body could fit.

"So if you ain't brought the kids, why you make me come out here on my lunch break?" Tooth asked, still staring at them fries as he chowed down.

"I gotta tell you something." I tried to steady my breathing, calm down my secret hoping that he'd be happy, that he'd say he was waiting to tell me, but he was buying us a house with all his savings, and he wanted to take me and the twins home to meet his grandmama and he wanted us to be a family.

I know you wondering why I was still betting on a grown man who clearly didn't know better, but you gotta remember my hope wasn't just for me. It was for my babies. Part of me was still wishing on a dying tree that I could give them the family I thought I'd had before it all fell apart.

"Good," he said. "I got something to tell you too."

"Really?" Maybe it would happen. Maybe he'd step up and we could give Luck and Lion what they deserved. Something intact. Something sacred.

Tooth nodded. "I actually just got a new place, moved in a couple weeks ago."

My jaw felt like it might wiggle loose and separate into top and bottom. "You bought a house? Please tell me it got two bedrooms."

"Renting, but yeah," he said. "Two big bedrooms, up close to the shop, and we just got some mattresses from that flea market in Pensacola and we was thinkin' maybe we'd go in on one of them big flatscreens that cover the whole wall."

Like always, Tooth snapped my hope in two and I remembered who he was. My torment stirred.

"We?" I coughed. "You got a new girl?" I was ready to stand up and throw them fries all over him, slap him silly.

"Whatchu talkin' 'bout? I don't got no woman but you."

"Then who's we?"

"Me and my boys. All five of us workin' at the shop rented out a whole goddamn house, and Trey and Slim and I sharing one room and Ricky and Deshawn sharing the other, and I was thinking that I could have the kids one or two nights a week. Just not on no weekends, 'cause you know the boys and I like to go on out to the city. And not on Thursday or Monday neither, 'cause I can't be missin' no football games with the season just starting. Whatchu think?"

As I listened to Tooth, trying to make sense of what the fuck he was saying to me, the door to the McDonald's opened up and Missus Woods walked in with some girl with natural hair trailing behind her. Prob'ly some stray relative come down for labor day. I smiled at Missus Woods and she smiled back, but I knew she wasn't down for none of the Girls or me, since she was friendly with my momma and her bunch.

I watched over Tooth's shoulder as they went up to the register and ordered, and I almost started laughing in Tooth's face when I saw their food coming out and Missus Woods grabbed her burger and fries and the girl picked up a salad in the same little carton they usually put the fries in. Nothing but iceberg lettuce and three cherry tomatoes up in that salad, and the girl looked happy as hell, sitting down in the farthest booth from us.

"Whatchu think, Simone?" Tooth asked again.

I turned back to him. "What do I think? Here I am, thinkin' you might actually do something to make us a family like I been askin' you to since the day I pushed two babies out my coochie and now you tellin' me you want me to let the most precious things I got sleep next to some strange men I don't know?"

Tooth threw his fist down on the table. "Bullshit, Simone, you know my boys. It ain't no different than you leaving them with your Girls."

"Just 'cause they try to fist-bump me once every couple months don't mean I know shit about your boys. And it's not nothing like the Girls. I won't leave my daughter alone with some old men I don't know nothin' about."

Tooth's eyebrows knit. "What you mean, old? You know me, you know I ain't no kiddie-lover and my boys ain't neither."

That's when I understood what I'd said. Not just what I'd said but what I'd meant. I couldn't leave my daughter with some strange grown men like I'd been left with Tooth. I couldn't let her grow up thinking it was normal to be alone with someone who had learned how to drive a car at the same time that she was still pissing her bed at night, someone who she would meet years later and who would claim to love her when really he wanted to own her. I couldn't let my son learn how to slink into a room like his dad had, sit down among the boys and learn all he had to do to feel powerful was clench a girl in his fist and never let her go.

And if I couldn't leave Luck or Lion in the house Tooth wanted, in the life Tooth wanted, learning the lessons of who he was and how he'd survived, how was I supposed to tell him there was another child that would tie us together, another child who would make it harder and harder for me to do what needed doing, to leave him. I couldn't bite into that peach thinking it might taste sweet when I could already smell it was rotting inside.

"No, Tooth. They ain't coming to sleep in your frat house. You wanna see your kids, you can come see 'em anytime, but you gotta come to me."

"The fuck you talkin' 'bout, Simone?" Tooth stood and I thought he was gonna hit me or something, but instead he came over and slid into my side of the booth, grabbed one of my hands. "I put in six goddamn years witchu. I stayed even when most niggas would've left. C'mon, baby, just let me have my kids come over." He moved his hand from mine down to my thigh and squeezed, and I pushed him away.

"No. I don't wanna be doing that no more. Not with you." I started to stand, but he was in my way. "Let me out."

Tooth looked at me for a moment, his eyes the color of the bayou just like his babies', staring at me like he wanted to rip into me. Then he slid out of the booth and let me out. I leaned over and scooped up my carton of fries, taking them with me, past Missus Woods and the salad girl, out of the McDonald's and into the early-September air, leaving him there, standing, watching me go.

I didn't know it then, but leaving Tooth in that McDonald's with the salad girl and Missus Woods would change everything, sweep me into a mess that went beyond Tooth or me or this thing growing inside me. I'm telling you that so you can stop yourself from thinking this whole thing could've been prevented if I just hadn't met him for those fries. Like all things, you can't know until you know.

In that moment though, when I marched out into the parking lot and keeled over, vomiting my insides out till they spilled across the hot asphalt, I felt free. When I rose, I put a fry into my mouth and got to walking. This time, it was just me and this thing growing inside me. And I was determined to get it out.

# ADELA

THIS WHOLE PREGNANCY wasn't anything like people described it. All I felt was sore and tired, a kind of fatigue that couldn't be slept away, a soreness that didn't end at my boobs or skin but went further, creaked at my joints and rubbed up against my ribs.

By the time I'd gagged up bile, cleaned myself, and gone upstairs to the kitchen, Noni was already up and swaying by the stove, stirring the largest pot I'd ever seen and crooning some song I'd never heard about some man I didn't know. Whatever was in the pot smelled rank.

She grinned at me when I entered the room. "You alright, baby? I made you some coffee and I know what you thinkin', but them doctors is lyin' 'bout 'you can't have no coffee or fish or wine.' All the women in our family done ate just the same when we big and we been fine. But if you worried, I made sure it was the smallest cup we had."

The cup was filled to the brim with coffee that Noni had already poured ice, cream, and sugar into, so I couldn't ask if she had any nondairy options, even though I already knew she wouldn't.

"What is that?" I nodded to the pot on the stove, still simmering. "It smells awful."

"This right here is a mixture of dog fennel and ginger. Might not smell all that pleasant, but it's about to get Mr. Levi his regular bowel movements back. I've got some more dog fennel leaves here, if you want to rub 'em up on your clothes so none of them bugs will come biting."

In a mason jar on the counter, leaves showed themselves through the shimmer of glass.

"Are you a witch or something?" I laughed.

Noni turned to me, serious, her cream-colored hair slick with gel. "This land's got a whole lot you might not know about, but our family's been pickin' leaves and grindin' seeds and findin' all kinds of ways to soothe a burn and slow a heartbeat for far longer than either of us been alive. Every day, before you wake up, I go on a walk, picking whatever I can find and drying leaves and crushing bark, and if you ever get so much as a cold, I'm gonna go up on into my bedroom and find you exactly what you need to feel better. So don't go disrespectin' my tea just 'cause it smell a little funky."

With that, Noni switched off the burner and screwed the top back on the jar. "Now, I already ate, but you help yoself to anything you want. I gotta get goin' to clean the Mulberrys' house real soon, so I'm just gon' leave the tea here to settle for Mr. Levi this afternoon, but don't worry, you don't need to watch it."

"Okay," I said, and maybe I thought Noni was crazy, but I also just didn't want her to be mad at me, because she'd shown me kindness even when I had done nothing but mope around her house, and I didn't want her to think I was ungrateful. I tried to stay away from the tea, though, grazing the blue tile counters with my fingers, making my way to the fridge.

I grabbed a tomato with a lump on top that looked like a hat and three eggs and opened every cabinet in Noni's kitchen until I found two bowls.

"You want me to leave out some yarn for you?" Noni asked. "Knitting passes the time."

I shook my head, my back turned to her as I set the bowls down.

"I was thinking I would head up to the pool today. It's been forever since I got to swim in a real pool, and I looked it up and did you know there's a pool not even half a mile from here?"

Noni cackled, smacking her thigh as I broke an egg open on the edge of the counter and poured the inside right into the palm of my hand held over one of the bowls, opening my fingers so the egg whites could drip through into the bowl, desperately trying to pull the yolk with them, but I held it back. Careful not to break it, to handle it with care as I placed it into the empty bowl.

"Why are you laughing?" I kept my eyes focused on the bowls, repeating my process with the other two eggs until I had a bowl with thick translucent yellow that looked just like vegetable oil and another with three rounded yolks that had somehow made their way toward each other, three round globs pressed close and glistening, like they needed some companionship outside their shells. Like it was too much to bear alone.

"No reason, no reason," Noni said, but I could hear the amused grin in her voice. "I think that's a great idea, baby. You need directions?"

I got out a plate and cut up the tomato, then made my way over to stand by Noni at the stove, heating a pan and trying to breathe through my mouth and not my nose to escape the smell of dog fennel.

"I looked it up, but I don't get reception in, like, half of this town, so it'd be nice if you could tell me where to go, just in case."

I poured the egg whites into the pan, laying tomatoes and a slice of American cheese I'd found in the fridge door on top.

"The pool's up in the community center, which mean you just gon' walk on down the road and turn right at the schoolhouse and when you see Ronald's Bait, you'll know you just a hop, skip, and a jump from the pool."

I squinted at her. "But I don't know what the schoolhouse or the community center looks like."

Noni dropped five whole allspice berries into her pot and tsked.

"You ain't got no sense of direction, do you? This town barely bigger than your thumb."

I sighed, deciding I'd rather get lost than talk in circles with Noni, and scooped my omelet onto my plate. I ate it standing up in the kitchen, sipping on my sweet iced coffee and looking out the window at the Florida sky, its clouds dense but fluffy, like whipped egg whites in a stretch of pale blue. I despised that sky, its cutting rays, how they made it through layers of my skin.

It was a lonely world, Florida, and I was on the outskirts of it, catapulted onto a shore that radiated disdain, full of people who were supposed to be family but felt more like relics of a life my dad had died in and then sent me to as a punishment, to live among his ghosts.

Even by the beach in a paradise that had never met ice, the sun was taunting me. I was supposed to be golden, that's what my mom called me, her golden girl, but now I was as dark as all the other people here and I knew it was judgmental and mean, but I didn't want to be like them. I wanted to go home. And this omelet was just more proof I was as far from home as I could get.

Noni left the kitchen and came back a few minutes later in an apron, with a bucket of cleaning supplies in her hand and a wig fastened to her head.

She kissed my cheek. Every time she touched me I felt a flurry of warmth and I wanted her to hug me, hold me, but it felt like defeat, to lean into her, so instead I leaned away. She squeezed me quickly anyway. "Alright, chile, I'm headin' out. You have a good swim." She laughed low and shook her head. "Don't wear that high-neck thing you got on at those competitions, you hear? Gonna give you tan lines."

I nodded even though I knew that was all I'd brought and all I'd consider wearing, listening to Noni's feet pound down the hallway and the red front door shut behind her. Alone again, I put the plate in the sink with the empty egg white bowl and then stared into the bowl with the yolks. I didn't know what to do with them, to throw them out or put them in the fridge, or leave them in that bowl, but it felt wrong to watch them break one after the other, alone at the bottom of the basin, so instead I took my fork and punctured each one, stirred until I could no longer tell the difference between them, and then poured the liquid down the drain of the kitchen sink. They went down together, as one mucus-orange reminder of a thing never come to fruition.

Satisfied, I left the kitchen and removed piles of magazines from the plastic-covered couch so I could lay down and, somewhere along the way, I fell asleep.

◆ ◆ ◆

Hands cupped, head tucked down, pushing the water away from the body, neck reaching up, gulping, back down. Dodging the ten-year-old boy with his eyes squeezed shut playing Marco Polo. Resisting the water, hands to sides, next stroke. As I emerged for my next breath, one of two tween girls having a water fight scraped her hand across the surface of the pool, pushing water up in a splash with her, right over her friend and into my open mouth.

I swallowed chlorine as I went back under, lungs hot and struggling for breath, coming back up to tread and say, "Be careful, God," to the girl in between coughs. I freestyled to the edge of the pool and pulled myself out, removing my goggles and swim cap and placing them on top of my towel. Like always, the water had still found its way to my hair, where it would dry and mat the lower layer for me to delicately pull apart later.

I sat down in the cleanest corner of dry cement I could find. I'd found the community center pretty easily, since there didn't seem to be more than a few functional buildings in Padua Beach and both the high school and the community center, low brick buildings with green metal roofs, had signs it looked like the town had put all its money into making only to have letters fallen off and painted over.

The moment I arrived at the pool, I understood why Noni had laughed at the thought of me in it, me thrilled to slip into the silky water and glide. This pool wasn't anything like the pools I swam in at home. It was probably less than half of an Olympic-length pool and there weren't even any swim lanes, so I was forced to weave through a maze of children just to make it from one length of the tiny thing to another.

I couldn't focus on the glitter of sun on top of the gaps of water not occupied by bodies. All I wanted was to sink into the complete stillness the water brought me, no thoughts that weren't about the stroke and the gurgle of sound somewhere far off. But in Padua's pool, I was distracted by the thumping current of a pool crowded with children kicking in whatever direction would keep them afloat, and none of the sounds resonated through the water like a lullaby. Instead, they screeched and pounded at my ears. So I got out. At least there was an umbrella by me now, though, so I was shaded from the harshest reach of the sun.

As I was drying off, watching all the kids and their parents in the pool, a scattering of Black and white patches, rarely blurring, I saw the lifeguard, the whistle around his neck twisted between his fingers.

I had a bad habit of falling in love with lifeguards who wanted nothing to do with me. It was part of swimming, all of us gathered together on the sidelines of the pool giggling about whatever older boy sat high above us, peering down at us like a beacon of all we couldn't have. Dry, gorgeous, and so out of reach.

After I admitted my feelings to the college lifeguard at last year's summer intensive and he turned so red I thought I might have to call an ambulance, I vowed never to look at a lifeguard again. But the second my eyes grazed over the lifeguard at Padua Beach's community pool, they paused. Because I knew that face. One of the only faces in this town I knew. He didn't seem to see me, so I stood up and slipped on my flip-flops so I didn't risk a fungal infection, making my way around the pool to where he sat in a chair under another umbrella. The lifeguard stand was directly under the sun, high enough up to touch it, obscured only by the feverish red of that umbrella.

He saw me coming and he perked at the sight of my face, or my body, or both, looking me up and down in my sport swimsuit, me and my dripping hair. I didn't expect him to even look at me, but now he was grinning, and the pool might have one good thing going for it, in the gleam of sweat on his forehead.

"Chris, right?" My feet squeaked in my flip-flops as I shifted my weight into my hip. "I didn't know you worked here."

Chris stood, placing his lifeguard buoy on the folding chair and edging toward me. "Yeah, I work here on the weekends."

"You swim?"

"Course I swim. I saw you in the water too, but I ain't known it was you with them goggles and cap on."

He laughed and for the first time since I was ten, I was embarrassed to have been seen swimming, in my cap. But Chris must have understood, because he loved the water too. Look at him, shirt still wet in patches like he'd come straight out of the ocean and hurriedly thrown it on, his sweat dewy and turning a light green shirt the same shade as all these pines. He might have been the only person in this whole state who could understand me.

I bit my lip. "Well, you're at work, so I don't want to distract you."

"No, wait, I wanna talk to you. C'mon, sit next to me." He flashed his teeth at me and that's when I saw his shark tooth, set on the top row in front of another grown tooth, a dagger that somehow made his smile more endearing, and I wanted to sit next to him.

Chris bypassed his folding chair and sat on the edge of the pool with his feet dangling into the water and I followed, slipping off my flip-flops and sitting beside him with my feet in the water too, even as the children splashed up into my face, even as I worried some kind of rare bacteria would crawl across the concrete and infect me.

I stared out at the pool, nervous to even look at him, but when I glanced over I saw he was looking at me the same way he did in that McDonald's, his eyes squinted just enough I felt safe in their sliver of brown, a smile so slight and present it made it look like his whole face was one soft, constant beam of light and it was all for me. He wasn't thinking about anything but me.

This was the first of my mistakes. To believe that his eyes were the most honest thing about him when really, it was his hands. The way they crept toward the tenderest parts of me when I was so focused on his gaze I didn't pay attention the way I should have. Maybe if I had known the Girls back then, it would have been different. But I didn't know them as anything more than a mirage and Chris was right in front of me, staring right at me.

I returned my attention to the pool, where a father held a six-month-old in a floral sun hat up into the air, where she shrieked and then, when I thought he was going to maybe hug her or let her feet touch the water, he instead blew into her face and dropped her. Just like that.

"No!" I cried out. No one but Chris could hear over the muddled screams of the children and the churning water, and he whipped his head toward the pool.

"What? Something wrong?" Chris placed a hand on my thigh, as if to protect me.

I pointed to the corner of the pool where the baby had gone under and that's when I saw her small cupped hands, rising to the surface, her on her back, sucking in air again. The dad scooped her up and kissed each cheek and, once again, she shrieked in delight, small crescent dimples appearing in her face.

"He just—that man just dropped his baby into the water," I stammered, now returning to an awareness of Chris's palm against my thigh.

Chris laughed. "That's how you teach a kid to swim, girl. Ain't no way to learn if they don't try. Besides, babies born knowin' how to swim. They swimmin' in they mama's bellies for longer than they been out in the air, in that amniotic sac and shit."

I laughed. "How do you know that? I've never met a guy who can say *amniotic sac*, let alone knows anything about them."

Chris shrugged. "I'm real good with kids." He added, "And I value the female body, Adele."

"It's Adela. Uh-del-uh."

"For sure." He squeezed my thigh just a little. "Listen, I don't wanna make you uncomfortable or nothing, but the moment I saw you, I knew you was something special, and I feel like you showin' up here just fate, know what I'm sayin'? So I was thinkin' maybe you'd wanna come out with me later? I can show you 'round Padua."

I looked up at him and he was still staring at me with that same unrelenting focus. I wasn't sure if I'd heard him right. Was he asking me out? It was impossible the most handsome guy I'd ever seen, at least the most handsome Black one, who was also a lifeguard and talked to me in the delicate language of wind chimes, his voice subtle and calm and sure, could like me back. I wanted to reach out and touch his mostly shaven beard, was sure it would feel like a flower petal rubbed between two fingers.

Chris was nothing like any boy I'd ever thought I loved. He was nothing like David, the boy responsible for what was happening inside me. David's beard had been new and rough, so rough that the next morning I woke up with an irritated red chin from where his beard had scratched up against me in those sloppy kisses.

Chris wasn't anything like that. He thought I was special from the first moment he saw me in that McDonald's, when Noni kissed my head and rushed off to her next job and I sat there, finishing my salad, and the next thing I knew, this Black guy with a shark tooth necklace and acid-wash jeans was sliding into the booth across from me. I thought he might try to mug me, but then he smiled.

"I don't wanna disturb you or nothin', but I just saw you was sittin' here alone and I don't think no woman should never have to sit alone," he said, and I watched his eyes dart around the room and then land on me, his knee bouncing up and down and causing his single hoop earring to tremble. He was concerned for me, for my safety, nervous but prepared to dart up and make sure nobody hurt a lone girl in a McDonald's.

He reached out his hand to shake. "I'm Chris." It was such a normal name. I'd expected it to be something scary like Bull or maybe Tyrone.

"Adela," I said, placing my hand in his. Instead of shaking it, he pulled my hand toward him and leaned down so his lips were kissing the top of my hand, and when he let go the entire surface of my hand was covered in saliva. No one had ever done something so charming and kind, kissing my hand and making sure I wasn't sitting alone.

"Can I ask you something, Adela?"

I nodded.

"You like fish? To eat?"

I thought he was going to ask me where I was from or if I had a boyfriend, but maybe this was a southern-boy way to ask someone out.

"Uh, yeah," I said. "I guess."

"What kind of fish you like?"

"I don't know, cod?" All I knew was cod had less calories than salmon.

It's not so much I wanted him to cook me a fish as I wanted someone to care enough to buy one from a market and season it just for me.

"Cod, aight. So if I went out fishing and I caught a nice big catfish, like two feet big, and you was hungry so I brought it to you, put some cajun spices up on it, grilled it, put it in front of you, you gonna say, 'Nah, I like cod. I won't eat no catfish'?"

Chris tapped the table with his fingernail. "Here's my real question for you. If I put a catfish in front of you after spending my time catching it, what you gon' do? Eat the catfish or tell me to go back out there and catch you a cod even though there ain't no cod in the water?"

He wasn't asking me out, he was asking me about fish. But at least he was asking me something at all, so I thought about it, trying to take my time, since I could tell it really mattered to him that I give him an honest answer, one I'd fully thought out. After a minute, I said, "I'd eat the catfish. It's not like you can catch a fish that's not in the water."

"Exactly," he said. "And that's why you a good girl, Miss Adela. I can already tell."

◆ ◆ ◆

Now I considered Chris's proposition, going out with him later, and I was about to tell him that no, my noni wouldn't like that and I wasn't sure I should be dating anyone anyway in my condition, but then I smelled the tuna.

The father with the baby girl in the floral hat and two other kids sat on towels a few yards away and the father had taken out plastic-wrapped tuna sandwiches and opened them for the older children. The smell of that tuna drifted all the way through the thick smell of chlorine and sunscreen until it was all I could think about. The second wave of nausea came as fast as the first and all I could do was keel over and allow the mouthwatering cramping to rise up and out of my mouth, tomato-colored vomit spilling right into the pool.

The moment the nausea passed, I realized what I'd done, and the humiliation washed over me. All the children in the pool were screaming and rushing to get out; Chris had quickly removed his feet from the pool and gone to grab the megaphone, shouting through it, "Pool's closing, pool's closing, all y'all make your way to the exit."

I was stunned that I had done it, so stunned I squeezed my eyes shut and didn't remove my feet from the pool, staying as still as I could, as though that would reverse what I'd done. After all the other people had left the pool, Chris crouched down next to me, wrapped a towel around my shoulders, and said, "C'mon, Adela," and when I still didn't move, he picked me up and took me to where he had laid his long red buoy away from the pool and sat me on top of it, like a bench. "Just wait here," he said.

I opened my eyes and watched as he began the process of straining the water, the net reemerging filled with chunks of vomit, dirt, and leaves long dead and fallen, and Chris placed all the dirt and vomit into a plastic bag. Then he continued this process, his biceps pulsing, until I could no longer see anything but rust and too-fine sand at the bottom of the pool.

He disappeared into the community center for a few minutes and, when he reappeared outside, he was smiling again. He fiddled with the skimmer and added chlorine tablets, something I'd seen a million times but never because of me, and I ducked my head and looked at my ashen shins. In a moment, he was beside me, sitting on the buoy.

"Look at me," Chris said.

I looked up. He was still staring at me the same way, even after I threw up red in his blue pool. "I'm sorry, I don't know what happened."

He ignored my apology and his voice turned suave. "Can I at least take you out? How 'bout Monday?"

I shook my head, couldn't believe he'd still want to do anything with me. "I have school Monday. Don't you?"

Chris laughed. "Nah, I'm not in school no more."

I wasn't sure I could be around somebody who dropped out of high school. "You graduated, though?"

"For sure. My grandmama made sure of it."

I was relieved. He was just a little older than me, maybe he even had plans to go to college. I always thought a college guy would be better for me, more evolved, more ready for me, and here he was.

I felt a steady buzz rise in me, like when I was ten laps in and began to think of when I would be done, when I would hit the end of the pool and push off for the very last time, and I wanted to prove myself. I wanted to be the best. It wasn't often a boy liked me, and now this guy wanted to see me, wanted to show me his town and cook me catfish after a long day. Not every girl could say that and for a moment all my worries became masked with the jitters of a simmering desire and the hope that I could have what every girl wanted: someone to love her, protect her, clean her vomit out of the pool and not make her feel bad about it for even a moment.

Chris smiled and his shark tooth glistened in the sun and I remembered myself. I was pregnant. Crushes and dates and the allure of want were for girls who hadn't already wasted their desire on boys who trampled over them and disappeared, leaving us with nothing but school transfers and staggering nausea. Chris wouldn't want me. He couldn't. And it was better to not even try.

"Sorry," I said, standing up, smoothing down the frizz my hair had dried into. "I have to go home." And before he could say anything, I left him, sitting by the pool that had once held my insides and now held nothing but chemical water, transformed to a miraculous ice blue.

# EMORY

**S**MART GIRLS AREN'T supposed to get in trouble. I knew that, but I didn't care. I couldn't help I was at the top of my class, just like I couldn't help the tongue that lashed from my mouth like an iguana's. The week I went back to school for the first time since I had Kai, the only thing I was thinking about was Adela. Her and what colleges I was gonna apply to. But mostly her.

Adela was the seed of so many beginnings. A pollinator for everything that would bloom and multiply and outgrow us. But what came with Adela, with beginnings, with the spread of wild blooms, was a little bit of sting. A little bit of trouble. So it was only natural that the first day I spoke to Adela, face-to-face, also happened to be the first time I'd ever been called into the dean's office.

Mrs. Simmons, the dean of students, was one of those women whose favorite day of the month was when all her magazine subscriptions came in. I bet she had all of them: *Elle* and *Cosmopolitan* and *Sports Illustrated* (for the swimsuit edition, a miserable time of the year, when she prob'ly sat down with her vat of wine and flipped through the pages just to rot in the sulfuric waste of her self-esteem) and some of the more obscure ones too, like *Private Islands* and *Positive News,* for when life got tough and Mrs. Simmons just really needed a pick-me-up. That's how I imagined her, anyway.

Getting called into Mrs. Simmons's office didn't necessarily mean you were in trouble, 'cause Mrs. Simmons was conflict avoidant and would never lead with that, but it was never a nice way to spend a period, especially in the only high school in this town and the one over, where Mrs. Simmons probably had hundreds of kids to indirectly scold and still chose you.

I was good at school. I got into tiffs with my teachers sometimes, but they tended to let it slide because my work was good and my effect on their overall test scores was better, so the Friday of my first week back at school was the first day I'd ever been called out of class. I'd nearly made it through the week without mishap, besides a few times when Kai woke up and started crying in the middle of a Government lecture or my tits started leaking through my shirt and I had to wad up toilet paper and slip it into my bra. But still, I was starting to think that Grammy was wrong, that I could really do this. Especially with Kai feeding, I was feeling like a good mother. A good student. A good girl.

And then Mrs. Simmons showed up at the end of my favorite class, Biology, and told me she'd love to see me in her office, glancing down at Kai curled up and wrapped to my front in one of Grammy's zebra-print scarves.

Now Mrs. Simmons smiled at me in her little office, which was definitely meant to be a janitorial closet, her sitting in her office chair and me sunk into a beanbag chair across from her, which was causing the back pain I'd had since Kai was born to flare like a lizard's neck at the sight of a starved hawk.

"So, Miss Reid, I can see you got a whole lot goin' on, what with the child and all, and you know Jayden's like a grandson to me, yes he is, been friends with his grandmama all my life," Mrs. Simmons started, going off on a tangent about how Jay's grandmother and her met back when this school was only for white people, and that's when Mrs. Simmons nodded at me and I shrunk back in the seat even more.

All these old folks only cared about race, but not me. I cared about people and animals and things more innate than color. It was primitive, seeing things all black and white. I prided myself on being evolved.

Mrs. Simmons continued, "Anyways, I do have to tell you that, unfortunately, you can't be bringing no baby to school. A few teachers and students have come to me expressing their discomfort and I just can't endorse a disruption to our learnin' environment." Mrs. Simmons left the last letter off every word so it bled into the next, then she leaned back waiting for my response.

"That doesn't even make sense," I said, and if I was a lizard and she'd turned hawk, then she was a threat to my young. "'Cause he sleeps all day and if he's fussin', I take him into the hall. Besides, isn't there some kind of law that says you can't be discriminating against me 'cause I got a child? Maybe I'd know if you didn't pull me out of Gov just to sit here and listen to this mess."

Mrs. Simmons sucked her big bottom lip under her top one and started rifling around in her desk drawer. I thought maybe she was looking for one of her magazines to calm her down a bit. But then she pulled out a brochure and passed it across the desk to me. Kai let out a mewling sound like he did when he was hungry. I loosened the scarf so I could unclasp the front of my bra and do what Simone taught me, touching my nipple to his cupid's bow until he yawned and then stuffing it in his mouth.

When I returned my gaze to Mrs. Simmons, her eyes were fixed on my tit. "What, you never seen a woman breastfeed before?" I asked, then tried to lean in enough to read the front page of the brochure before falling back into my chair. "I'm not goin' to some reform school, Mrs. Simmons. I'm your best student, I don't need that."

She pushed the brochure even closer to me so I could see the two girls on it, one African American and one probably Puerto Rican, holding hands in front of a tree that I'd never seen before in this part of Florida, maybe some kind of dwarf magnolia, the African American girl pregnant and the Puerto Rican girl with a toddler on her hip. When I saw them holding hands like that and smiling, I knew the picture was fake. Which probably meant the school couldn't get any better photos 'cause all the real girls were sad and refused to hold hands.

"You could at least try to cover up now, Miss Reid. We value modesty here. And the West Florida Hope Center isn't a reform school, it's the only school in this county that offers the Teenage Parent Program to support young ladies like yourself. They have over a dozen young mothers, and they partner with a daycare and all you gotta do is switch over there. I'd help you set it all up." Mrs. Simmons tapped her gels on the table and nodded, and I knew she thought she was being nice, but what would have really been nice was if she offered to hold Kai so I could go take a piss on my own for once.

"I'm sorry, ma'am, but you don't understand. I only have one year left and I'm gonna graduate at the top of my class and go off to college next fall. Changing schools, especially to some reform school an hour away, would mess up all my plans. Besides, I don't have a car or a license and I can't be living so far away from my grandparents and my friends and Jayden."

Mrs. Simmons clasped her hands together and sighed, looking down at her thumbs. "I think we need to . . . adjust your expectations. You made some choices, Miss Reid, and those choices have consequences. Yours is that you're probably not gonna go to college, at least not anytime soon, and certainly not to any school where you'd be living on campus. Let's be more realistic, hmm? How about you transfer to the West Florida Hope Center and you work on graduating, and then maybe you can take some classes at the junior college next fall?"

I stared at her. She didn't even have the gall to look back at me, and I was so tired of being ignored like I was a window, a sheet of glass for birds to slam into, again and again. I slapped my hands down on her desk and started shimmying up and out of my chair. "Well, Mrs. Simmons, I knew you were a bitter old woman, but I didn't know you were so jealous of me you'd go to such lengths to make sure I don't succeed. I'll be keeping my baby with me and if anyone's got a problem with it, they can bring it to court or something."

I don't really know why I said that. I certainly wasn't in a position to go to court and pay any lawyer fees, but it seemed to do the trick. Mrs. Simmons went quiet, removing the brochure from her desk and tucking it back into a drawer. I took my tit out of Kai's mouth and tucked it into my bra, retying the scarf so he was secure, and I wished Mrs. Simmons a good rest of her day as Grammy would tell me to do. You catch more flies with honey than vinegar, she'd say. Then I marched right out of there, imagining Mrs. Simmons's pouty face when she gave me the apology I was owed come graduation.

◆ ◆ ◆

It was lunch now. I knew 'cause nobody was lingering in the halls and all the classroom doors were swung open to try to get some airflow in this September heat. I wove through the hall to the back door, bouncing Kai until his eyelids slid shut again, and made my way out to the lawn.

Padua Beach High was less than a mile from both the beach and the bayou and just about a mile from the dune lake. Half the kids went to smoke or take a dip in the water or down some moonshine during lunch, and those of us who wanted to do our homework or scroll our phones or just didn't have anything better to do sat out at one of the six picnic tables and contemplated whether any of this was really worth it.

I used to be one of the people who went to the beach during lunch, with a group of girls that lived on the seaside of the highway, in new-build houses that had two or three stories. Girls who lived in the kind of house we used to. The one I knew Pawpaw still dreamed of when he fell asleep eating dinner in front of the TV.

Those seaside girls and me would strip off all our clothes and dive into the ocean, then grab something from Earl Ford's fish shack, and ~~half the group would ditch the rest of the school day. The other half~~ of us, me included, would head back to school and put everything we had into trying to remember which countries were on what side of World War II.

At the end of my sophomore year I met Jayden. After we got together, I'd abandon the seaside girls once or twice a week to sneak off with him. We'd go to the edge of the bayou and fuck in the tall grass. All kinds of bugs would bite my ass and Grammy would have to apply salve later, after she scolded me about my tiny bikini and the karmic justice God enacted when a lady showed too much cheek.

But now Jay and I weren't together. And, even if we were, he wasn't in school anymore. He was working in construction on a hotel renovation over in Panama City and, even when he was in Padua Beach, I didn't really want to see him. Not like I used to. Drooping at his scent. Going wild at the sound of my name in his mouth.

After the seaside girls found out I was pregnant with Jay's baby last spring, they slowly stopped texting. Stopped inviting me to go dive into the ocean at lunch. Stopped speaking to me at all. I wasn't sure if it was because he was African American or even poorer than me, or maybe 'cause their parents didn't want them to catch the pregnancy disease, but in the end it didn't really matter. They were never my friends anyway. I was always gonna be alone.

At least before the Girls scooped me into their coven and showed me how to be warm without the body heat of all the people who'd left me. Except the Girls had all dropped out of school, or took online classes from shared computers with babies drooling wet patches on the fronts of their shirts, or got their GEDs, so even with them in my life, on school grounds it was just me and Kai.

Every day this week, I spent lunch sitting at an empty picnic table, nursing Kai or begging him to sleep, watching boys in camo dip and spit into the dirt, and when Kai was securely in a milk-induced doze, I'd pull out my notebook and start working on my college essays.

Padua Beach High didn't even bother putting brochures in our homerooms for any colleges outside of Florida 'cause they didn't think any of us could possibly get in anyway. I'd done my own research and had a list two dozen long of places to escape to. I was gonna go. I didn't care where, so I figured I'd apply to them all. I was gonna make a whole lotta people suffocate on the echo of their own words. I was going to do it all.

Despite Mrs. Simmons, today was a lucky day. Today, when I walked outside the school building, Adela was sitting at one of those picnic tables.

I'd been hoping she'd come sit outside at some point after I saw her walk into my senior Government class on my first day back at school even though she was a junior, that back even more sculpted up close. But all week I'd spied her having lunch inside, hunched at a desk in her homeroom class doing her schoolwork. I'm sure her teacher wasn't too pleased by that, but it didn't seem like she knew any better. She wasn't from here.

After Mrs. Simmons, I was thinking about going straight home and climbing into bed instead of returning for afternoon classes, but the sight of Adela made me change my mind and beeline for her and her shaded table.

"Mind if I sit with you?" I asked.

She shook her head, quickly taking in Kai on my chest. "Go for it," she said, and her voice was like rubbing velvet the wrong way. Not smooth, but captivating.

I sat across from her and pulled out the plastic bag I'd put three johnnycakes and a microwave corn dog in this morning and set it on the table with my notebook and pen. I pretended to read over a paragraph, skimming it with my pen, but really I was just thinking about her. Who she was and why I itched with the bristling sense of fate when I saw her.

I'd never had a friend I cared much about before. Except maybe Simone, but she was family. I'd never had somebody who I wanted to listen to as much as I wanted to talk, and it didn't make sense that this girl the color of silt from a suburb I couldn't comprehend could be somebody I was meant to know, but I was sure she was. Surer than I was of the thud of my own heart hitting the bottom of my stomach when I realized for the first time my child was real and mine.

I took a bite of one of the johnnycakes and found it had lost all its smooth crunch in the sweaty hours in my bag. All I tasted was soggy cornmeal. Ever since I'd gotten Kai to latch last week, I'd been starving, so I ate the whole thing anyway. And then another. And then, after half my corn dog was gone, my stomach wasn't churning anymore, so I put the other half back in the plastic bag. I could tell Adela was watching me from across the table, even as she was typing something on her laptop.

"Where's your lunch?" I asked. "Don't you eat?"

She laughed and I could tell I'd embarrassed her.

"I'll eat when I get home," she said.

I shook my head and pushed my food toward her. "You should eat this. It's hot, we don't want you passing out."

"Thanks," she murmured. I watched her open the bag and take out the johnnycake and tear off a bite so small, I'd even consider feeding it to Kai at only one month old, and then she placed it on her tongue to dissolve and nodded. "It's good. What is it?"

I could tell she didn't really like it, but I appreciated that she was trying to be polite, especially to some random girl with a baby. "It's a johnnycake. Or some people call them hoecakes, but my grammy says that doesn't give off the right impression."

Adela laughed for real this time.

She reached her hand across the table and said, "I'm Adela," even though I already knew. I'd listened for her name when they took attendance in Government that first day back at school and chewed it around in my mouth every day since.

"Emory," I said, shaking her hand and feeling funny, like we were on *Law & Order* or something. "Where you from?"

Adela tucked a piece of fried curl behind her ear that resisted and sprung right back up as she said, "Indiana. But my dad's from here."

"My family's lived in Padua for generations, so I know all the folks around here. What's your last name?"

"Woods."

"Like Eve? You Eve's daughter?"

Adela shook her head. "Granddaughter."

I beamed. "I hear Eve knows how to make a window sparkle. And, once, my grammy's brother's stepdaughter bought a dress Eve made for her prom and it might just be one of the prettiest dresses I've ever seen."

Adela nodded and returned her eyes to her computer. I worried she was done talking to me before I'd even gotten to tell her anything about me. She probably thought I was some hillbilly's daughter who fucked everyone she saw and forgot to use a condom. But she had to know it wasn't like that. She had to.

I twisted my body so my back was to Adela and Kai's wrinkled sleeping face was visible.

"This is Kai," I said. "He's almost five weeks and these teachers are trying to get me to move to some reform school or leave him at home, but I've got other plans, Adela. Actually, I'm writing my college applications right now." I tapped the notebook with my pen and faced her again after I made sure she'd gotten a good look at Kai's round face, bubbles escaping his lips.

"Really?" Adela asked. "Where are you applying?"

I grinned wider. She was hooked. "Everywhere," I said. "I got a fee waiver, so I figured I'd just apply wherever's got a good Biology program and looks pretty enough for me and Kai. All the UCs, Miami, NYU, Hawaii. Oh, and Emory University, of course, 'cause wouldn't it just be cool to say, 'Hi, nice to meet y'all, my name is Emory and I go to Emory.'"

She giggled and it was the same whimpering jingle as a snowy tree cricket's wings rubbing together in the night.

She took a full bite of the johnnycake and after she swallowed, she said, "I'm hoping to go to Stanford or UCLA." Her neck hinged and dropped. "Actually, I was supposed to be scouted this year, but since I'll be here, I'm just going to have to hope they'll take me anyway."

"Scouted? Like, for cheer? I know a girl who did that."

Adela shook her head, mouth full of corn dog that she seemed to suddenly devour. "For swimming. I want to go to the Olympics. That's the goal anyway."

No wonder that wave hadn't taken her under. She knew water. She lived in it. I was just about to ask her if she wanted to go swimming with me sometime or if she wanted to come over and study with me this weekend, since maybe Pawpaw would think Adela was different from all the other African American girls at my school, better than the Girls, because Adela had dreams. Then again, maybe he'd feel like someone as pretty and smart as Adela was some kinda threat to Grammy and him and the life they'd gone to war for, so maybe it was better to keep her to myself.

I didn't get to offer anyway 'cause Raymond Stewart spit out his dip and hollered, "Gator!," his lips puffed out so you could see the black of his tongue. Everyone at the tables stood, grabbing backpacks and sodas and stray pieces of paper, and sprinted to the door that led to the auditorium. I stood to do the same but when I looked back, Adela was still just sitting there, her eyebrows one wavy line, munching on my corn dog.

"What'd he say?" she asked, and I realized this girl prob'ly didn't understand half the things anyone said in class. Didn't know how to read through the way we led with the back of our tongues in every word so the vowels came first and everything else trailed behind.

I tugged at her hand, holding Kai to me and scanning the grass for the alligator. She was over at the other end, by the vending machine, a good eight feet long at least, and I knew she moved fast, that she could be beside us any minute. "Ga-tor," I said, sounding out every part until Adela's eyes split open in panic and she slammed her laptop closed and shoved it into her bag and then you wouldn't believe what this girl started doing.

Right in front of me, Adela started running in zigzags across the lawn. She looked like a rag doll or something, her limbs flying and every turn of her heel slowing her down. If anything, she was getting the gator's attention. I ran up to her, holding Kai's head to my chest, grabbed her wrist, and pulled her straight with me across the dirt to the auditorium door. I pushed her inside, that alligator still out there, now having climbed on top of the table we were just sitting at as I yanked the door shut.

◆ ◆ ◆

In the auditorium, the whole school gathered, at least everyone who was still on campus, as we waited for the alligator wranglers to arrive and haul her out. Adela was shaking on the floor in the corner and I was trying to calm her while, once again, nursing a ravenous Kai.

"It happens sometimes, Adela. We're right by the water, so it's kinda like we're neighbors," I said, reaching out to touch her knee and then retreating.

She shook her head. "It was so . . . big."

I was trying to soothe her, but to tell the truth and shame the devil, I was glad to be trapped in a room with her. Being near Adela made me feel something. Something more like I'd felt before having Kai, almost like being in the ocean at just the right time of day, when you could look down at the water and see the sunlight threaded through it, the ripples making constellations out of light so it looked like a spiderweb of lightning beneath a shimmer of blue. She made me feel like that, and I liked it.

"If it helps, that gator was only about eight feet, so either it was a youngin or a female and either way, that's a little less scary, don't you think?" She shrugged. "Why'd you run like that from her?"

"I heard you're supposed to run in zigzags from an alligator."

I laughed. "That don't even make sense, 'cause gators have eyes on the sides of their heads, so the only time you're out of sight is when you're in front of 'em." Kai grasped onto one of my fingers and held tight. "You wanna know something else about gators?"

She shrugged again, but I knew she did.

"They don't have normal sex chromosomes like we do, so instead the sex of the baby gators gets decided by the temperature during incubation. So, one little degree can change the whole thing, and then there's a gray area, somewhere between eighty-six and ninety-three degrees, where it's a toss-up. Could be a boy or a girl."

She squinted at me. "How do you know all that?"

I smiled. "I told you, I'm gonna major in Biology."

Adela sat up more fully. "You know, you're the first person to talk to me for more than a minute this whole week? So thanks, for talking to me and for, like, saving me from an alligator attack."

I wanted to tell Adela that I'd been meaning to talk to her since the moment I saw her and if I wasn't so nervous, I would've gone up to her on my first day back at school or maybe even when I saw her on the beach last week. But I didn't want to scare her or seem overeager, so instead I said, "She wasn't gonna attack. Not unless you tried to hurt her. Isn't that how we all are?"

She got it. I knew she did. We stared at each other for a moment that made the blood in my veins swish. When you meet someone who already knows the temperature of the life inside you, there's almost nothing left to say. But, at the same time, you want to tell them everything in every language that's ever existed. Call it destiny or soulmates or best friends, but Adela was the other pea cocooned in my pod, the twin flame hissing with the same fervor as mine, a feather plucked from the same squawking bird.

I was gonna talk again, ask her about where she came from, when Kai started fussing. I tried sticking a pinky in his mouth to soothe him, tried burping, tried everything, but he wouldn't stop. Adela stared at her phone and then when Kai was just quieting, Mrs. Simmons got on the loudspeaker and said, "The gator has been detained. All y'all head to class."

Adela stood and slung her bag over her shoulder, and she smiled at me, a smile that meant goodbye, but I couldn't let it end like this. I needed my shimmer, my treasure.

"Wait!" I called. "I promised some of my friends I'd meet them at the lake after school and I thought maybe you'd wanna come?"

Adela glanced down at Kai, and I wondered if she was just being polite, if she had planned not to ever talk to me again, but then she looked back up at me and nodded.

"Yeah," she said. "I'd love to."

# SIMONE

YOU'RE GONNA THINK I was unkempt and irresponsible and just plain mean from what I did next. And that's fine, 'cause maybe I was. But maybe I had a right to be, after so many years spent keeping it together.

The day didn't start as nothing more than another day in the sun but by the time we made it to late afternoon, I was already onto my fourth swig of Tori's uncle's moonshine, watching the world go fuzzy in a blanket of heat.

Luck and Lion was on their second hour of building themselves a boat out of palm fronds and branches and someone's stray flip-flops they'd found in a bush.

I kept my eyes on them even in my drunken daze, I swear.

Lord, I loved them kids more than I ever could've imagined. It was a love I ain't known how to describe to none of the pregnant Girls who came along asking, not till Jayden sent Emory to me and I described it like this: Loving them kids was like holding my breath. At first it almost hurt but now it was simply how air moved through me, held in place while they was sleepin' or screamin' or slippin' in the bath bucket.

And then there was times when they knocked the wind outta me, when a sizzling laugh or a sticky kiss or a lopsided jump could plow right through me and unleash breath, and that release was enough to sustain through the continuous tight clench. They changed the very way I sustained life, right down to the brilliant gnaw of breath.

That's how I knew I couldn't have this other baby. 'Cause I loved Luck and Lion with all the air in me and I didn't have enough wind left for another child if I wanted to keep breathing myself.

Still, it wasn't that easy.

I called Planned Parenthood in Tallahassee this morning. The lady on the other end of the phone asked me what I was calling for and I said, "Look, I'm pregnant and I need you to abort this fucker out of me as quick and cheap as you can."

She didn't laugh, but I think I heard her snort.

"You're looking to have an abortion, ma'am? Do you happen to know when the first day of your last period was?"

I sighed. "If you wanna know when I got knocked up, it was August eighth at two p.m. and it was real muggy out that day, and I counted and I know that means I'm what, four weeks and a couple days?"

"I appreciate all that information, ma'am, but we calculate based on your menstrual cycle." She said *menstrual* with the *u* all drawn out and if I wasn't nervous I prob'ly would've laughed.

"It was like the very end of July I think."

"Oka-ay." I could hear the lady clacking on her keyboard and next she rattled off a bunch of shit about laws and policies and procedures, but all I cared about was how much time did I have and what was it gonna cost.

"About six hundred dollars, ma'am. We can get you scheduled now—"

"Now? I don't have six hundred dollars now."

She started talking about access to financial assistance, said I could apply for it at my appointment, but I already knew there was no way I was driving three hours just for the chance that maybe these white folks would take pity on me and decide I needed the help without no tax return or paystubs to show for it. I'd figure it out myself.

"I just need some time," I said. "How long do I have?"

She sighed apologetically. "You can get an abortion via medication up until eleven weeks after your last menstrual period, which would be a little under six weeks from now. After that, you have four weeks until you can no longer receive a legal abortion, surgically or otherwise, in the state of Florida. You'll need to come for your initial appointment in person, wait at least twenty-four hours per Florida law, and then you can have another appointment where you'd be given the medication."

Two appointments a day apart, three hours away, six hundred dollars. It would be nearly impossible, but those first months with the twins felt impossible to survive too and I still made it here.

"Ma'am? Would you like to schedule an appointment?"

"Yes," I said. "Yes."

I'd do anything.

I hung up and knew I was already on the cliffside of this thing and I was liable to fall off any moment, only one month to make seven hundred dollars to cover all that gas too, and drive three hours to extract this thing from where I could already feel it burrowing inside me.

So that's how I decided that before I started scrounging for money, I could have a day to unravel, go to the dune lake, and drink so much liquor I thought my hair whippin' in front of my eyes was lightning.

The Girls fixed the stereo this morning, so it was blasting from the windows of the truck again, and when I tell you Megan Thee Stallion knows how to get me going just like Kelly Rowland, I mean I got my fingernails digging into the dirt and my ass throwin' it back in a circle the way it was intended, and all the Girls was cheerin' and every once in a while one of the toddlers would start bobbing and bouncing to the music and we'd chant, "Go Cece, go Cece!"

I was catching my breath, sitting in the shallows of the lake, tying branches together with swamp lily stems for Luck while Lion painted the flip-flops in muscadine grape juice, when Emory arrived. Trailing behind her, the salad girl from McDonald's kept her eyes on her feet, like she was checking for dog shit before each step. Jamilah turned the music down and everybody paused, eyes on the salad girl.

When Emory made it to the truck, she stopped and turned to grab the girl's hand like she was claiming her, and Em looked around at us and nodded proudly, like bringing some girl clearly not from here and without no baby was some kind of gift for us.

"Y'all, meet Adela. She's new."

Nobody else said nothing, all of us just staring at her. April offered herself up first, taking a sip of her beer and bouncing her son on her knees. "I'm April. This is Jamilah." She nodded to Jamilah beside her and the salad girl—Adela—smiled like she was shy even though I could tell she wasn't and waved once with her free hand.

Tori and Crystal said, "Hey," and returned to their game of cards in the truck bed, letting each of their kids take a few cards for themselves, even though Cece, Crystal's daughter, just stuck them in her mouth and sucked.

That left me. Emory pulled Adela toward the shore of the lake where me and the twins was and paused in front of us, Emory's eyebrows raised.

"What, girl?" I asked. "Can a bitch get some personal space, damn."

Adela stepped back, but Emory tugged on her wrist and stayed put. "Be nice, Simone," Em scolded. "Jay always said you had an attitude when you were jealous."

"Jealous?" I handed Luck the panel of branches tied together and stood in the water so they could see I was taller than them, older than them, that I wasn't nobody Emory wanted to fuck with. "You only allowed here 'cause of me, Em. Watch what you say."

Emory sucked her cheeks in and I knew she was about to cry, and part of me felt like I should hug her or say I was sorry, but I didn't want this girl, Adela, thinking I was soft, so I kept my chin raised and turned toward the girl.

"Look, Em's like my sister, so if she cool witchu, I'll be cool witchu. But if you fuck with my babies or my Girls, then we finna have a problem." Adela nodded once, her eyes a bleary vent for her fear. "You want a beer?"

Emory wiped her eyes even though I didn't see no tears and nodded. "C'mon, Adela, I'll get you one."

But apparently, the salad girl didn't drink 'cause I watched her on and off for the next three hours and she didn't take one sip of that beer, not when the rest of us was whining our hips and taking turns reciting verses of "Get Ur Freak On," not when Luck and Lion insisted everyone try gettin' on their boat and goin' on a pirate quest, not when we all shrieked and toppled from the boat when it inevitably sunk and sent us face-first into the dune lake.

The sun retreated from our sight and pulled all light with it. We constructed a fire, brought out the camp stove, and I cooked up some rice while Crystal fished with her spear like her momma taught her till she caught a big old bass, and then she scaled it and I cooked it up too. After all the kids was fed, we laid them down in blankets in the truck and wrangled them to sleep.

Then the rest of us Girls sat and drank in a circle by the fire except Adela, who just looked at her beer can, and as I took my eighth—or maybe ninth—swig of moonshine, Emory called from across the circle, "You sure you should be drinking like that, Simone?"

I looked at her. She had her head in Adela's lap and Kai still strapped to her chest. I remembered wishin' I could carry my babies like that, but it wasn't so easy with two. Before I had them, I wanted to exclusively breastfeed and sleep train and never feed them no preservatives, but it wasn't like I had no choice when suddenly I was raising two babies in nothing but my kind-of-boyfriend's old truck and selling my breast milk was the only way we could make any extra cash.

I didn't have no choice but to co-sleep beyond a year or two or three, since we was sleeping together in a truck bed anyway, and I fed 'em whatever we could afford with my money and Tooth's EBT while it lasted and whatever else he gave me when he was feeling nice. Emory got to do it just like she wanted and here she was judging me.

"Mind your own business," I spit. I knew she was talking about the pregnancy test. She'd found me after I took it, out by the water, saw each line, and gaped at me like, *Look what you did, Simone, look what you've become.* We ain't talked about it since, but now Emory was tryna bring it up in front of all them, make a scene just for the salad girl to watch.

I stared off as April waded into the lake. She cupped her hands, splashing some water on her face and waving Jamilah over to kneel in front of her so she could wash her baby locs for the first time this month. The dune lake was the only place you could really wash all that salt water from the Gulf off you if you didn't wanna fight with your brothers over the shower, and Jamilah's brothers was always showering.

"Why can't she drink?" Jamilah called as she closed her eyes and waited for the cool water to spill down her face.

Emory sat up and looked at me like I'd betrayed her. "You didn't tell them?"

"What, you pregnant?" Tori laughed.

I shrugged. "Guess so."

"Oh shit," Crystal said, downing the last gulp of her Gatorade.

"Wait, then why are you drinking?" Adela asked, running her hand through her hair like white girls do, even though her hair barely budged, and I wondered if she even knew what she looked like.

I held a hand up and everyone hushed. "What I drink ain't nobody's business but mines."

"Yours and your baby's," Adela said, her voice an entirely different texture than it had been the past few hours, when she'd sounded like a wheezing balloon. Now she sounded so sure, her voice blowing the fire's smoke in the opposite direction, and I was just about ready to slap her.

"And Tooth's," Tori said.

Crystal shrugged. "I hear a drink or two don't really matter much."

"But ten of 'em does," Emory said.

Adela leaned toward Emory and asked, "Who's Tooth?"

"He's my children's wack-ass daddy," I called across the circle, the smoke veering from its path and soaring toward Adela, making her hazy. "And we ain't together so he don't get to say nothin' 'bout what I do or don't do. Goddamn, all y'all really gotta stop."

Everyone quieted again and all I could hear was the sound of water dripping from Jamilah's head back into the water as April washed out the shampoo. Then that salad girl just had to butt in and make things worse.

"It's really not okay to drink, especially in the first trimester. It could mess up the baby."

I glared at her shape through the blur. "Luckily, I'm not keepin' the baby."

"You serious?" Emory asked.

They all looked at me now like I'd been looked at so many times, like the wrong kind of mother. This was how one mother looked at another when pride made us tender and all we wanted was to be good. Right. What I'd learned, though, is I'd always be the wrong kind of mother, and this look waltzing across the other mothers' faces was by nature always gonna be for me, but I refused to let it be mine. The Girls ain't never gave me that look all at once, and I didn't think they was like that, but also sometimes when we looked at each other, all we could see was ourselves.

"If I can get the money for it, yeah," I said. "Unless you don't want me to, 'cause I really be tryna make sure you happy first, Em," I sneered.

Emory frowned at me, but then she looked down at Kai and when her head tilted back up, her face had broken open and she nodded. "You should do what you wanna do. Let me know if you need help."

"Wait," Adela blurted again. "If you're not completely sure, if you don't even have the money yet, then you shouldn't be drinking. Besides, there's always adoption if you don't want to keep it. That baby could make someone else really happy."

This time, we all turned to glare at her, everyone except Emory at least, and Tori was the one to speak this time. "This isn't *Juno*. Nobody wants no high school dropout black girl's baby, especially no one who got the kinda money it takes to adopt."

I added, "And before you say there's always foster care, you better think about what you saying. This not no Annie situation you signin' that child up for, and I can't be having that kinda shit on my conscience."

Adela shrugged. "I still don't think you should be drinking. It just confirms what everyone else already thinks about you."

Even as drunk as I was, the moment she said it, my eyes sobered and my lips, chapped and split, quivered, teeth growing sharp. I stood up and stumbled toward her. As I lunged, half of me was thinking about how I didn't want Luck and Lion to wake up and see me beating this bitch up, but the other half of me was flooded by the gaudy heat of rage, and next thing I knew I was ripping a clump of hair from this salad girl's head and my nails tore along her neck and came up filled with bloody cells.

I know you prob'ly see me as just another black girl gone off the walls, but really, I reacted with the sour spit of any woman who was tired of being scrutinized like a pit bull lured into a fight.

Next thing I knew, Tori was prying me off her and Emory was holding Adela to her side and pulling her away from the lake, away from the clearing, away from the truck, and I was on the ground, sobbing till my braids was sticking to my cheeks and Crystal was holding me and telling me it was gonna be alright and I wanted to call

Momma and Pops and Jayden and go somewhere where someone would wrap me up in the crackle of a soft voice and cook me something sweet and tell me it wasn't my fault, none of it was, that I was doing everything I knew how to do and everything I didn't.

But instead, I fell asleep in the sand by the dune lake and woke up with water licking at my toes and my babies asking me again if they could build another boat to ride out on Luck and Lion Lake. And still I smiled, held my breath taut in my lungs, and said yes. For them, always yes.

# ADELA

SHOULD HAVE known following Emory to the Girls was a perilous journey to take, one that would only end with me limp and mutilated on a forest floor. But Emory was kind and smart and the only thing close to a friend I could imagine having here, so I followed her away from the school, not knowing she would make me walk for almost an hour down the side of the highway before she finally turned left.

Then we were thrust into dense forest, climbing through undergrowth and mud from last night's summer storm that soaked through my white Keds, and I could smell all the wild creatures who harbored among these trees and fed off the nearby lake. I felt exposed out there in the middle of nothing and so much, and this is when I should've known to turn around like I sensed the edge of the pool in my backstroke and somersaulted before my skull cracked on the pool's wall, but I didn't. I continued on, Emory the only thing protecting me from alligators and wolves and crazy teen mothers.

I'd never heard of a dune lake before, some kind of weird phenomenon where a lake formed with a channel to the sea nearby, and I wondered why you'd want to swim in a lake when that massive aqua ocean was right there, but I guess the Girls liked the dirty lake because when the trees parted, there they were, sprawled out on a bed of sandy loam, drinking.

I'd drank before, at parties and stuff. I just didn't believe that a pregnant woman should be drinking. It was unsafe, the CDC and every pregnancy book ever made said so, I knew because I'd started to read them, the horrifying thrill in each phenomenon of body sparking my teeth to chatter and grind at night.

I understood you couldn't do every little thing right, but I also understood there were some things you shouldn't do and drinking while pregnant was one of them. I didn't want them to think I was a prude or stuck-up, though, and I also didn't want to tell them I was pregnant, since then they'd for sure try to recruit me like some kind of cult, so instead I held a beer in my hand and didn't drink it.

Simone watched me the whole night, her stare scanning at first and then invading, existing only in the wake of her pupils rippling up and down, across and then through me. I could tell she scared Emory a little too because when Simone raised her voice at Emory, I felt her flinch in my hand. Emory had taken hold of my hand when we walked into the clearing, a southern sweetness and a protective declaration to all of them that I was here and I belonged, if only in tandem to her.

Before Simone attacked me, I was considering replacing my old best friend with Emory, getting Emory to put her son down sometimes so that we could take pictures together on the beach to post, guiding Emory through a crooked attempt at a butterfly stroke, and letting her slip her clammy hand over the rotund growth of my abdomen.

But then I felt Simone's nails ripping into my neck, her body weight knocking the wind out of me and reminding me of the child I was growing instead of just the sacred sculpture my body had become, a trophy to be sheltered, nurtured, never threatened. Then all I felt was burning, my body ignited by the force of hers, and pain was the only sound, everything so quick I saw nothing more than a blur of blond braids and Simone's yellowed teeth before Emory hauled me away and I was sobbing in a heap by the side of the road while she tried to hug me without crushing her baby between us. Her hand in mine hadn't been enough and she knew it, but she kept trying to touch me and I didn't want anything to do with her, them. These Girls were vicious.

When I found words through the saliva and shock, I screeched out, "Get away from me! I don't want to be anywhere near you or your crazy fucking friends." I choked on my own mucus and when Emory still didn't move, I glared at her through layers of tears and panted, "Get. Away. From. Me."

Finally, Emory, her face collapsing at the center, rose and slowly began to back away, disappearing around the bend of the highway.

◆ ◆ ◆

After the vomit reduced to pure stomach acid and I could remove myself from the toilet, I fell back onto my bed. It was dawn, the morning after Simone attacked me, and the bruising on my cheek was worse than the scratches on my neck, the throb making me strangely aware of the bottom of my eye, and I was done. Done with the Girls. Done with this pregnancy. And definitely done with Florida.

Mom answered the home phone like she always did, the moment before it went to voicemail. "Hello?" I knew she'd been up for at least an hour, but her voice was still groggy like she hadn't yet spoken to another person today, and I missed being the first one she talked to, when we used to have coffee together on the front porch and watch the neighbors jog by.

Mom was more focused on her job and practical things—adding fertilizer to the zinnias in the garden and scheduling dentist appointments—than she was on me and that worked, mostly. Then we didn't have to be seen out together too often, when strangers would ask if I was adopted or if my dad was just Black. Neither of us liked it, so we just stopped going out together and then slowly stopped talking much at all, except for in the morning.

"Hi, Mom." I hadn't talked to either of them since I left. Noni called them once a week to update them that I was still alive and still pregnant and, as far as I knew, if both of those things were true, they saw no reason to speak to me. At least they hadn't called and, until today, I hadn't either.

"Adela." Her voice betrayed nothing, like walking on the basement's linoleum floor, my mother was relentlessly cold.

"Can you wake up Dad?" I asked, and I knew she wouldn't have if she hadn't heard the tremble of my voice falling off the edge of tears, but the phone went blank and a long two minutes later switched back on with Dad's voice.

"Adela? You're on speaker. What's wrong?" Dad was so diplomatic, a corporate attorney who used *Not to my knowledge* to answer pretty much every question. "Your grandmother hasn't called in a few days. Is her health deteriorating?"

"Her health? Noni's only like sixty-five and she's fine. It's me. I'm what's wrong." I tried to keep my tears silent, but they were the kind that forced their way out in a whimper and a tight bellowed sob that lodged in my throat, jammed beside the indigestible shame I couldn't swallow.

Mom and Dad didn't say anything, just listened to me cry, and I imagined them staring at each other, silently fighting about who would handle their grossly emotional pregnant teenager. Dad lost.

"Is it the baby? Are there . . . defects present?" he asked.

I kicked the sheet from my body. It was damp from a night of steeping in my sweat. "No, Dad, I haven't even had my doctor's appointment yet." Part of me wished there was something wrong with the baby; maybe then they'd let me come home. "I just really hate it here. I don't want to be pregnant anymore. I want to come home. Can I . . . maybe I could get an abor—"

"No." Mom's voice cut in. "You have a life in you, Adela. You're in Florida and you'll stay there because it's the right thing to do. That's God's child growing in you, and it will make some family very happy.

Besides, your grandmother said you're doing well, swimming a lot, doing your homework. I don't see why you need to come back before it's time."

"Because this isn't my home. And the people here are awful. Dad, you always said you hated Florida, you have to know this place can't be good for me. I mean, what if I end up like them?"

Dad laughed, a chuckle croaking through the phone while I cried at seven in the morning, and I think I felt my cheekbone turn violet, the bruise spreading through my body. "Honey, you're nothing like them, at least not to my knowledge. Regardless, you'll only be there for the rest of the school year and, if it was so important to you to remain at home, you could have made some different decisions that wouldn't have led to your current . . . situation. Unfortunately, things are the way they are."

"Are you fucking kidding me?" I wasn't sure I'd ever swore in front of my parents before and I could imagine Mom's eyebrows leaping up, Dad's fist clutched to his chest like I'd given him heartburn, but I didn't care because he was breaking my heart, and I didn't understand how they could leave me here like this.

Mom cleared her throat. "Since it appears you have not, in fact, learned your lesson, your father and I are going to hang up and you can take some time to think about your behavior."

Dad interjected. "We're trying to protect you, Adela, it's not a punishment." They were delusional, convincing themselves they'd sent me away for my good and not theirs. I knew they would rather live without me than choke on the image of the three of us, together, as my body grew to house another. They were humiliated.

Dad continued, "We sent you to your grandmother's in order to give you a life where you don't have to raise a child at sixteen years old. In a year, you'll still be able to pursue your athletic career and have a family paying for your bills, so consider yourself lucky. Very lucky."

And then they hung up. Just like that, the phone call done, and here I was, still in this basement room with a swollen cheek and a stir of nausea rising and falling, and apparently, I was lucky. Very lucky.

◆ ◆ ◆

The sun was a hanging fruit in the sky and Chris was late.

I was standing there in front of the community center, watching the sun set and cursing Mom and Dad in my head, grinding my teeth until my wounded cheek ached so bad I had to release. I was trying to maintain my grasp on the seething anger I'd felt on the phone this morning, even as it slipped into grief, because I knew the only thing left to feel would be weights strapped to my ankles in the deep end, helplessly sinking.

I was about to start crying when my eyes, caught onto the figure coming toward me, straight toward me, with the glaring sun tucked under his arm, but then his body blocked the light and it was just Chris, smiling at me.

"Hey," he said, and when he showed his shark tooth, I relaxed.

Then I remembered my face, the swelling still obstructing my vision, and I got shy, ducked my head. I felt the moment when he got close enough to notice, took a finger and traced the slashes on my neck, the trail of purple across my face. "What, you getting into fights now? When I can't do nothing to protect you?"

I lifted my hand to my neck to hide it. "Would you believe it if I told you I'd been attacked by an alligator?"

He laughed, brushing small specks of sand from his hands. "Nah, girl, I seen some catfights in my life and them scratches is straight from a crazy bitch's nails."

"Yeah, well, I was almost attacked by an alligator. And then I was actually attacked by an insane girl."

I thought Chris might ask for more details, but, instead, he reached his hand out to me.

"My car's in the lot. C'mon, you can tell me all about it over dinner."

I took his hand and for the moment I didn't care that I looked like I had just taken a beating or that Mom and Dad had abandoned me and were uninterested in my pleading to come home, because I wasn't alone and Chris's hand wrapped around mine was enough to make this day worth remembering.

◆ ◆ ◆

"Tell me something about you," Chris said, half his face lit up yellow from the glow of the Waffle House sign. He was so beautiful, it made me feel like I'd swallowed just enough pool water to enjoy the swash of it whirlpooling inside me but not enough to make me sick.

After my call with Mom and Dad, I marched to the community center and called over the fence to where Chris sat in his faded red swim trunks. *Hey. Are you free tonight?* He'd only seen shadows of me, but still he'd said yes, and I'd waited two hours reading outside the community center, waiting for him, before he finally walked around the corner. And now we were here, in his car in the Waffle House parking lot, after a full driving tour of all Padua had to offer in its two square miles.

"I swim." It was the only thing I could think of. The only thing that had ever been important about me.

"I saw that, you and them goggles."

I giggled and the little pine tree air freshener dangled on his dashboard. "No, I swim, like, competitively."

"Ah, so you a lil' mermaid now too, huh?" He grinned, shook his head, and his voice sunk lower, honest and gravel. "Every time you say something, I think I can't get no more impressed. And then you blow me out the water."

I ducked my head and looked at my lap. I'd worn heels but I slipped them off in the passenger seat of his car and now I was folded up, both of us leaning into each other, and I never thought a Waffle House parking lot could be romantic, but here I was.

I laughed. "Definitely not a mermaid."

"I swim too, you know. Not competitively, but enough that when I'm surfing, I'm not about to drown."

He swam. He surfed. He fished. If he knew the water, I thought maybe he could know me.

"You ever surfed?" he asked.

I shook my head, sipped the milkshake he'd bought me. I wasn't sure I was going to drink it at first, but one taste and I couldn't stop guzzling it. Like him, I just kept wanting more.

"Maybe I could teach you sometime."

He had something to teach me. He cared enough to watch me flail until the moment I learned not to and soared.

"You were the first person in this town to be nice to me," I whispered.

He stroked my hand. "This town can be rough for people like us, Adela. You and me, we like to do things our own way. Like when you swimming and you gotta follow your own stroke, not the person next to you. A lotta these folks don't get that here and so they don't understand nobody who wear no goggles and cap to the swimming pool or somebody who wakes up at dawn every day to surf like me."

Chris slipped a hand right above my knee and kept it there. It didn't make me nervous like it had the week before. Instead, I felt safe like a small cub in a cave, the dark of the car consuming, just his face lit up. He moved his fingers higher, toward my thigh.

"Can I tell you something?" I asked.

"You can tell me anything." His voice was soft, but not too soft. Like corduroy.

"Nobody's ever asked me out before."

His neck cocked back. "Nah, you lyin."

"It's true. You're the first person to ever want to go out with me."

"So you never . . . been with nobody?"

I looked into my lap, where his hand was rested heavy, so close to my stomach. I knew I should tell him the truth, but I wanted him to think I was special. Pure. Untouched.

"Never."

"Why wouldn't nobody want you? You seen yourself?"

"Where I'm from, the school I went to, I'm not pretty. At least not the kind of pretty that gets asked out. Maybe if I stopped swimming, I might've lost all the bulky muscle and been able to blow out my hair and then boys might've wanted to take me to homecoming. But my dad wouldn't let me quit, not when he realized how good I was. Plus, I love swimming. I love it most without the timer, when it's just me in the water, but either way, it's always been enough to make up for being so ugly."

"Ugly? You better take that back, Adela. You think I'd want no ugly girl? You the most beautiful woman I ever seen in my whole life. You strong. You the only woman I ever seen who I think might be stronger than me and I bet you smart too. In fact, I know you smart. I like you just the way you is."

"You like me the only way you've ever seen me."

Chris removed his hand from my leg and tilted my chin to look at him. "You think I judge a fish on the way it looks? You think I only want a trout if it's the size of my foot or the color of the sunset's belly? I ain't saying all fish made the same, I'm saying I know the minute that little bastard pops out the water on a hook if it's gonna be a good one, gonna feed my family, gon' settle on ice and die happy. Just like you know every pool's not the same, but the water's always good no matter how cold or warm or yellow it might be. I like you 'cause you special. And no matter who you been or gonna be, you always special."

I didn't want to cry, but I couldn't help it. These last two weeks had left me touch starved and all I wanted was for someone to hug me and make me forget the mess I'd made, the dreams I'd scattered between Indiana and here, and now this boy was telling me he wanted me without condition and I believed him. I believed him enough to kiss him, and when he kissed me back and his tongue slipped warm against my teeth, I climbed in his lap.

I let him curl his fingers around my hips, let his lips search my skin and find soft, maimed neck. He was slow, and he looked up at me as he mapped my body, so I knew he could see me, and I was just about to let him slip a finger inside me when the jingle of the Waffle House door chimed. A flip-flop-clad family filed out, one after the other until all six kids made it to their car, parked a few rows away from us. I tucked my breast back into my bra and climbed off him, slid back into the passenger seat.

Chris wasn't shaken, though. He leaned into my ear and said, "Don't worry, we got time. You special, remember. I wanna do this right."

I gazed up at him and nodded and he smiled and kissed my cheek, and as he revved the car and I listened to the rumble of his voice telling me about every store and tree in Padua, I decided this would be the first man I ever loved.

# EMORY

W E AREN'T SPECIAL. Humans, I mean. Actually, we are special, but that's 'cause we know how to use our hands for basically everything and also we can form complex ideas about our environments. But, in a lot of ways, we're the same as any other animal.

Some people think humans have more complicated feelings than other animals, but I'd say remorse is about the most complicated feeling somebody could have and it's not a distinctly human thing. To regret.

A few years ago, some scientists did a study on rats and found that when the little guys took the wrong turn in a maze and lost out on a treat, they'd look back over their shoulders, brains sparking with a desire to turn around and reverse it. Scientists were all shocked, but I don't know why they would be. There wasn't a single being who made choices who wouldn't sometimes feel shitty about the ones they made. There weren't exceptions to regret. It was like breath, food, baby making. You couldn't be alive without regret.

I wasn't new to regret when I lost Adela right after I'd first got her. I'd had a life full of it, actually. But it was a different kind of feeling with her. A hot rush of remorse. Looking over my shoulder and wishing I'd never brought her to the Girls at all. Before her, I wasn't sad I didn't have a best friend, a person to fold into and feed my secrets. But once I met her, I hadn't prepared to let her go. Especially not so quickly.

Regret feasted on what was left of me like a falcon going after its prey's unhatched eggs. Swooped down and snatched the most precious part of me. I wasn't throwing a pity party or anything, but it hurt to feel the gaping absence. Kind of like when I first got the idea in my head that a baby would be all I needed, all we needed, and I changed my life forever. You couldn't undo something like that.

It's hard to explain what I felt about Jay 'cause I felt nothing. But also everything. It wasn't love, not exactly, but it wasn't lust either. He was just my most urgent pursuit, an electric tide to fill my empty days, and I liked him, at least for a while. That boy wanted me unlike any other. I'd never felt that before, not from no one, and I realized I liked it. I wanted more.

Suddenly, everywhere I looked, all I saw was the absence of that. My old friends didn't care about me enough to listen to me talk about the beaks of woodpeckers. None of those other boys besides Jay wanted nothing from me but the feeling of my breathless body beneath theirs. Grammy and Pawpaw kept me fed and loved me to pieces, but I knew they also resented me. I didn't blame them either. They gave up so much of their lives the day Ma dropped me on their porch back when I was just five. I wondered if they regretted it sometimes, taking me in. Prob'ly.

Then Christa happened. Christa was Grammy's second cousin's daughter and she'd just gone on maternity leave, so Grammy was covering for her, taking on her shifts at the dry cleaner's in the next town over. We didn't see Christa all that much before I turned seventeen, but when Grammy took over her shifts, Christa started coming over every week or so with her new baby—I think just to check up on Grammy and make sure she still had a job to go back to—but anyways, Christa would give Grammy her daughter to hold and Grammy would coo and sway and look like an eager bunny rabbit staring at that baby. I'd never seen her like that before.

After three weeks of this, I was sitting on the couch with my textbook laid out in front of me and Christa asked if I wanted to hold the baby. I shrugged, even though I wanted to, of course I did, she was real cute and everything, and so Christa passed the baby over, right into my arms.

Her legs curled up on my chest like a roly-poly and she had this thick, soft hair that smelled like fresh laundry and butter, and when I looked at her small face, I understood what Grammy felt. Nothing seemed to matter but this tiny person and you could just stare at her forever and love her even when she shit on you. I stayed like that, holding the baby, until Grammy said it was her turn. She stayed rocking the baby for another hour till finally Christa took the baby and left and there was nothing more devastating than the sagging air in our house after that child was swept out the front door.

So when I stopped taking my pills, I thought I was giving my grammy the gift of a baby that she hadn't even gotten when I came around, since I was already old enough to go to school. I thought that's what she wanted, and then our house would always be so full and bursting with hope, like when Christa's baby came around. I was gonna have someone to love and to be loved by in the way Jay loved me. Completely and without condition. That's what I thought I was getting when I stopped taking the pills. When I took the pregnancy test. When I decided I was gonna name my daughter Gemma after the treasure spilled at the bottom of our sea.

But that was before I told anybody, before I started to feel suffocated beneath a love I couldn't return. Before I gave birth and realized I got a lotta love from Kai, with Kai, but I didn't have no one to cover my shifts at school. I didn't have extra hands to hold that baby and fill him back up with love and no one seemed to care what I was losing 'cause they all believed I'd done this to myself. And I guess, in simple terms, I had.

I never regretted my child. But if I could've turned around and walked back in the direction I came from, I would've. Still, here we were. And despite how we'd gotten here, despite the possibility of my first best friend reduced to sawdust and a bloody patch of dune lake dirt, I was determined to be happy.

If I was a lizard and this whole world thought I was prey, then I would be the type of lizard who was smart enough to swallow my eggs and keep 'em tucked into the pouch of my stomach before I ever let somebody come and crush 'em.

I would focus on Kai. *That's what any animal would do*, I thought. I knew what I felt wasn't distinctly human, but some days I thought it'd be better to be some other kind of critter so even if the regret still spiked a hole through me, I prob'ly wouldn't remember it an hour later. The way those rats in the maze would when their little brains blessed them with forgetting.

◆ ◆ ◆

We sorted through boxes of clothes in Jay's church's basement while all the church ladies snickered at me around us. Jayden had Kai wrapped in one of his ma's shawls on his chest, the way Kai liked best, and after three failed attempts, I'd finally let Jay hold my hand. My mind was always changing about him, me, us, and I was liable to float into a new world of feeling before I even realized my feet were off the ground.

Today I sort've thought I might love him. So I let my palm slip into his as we moved to the next box and Kai mewled. There wasn't no use fighting my feeling. Like Grammy always said, fighting without no reason's as useful as a trapdoor in a canoe. Or maybe as useful as a rat regretting not picking up the cheese now in his brother's stomach. It doesn't do nobody no good.

"I thought you said they wouldn't care if I came," I whispered to Jay.

I'd agreed to go to his church's clothing drive 'cause Kai was only five weeks and already fit into his three-to-six-months onesies. He was in the ninety-eighth percentile for height and I knew I needed some bigger clothes fast, before my breast milk turned him into a baby gorilla. Jay said the church's clothing drive was free and everyone would be real friendly and welcoming, not like his parents at all. He said they would care that the baby was here and taken care of and being raised in a Godly fashion. But I was being looked at like a vulture in a crowd of bird-watchers. I didn't feel welcomed at all.

"They don't," Jay whispered back. "They just don't have a lot of white folks coming in here, that's all."

I shrugged. No one I knew had ever been inside the Baptist church. We were Methodists or Catholics, sometimes Evangelical, but none of my family or friends were Baptists or knew Baptists, almost like we weren't all Christians at all. I didn't think it was a race thing, though. More like a matter of faith that happened to coincide with sides of the highway and skin color, but not entirely. We had African Americans at our church. Two families, in fact. One came from Oklahoma and the other from Ghana. We welcomed them with open arms. Not like this.

"Maybe we should go," I said.

"Just wave and say hi and everybody'll hush and get back to business. They just wanna make sure you friendly."

I looked up at an older couple rolling pairs of socks at the next table and smiled. "How y'all doing?" I said, prepared to prove Jay wrong. But then the lady set down her last roll of socks and wove around the table toward us. She grinned and squeezed Jay's shoulder.

"We just fine, baby, thank you for askin'. Real nice to meet you, sweet thing you is." She wasn't sarcastic about it at all, and she looked at me like Grammy did when I showed her my report card. Proud. Then she turned to Jay. "Jayden, baby, when you comin' back to run youth group? The youngins always looked up to you. We'd love to have you back sometime." Her gaze fell to Kai. "Maybe one day this little fella can join group, hmm? I'm sure y'all raisin' a fine young man."

"Trying, ma'am. We 'preciate your generosity." Jayden's tilted smile could soften a whole room like butter on a warm day. He gestured to the baby clothes in my arm. "They grow fast."

"Sure do," the lady said. "You was that small once. Feels like not more than two moons ago. You tell your parents hi from us, now, and we'll see y'all at service Sunday." She turned toward me and there was nothing but warmth woven in her face. "You welcome to come too, sweetheart. I know not everyone been thrilled about the . . . situation, but you always welcome here. I'll make sure of it." She squeezed my arm like she'd squeezed Jay's and walked back to the table where her husband was standing.

Jay was right. The whole room stopped staring, at least not more than anyone else in town, and we were free to sort boxes under the peaceful watch of the kindest Baptists in all of Florida.

"She was so nice," I said. I held Jay's hand tighter, instead of just letting my fingers hang.

"Yeah, she is. Not all them like that, 'specially at service when some of the folks who don't really got no faith go, but most people are more like Mrs. Carol." Jayden pulled a fuzzy thing from the nearest box and unraveled it. It was a bear costume, two curved ears sewed to the top. "For Halloween? I'll be papa bear if you be mama bear."

I laughed and when I saw Jayden today, I saw a maroon lake glimmer at sunset. A brazen young pine emerging from honeysuckle threatening to choke it. A single pure egg guarded for life.

"Yeah," I said. "I'd like that." Brown bears had always been my favorite. Grammy used to tell me the story of Goldilocks at bedtime the night before my birthday and Christmas and Easter, and Grammy would call Goldilocks "Emmylocks" and I would giggle, but really I didn't wanna be Goldilocks. I wanted to be one of the bears.

Now I knew brown bears were loner animals, didn't like being around each other much at all, but all the stories about them came in forms of family. Mama, papa, cub. Lonely till they found the ones who made loneliness not worth the familiar gnaw. When I was young, I wanted to be the cub. Now I thought maybe I wanted to be the mama. I wondered if it was possible for that to be us. Me, Jay, Kai. Mama, papa, cub.

# SIMONE

THE FIRST THREE months of Luck and Lion's lives, I was alone. Me, the babies, sometimes Tooth, and that truck that cocooned us. Motherhood makes you lonely, but more than that, having everyone turn away from you in the moment you need them most is a betrayal that lingers like a chipped tooth, for you to drag your tongue over and remember all that was lost and wouldn't return.

I didn't think none of my family would ever know my babies, call their names, understand the downy fuzz of their cheeks or the way it shed as they grew. I didn't think none of my family would ever want nothing to do with me again, after I left. After they made me leave. Jayden not choosing me hurt most, though.

If you not your mother's only child, you know there's not nobody in the world that can understand the dirt you fought to grow from like your brother. Jayden had been there, in the same bed, in the same trailer, shared the same breath and buckled under the same righteous thunder that my parents wielded best. He understood what it meant to love and hate them, to be their child, and still he chose to stand by them instead of me.

I spent most of my life scooping the blame from Jayden's shoulders and letting it curve my back into a hook. When he broke Momma's favorite mug throwing a ball across the trailer with our sisters, I picked up the ceramic pieces, glued them together, and told Momma I was sorry I'd ruined the thing she loved the most.

When some older guys ripped the skin from Jayden's chest so he was deep brown with a map of raw pink lines, I dressed his wounds and told Pops I'd seen a racoon attack Jay, right in broad daylight, after Jayden tried to chase it from the Cruz's cooler.

When Jayden started sneaking out to see the Jeffreys girl across Beach Row and he got caught and pulled back to bed by his T-shirt, I told Momma and Pops that the girl was a sweetheart and they mostly shared their favorite Bible verses and admired the stars spotting the sky together, even though she was known to be a pick-me and she prob'ly couldn't tell you the difference between Isaac and Isaiah if her momma's best wig depended on it.

Me and Jayden was close when we were little, and then we frayed. We didn't have much in common, but that ain't what family's about. I was the blistering bark that enclosed Jayden's tender red center and he'd been the soft middle of my world, the only person I knew wasn't never gonna hurt me. He was gentle, would sob before he screamed, cower before he clawed, and in a family where we stampeded, trampled, or fled at the first sign of smoke swirling the air, he was my safe haven.

But when I left, he didn't follow me out the door. And maybe I shouldn't've expected him to, he was only thirteen and he always did choose the path of least resistance. Still, I felt myself splinter when my birthday passed and he didn't call. Shed bark when I ran into him at the Tom Thumb in the gum aisle and he didn't even smile. Crumbled when my twins was born and he wasn't there to see it.

Those first three months as a mother were a lesson in how to lose my own core and I was prepared for the rest of my life to be hollow too, for the only family I knew to be the ones who came from me. Just when I'd gotten used to it, my brother reappeared in the spring bloom.

I don't know how he found me, 'cept that it was a town the size of a butter bean and if you looked hard enough you could find just about anyone. I was giving the babies tummy time in the truck bed, parked by our favorite strip of beach. A breeze roamed the air, rare for us, and every time it flushed the sky, Lion would open his mouth and laugh and Luck would sneeze. She'd just sneezed so hard she had to rest her little head on the blanket, her neck tired from resisting the sky above her so long, when Jayden walked up. I almost didn't recognize him. He was nearly fourteen and puberty had stretched him into somewhere closer to a man than the way I'd always thought of him, a small deer.

"Hi, Money," he said, and his voice was stones beneath a foot, low and crackling.

I was prepared never to know my brother again. When you give up hope and then watch your biggest dream resuscitated on a windy day when you least expected it, it's almost like meeting somebody once dead. And my ghost brother was standing in front of me with his hands stuck in his pockets and a question carved in his face.

"Can I . . . ," he started, coughing to shake the dips from his voice. "Can I hold 'em?" He shrugged toward the twins, both of their necks craned to look at him, this stranger making sound and breaking the usual echo of my voice and the rush of waves.

When my ghost spoke as soft as my brother, it rattled me so much I forgot to respond until the breeze returned and Lion laughed, Luck sneezed, and I stood. "Yeah. Yeah, of course."

I jumped down from the truck bed, opened the back so he could sit with his legs dangling, and placed Lion in the crook of his arm. Then I gathered Luck and tucked her into his other arm so they was both cradled, his head switching from looking at one to the other, the twins' toes touching so in his arms they made the shape of a heart out of his shoulders.

Jayden glanced up at me and his eyes was pooling. Soft boy. Raw heart.

"They perfect," he breathed.

I smiled, remembering that day when they swam from inside me, when I chewed through their cords and touched their skin still damp with fluid. "That's what I said."

And in that one moment, my brother's tears promised to stay by me, to find a way to know me and the children that came from me, and I promised to forgive him for those months he didn't know how to love me 'cause I knew what it was to be our parents' child, to want them to think angel of us. I knew what it took for him to show up, a budding man, and take an ounce of the blame from the place it called home on my back and let it weigh down those shoulders that held tight to my children as the breeze rolled back in. Lion laughed, looked up at his uncle's wet face. Luck sneezed, delicate and squeaky. Jayden smiled again.

◆ ◆ ◆

One thing you gotta know is I'm resourceful. I built a whole world in the back of a truck and if I had to rid myself of a child with nothing but my hands and my Girls, I would. But I was running out of ideas.

April shrugged. "I don't have extra," she said. "None of us do."

Jamilah's daughter hung on her nipple and sucked. Jamilah shook her head.

I turned to Tori. "What about you? You weanin' him, right?"

"Yeah, 'cause I got less milk the older he gets. Sorry, Simone. We can't help you."

I shook my head. This was the only thing I could think of, the milk, and even though I knew they'd all help me, 'cause I told 'em they owed me, which they did, I also knew they couldn't produce milk just 'cause I said so.

Selling my extra milk was how I'd made enough money to fix up Tooth's truck and turn it into a home back when the twins was infants. It didn't require nobody thinking I was worth a hire, especially when the babies still needed me close enough to touch at all times. But eventually my milk dried up and there was nothing left to sell.

I needed quick money for Planned Parenthood, and I knew I could rely on all those folks out there who had some kinda breast milk fetish, thought they could cure their eczema in a bath of some titty milk, or just didn't have their own for their baby. The only thing I needed was the milk itself. And I had none.

"You know who's got milk," Crystal started, hesitant. "Emory."

"No Emory. Not after last week."

Crystal shrugged. "She's got a freezer full of milk she won't be able to do nothing with real soon."

"I won't do it," I said. I wasn't about to fold and call Emory. But I would call the next best thing, the person who could get me that milk without making me beg the girl who hated me right now for it.

So I picked up the phone and called Jayden.

I was lucky he answered and luckier he hadn't left for Panama City yet, was still dozing in bed. I knew 'cause I could hear Momma's voice in the background and my throat throbbed. I asked Jay to come stop by the lake where we was parked and eventually he agreed.

An hour later, Jay's white pickup pulled in, the back full of wood scraps and tools he'd rented after I told him a father materializes with a binky and an armful of patience without never having to be called. He was a good dad. Great, even. If Emory let him, I knew he'd be there day and night through every feeding and fight to sleep. But since all he could do was show up every weekend with some cash and gifts, he never missed a chance.

Jayden stepped out, wifebeater and Timberlands on his skinny little body, and, like always, it hurt to see him. A pulsing ache like pushing a week-old bruise as he slunk toward me, neither of us knowing whether to hug or not and so we only did it halfway even though I wanted the whole thing. I wanted to be enveloped.

He stepped back and Jayden's widow's peak reached for me like a bird's beak, his sideburns longer than the top of his head 'cause I wasn't around to sit him down and buzz it even, 'cause we was living on two different planets in the same town. Lil Jayden grown half-big, got a job and a baby and still came home to a plate of Momma's home-cooked pork and fresh sheets at the end of the day. Lil Jayden still nursing the heartbreak Emory left him with over and over again, still afraid to look at a woman with her nipple shoved into a child's open mouth, still afraid to call himself afraid.

Jayden looked off into the line of pines and marsh noises to avoid looking at Jamilah, and he winced. "Damn, y'all couldn't cover up before I came? I ain't wanna see that shit."

"It's just a titty," I said. "You seen a titty before, right, Jayden?"

April giggled and Jayden looked down at his Timberlands. "Why you ask me to come here, Money?"

When Jayden was two, he couldn't say my name, so he started saying *Money* instead, and even when his lisp faded, he kept calling me it. When our little sisters were born seven years after Jayden, they heard him call me Money so often they started calling me it too, thought it was my name.

"I need help. I don't wanna tell you what for 'cause I don't want no opinions about it, but I need some money and I decided to sell some breast milk, but I don't got any. I need you to get Emory to give you her extra supply. But you can't tell her it's for me."

"You want me, a grown man, to ask my girlfriend for some titty milk? And say it's for me?"

"You ain't grown," Tori called, cackling. I glared at her and held my hand out in a warning.

"You know she's not your girlfriend no more," I said.

"Don't matter what we is right now, she still mine." Jayden's forehead split into lines. "What happened? Y'all was tight last week and this week she ain't stopped callin' you all kinds of names."

I wanted to tell him what happened was his white-ass bitch walked up on me with some light-skinned girl I don't know and then both of them got on my ass about something they shouldn't have no opinion on. I wanted to tell him I had two babies before I got my own driver's license, and I didn't wanna have another the same year I had my first legal drink.

I wanted to tell Jayden that Momma and Pops treated me like salt water to gargle and spit out while he got everything, even if the salad girl was right and everyone else thought my everything was nothing at all. I wanted to tell him that I was so much more than she thought of me, than they all did, that when my babies looked at me, they saw infinity: a blood source, a tsunami of warmth, two arms to be tucked beneath.

But all I could get out was "She don't respect me," which I guess was true too.

Jayden scoffed. "She don't respect nobody, Money. You know that."

"Then why you still love her?" Emory and him never made sense to me. Out of all the girls in this town, why choose the one who don't want you?

Jayden pulled his vape from his back pocket and took a puff into his mouth, still staring out at those trees like my face was too much for him. The only one he ever looked in the eyes was Emory.

"Well, she fine as fuck." Jayden licked his lips and grinned, thinking I'd let him be this chickenshit, pretendin' like he ain't felt all he felt.

I shook my head. "We both know that girl got thin-ass fake blond hair and prob'ly ten generations of incest, boy. You ain't love her 'cause of how she look and, if you do, it's prob'ly just 'cause you ain't like yoself, huh? Or maybe 'cause you don't like Momma? Or me? 'Cause Em just about the furthest-lookin' thing from us you gon' get and you might be the only boy who wanted her even after she fucked you, so why, Jay? Why you still pickin' her flowers on your anniversary like she ain't broke up with you six months ago?"

Jay crunched a twig with the tip of his boot and looked at the ground before finally meeting my eyes. "I love her for the same reason you love Tooth." He shrugged. "It's easier to love her than to hate her."

And that was when I couldn't look at him no longer, when I shoved my hands inside the back pockets of my cutoffs and glanced back over at the Girls, all of 'em pretending they ain't heard what Jayden said, and in this second, I knew it was true, but I also knew that admitting he was right wasn't an option I could live with tomorrow, when Lion asked me if Daddy was gonna come by and eat s'mores with us and Luck used her hair to tie around her chin and said *Look, Momma, I'm just like Daddy.* Tomorrow, I needed to be able to nod and say *Yeah, baby, Daddy can come help make sure your marshmallow don't catch on fire. Yeah, baby, I'd love if you grew up to be just like him.*

"You know I'm right. But if you ain't wanna know the answer to a question, best not to ask it," Jayden said. "Now, I 'preciate you callin' me out here to ask for my help, but I can't do nothing for you even if I wanted to. You know Emmy's grandpa not gon' let me up in his house, even if I was willing to ask my girl for her milk."

I rolled my eyes. "She's still not your girl."

He waved me off. "You go on and apologize to Emmy and she'll let you have whatever you want."

"I'm not sorry, though."

"Don't matter. You know all she needs is to hear you say it. She prideful."

Before I could respond, Luck ran up behind me with a small bird's nest in her hands and shouted, "Momma, Momma, Momma," until I kneeled to look at it with her.

"Baby, there's an egg in here," I said. It wasn't bigger than an eyeball, spotted and kind of green, and I bet she hadn't never seen an egg like that before.

"To eat?" she asked, her eyelashes stretching to each end as she looked down at her nest. She was normally so prone to destruction, knocking down anything she could find and giggling, running in circles till she inevitably ran into the trunk of a tree. She was indestructible. But, with the nest, she was gentle, careful not to drop it, slow.

I shook my head. "No, Lucky, that birdie's momma's prob'ly

lookin' for that egg 'cause that's her baby, like you my baby. Where you find it? Can you put it back for me so the momma birdie can find her baby?"

Luck pointed to a mulberry bush on the edge of some fence that'd been covered in vines and taken over in the past decades, the marsh consuming as it always did. Luck started half skipping back to the bush, her legs wanting to prance but her arms careful not to upset the nest or its egg. I straightened and looked back at Jayden.

"Fine," I said. "I'll make good with Em. You still owe me a favor, though."

Jayden nodded and looked like he might try to hug me again, but he didn't. He turned around and walked straight to his truck, careful not to glance at the Girls and their titties as he reversed and disappeared into the trees.

• • •

It took a lot to get Emory to meet me, but when I reminded her that I'd held her stomach up with my hands those last weeks when Kai's weight pulled at her back, that I'd seen the way one of her labia dangled when she spread her legs wide for me to wax it, that I'd sucked on her nipple just last week to get a clogged duct to flow again, she agreed to meet in the Walmart parking lot where her grammy worked.

I walked all the way from the lake, since I didn't want to pack up the Girls and bring them all here. I'd sweated out all the beer and water I'd drank the night before by the time I got here, and the bag of Goldfish I'd brought to ease my nausea was empty when Emory came out of the Walmart entrance with Kai still strapped to her. She traipsed toward me, joined me where I was collapsed against the side of the store, and leaned against the trash can opposite me.

"I can't believe you did that," Emory said, trying to cross her arms but finding herself unable to with Kai's body in the way. "You ruined everything. Adela doesn't even wanna talk to me anymore, 'cause she says I'm just as crazy as you, but you know I'm not. You've always been the crazy one, your whole family is, and I'm done with it. Done."

But Emory didn't move, which meant she wasn't done, she just wanted to see my face knot up. She wanted to see what I'd do next.

I tried to remember the good moments with Emory, when she sat beside me on the beach and wrote my name into the sand, when she knit Luck and Lion matching hats for their fourth birthday, when she consoled me in the middle of the night the last time Tooth forgot to pick up the kids for their fishing trip and I had to explain to them how a father can forget his children.

I heaved a breath and swallowed my contempt for all the worst parts of her, remembered in some backward way she was my sister. "I'm sorry I got so mad. I was drunk and I ain't needed to jump her or nothing, so I'm real sorry. I'll apologize to her too, if you want."

Emory looked at me, her lips still poking out, her eyebrow still bowing. "I get why you don't wanna keep it. Trust me, I do." She looked down at Kai and when she looked back up at me, her cheeks pillowy and red, she looked younger than she had since the day she felt her first Braxton-Hicks and wailed at me. "Just, try to be nicer, okay?"

I nodded, even though part of me still sorta wanted to punch her, but the other part of me wanted to hug her, so I compromised and did nothing. After a minute, she started to say goodbye, but I stopped her. "You know how you said you was happy to help me? Well, I need you. Actually, I need your milk."

She looked down at her chest and back up at me, and even though we weren't talking five minutes ago, I knew she'd do it for me. They all would. We understood what it was like to not have no help, to be entirely alone, but with each other we vowed not to leave, and as much as there was times when it didn't feel like it, Emory was one of us. Always would be.

# ADELA

WOKE UP AT DAWN for our third official date. The second date Chris took me back to his place and he was so sweet to me I disregarded the strewn clothes and three roommates, focusing only on his lips melted against mine. And now we were here, on the beach, and he was the picture of everything I'd always wanted, an orange surfboard beneath his arm and eyes that never strayed from me.

"You ready for me to teach you how to surf?"

There was something about Chris. Maybe it was the way he rocked his jaw side to side when he wasn't talking or the creamy whites of his eyes or how I could imagine him as a toddler, gripping his mother's pointer finger and leading her toward this ocean. I couldn't help but want to be his. When I was with him, the pregnancy disappeared. The loneliness evaporated. Florida became a possibility for alternate universes, alternate endings.

I followed Chris toward the tide.

His tattoos covered his torso, and I didn't normally like tattoos, but on him it made me want to graze the peaks of his body, the outline of his ribs showing briefly beneath a dragon and the words *Only God Can Judge Me*. When I asked him about the dragon, he said it was his protector, made him breathe fire when he was angry, and he told me it would help him protect me too. I think I might have blushed.

He was a good teacher, didn't use a lot of words but would get on the board and show me where to place my feet, how to crouch and follow the white rush of wave, and then he'd give me his board and let me try. The first three times, I immediately fell backward and my spine hit the shallow bottom of sand, causing me to draw in a breath of hot salt water and cough it back up. Chris rubbed my back, his hand slipping closer to the horizontal stretch marks where my hips grew wide beneath my bathing suit. I giggled and moved away from him to try again.

The fourth time, I was able to get my feet farther up on the board and crouch low, and I felt the exact moment when the board started to glide along the wave, when it lifted me and I felt what it would be like to walk on water, just a layer of foam between me and it, and it was exhilarating.

Chris picked me up and twirled me around and I instinctively wrapped my legs around his torso and let him kiss me, let him kiss the scratches on my neck, let my body grow hot even in the crisp morning, before hopping off him. Part of me wanted to ask him to take me back to his car and touch me bent over in his backseat. But I also wanted him to treat me like I was special. I wanted him to talk to me about the ocean, about the fish. Only then could I let him know my body the way he knew water, the way we both did.

After an hour of catching and chasing, catching and chasing, the waves started dying down and he asked me if I wanted to see something and I said yes, even though Noni would be waking up and calling down for me to come eat breakfast now.

He took my hand, laced his fingers through mine the way I'd seen my friend Lindsay's boyfriends hold her hand, so the sweat between our fingers grew sticky and it would hurt to pull apart. Chris led me up the sand to where the dunes made mountains between us and the road, and he helped me not trip as we climbed one dune and then wound down a path until we were standing in a little crater between two dunes.

It was cooler down there, hidden from the height of the sun, and Chris leaned his surfboard up against the tall side of the crater and pressed me to it, soft, careful not to mess up my hair. He kissed me, his hand still locked in mine, and I wanted to be close to him. I wanted to know him as deeply as the sea knew these dunes, perpetually chasing each other.

"We don't have to do nothing," he breathed between kisses. "I meant it when I said I wanted it to be special. For you."

I leaned back and looked up at him. "This is special," I said. "I want to."

He asked if I was sure, which made me all the more so, and the next thing I knew his shorts were around his knees and he was pulling at the crotch of my swimsuit.

"It's too tight," I said. It made me wish I had a bikini.

"Take it off, then."

I didn't want him to see me so exposed, reduced to nothing but skin, even if he saw the small protrusion of stomach and didn't know it wasn't there a month ago and would only grow from here.

"Let me just change really quick," I said, ducking from beneath him. I rifled through my bag and pulled out the dress I'd worn over my swimsuit on my way to the beach. I pulled it on and then carefully maneuvered the suit off until it was a wet bunch in my hand. I let it drop to the sand.

"You modest, huh?" Chris smiled. "I like that. Not a lotta girls like that no more. You different."

He still thought I was special, even when I didn't own a bikini and I was too afraid to let him see all of me. I turned back to him and kissed him, not like I had in his car the first time. This time, I kissed him with force, like I wanted to devour him, because I did, and I reached between the two of us and felt him hard and he whispered how beautiful I was as he lifted me up and pressed me to the sand wall and did what no one else had ever done: before he burrowed himself inside me and grunted, before he told me to get on my knees, before he held a thumb to my windpipe, he took those calloused fingers and circled my clit, made my head swarm.

Made me sweat and want more and I almost couldn't believe that it could feel like this, that this is what it was to be special, to be loved. He fingered me next, kissed me slow and then quick and then slow again, teased a nipple between his teeth. Not once did he try to lift my dress, though. He worked around the fabric, twisted it in his fist, grazed his arm against the hem as he touched me.

When he finally leveled his pelvis to mine and pushed, it only burned for a second. And after that second, I started to like it. Not for the feeling exactly, but for the way he nuzzled in my neck as he thrust, for the way he kept one hand always laced in mine, even after he came into the sand, even after he pulled away.

"You're perfect," he breathed. I wished we were in a bed so I could curl into his chest and fall asleep. I wished we could stay there forever.

Chris pulled his shorts back up. "Don't want your grandmama gettin' mad, though. Lemme take you home."

I picked my wet suit off the ground and put it in my bag, painfully aware of the sand in my ass crack and the fact I had no underwear, but it didn't matter because Chris didn't stop liking me after I let him have my body. He lifted me up out of the sand crater like a small child and held my hand the whole way back to his car.

The drive was short and I didn't know when I'd be able to sneak out and see him next, so I had to ask the question I'd been working up to, just in case this really became something.

"Do you think you'd ever want to have kids?"

Chris's eyes were locked on the road, but one hand stayed in my lap, still wrapped in mine. He cleared his throat. "Actually, I got kids. Two, but they mama's crazy and we're not together or nothing, don't worry."

Two kids? He must have had them when he was my age, one after the other, and I didn't know if I should be upset or relieved, if this was a sign he was mature enough to be a father or a sign he was not mine to have, that he already had a family of his own. But I don't think I was really angry or even comforted by the idea of him already having kids at all. Instead, I was jealous.

I tried to sound casual. "How long were you with their mom? You must've been young when you got together."

Chris shrugged. "Not that young. Twenty, maybe twenty-one."

"Twenty-one?" My whole body contracted at once, seized and held itself as I knew the question I was about to ask was not one I wanted answered. "Chris, how old are you?"

He glanced over at me and then back to the road and I couldn't figure out what his face was saying. Was he as scared to tell me as I was to know?

"I just turned twenty-seven."

Twenty-seven. I let my head fall back on the seat and stared ahead. Cement, gravel, dirt. Weeds and willows. I let the landscape change and felt myself morph with it. Fear, rage, disappointment, the tug of hope. I knew I had every reason to never speak his name again the moment I left his car, but when I looked back over at him and the glare of the sun dancing on his temples as his gaze moved back and forth, from me to the road, me to the road, I realized I didn't want to.

He was quiet when he spoke. "I thought you knew."

I nodded, leaned over, and kissed his cheek. "Of course I did. I just thought you were twenty-six." It wasn't true, but I just wanted to see the sadness melt from his face. I just wanted to forget it had happened and think instead of the way he touched me in our cove of sand.

"I'm sure you're a great dad," I said.

He pulled up to the community center, where he would drop me off.

"I think so. But I wanna have more kids. With somebody more like me, you know?" He smiled, earnest. "I don't got no doubt you'd be a damn good mama, Adela."

And for the first time, I thought, yeah, maybe I would. Maybe his dragon would come out and create a barrier between the world and us, our family. Maybe his age meant all of this was even more possible, that he could be mine and I could be his and we could make a family that was ours. I could cook the fish he caught and follow him deep into the ocean, stand at the height of the wave and be unrelenting, beside a man who would love me despite it all. Maybe he was exactly what I'd always hoped for.

◆ ◆ ◆

"You ready, sweetie?" The doctor raised the wand up so I could see its full length and my legs snapped shut at the sight of it.

My parents insisted I go to the obstetrician every four weeks of the pregnancy, and I'd spent the first weeks in Florida arguing with Noni about not wanting to see the only ob-gyn in the county, since I knew that he would tell somebody who would tell somebody and next thing I knew, the whole school would think I was just another one of the Girls.

It took weeks for Noni to be able to find an appointment and take the day off to drive me all the way to Tallahassee for it. I was just happy to get out of school early so I didn't have to deal with Emory staring at me, her pupils quivering and begging me to talk to her.

But I didn't know they were going to hold up this long wand and tell me that it was going to go inside me.

"Can't you just rub it on my stomach?" I asked, squeezing Noni's hand.

The doctor, a middle-aged white woman with the biggest lip fillers I'd ever seen, smiled softly, which made her look like she was about to cry or burst out laughing, and said, "We won't get a very good picture this far along if we don't go in transvaginally. Mm-kay?" And, just like that, she pulled a latex glove over the wand so the other four finger holes just flapped around at the bottom and lubed it up, putting my feet in these little holders, lifting under the paper sheet she'd given me, and then sticking that rubber glove wand directly inside me.

I grunted and Noni whispered, "It's not like you ain't had nothin' up there, Delly, just relax."

So I shut my eyes and let the feeling subside to a slight pressure, and I tried to picture myself in the water, started counting strokes. One, the delicate blow of bubbles with every breath. Two, the sweet sting of my rotator cuffs swinging in a butterfly. Three, Chris's face as I came up for air on that surfboard.

Chris had probably been in a room like this one, with some other girl, when his children were so small they could only be visible by a stick shoved deep inside that girl. I got so lost in the water and Chris and wondering what this other girl whose children he'd fathered was like that Noni had to squeeze my hand and whisper, "Look," for me to flash open my eyes.

On the screen, the doctor was pointing to a black hole in the white static of the image, and inside that hole there were three white blobs. She froze the screen and dragged a cursor across the two connected blobs, turned to me with her lip fillers flipping up in her smile like a duck, and said, "There's your baby."

"That thing? That's a baby?" It just seemed too inconsequential, too fuzzy, to be a real human.

"Yes, sweetheart. Your baby," the doctor said.

I pointed to the other white blob above the ones that were apparently my baby's head and torso. "What's that thing, then?"

"That's the yolk sac. It's what's feeding that baby and keeping it alive until it grows a placenta."

The doctor kept taking pictures at different angles, muttering measurements as she inputted them into my chart, and then she found the heartbeat and let me listen to it, but that wasn't what got me, wasn't what stilled everything else and rushed through me like the howl of wind a car leaves behind as it barrels down the road. And

I was standing in its wake, cold. Like I'd been in the water for hours, my skin pruned, and my body made of soft flesh and crevices eager to break open at a too-harsh touch.

It was not the heartbeat that did this, but that third white blob and the deep black surrounding it. All the nausea coursing through me had meant nothing until now, when it became evidence of my body constructing not only that little thing that would probably become a baby but my body creating this other small thing that had channeled me and the spasms of my body into keeping something alive.

I thought of those three yolks I'd punctured and poured down the drain weeks ago and wondered if my little yolk sac would run yellow if this doctor split me open. And that black around it was my own body of water, floating this would-be baby around inside me, and as small as I felt in the ocean, I wondered if this would-be baby felt small inside me too. I knew it didn't feel anything yet, but it would, if I let it, if I didn't try to stop it. If I cared enough to want to hear one day how it felt to exist in my body's sea.

"I know you said you didn't get your period regularly, so we were estimating based on the presumed date of conception, but it's looking like this baby is measuring a little small at about seven weeks right now instead of eight, so the new due date looks like it's going to be May fourteenth, 2024. A good birthday, don't you think?" She started typing this up and then printing the little photos from the screen. "Are you thinking of names yet? I know it's early, but some people already have 'em picked out."

I squeezed Noni's hand tighter. "Uh, no, I'm not sure that I'm even going to have anything to do with it. You'll name it, right, Noni?"

She looked down at me. "Whatever you want, Delly. You don't gotta know right now. Let's wait till you big, hmm?"

Big. Yes, I was going to get big. I was going to get so big I wouldn't be able to hide it from anyone at school or Chris or myself, even. And, at some point, I was going to have to make a choice and that choice would change so much, and the moment the doctor handed me the photo of my three blobs, I burst out sobbing. She pursed her lips and left us alone in the room so I could pull on my panties, but I didn't move. Noni scooped me into her chest and said, "I know, baby. I know."

While Noni went to the bathroom, I waited for her outside the car and dialed Lindsay's number. Lindsay was my closest friend back home in Indiana, and even though we'd only texted a few times since I got to Florida, I still thought of her like that. My best friend. The person you call when you panic. Lindsay didn't pick up until the last ring and then, just when I was sure she wouldn't, she answered.

"Del? Why are you calling me? I've, like, literally never talked to anyone on the phone who wasn't, like, my mom. Do you want to FaceTime? I've got an hour till practice."

"Um, I can't. I'm waiting for my grandma."

Neither of us said anything for a minute. I listened to the sound of running water that I realized was Lindsay peeing and then a flush.

I broke the silence. "I'm having, like, the worst week. Will you just tell me something, distract me? Like has Violet been made captain yet? Has David said anything to you about me?"

Over the past weeks, I'd been scrolling my phone and looking at the photos of people in my class posting homages to the summer, bikini shots at hotel pools, and sunglasses hiding all traces of difference in their faces. I hadn't posted since my last swim competition in July, and I wished I had something good to post, something that would feign normalcy without giving me away. But Dad was clear: no one could know I was in Florida. They'd told the school I was going on an opportunity abroad after Coach said it would be best for my athletic career if we kept this to ourselves.

Even with all the lurking I'd been doing, I couldn't figure out any real information: Who was dating who now? Was Violet excelling without me? Had David thought of me last week and decided I might have been worth more than a single fuck?

Lindsay's voice went high. "Um, well, I'm not really sure, but, uh, you should probably know that people are talking about you. I mean, people have just been coming to me asking if it was true, that you were, you know."

"That I was what?"

"Del!" Lindsay's tone implied it should be obvious. "You know, that you're . . . with child, or whatever."

"Oh." I hadn't thought about Violet telling anyone else. Or maybe Lindsay had told. Or Coach. It could have been anyone, looking for some good gossip to pass the slow midwestern days. I was instantly humiliated, maybe even more than I had been when I threw up in the pool in front of Chris.

"I told them it wasn't like you were one of those Jefferson High girls, you're not ghetto like that. And I tried to explain that it wasn't very feminist of them to put all of it on you, 'cause it's David's fault too, but David says he's not even the dad."

I didn't think I cared until she said it. But it punctured right through me, and I felt all my feelings leak from a hole in me that couldn't be patched.

I'd thought David was going to be my first love. Some days, I still thought he was. I didn't have a lot of extra time, outside elite training and swim practice and school, but whenever I caught a single moment of breath, I thought about David. His hair all rusty brown, his eyes golden green, his smile clumsy. I memorized his class schedule and lingered in the halls between periods just to run into him. He barely even looked at me, until I went to the only non-swim party I attended in all of high school.

It was the squishy center of summer and me and Lindsay went to her ex-boyfriend's house because he was throwing a rager for all the kids who weren't vacationing or doing summer programs. I didn't drink or smoke or anything, so I stayed back on the edges of the party while Lindsay ran wild. By midnight, the only people left in the living room were me, David, and some freshman boy I didn't know.

David and the freshman were playing a football video game on the TV and David beat the freshman. He threw down the remote and got up to get a drink. That's when David looked at me.

He was high, I could tell because his golden-green eyes looked like they'd been dipped in the soapy liquid kids blow bubbles out of. *You look good tonight,* he said. My hands sweat cold. *You want to go upstairs?* I nodded. David took me to Lindsay's ex's parents' bedroom. He laid me down on their bed and when he said he didn't have a condom, I shrugged and said it was probably fine. I only got my period a couple times a year anyway, and I hadn't had it in three months. He smiled down at me and said, *You're cool, you know.* I kissed him and thought I was in love.

Now I wasn't sure if I was stupid or if, maybe, we would've ended up together if it wasn't for the pregnancy. It was humiliating to think he might know, though, that he might be out there wishing he could take that night at the party back.

"David knows?" I asked.

"How could he not? Adela, don't be dumb, you knew what was going to happen when you decided to have a baby at sixteen."

"I didn't decide to do anything." Lindsay was always doing this, blaming me for things, eager to know my secrets only to turn around and judge them. I didn't want to get pregnant. I guess I just didn't do enough to prevent it. "Well, you can tell them all I'm having a great time here. I live right on the beach and I actually met a guy. So David can go around saying he's not the dad all he wants. I have someone who I'm sure would kill to be my kid's dad."

I was sure Chris would too. Especially if he found out when it was too late for him to have an opinion on it. He already had kids, what was one more?

"Really? Who?"

"His name's Chris. He's more . . . mature."

"Oh." Lindsay was mad, I knew because she started clicking her tongue. "Well, I should let you get back to your *mature* life."

I listened to the silence, thinking she'd retract it and apologize, but she didn't. "Fine," I said. "My new friends are waiting for me anyway."

I hung up first so Lindsay couldn't, and even though I hadn't planned on seeing any of the Girls again, now I felt desperate for someone who would understand, someone who would know what it means to have just seen that little yolk sac and be changed in the aftermath.

Noni arrived back at the car and we both climbed in and got back on the highway. After an hour of listening to her old-school radio, I spoke.

"Can we make a stop on the way home?"

"Where you wanna go? I don't got no McDonald's money on me right now."

I shook my head from the passenger seat, where Noni said I could ride just for this one trip. "Will you take me to Emory Reid's house?"

When I knocked on Emory's door, I was ready for her grandparents to answer, to explain who I was and charm them if I needed to, but neither of them showed up on her porch. Emory came to the door instead, without Kai, the first time I'd ever seen her without a baby strapped to her, and she immediately started pushing her greasy hair away from her face, her roots growing in dark brown, her forehead squirming, and I didn't have the words, not yet, so I handed her the little photo of the ocean in my body and, this time, when Emory reached for my hand, I didn't hesitate. I let her take it.

# EMORY

ADELA WAS SENT here just for me. I knew it from the minute I saw her. Her pregnancy just confirmed it.

I mean, I'd been compelled by the nature of life since I was born. Not how or when we became, but why we became. The specific natural selection that made us into ourselves. How our cells arranged to create life capable of enduring the hellscape that was this world. It fascinated me, always had.

Pawpaw was a believer in not asking questions, trusting God had it handled. He thought science was the crutch we leaned on to justify all our bullshit. There were times I agreed with him, mostly when I was trying to explain something that just didn't make no sense, but that was before Adela.

When Adela showed up at my door with an ultrasound photo, I knew it was more complicated than anything Pawpaw thought. I mean, I couldn't fight the undeniable nature of destiny that was Adela on my porch. But it wasn't just destiny. Life was the meeting of an organism's undying persistence to survive and that funny little thing called faith. I believed it now.

Adela, pregnant. I had to admit, there was a sliver of me that was jealous of whoever had a claim to that baby, to being a part of her forever. But mostly, I was grateful for all the seconds that collided into moments and then days of me and Adela, together. My best friend.

The salvation of a life that had been chipping at all its edges since Kai was born.

But I'd seen how quickly Adela could leave, so I didn't let myself get too comfortable. Like a penguin on a bed of ice floating toward the equator, I thought every day might be my last with her, and when I woke up to her text or call or face in the hallway at school searching for me, I had to remind myself that life endured, that she was here for a reason and, at least for the moment, she was mine.

Moments with Adela when we were alone, sitting at a picnic table during lunch or wading into the Gulf or splayed across the cold floor in her bedroom, kept me satiated for all the other moments when she wasn't around. When Mrs. Simmons brought me into her office each week, insisting I wasn't allowed to bring Kai to school. When I returned home in the evenings and Pawpaw started going at me about how I never cleaned Kai's spit-up and how it was all over the carpet in the living room like his beer hadn't already turned it brown and sour. When Jay called me, pleading for me to get back with him, as if I could ever do that with Adela here. I wasn't lonely anymore. For the first time in my life, I had a best friend.

Every time I got to hear Adela's giggle or watch her scarf down some food, I felt the life return to me. But I knew she would be gone soon, for an hour or a day or maybe forever, so I had to store whatever I had of her inside me. Like a cactus stores its water in its core. Rationing to my veins through mirages of her skin around the corner of a hallway and the sound of her velvet voice in the deep parts of the night as Kai screamed.

Adela disappeared for periods of time, in the mornings and on the weekends. She wouldn't even answer her phone. I would go by her house and ask her grandmother where she was and her grandmother would always say, "She's with her friend from the pool," but when I asked Adela who her friend from the pool was, she shrugged and said, "No one." I didn't want to push her away, so I left it at that, thinking maybe she was just alone, in the water somewhere, away from her phone.

But on the weekdays, she was mine. I used every second I had with her, asking her to read my college essays, showing her how to burp a baby, and trying again and again to get her to give Simone and the Girls another chance.

It was on one of these weekends when Adela disappeared, October and the peak of storm season, when we started hearing murmurings of the hurricane. With it, as though Kai could feel it coming, a fever came over him.

I wouldn't wish a sick infant on no one, no one at all. He'd cry with such ferocity, his face turned red. His sharp nails clawed at his cheeks and ears and hair and then turned to scratch at my cheeks and ears and hair, forcing me to suffer with him. There was no end to it. No matter how many lullabies I sang. No matter the forceful push with which I stuck my nipple in his wide, sobbing mouth. The cries wouldn't stop.

He'd sleep for only ten or twenty minutes at a time before he'd start writhing in a lazy sweat and his eyes would blink open mid-roar. I had no idea this much sound could erupt from such a small body, this much sickness circulating inside a person so new.

I skipped school on Monday, then Tuesday. Adela called each day asking where I was, when I'd be back, and I had nothing to tell her. The fever would die down only to return again at night. In the middle of the night on Tuesday, Pawpaw banged on the door to my room and then swung it open, his hair a frizzy disaster around his bald spot, his eyes manic.

"I can't do it no more," he said. "Y'all gonna have to leave first thing tomorrow."

I was on the bed blowing cold air into Kai's face to try to get him to cool down, so exhausted I couldn't make sense of what Pawpaw was trying to say.

"What do you mean, leave?"

Pawpaw held his head in his hands, his eyes glancing wildly around the room. "I can't get no sleep with him cryin' all day and night and with this storm comin' I won't be trapped inside with no sick baby, I just can't be doin' that, not at my age."

"Pawpaw, you're only in your sixties." I continued blowin' on Kai, but when Pawpaw didn't leave in a huff, I looked back up at him, and he was serious. "Where you want me to go? You can't kick me out in a hurricane."

"Don't be a sidewalk sissy now, Emory. Go stay with one of those girls, call his daddy, I don't really give a rat's behind where it is you go, sweetheart. Just get out my house so I can get some gosh darn sleep." Pawpaw slammed the door shut behind him, which, of course, only made Kai cry harder and I was right there with him, our tears running into a single wet pool on my chest.

◆ ◆ ◆

On Wednesday, they shut the school down. All the nonessential businesses closed up. Sandbags were laid out, people clutched their children close, and I stood out in the warm, dense rain, attempting to hold on to the umbrella in the wind only for it to blow upward and let all that rain rush in on us.

When Jay pulled up, I swung my bag full of Kai's stuff into the middle seat of the truck cab, closed the umbrella and flung it into the footwell, and climbed in. The moment of rain on Kai's head quieted him for a moment, but once I shut the car door, the little demon in him reemerged and he cried so hard the purple veins at the back of his throat showed.

Jay beamed at me, one hand on the steering wheel. "This fate, Emmy. I got the day off work, and I was just thinkin' 'bout you when you called."

I glared at him. "Your son's so sick I haven't slept in days, we're in the middle of a hurricane, and I just got kicked out of my house. It's not fate, Jay, it's karma."

I shoved Kai into his arms, and he took him with ease. Jay was too nice about it all. It made it hard to resent the fact that I had to deal with his child all day and all he had to do was send me some money every week and beg for my love.

I knew that wasn't entirely fair. I mean, Jay would drop anything for Kai and me. But all I had to keep a border drawn between me and him was a curdling resentment and I wasn't about to let my guard down.

"His doctor's expecting him at urgent care, thinks maybe he's got an ear infection or something, but you're gonna need to take him," I said. "Your sister needs me to go do something with her, but I can meet you back at Beach Row right after I'm done. I know it'll be tight with us all in the trailer, but I really appreciate your parents coming around."

Jay glanced away from me, at the steering wheel. That's how I knew him saying his ma had changed her mind and they were gonna let me and Kai stay with them was false. He just wanted to get us in his car, orchestrate a second chance for him as though we'd ever had a real shot the first time. He lied to me.

"Are you fuckin kidding me—" I started.

Jay folded. "I'm so sorry, Emmy, it's just I was working up to talking to 'em when you called, and I was sure they'd be fine with it. But when I asked Momma and Pops, they said they can't have y'all with us. But we can still meet at the Beach Row entrance later. I'll just keep Kai in the car till then."

I shouldn't've believed him in the first place. His family didn't have space for me and Kai inside usually, didn't want us anyway, but I figured it would be different in a hurricane.

"And you just said okay, I'll let my baby and his mother sleep out in a hurricane?" I crossed my arms. "You're such a pussy sometimes."

This morning, Simone called and said that they were all planning on staying at Tori's boyfriend's place, but his place was already flooding and now none of the Girls had nowhere to stay, and Simone's appointment was this afternoon. They were all camping out in the hospital waiting room for now, but eventually someone would notice they didn't have anyone to visit and then we'd all be out cowering in the dunes, us and the kids. Jay was my last option, at least the last one I thought might work. I shook my head. I could barely look at him. Now I'd have to go to the only person I had left and ask her something that might make her hate me again.

Jay tried to lean over and kiss my neck, but I pushed him away, fishing into my backpack and pulling out two full bottles. "Take Kai to the doctor in an hour. Feed him every two hours, burp him after, and try to get him to go to sleep. I'll pick him up from Beach Row before dark and don't worry, I won't try to come inside."

I grabbed the umbrella and leaned in to kiss Kai's forehead. As I opened the door to get out, Jay's voice broke—"Emmy, wait"—but I closed it in his face. I wasn't sure how many more times I could handle breaking this boy's heart. It was getting plain embarrassing. For the both of us. Like Pawpaw sometimes said, if Jay fell in a barrel of tits, he'd somehow come out suckin' his own thumb. But he kept on divin' anyway. And I was getting real tired of turning him away.

◆ ◆ ◆

I waited on Adela's front porch until the red door opened and her face showed pale. She'd been throwing up again.

"I've been texting you for days. Are you okay?" she asked.

I shook my head.

"Come inside." She opened the door wider for me, but I stayed on the porch under the sliver of protruding roof keeping me dry. Adela's eyebrows reached for each other in the center of her face. "What's wrong? Where's Kai?"

"With his dad. Look, I'm gonna ask you something and I need you to consider it, okay? Can you do that?"

She leaned forward and I wanted to fold against her chest and beg her to take me in, but the rain was pouring behind me and I knew if I did that, if I overstepped, I'd be worse off than I was laying out in the flood of rain. After all, she was my drinkable water, and there was no life without her.

"Of course. Are you sure you don't want to come inside, just to stay dry?"

I shook my head again. "In about five minutes Simone's gonna pull up and I'm gonna need to go with her to Tallahassee to the clinic and, when we come back, we're gonna pick up the kids and the other Girls and then we're not gonna have nowhere to go." I paused, looked up at her. "Can we stay with you? Just till the storm's over?"

Adela leaned back. "*All* of you?"

I nodded, sniffed in the wet, electric air.

Adela crossed her arms. "You can stay. My noni's taking some kind of sleeping pill, she won't even know you're here. The Girls can stay too. Just not Simone. Not after what she did to me."

I was considering saying okay, thanking her and falling into her arms, but then Simone's red truck pulled up outside the line of trees around Adela's house. I could feel the engine, the buzz of my phone with the text I knew Simone had sent telling me to hurry up. I pictured Simone and the twins in the back of the truck tonight. Rainwater filling the truck bed till they were swimming in it. I couldn't leave Simone like that.

I clasped my hands together. "Please, Adela. She's pregnant, just like you, and she found a way outta it, that's why we gotta go to Tallahassee, so she can have her appointment to get the pills, and I can't let her do that alone. What if it was you? What if it was me? How could you let me do that alone?"

She stared at me and I couldn't read her. She got like that sometimes, cold and judging, analyzing me with those narrow eyes, and that's when I was most aware of how much I needed Adela. At the possibility of rejection planted deep inside her eyes.

"If it was you," she started, "I wouldn't let you do it alone. But if you were me, what would you do? She *attacked* me, Emory." Adela placed her hand on her stomach, where the smallest slope was growing.

I thought about it. If I was Adela, if my skin glowed like that, if I had those mountains of muscle on my back and a chin that never dropped, would I let a girl who pounced on me in my house? I wasn't even sure Adela thought of Simone as a girl, as much as she thought of her as that alligator she'd tried running zigzag from: something set out to hurt her, as though it was in its nature. If I thought a creature built to kill was after me, I wouldn't let it in my house till it proved it could do something besides terrorize me. That there was something in it distinctly kind, caring. Human.

"What if Simone could help your nausea?" I said. "She did it for me, when I was pregnant, did it for all of us who had it real bad, and if you let her, she'd help you. I know she would."

Adela's top lip curled inward, and her voice got low. "The medication the doctor gave me was the only thing that helped but it made me so dizzy I couldn't even see, so I stopped taking it. How am I supposed to believe some crazy girl could fix something a doctor couldn't?"

I shrugged. "'Cause Simone's had to survive without nobody to help her." My phone buzzed again, Simone growing impatient. "Either way, I can't stay with you if you won't take all of us in. I won't."

Adela stared at me, deciding whether or not to test my bluff, and then she opened her arms, reached out for my hand, and brushed her thumb across my palm. "Okay," she said. "Simone can come too."

In moments like these, the way I felt about Adela didn't make any sense, not even to me. Maybe this was what true friendship was like, when your body overflowed like a pond after rainfall, fish spilling from my stomach, jumping and flailing out of the water. When there was no way to contain all the life in you and you almost didn't care.

All I wanted was to be close to her. Kindred spirits or whatever. But sometimes I thought it might just be me. Maybe I was overly attached to Adela. Even now, on her steps, the urge to hug her slashed through me when anybody else would've just smiled and said thank you. I didn't know how to make sense of it, so I just squeezed her hand once.

"Thank you," I said. She smiled at me, and I squeezed her hand one more time before backing off the porch, into the rain, dashing beneath the arch of trees to Simone's truck, and slamming the truck door shut behind me to keep out the rain.

When I looked over at Simone, I could see the fear ripe on her face.

"Don't worry," I said. "She'll take us."

Simone's face arched. "Me too?"

I nodded. "She's not what you think, Simone. You'll see."

Simone didn't protest as she pulled out onto gravel awash with water, sped down the road to the highway, where we both gazed in front of us as far as we could see.

It was raining like a cow pissing on a flat rock. That rain pounded and spit at the windshield, both of us bracing for the next moment and then the next, when the rain would tornado us, not taking a single real breath till we pulled into the parking lot behind the Planned Parenthood, and when I saw it I reached for Simone's hand, the way I knew I'd want her to hold mine, the way I knew I'd insist on holding Adela's if this was her, and for the first time since I'd met Simone, she didn't shove me off, 'cause she saw it too and it was devastating.

Right through the center of the clinic building, a tree had fallen. I looked over at Simone and I thought I saw a tear glisten in her right eye, but I never saw it fall.

# SIMONE

W HEN I FIRST learned I was having twins, I didn't understand
how that happened. I bet you think I'm dumb for that, but
they don't teach you this shit in school. I kept asking the doctor if they was identical and he kept shaking his head and explaining
that if they was identical, the egg would've split in two. But my egg
didn't split, there was just two eggs that wanted to hole up in my
womb, two placentas and two cords to go with them.

When I saw the pine tree sitting right in the center of the building
I was supposed to be in, I thought of that day in the doctor's office at
fifteen, holding on to Tooth's hand, imagining my egg splitting right
down the center when really my babies were two separate things
from the beginning, who'd both chose to exist in my body. Finding
me at the same time, it was an act of fate. Not like this. This was the
devil raining down.

The tree was cutting the building right in half like a knife, both
sides empty and dark, and I guess I should've been happy it didn't
seem like no one was inside, but instead I felt dumb that I ain't even
considered they'd close down for the hurricane.

I tried calling them from the parking lot, again and again, but no
one answered, and Emory, still holding on to my hand and shaking
her knee in rhythm to the torrential rain, squeezed my palm after I
hung up for the third time, reaching voicemail again.

"It'll be okay, we can come back next week," she said.

"No we can't." I ripped my hand away from hers and leaned my cheek against the glass. All sounds were muffled, like crystallized honey clogging my eardrums. "We both know they not gonna be able to fix it and open again for at least a few weeks, and by then I'll be too far along, they won't give it to me. Fuck, Em. What am I supposed to do? I can't have another one of his babies."

Last night, I called Tooth to ask if he could take the twins today, and he started going off on me about how I don't get to decide what he does, and then I heard a giggle in the background and I knew he'd found a new girl. I hung up and resolved that I would figure it out, do whatever it took, hurricane or not. For Luck and Lion. For me.

Emory'd come through today, having Jayden take Kai so she could come with me, and somehow managing to convince Adela to let us all stay with her, even after what I did. I was so close to making it all happen, to doing the thing they tell us not to do right before they scold us for daring to wear a tank top in the summer heat and reveal the bump that so shamelessly mocked them.

I was so close, after weeks of driving around and selling Emory's frozen milk to whoever was willing to pay. I'd been so proud of that money, even if it wasn't my milk, and I had just enough left over I could buy Luck and Lion a Christmas tree in two months. A small one, maybe two feet, and we'd have to keep it in the back of the truck, but I could already imagine seeing the bumpy roof of Lion's mouth as he grinned wide at the sight of it.

But now all those bills were worthless 'cause they couldn't begin to pay for a lifetime with the thing I had fighting inside me and I didn't know what to do. All I knew was Luck and Lion were hours away and they needed me, so I revved the truck again, swallowing the ache to scream, and didn't listen when Emory suggested we wait for a pause in the rain.

The worst part of driving in a hurricane wasn't actually the way the rain obscured even the few inches beyond the windshield, or the depth of the water you thought was just a puddle till you felt your front wheel dip all the way down into it, your back wheel sliding across and threatening to send you skidding. The worst part of driving in a hurricane was the wind.

The wind thrashed, tormented, made mockery of the weight of the truck, the slick dripping metal as it effortlessly blew us into the next lane. I had to wrestle, gripping the steering wheel, murmuring prayers and pleading for the wind to blow us forward, straight ahead, back to our children.

Motherhood was a constant supply of adrenaline, a goddamn phenomenon of logic, I thought, as I felt the wheels skid. I let up on the accelerator until I felt ground beneath us again.

I read a book once about a girl named Linda who escaped her plantation but stayed there, on the property, hiding in the crawl space for months. I read it, curled up in the library, Linda looking through the little hole and watching her children age down below, Linda waiting for opportunities even as they passed her by, heart caught like a hangnail on the hope of those babies, and I nodded. Yeah, that's what it was. Motherhood made you believe blindly, hope endlessly, behave irrationally, as long as it meant those children tucked safely in the pocket of your love.

I was crazy, like Linda, and I knew it as I drove hours through the hurricane, but it didn't matter none 'cause, for Luck and Lion, I lived in the promise I'd made the moment I'd birthed them: to pull a world that was good to them from the depths of its horrors. I owed them the impossible.

Emory clutched on to her seat beside me and shouted across the chorus of rain. "I don't know if we can make it back like this."

"We have to," I said.

We didn't get to make no different choices. That was motherhood. Emory was still new at it, considered for a moment letting Jayden and Kai stand outside my parents' weighed-down trailer as he pleaded for them to let him inside. They wouldn't, though, not with a child born outside of something bound by time, contract, history, and even if Jayden convinced himself they had all that, I saw the way Emory averted her eyes from him, the way they settled on Adela.

"What if we pulled over and called Adela, got her to go pick up the kids?"

I shook my head. Emory was being stupid, selfish. She didn't get it like I did, like Linda did. And when she finally understood, I knew she'd wish she could go back to not knowing 'cause it'd be too much for her, suffocating on love. "Storm's only gettin' worse and could last days. I don't know 'bout you, but I can't be leavin' my kids without me like that, especially in some girl I don't know's house. If you want me to pull over and let you out, I will, but I'm going home."

And then, in front of me, I saw what I thought might be a glimmer of sunset, a faint pulsing orange tint in the shadows beyond the rain. But Emory must've been able to see it for what it was 'cause she let out a hell of a screech, the kind of sound that didn't need no words accompanying it 'cause it reached the body before I could even form a thought, and my hands whipped the steering wheel away from the glimpse of what was not a lowering sun but the blinking hazards of an SUV in what had been my lane, was supposed to be my lane, that car sunk into its own crater of water, unmoving, obstructing anything that dared to venture across a highway in a hurricane. I'd been one ripping eruption from Emory's vocal cords away from slamming right into it, not seeing it until it was too late.

And, still, I didn't have no choice but to drive on.

Emory didn't speak again, didn't protest even as we passed by two cars on the side of the road, the first car's bumper battered to a naked scrape of silver and the second car's wheels invisible beneath the small lake of water that had filled a crater-sized pothole. Made me think of Luck, throwing herself from the rope into the dune lake. Made me drive faster.

I knew we had to get home, that no matter what this thing inside me became, no matter what destruction the hurricane descended to wreak, we couldn't think about nothing but the abyss of fear in a child's pupils when they were sure their mother wasn't gonna return.

◆ ◆ ◆

"What about a coat hanger?" April offered.

I'd been thinking the same thing, I think we all had. Still, no one responded, let the sound of the rain resound in Adela's basement, where we gathered, spread out, blankets protecting our skin from the cold of the linoleum.

Adela finally shook her head. "I don't mean to interfere or anything, but . . ." She glanced at me and when I didn't glare, she continued, "A coat hanger is only a good idea if you want to risk bleeding out down here. And even if I didn't care if you stained my noni's floor, I don't think you want to let your kids watch that."

Adela retreated back to her hunched spot under her blanket, leaned up against her sofa bed, the same position she'd been in since I gave her the handmade sea bands, and she put them on her wrists and sank into the relief of not feeling nauseous for the first time in months.

When we all came down here and Tori pulled out the liquor and weed from her pockets, ready to get the party started, I could tell Adela hadn't realized we'd be partying, hadn't never thought you could do nothing in a hurricane but stare at the wall and pray your house didn't get swept away. But since she had the bands on, she'd never looked so relaxed.

It was night now and we had candles scattered around the room, everyone trying to keep a hand or a flashlight on each kid before they ended up sucking on some exposed pipe. Emory was as close to Adela as she could get without intruding on Adela's blanketed sphere, and I could tell by the way she leaned that she wanted to be closer. We'd barely made it back when the rain picked up and if I wasn't panicking about the inevitability of my life, I'd be grateful just to be dry.

Emory nodded. "Adela's right, it's not smart."

I looked up at her and, for just a moment, let her see it all. The creeping suspicion that I would not get to have a choice in this, that a child would be born and no matter how much I loved that baby, another child would take something from me and my children's lives that could never be returned. Like a lost tooth, you can get a fake one put in, metal screwed into the base of a gum, but your body won't never forget what is missing, the bone that could have been in its place. I whispered, just loud enough they could all hear, "I don't know what else to do."

"What about the vacuum suction thingy? They could take it out like that after they fix up the clinic in a few weeks, right?" Jamilah proposed.

Crystal took a sip of her beer. "I wouldn't count on it. They can't do nothing for you after fifteen weeks, it's the law, and how far along are you, Simone?"

"Eleven weeks."

Tori nodded. "Yeah, I wouldn't risk that. What about a different clinic?"

"The next closest clinic is in Mobile and they don't do abortions. And even if I could do a six-hour drive to somewhere else, the limits in the next four states are even less than fifteen weeks. I don't got that kinda time."

"So what do we do? If the clinic ain't an option and you won't use no coat hanger, what are you supposed to do?" Jamilah asked.

I kissed the top of Lion's head as he flipped through a picture book in my lap, a flashlight tucked under his little chin.

Crystal set Cece's sleeping frame onto a blanket on the floor. "My grandmama told me something when I was pregnant, about how her sister got knocked up by some white man when she was young and her mama made her a special tea. I think it was made of sage or something, and her blood came just like that. I wanted my Cecilia, but Grandmama said that plenty of women in the family'd done the same and ain't nothing bad happened as long as nobody went around blabbing about it."

I nodded, remembering something. "I read in some book, years ago, about cotton root being used for centuries to make your period come, back when our families was bred like chickens in a slaughter house." I tucked a curl on Lion's head behind his ear and glanced over to check that Luck was still fiddling with a Rubik's Cube beside me. "But it don't matter 'cause I don't know where I'd find any of that shit anyway. I can't tell the difference between no eucalyptus and bay leaf."

I guess it's fitting that Adela would be the one to destroy me and save me at once, to come in at all the right and wrong times and change everything without me even knowing, and this time, when she spoke up, I could imagine the thing inside me breaking open like the tree through the clinic building, this time at my own hands, a welcome spill.

"My noni grows a whole bunch of herbs and plants and she dries them out and puts them in jars. I've only ever seen one or two because she keeps most of them in her bedroom, but I bet she'd have something. Em, you know plants, right?"

Emory tilted her head closer to Adela. "I know animals mostly, but I know a little about some plants. Rue might work if you can't find anything else. And you'd wanna make it a tea but don't put too much in, 'cause these plants are toxic, that's why they can kill a baby. You wanna make sure it doesn't kill you too."

"How much is too much?" Adela asked.

We all looked at each other, eyes to eyes, and found no answer. We wouldn't get one, couldn't, would have to walk in blindly like only a mother knows how to do. All their eyes landed on me and waited for me to decide, a final declaration of what I wanted, what I was willing to do for myself, for my children.

You might think it's dangerous, naive, misguided, to do it like this, but it is more dangerous to birth a child into this world unwanted. At least it is to me and, at the end of this hurricane, I was gonna be the only one who had to sit in that truck with what I'd done.

"Okay," I said. "Tell me how to get these herbs from your grand-mama."

# ADELA

WHEN THE RAIN started to pound, Noni entered her hurricane zone. She guzzled a sleeping tonic, lit candles around the house, said a prayer in each room, and then went into her bedroom, swearing she wouldn't be coming out until the hurricane was over.

I'd never snuck anywhere in my life. I'd lied to find a loophole, created a story about where I was going and who I was going with, but I'd never opened a door I wasn't supposed to walk through and tried not to make a sound.

I cracked the door to Noni's room, Simone right behind me, and found Noni where she said she'd be, asleep in bed and fully dressed, in raincoat and boots like she was prepared to brave the storm even in her slumber. My heart crackled in my chest, and I wasn't sure I should be doing this, breaking the only rule Noni gave me: not to go into her room. But Simone was behind me and she needed this, so I waited a moment, then when I was sure Noni wasn't going to wake up, I slipped fully inside, Simone right behind me, and we finally got a full view of the room.

Noni's room wasn't anything like I thought it would be. Her whole house was full of things that had seemingly no place or purpose, piled on any available surface, and I thought her room would be more of the same, but it wasn't.

Bookshelves lined the walls, but there were no books. Instead, the shelves were occupied by mason jars containing all kinds of things meant to live outdoors and now dead and shoved into glass in my grandmother's bedroom: leaves and liquid, strange fluff and flower petals. Her room was bare and painted eggshell white, blank and still as an empty pool, the only decoration her wall of jarred plants.

Sage, cotton root, rue. I didn't know what any of them looked like. I glanced back at Simone and shrugged, so she stepped toward the shelves and started to read labels. I joined her on the other shelf. Raspberry leaf, black cohosh root, mint. Pine bark, sassafras, turpentine oil. Finally, rue. I grabbed the jar and unscrewed it, leaning my head in.

The smell leaped out and slapped me. I gagged and screwed the top shut again. It was sour, yellow flowers curled in the jar, making it feel almost hopeful, a false sense that it could save you.

Simone was holding a jar full of clary sage leaves, and our eyes met. She looked different than she had at the lake over a month ago now, different than she'd looked when she slipped the nausea bands on my wrists in the basement only hours before. There was a determination planted squarely in her eyes and, right behind it, a cave of fear black as oil, and I understood her for the first time.

She was battling the same thing as me, watching herself expand, and I imagined for a moment what it would be like to be as brave as her, to choose something that would shed all the complication from my life. Let myself lay my head on Chris's chest in his twin bed and focus on trivial things, tracing his tattoos, arguing with his roommates, laughing at the smirk painting his face right before he tried to undress me.

But that was not the life I was barreling toward, and I realized it wasn't the one I would choose anyway. If the baby wasn't taking refuge in my body, I would be back home in a pool, breaking down muscle after muscle just to reconstruct them bigger and better than they'd been before. Without this baby, there was no reality of Chris or Emory or the winding shores of Florida where the ocean I'd discovered caressed its sand. And for the first time ever, I was grateful for it and all that it had given me. Even Simone.

◆ ◆ ◆

The air bubbles began to percolate, small at first, floating to the surface, simmering up from the bottom of the pot as we waited in the kitchen, Simone and I fixated on it, close enough to Simone's camp stove to feel it warm our cheeks.

"How did you know?" I asked her.

"Know what?" Simone wasn't as defensive as she had been when I first met her and, as we watched the bubbles follow each other up to the surface of the water, I started to think Emory might've been right, that she wasn't so bad after all.

"That you wanted to keep your twins." I nodded to the mug half-full of sage and rue, ready for hot water. "That you didn't want to keep this one."

I knew I was going to carry this pregnancy through until the day the child pressed on my pelvis and begged to see light, but I didn't know what I might do after that. I'd been thinking about it a lot, as my image of my future bleared like the sky awash with hurricane.

The closer I got to Chris, the further I got from Indiana and David and chasing gold. Now I dreamed in the emerald hue of the Gulf, rushed to call Emory after every episode of *Shark Tank* and tell her a new idea I had, started to wonder if this baby's nose would be hooked or round or flat. If it would be mine or not.

Simone looked away from the pot to me. "I'm different than I was when I had Luck and Lion. Older. Better. And, if I coulda given them this version of me for those first years, I would've. But I ain't known that back then. All I knew was the man who loved me wanted those babies and I couldn't help but want them too, and I'm real glad I did, don't get me wrong, but now I know different, and I bet if I had this baby now, in ten years I'd wish they coulda had that version of me instead. So maybe that's why. But . . ."

Simone trailed off and looked into the mug. When she returned to look at me, her brows knit together. "But maybe the real reason is I just got a feeling. It's not the right time, not the right person, shit, maybe it's not the right baby. All I know is I don't wanna give my body to this child, trade my idea of my life for something else in the name of someone else. Maybe the only real reason I got is I'm tired and I don't wanna give up nothing else."

I tapped a nail on the counter in rhythm to the rain and thought about it. I knew I was going to give my body to this child and, honestly, it was a relief, to not wake up before dawn to freeze in an indoor pool without even a view of the rising sun, to eat whatever was put in front of me and not worry about how I might morph. It was after the baby was born that I wasn't sure about, an option Simone never had.

"If you could've given the twins to someone else, someone who would have been good to them, would you have?"

She shrugged. "I don't know if I can answer that 'cause now they mine. They'll never be nothing but mine to me. But if I coulda had it different, I woulda wanted to raise my babies where I grew up, with my momma and my pops, and I coulda learned how to open a business or just slept in sometimes and not worried 'bout what would happen if Lion learned how to climb out of the truck in the middle of the night and ran toward the water.

"But really you gotta ask what you want for yourself. 'Cause me, back then? I don't think I wanted nothing different, woulda been somebody's momma one way or another, my sisters or my boyfriend's or my child's. But now? I want different now. You can't predict what's gonna happen, Adela, but you can take a good look at yourself and be honest bout who you are and what you want. At least that's what I'm doing."

The pot began to rumble and then all those small bubbles became larger currents of air filling the basin, and I turned off the burner. Simone took the hot water and poured it into her mug, and we watched the water brown until it was the color of dune lake water. We both looked to each other, a silent prayer that we had put just enough in, not too little or too much, before Simone blew into the cup and gulped.

# EMORY

I T WAS MY TURN in Truth or Dare. I chose Dare, expecting someone to make me lick a pipe in Adela's basement or something gross.
I figured it couldn't be nastier than anything else I'd done, growing
up poking at hardened fox shit and turning myself into my own best
companion.

When I chose Dare, I wasn't expecting Adela to immediately call
out, "Me! I got one!" None of us had ever heard her talk so loud,
heard her tongue so quick to loop and run, and then she said the last
thing I thought she might say.

"Em says she doesn't think she'll get into Stanford and so she
won't even apply, but that's where I want to go, and she has all the
essays already written. So . . ." She smiled sly, like it was the biggest
risk she could think of taking, and said, "I dare you to apply. Early
action. Right now."

I rolled my eyes. "We don't even have power. Even if I wanted to,
I can't get online."

Adela grinned. "I can." She stood up and stepped across the sleeping babies, flashlight scanning, and when she made it to her bed, she
got on her knees and started looking under it, pulled out her slim
MacBook and tucked it under her arm, and returned to the circle.

Next thing I knew, Adela had turned on her hotspot and shoved
her laptop onto my knees, and the rest of the Girls joined in cheering
me on, deciding they didn't care if it was college or the lottery. It was

something to gamble on and they were in need of a leap of faith. A moment of undelivered hope.

I signed into my email and retrieved the typed-up essays and information I'd sent to myself from our desktop at home, the one Grammy was always hogging to chat with women on the internet about her crochet. I logged into the application portal, then looked up at Adela.

"The deadline's in a week."

"I know," she said. "I was going to bug you about it, but Kai got sick and I didn't want you to feel bad. But this is perfect, Em, we'll get to go to school together. In California."

Adela and me, together. The image of it propelled me forward— us on the other end of the country, still walking side by side, sand crunching beneath our feet—even as the Girls moved on to the next round and Simone fell asleep waiting. Even as Jamilah was dared to eat a raw egg and Crystal confessed that she was going to try to get a job, a real job, and then she'd have to put Cece in the Early Head Start, so once she found a job, she wouldn't be around so much any-more. When Tori started crying, I continued to fill in answers about my activities, struggling to find any that didn't include being Kai's ma. And finally, when Simone had awoken and Adela was about to take another turn at Truth or Dare, I looked up.

"All I need to do is click submit," I said.

The Girls gathered around behind me, shoulder to shoulder, cheek to cheek, and I moved the cursor to the submit button and clicked. Waited. The page loaded, hurricane fully whipping around the house and interfering with Adela's hotspot. I felt us all hold our breath, the way we did when pregnancy tests worked to show their lines and, finally, the screen switched to a confirmation message, and we all let out the air grown warm in our cheeks.

Adela turned and pulled me into a hug, squealing in my ear. It made my whole face hot. Even though I didn't know if I could make

it in or if I could move to California or if I wanted to tow a toddler along with me, it didn't matter anymore 'cause I got to sink into
Adela's arms for a moment, and when she pulled away and giddily
declared that she was choosing Truth, I had to ask.

"I got one," I said, trying to make sure my voice didn't sound too
shaky. To tell the truth, I was shitting myself as the words came out.
"Have you ever been in love?"

Adela and I had avoided all discussion of how we each got pregnant, what life was like for her in the hours between when I saw her,
whose sweat she'd wiped from her cheek yesterday or last month or
last year. I wasn't all that sure I wanted to know, but the ache that
came with having Adela as my best friend had turned from a welcome obsession to a crazed swirl at the bowl of my body every time I
looked at her.

The truth was, I wanted to know her everything, even when she
only gave me fractions.

Adela shifted to sit up and fiddled with the blanket April had
given her, eyes cast down, but then I saw her lips squirm and when
she looked up at us all, there was a shadow of a smile on her face, her
trying to hold herself back from beaming. I gripped on to Kai's little
hand and tried not to squeeze.

"Actually," Adela said. "I think I'm in love, like, right now."

My stomach seized and rippled. My fingers twitched. I started
sweating like a whore in church. The realization came quick and
feverish. All that time with Adela and time spent thinking about
Adela collided at once into one pure thought: I loved her. Not like
a friend loved a friend or a mother loved a mother but like Jay loved
me. I wanted her.

And suddenly, it all made sense.

This was what it was like to be down bad for someone. Like when
Kai was first born and I was so mesmerized by him I couldn't help but
stare at him all night, even as he slept. Especially as he slept. But then,

the next day I would feel like shit, wishing with every drooping part of me I hadn't stayed up all night looking at him, and still, inevitably, I would do it again and again.

That's what loving Adela was like: being consumed by her. Wanting nothing more than to think of her and be in her presence until, suddenly, the moment she was gone, and I sat alone with the absence of her beside me. That's when wanting her began to hurt, like a rock caught between esophagus and stomach. I'd spent all our time together waiting for something, I just didn't know what. Until now. I was waiting to know if it was possible to love her. To have her love me back.

All the Girls started giggling and gushing and pushing Adela for more information, but Adela shook her head and said she wasn't gonna tell, not yet, 'cause it wouldn't be fair to tell us all about who-ever it was before she even told the person she was in love with that she was in love with them, and I was on the edge of crying or grin-ning like a wild woman myself when Adela glanced over at me and winked.

She loved me.

All this time, I'd been spiraling. Loving her and pretending I didn't. Thinking I couldn't ever have her or, if I had her, I couldn't ever keep her. Loving her with my hand wrapped in hers. Loving her as she hushed my baby to sleep on the chest of the body carrying her own. Loving her as I looked over and couldn't decipher if she even thought about me in the dead pit of night. And now, I finally knew. Even as the rest of them moved on, even as I told myself I would let Adela tell me on her own time, confess to me alone, just the two of us, I couldn't help but smile.

Until Simone's first moan ripped out across the room and my smile dropped. When I looked up at the closest thing to a sister I'd ever have, she met my gaze, and I knew it was time. We all did.

# SIMONE

A BATHTUB WITHOUT WATER feels like a cold palm, cradling you frozen. Capable of one squeeze that could kill you. All I wanted was a little warm water and, even if the Girls could boil some, Emory wouldn't let 'em, not even when I begged, clammy sweat accumulating beneath my titties from the grip of cramps splitting in my pelvis.

"I'm sorry," Emory whispered, wiping my forehead with a cold wet rag. "You might get an infection if I add water."

Emory was crying too, and I couldn't handle that shit, so I snapped at her to stop and even though the tears kept bubbling up in her eyes, she paused them right at the edge of her waterline.

Nobody ever told me it would hurt like this. Maybe it didn't, if you did it the right way, but the only right way was the way that ended with me the only living thing in my body. You can judge all you want, except anybody who had to swallow that pain knows it was far from the easy way out.

I felt the next seize approaching in my low back and I could feel this one was gonna collapse me. Through my teeth, I groaned, "Don't. Let. Them. Hear." I looked to the bathroom door. Behind it, April, Jamilah, and the kids were caught in the tide of sleep and, out of all the Girls on this side of the door, Adela seemed to understand.

I just didn't want my kids to hear me cry.

She scrambled from her spot kneeling at the foot of the tub, scavenging through cabinets in the bathroom, the flashlight in her grip dimming as it got closer to death, and she found a clean sponge right as the height of the wave took me over, stuffing it in my mouth as I ripped into another guttural roar. The sound couldn't be heard past the hums Tori and Crystal began singing to me.

When I drank up that tea, I was ready for the pain, for the rusty metal flavor of blood, and yet I'd sat there in Adela's basement for hours and nothing happened. I'd started to think it wasn't gonna work and I was gonna have to have this child and tell Tooth and adjust to an idea that whatever was cooking up inside me was gonna become a baby, my baby, and as the Girls played Truth or Dare, my mind wandered off to whether the baby would be a boy or a girl.

I thought it would be a girl, couldn't imagine anything but a girl, wondered whether that girl, at fifteen, would learn the precise method of measuring the area of a circle or what it felt like when you realized, mid-fuck, a grown man was inside you and you'd welcomed him to be there.

I met Tooth the way anybody meets anybody in this town: by the water.

I was fifteen and Momma let me wear a bikini for the first time in my whole life as long as I wore a cover-up over it, and I'd strutted onto the beach, tugging Jayden and my sisters behind me. Jayden was twelve and the twins were five and Momma told me I had to take them to the beach while she cleaned up 'cause she just needed a break.

I wasn't happy to be stuck with the kids, so I made them bring their boogie boards and, when we got to the beach, I took off my cover-up and told Jayden to keep an eye on the twins while I took a walk. That's all it was, really, just a walk.

I'd planned on finding a nice, quiet place to sit and read my book— I was starting to read bell hooks's *All About Love* at the time, 'cause the librarian at school told me all young people should read something by ms. hooks, and it was as good as anything at occupying my attention while the sun greeted my belly button for the first time in a decade—

and so I got to walking along the winding shore where the sand was tamped down by the sea and my feet didn't sink too far into it.

The Gulf diverts about two miles east and I hadn't realized I'd walked that far until suddenly I was following a path inland, where the wind blew the sea into the channel leading to the dune lake.

I climbed up the sand and right by where the channel flared into the lake, I saw Tooth. His feet planted on the sandy portion of lake right before the marsh grass took over and his hands firmly stuck to the handle of his fishing rod as he cranked it, front teeth biting over his lip, his shoulder muscles shaking.

I stood there and watched him as he reeled it in, the fish flying through the air and his hand reaching out for it, grabbing it by the inside of the mouth and releasing it from the hook. It was a good-sized trout, a little less than a foot, and I wasn't gonna go up to him, I really wasn't, but then he did something I never expected. He took the fish he'd just fought the cramp of his muscles for, kneeled at the edge of the lake, and released it back into the water.

What I didn't know at the time was that he ain't let that fish go 'cause of some sort of mercy. He released the fish back into the water she came from 'cause she was too small to be worth all the scaling, what it took to make a fish ready to eat. He wanted something bigger.

I was fifteen, though, and I was intrigued by the cute guy fishing alone, his kind fingers, his bare stomach, and so I kept walking up the sand till he looked over and saw me. And when he saw me, he flashed a smile.

"Love, huh?"

My face grew warm. "What?"

He laughed and his crowned tooth glinted in the sun. "The book. You lookin' for love?"

It was my turn to laugh, embarrassed, and I was about to tell him no, but I didn't want him to think I was closed off or nothing, so I straightened my neck and said, "Maybe. How 'bout you?"

His eyes traced over me. Moles, stomach, ashy shins, before

returning to my eyes. He was as handsome as all my friends said, the bait boy sending tremors through me as he shrugged. "Who couldn't use a little more love?" He said it so soft it sounded like poetry, and I'd always loved a symphony of words. "You ever been fishin'?"

I glanced back at where I'd come from, thinking of Jayden and the twins, probably still out in the water on their boards, not even aware I was gone, then I looked down at the book, before finding Tooth's eyes again. They were pinned on me. I shook my head, smiled back.

"Teach me."

I never did finish the book. Maybe if I had, things would've turned out different.

◆ ◆ ◆

Once I got Lion to sleep, while the Girls were still mid Truth or Dare, I started to think maybe I would have a boy. Maybe that boy would grow up and do to some girl what Tooth had done to me, whatever it was he'd done, and I knew that I would still love that boy with all of me, but, God, I would feel disgusted at the sight of him too.

I still don't know the exact day I conceived the twins, since I was with Tooth damn near every day and he insisted his balls would color blue if we didn't get down to business the moment I walked in the door. I should've known it would happen eventually, but I was young and Tooth didn't like condoms and he always pulled out right in time. It's funny, making the same mistake twice. Somehow, I still thought it was impossible, that there wasn't no way I could get pregnant by the same man twice. But I did, and, this time, I knew the exact day I conceived 'cause it was the last time I ever let Tooth touch me.

Tooth and I weren't together, not really, but I wouldn't say we was broken up neither. We was in limbo, and I both angered at his scent and melted into him at the sight of his eyes registering me, his words tracing me like that first time at the beach. It wasn't what he said but how he said it, and like a tsunami, it devoured everything in sight.

I couldn't help it. But I'd sworn, mostly to Emory, that I wouldn't fuck him again, and I'd kept that vow for two months before the day I broke it.

I didn't do it 'cause I wanted him back and it wasn't a hate-fuck, not really. I did it 'cause he was all I had left from my childhood, messed up as it was, and that day I'd been reminded of that with a quick blow to the gut.

It was summer and I'd finally gotten around to filling out all the Obamacare documents, so I could finally take the twins to the pediatrician. I felt bad 'cause I hadn't taken them since a few weeks after they was born, but at least I was doing it now, and I walked into the same doctor's office I'd gone to my whole life, each of my babies holding on to one hand, as I told them about how they'd get a lollipop or something from the doctor and secretly hoped they'd give me one too.

We was sitting there, Luck and Lion playing in the kids' corner as I filled out all kinds of forms for them, waiting on the doctor, and that's when Momma and Pops walked in, Jayden trailing behind them.

I heard Pops's voice before I saw his frame, him spitting, "And what if you got some kinda STD from that white girl? You gettin' tested, boy."

Jayden was two weeks to eighteen and I should've known they'd try to get him in to see the pediatrician before he had to switch doctors, should've asked Jayden when his appointment was so we didn't accidentally overlap, but by the time they walked into the waiting room, it was too late.

I stiffened. Momma and Pops both stopped in the doorway when they saw me, before Momma's eyes glazed over and she walked straight to three open seats and sat down, grabbing an *Essence* magazine and beginning to flip through. Pops followed her, casting his eyes to the small TV displaying a baseball game in the corner, and that left Jayden.

I knew he wasn't gonna come say hi to me or the kids, not even when they looked up and noticed their uncle JJ was standing there and ran to him. He said, "Go back to your momma," and turned away, sat down beside my parents. Later, he told me he just didn't want more trouble, as if Momma or Pops would ever punish him. He had always been their cherished son, always would be. It wasn't more than five minutes before the nurse called us back to her office and, by the time we left, Momma, Pops, and Jayden were already gone.

Afterward, I drove the kids to Tori's boyfriend's place, where she, Crystal, and their kids were, and left Luck and Lion there for the afternoon. Then I got back in the truck and beelined straight for the bait shop, where I found Tooth in the back room, just like I had every afternoon five years before, and I climbed on top of him and fucked him, thinking it would make me feel like someone wanted me still, like I was fifteen and things were still right. But it didn't. All I felt was Tooth's thumb on my windpipe, his teeth on my nipple, his shout as he came, before I slipped out of the room with his cum still sticky on my thighs.

◆ ◆ ◆

Now, in this tub, I was sure that it was working, that this is what it felt like to expel, and this fetus, this would-be child, would never become a girl or a boy. It would not learn to dance or bake a cake that was the perfect balance of moist and sweet or find a thing that they wanted so much they would make a choice they wished didn't need making just to have it. And, in this moment, I was okay with that.

I let my head drift to rest on the back of the tub, Emory rewetting the rag with a water bottle and dabbing my forehead, the Girls humming tunes I couldn't place and didn't need to as I gripped the porcelain and closed my eyes.

The cramping escalated and I had to spit out the sponge and vomit into the plastic bowl Adela kept bath bombs and unused rubber duckies in and I felt unbearably close. Closer to myself than I'd ever been, all the tenderness of youth and harshness of womanhood crashing into each other, and I knew I wouldn't be able to survive this unless I let go of it all.

So I stopped fighting the hurt and let the raging vibrations take me. I slipped into a trance with the Girls' hums, closed my eyes and imagined the sound of hurricane rain outside was actually dune lake water, something alive, holding me up, waiting to capture my blood and disperse it into the ocean through a small channel that withstood all odds just to exist.

I expected the blood to come all at once, for it to flow straight out like a hose from my insides. But that ain't happened. It took at least an hour before I saw blood, waves clamping on to my abdomen and twisting, felt like hands, my body wrung out like wet clothes.

That first hour, nothing came, just cramps, and then, in the second hour, clots of blood the size of marbles and then quarters and then golf balls, the pain relentless, my hairline matted in sweat, limbs shaking, reminding myself to keep quiet and not wake the babies up.

My body forced me to push, just like it had almost five years ago, and part of me worried a live child would emerge, a full-grown baby cooked up from not even three months inside the womb, that I would have to raise that child or kill it with my own hands. But no child came out. Instead, the things that came from each push did not even equate to the breath it took to evict them, small gray bits of flesh and tissue, but mostly blood clots and pink.

I thought it was over when the next wave ended, only to find another one coming, a larger blood clot the size of an uncracked egg filling the tub, where Emory had poured just the smallest bit of cold water, not even enough to cover a single toe. Over and over again, the Girls by my side humming, Adela stuffing the sponge back in my mouth when it looked like a real bad one was coming, the cramping squeezing at my pelvis, until, finally, as the sun began to rise, we all looked to the water between my legs and realized the bleeding had slowed.

Emory dressed me in some of Adela's clothes, made a large pad out of three smaller ones while Crystal and Tori fished out the biggest blood clots and emptied them into the toilet with my vomit, flushing. Adela drained the tub and poured clean water and bleach over the stained parts of the porcelain, and then helped me into her bed, just as the kids all started to slowly blink their eyes open. Luck and Lion, half-asleep, climbed up onto the bed and into my arms, and fell back into slumber.

Emory leaned down to where I was tucked under the sheets and whispered, "It's okay. Go to sleep."

I was delirious with relief and fatigue and grief, and I hadn't felt such a medley of heavy since the twins was three and a half months old and stopped sleeping for weeks on end. I'd stay up all night hushing, rocking, pleading for just an hour of silence, sure I wouldn't last one more minute of Luck's deep-throated scream and then another minute would come and go.

I'd sob with them, pray like I was my momma and it was the only thing keeping me from chucking my babies into the ocean. But, eventually, the sun would always creep up and, like they could sense the golden light even before it glimmered on their skin, they stopped screaming and fell asleep. And I'd be left there, curled up in blankets in the truck bed, an infant tucked under each arm, awake. All the fatigued daze boiled down to that sunrise, pink as their pulsing lips.

This is what I felt, lying in Adela's bed, released from years of what could've become us. Awed I'd made it to daylight resting like a warm hand on my face, drowsy and uncertain of everything but this moment, this morning air, these purring bodies I got to call mine asleep on my chest.

Emory told me to sleep and even though I knew the hurricane was still tormenting the house, I felt like the sun had risen, breathed out a sigh and closed my eyes, a tsunami of desperation receding to reveal me, still standing on the shore, still whole and human.

# SECOND TRIMESTER

THEY SAY THIS *is the moment of complete peace. The gentle lapping between waves, a stomach swollen enough to rest a cup of tea. We'd say it's true, except for the ways our own bodies expose us. The bow of our bellies smooth and arched like a glorious moon that can no longer be eclipsed. In these weeks, we start to worry as much as we start to wonder: Who is curled inside us, who are we to be the sanctuary for someone to curl inside?*

*Us Girls wake in sweats to the first flutters of webbed hands tapping from our insides and our breath hitches. How miraculous. How alien. Suddenly, it is not a sacred secret—this thing, this small person within—but a truth demanding to be unleashed. A truth that will soon subject each of us to strangers' palms pressed to our stretchings. To cold glares that threaten to freeze over all our soft.*

*Still, we are at peace for these months. Hungry and without all the aching we'd thought would be forever. We conjure names for our would-bes. We dare to let our bellies hang to the wind. As time wears on in this era of relief, we prepare for what is brewing. That at some point, the tides will churn and up out our mouths will come every last ounce of air and, with it, a surrender to what is to come.*

*But first, one final moment of pure still.*

———◆———

# EMORY

BELIEVED IN MIRACLES the same way I believed that cardinals could flap and fly and rain could pour like the devil's pitchforks. I had to. If you don't believe in miracles, how are you supposed to believe your ma loves you from a far-off place you don't know nothin' about? Or that the child growing in you won't claw you to death from the inside? Or that somebody you know you shouldn't love might love you back? I was a believer in miracles, and that's how I knew I could save the orca.

I walked the beach at dawn, fresh air lulling Kai back into sleep. Normally I didn't walk this far east where the tide rose higher and the waves crashed more menacing than over west. But today I walked on anyway, led by the sparkle of pearly shells and the sun bobbing in the distance, and that's how I found her. Body a fighting clash of white and black, massive and half-buried in the sand.

Here's the thing about killer whales: contrary to popular belief, they won't kill you and they're not even whales. That's what happens to someone when the world decides something about you, grabs hold and morphs you into an illusion of yourself: suddenly even your name isn't your own. I understood that, and seeing the orca there, half-buried in the sand, I was sure it was some kind of tragic miracle, a sign just for me.

No killer whales were supposed to be anywhere this close to shore, let alone this close to Florida, especially without their roaming group of mothers prepared to mar and mutilate in the name of their young. There wasn't no reason she should've been real. Except the closer I got, the larger she loomed, and I knew, like a bee knows the hive it came from, I had to get her out of that sand and back to sea.

The first thing I did was call Simone. Then I called Jayden 'cause he had the shovels. That's how the three of us and our kids ended up on the beach at six in the morning, digging up a killer whale with the fierce desperation of time already running from us. Orcas couldn't survive long on land, the weight of their own bodies slowly killing them.

"This crazier than all get-out, Emory. It's dead." Simone threw down her shovel. "Can't you see that?"

"She's not. She just needs some water so she doesn't get too hot." I could see the white of her underbelly peeking out from the cleared sand, but she was still at least a foot deep all around.

I needed to keep her alive. Forget getting her back into the sea, maybe she was sick. If I could get her cool enough, then I could call the NOAA to come treat her and get her back out in the water in no time.

I threw my shovel to the side and waded in, dipped my cupped hands into the ocean, caught a handful of water, and threw it on the orca's body. "C'mon, help me!" I looked back to Jayden, standing a few feet away where the twins crouched beside him wide-eyed and thrilled, Kai strapped to Jay's chest. Simone, beside him, stared at me, but didn't move.

I kept dipping my hands into the ocean and throwing them in the direction of my orca, but not enough water stayed in the cup of my palms before it leaked back into the ocean. The water that did land on the orca's body slid off and the rest sprayed back into the sea. I picked my shovel back up and began shoveling water on her, covering every bare spot. Except, whenever I watered one spot, by the time I'd moved to the next, the sun had already turned it to vapor.

"Help!" I screamed, and I could feel tears scorching down my throat.

I heard Jay splash toward me, his hand meeting my wrist, gently pulling it. He took the shovel from my grip before I could tell him not to and I shook my head, I tried to say no, but my mouth was gummy with tears and spit.

"Emmy, you gotta stop," he said, his tone a soft purr like he was talking to a child. "It's dead. Look."

I looked at the orca and all I saw was how she should be swimming. How she was half-buried in the sand, but she didn't have to be. She could dive. She could sing. She could grow up and find somebody to love.

"No, no, I can fix it," I said. "I can bring her back to life."

I knew I was blubbering, but I also knew that Jesus brought Lazarus back from the tomb and that miracles only work in the absence of doubt and that Simone and Jay were destroying my orca's only chance. My only chance.

"Help me," I wheezed, my throat dry and cracking.

Jay pulled me back toward the shore, pulled me in the direction of Simone's truck, and when I looked to Simone to get her to see that I wasn't being crazy, I was responsible for a miracle, she just shrugged.

Neither of them understood. When I twisted around to look over my shoulder and saw the orca laying there, I knew too much time had passed. *She could've lived,* I thought. *If someone had just believed me, she could've lived.*

But they hadn't and they wouldn't and I didn't wanna sit in the truck bed and listen to them lecture me. I didn't wanna watch Simone glance at me like I was unraveling. So when Jay finally let go of my wrist, I ran. And when they called after me, I did what they had when I'd asked them to help. I ignored, didn't even bother meeting their eyes. If I was crazy, so were they.

◆ ◆ ◆

Adela walked belly-first toward where I sat by the bayou shore, on a boulder big enough for the both of us. She was wearing a sweatshirt, but even through it I could see the faint outline of her bump. She was finally really showing.

"What's wrong? Are you okay?" Adela sat beside me and only near the warmth of her skin did I realize I was freezing. All my clothes were soaked from the water and I'd run right here, not remembering until I got here that I'd left my son and my diaper bag and my house keys with Simone.

"Your lips are purple. Here." Adela pulled her sweatshirt off and handed it to me. For a moment, I believed in miracles again. Beneath her sweatshirt, Adela was wearing a cropped tank top. I'd never seen her in so little clothes before when we weren't swimming. She was, like, twenty weeks now, but she looked as big as I had when I was only fourteen weeks along and I had to admit I was a little jealous.

"I put on the first thing I saw when you called," she said. "Tell me. What happened?"

"I . . . there was . . ." I didn't know how to explain it. I didn't want her to call my miracle a failed fantasy either. There were some secrets you held for safekeeping and others you kept curled up in your fist 'cause you already knew they'd erupt as soon as the light hit them, like pavement smoking from the gaze of pure heat.

I knew if I gave Adela the story of my orca, she'd set it on fire, and I didn't want to know the way her eyes could burn through the softest parts of me. So instead of what I was really thinking, what slipped from my mouth was "Sometimes I regret what we did. At the hurricane party."

"With Simone?"

I shrugged. I'd meant the Truth or Dare, the Stanford application, but now that she said it, maybe Simone too. "Yeah."

We watched the water. Each glimpse of water I looked to appeared a different shade of copper, bronze, gold, shit brown. An ever-changing thing. Beautiful and then repulsive.

"Yeah," Adela said. "Me too."

"What if that's not how it was supposed to go? What if we played God when we weren't supposed to?"

"It's her choice, though," Adela said, readjusting on the boulder so her shoulder was leaning into mine.

I missed being this close to her. Sometimes it felt like her confession, that she was in love, hadn't happened. I'd tried cajoling her to tell me, getting us alone, but nothing happened. And then she'd gotten extra busy. She always said it was just family stuff with the holidays or that she was training but even I knew there was no way Adela was spending all that time in some pool, pregnant as she was. Especially since the town hadn't caught word that she was big yet. I knew 'cause they were all still calling her Missus Woods's smart granddaughter, taking senior classes at only sixteen.

I kept trying to distract myself from her absence. I'd gotten into two colleges already and spent my afternoons researching apartments and daycares for Kai in their towns, which only made the whole thing feel more unfeasible. I was trying to give her space, to let her come to me, but it wasn't working.

"Just like it's your right to apply to whatever college you want," she added.

"Sometimes wanting things isn't worth it," I said. I hoped she'd argue, tell me she wanted me. But instead she just let me talk. "It doesn't always work out the way you want it to and sometimes you're worse off for trying. Sometimes the possible miracle's not worth the risk. Try to walk on water and you might drown, you know?"

"Don't say that." Adela shook her head. My breath hitched. "Just because things don't always work out doesn't mean some things don't. Simone's fine. Happy even. And so are you."

I turned to her and stared her right in the eyes, squinted. "Am I?" I asked. Her brows knit. Didn't she know I loved her? It was driving me kind of crazy, thinking about her, worrying myself into a coil about all it meant. My whole life I'd been with boys. I liked boys. But I loved Adela.

I wasn't a lesbian or nothing though, so don't start thinking I'd ever be dyeing my hair rainbow or joining some kind of parade. It was just Adela. She was different. I couldn't help but love her.

I sighed. "Sometimes happiness feels like a snake in the grass."

When I turned my head away from hers to look back out at the bayou water, I saw it. A snake, head stuck up out of the water and bobbing like a dog as the length of him slithered and slashed across the shoreline. Adela saw it next, screamed, pulled her legs up onto the boulder with us. I wanted to tell her not to worry, that it was here for me, that it was a sign I needed to keep my mouth shut. The orca and now the snake.

But I couldn't tell her anything 'cause all my words ceased their ties to sound and I couldn't speak, think, breathe. There was a time I would've sprinted into that water, clothes and all, and tried catching the snake in the clench of my fingers, a time I would've risked venom and leeches just for a chance to touch it. But I'd learned my lesson a long time ago, so I stayed on my boulder beside Adela and didn't say a word.

◆ ◆ ◆

When I was five and Ma dropped me off at Grammy and Pawpaw's house in an opioid-fueled haze and never turned back, Grammy started sending me over to my auntie's house during the summer days so her and Pawpaw could still go to work. This was only a couple months before Pawpaw was laid off and we had to move across the highway into my auntie's house for good, but at that point I was just excited 'cause my cousins Timothy and Ron were the only kids I ever got to see, since I wasn't starting school till September.

Ron had recently gotten a pet and I'd never had a pet before, so naturally I followed Ron around, asking if I could hold Matilda the snake, and Ron kept saying no, that I was too young to hold her, which made me cry. But Ron didn't care if I cried, didn't hand over Matilda or nothing, so eventually I stopped crying and just watched red-eyed as Ron looped Matilda around his shoulders and fed her dead roaches.

That summer when I was five, I fell in love with Matilda the corn snake. Her orange length nearing four feet, her tail tapering off as she slithered around the corner to the kitchen. My auntie's rule was that Ron wasn't allowed to let the snake into her room or touch her stuff and so most of the time, we played with her outside, me and Ron and Timothy. Until halfway through the summer when Timothy got his Nintendo and then he spent all his time on the top bunk bed in what would end up being my room but was then Timothy and Ron's.

Us kids were alone most of the time, while my auntie worked, and since there was no school for Ron, who was in fifth grade, or Timothy, who was in third, it was like they weren't older than me at all that summer. Except I didn't get to touch Matilda and nothing had ever made me angrier.

It was the hottest day of the summer so far and Ron and me decided to turn on the hose out in the backyard. Even though the water had turned warm in the pipes, it was still cooler than the air. We stripped down, ran naked through the brush, Ron chasing me with the hose until it pulled taut at the edge of the property. Matilda was inside the house, in her tank where we could keep the temperature to a cool eighty. But I was dreaming of her, as always. Her scales bright orange like the center of a nectarine.

I was done playing with the hose but Ron wasn't, so he stayed outside and I slipped my dress back on and went in. Timothy was still in the bunk bed and nobody else was home, so I tiptoed to Matilda's tank and opened the top and I was just about to reach in and grab her when Ron called, "Hey!"

He was dripping wet in the hallway, still only wearing his soggy boxers, and I leaped back just in time for him to tackle me to the carpet of the living room.

"You not allowed to touch her! I told you that!"

I started sobbing and Ron got off me and shut Matilda's tank and then he sat there guarding it, watching me lay on the floor crying a damp river on the front of my dress. Eventually, I quieted down and that's when Ron's mouth knotted up and he said, "You really wanna hold her?"

I sat up quick, nodded, eyes wide and hoping.

He smirked. "Alright. You git to hold her if you do somethin' for me."

"What?"

That's when Ron showed me how he had a special hole in his boxers and the hole was for his penis, see? And he snaked this small fleshy thing through his boxers. You gotta understand, I'd spent my whole life up until that point with Ma and I'd never seen one of those before, so I didn't know the rules when he asked me to touch it. I was just thinking that Matilda would like to curl up under my hair like a blanket.

So I touched Ron's little thingy and it got kind of wet at the tip and the veins started showing and it grew just a little, kind of like a worm, and I laughed and pulled my hand back, but he told me that I had to keep touching it, petting it like a dog, if I wanted to hold Matilda. And so I did, until we heard Timothy hop down from the bunk bed ladder and Ron rushed to put the thing back through the hole. Timothy slumped in a heat across the hall to the kitchen, where he grabbed a handful of cheese balls, and I stood to go to the tank, but Ron yanked my hand back before I could open the top.

"Don't touch that," he said.

"But you said—you said I could hold her now," I stammered, reaching out again.

He swatted my hand and shrugged. "I changed my mind."

I never got to hold Matilda.

But I dreamed about her and I loved her and I wanted her to be mine more than anything. Almost as much as I wanted Grammy to have done something different than what she did, when I finally told her the promise Ron made me before he snatched my dream and crushed it in his fist.

# SIMONE

**Y**OU EVER WONDERED what happens after you abort a baby?
Life. And blood.

The blood came on and off for almost three weeks. I threw
a party with the Girls on the beach when all the spotting ceased to
nothing. In between songs and rounds of would you rather, I took
another pregnancy test down by the water, Emory standing by me,
and we both hollered like coyotes in the night when only one line
showed up. It was over, all my ugly feelings washing away with my
piss.

I ran back to the Girls, picked Luck up and swung her into the
air until she started hiccuping she was laughin' so hard, me laughin'
with her like I ain't done in months. That hurricane began and ended
so many things, but I'd spent every minute since then worrying it
didn't work, or that I was about to hemorrhage, or that somebody
was gonna come and lock me away for what we did that night in
Adela's basement. But now it was really over. Life was a steady trickle
by the dune lake and me and my babies was good.

Until the morning Emory called in December.

When me and Jayden showed up on the beach and saw her, I
knew Emory was having some kind of nervous breakdown, but he
was all hung up on her, so he'd do anything and I followed without
much question.

Now that Emory'd run off to God knows where and Jayden was

swinging the shovels into the back of his truck and shaking his head the whole time like he had a wasp circling his hair, I really started to think about it. That big-ass whale. I wasn't crazy, I didn't wanna save a dead whale or nothing, I just didn't believe in leaving a dead creature on the shoreline to rot. I decided I needed to bury her.

"Wait," I called across the parking lot to Jayden. "Take the shovels back out."

Jayden moved Kai from his chest to his back in the sling and passed the twins each a little shovel so they could help. We dug till the sand turned rock-hard, so compacted it was impenetrable. Jayden talked the whole time.

"I just don't get why she's like that. Not tryna save it but running away like that. Don't she know she don't gotta run from me?"

"I don't think it's like that, Jay. She's not running from you, she's running to whatever else she thinks gonna bring her comfort."

"And what's that?"

I shrugged, even though I knew. "Ask her." I felt bad for Jayden sometimes. He just wanted to be Kai's daddy, Emory's chosen, and Emory was never gonna let that happen. I bet he felt like I did, sobbing outside the trailer when Momma and Pops wouldn't let me in, still just wishing they'd open the door.

I kept shoveling, sweat seeping into my eyes and stinging. I shook my head to clear my thoughts and get the newest drops of sweat to fly from my eyelashes.

Eyelashes. Lion's were all curled inward like a spiral. Luck's reached out for me as she giggled so big her jaw fell open. All those eyelashes, fallen and flew away, and here we was, digging a whale's grave.

I didn't do what I did in that tub just to cut myself loose from Tooth so I could start really thinking about what I was gonna do, going forward. I know you'd think that, maybe even think that I was jealous of Emory and decided I shoulda graduated high school or even gone to college. But it wasn't like that. Not everyone has something big to run to. Shit, not everyone wants nothing that big, if you only count a dream like Adela's with that pool or Emory and all her animals.

I never had nothing like that, one thing I'd do anything to have, but I had little things. I had a million eyelashes long gone, wishes I'd made like any other young girl hoping for something beyond the mess we're given. And, once I had the twins, I had a fever unlike any other, a constant drive to keep them safe, to catch every one of their eyelashes and present it for them to blow away.

I was relieved, don't get me wrong, and I *was* running. But I didn't run 'cause I felt a flash of fury or flame, I ran 'cause I'd been stuck for so long and didn't even realize it and now I knew what I had to do. I would run, or jog really, 'cause it was what needed to be done. With intention. And I wouldn't bat an eye when my knee throbbed and my lungs blew up with red-hot air.

After five years of doing everything for myself—living out of the back of a truck, holding small hands, counseling Girls who I loved but who never loved me back the same way, like family—sitting in that bathtub surrounded by the Girls, letting them see me broke open and bleeding, I realized how lonely I'd been.

Loneliness is a young mother's shadowed hand, clutched to the gut and pulling even as she laughs with her babies, even as she bites off newborn fingernails and rubs lotion under the folds of an infant's neck, it always has a hold.

I was the oldest, the founder of the group, and the Girls followed by example. I knew that. I just never realized all that holding myself up left my bones sore and locked tight, joints creaking as I rested my head on the edge of that tub. So when it was all over, when I was empty again, I couldn't just return to how I'd been. I didn't want to.

For those moments in the tub, I realized it didn't matter what I was running from or to as much as it mattered that I finally pulled my feet from the sand and moved with purpose. And with that movement, all these small wishes I'd made over the past five years returned to me, and almost every one was something I'd been too scared to say aloud. Momma. Pops. Jayden. Home.

Eyelashes. Get one stuck in the whites of your eye and you'll feel the phantom of it long after it's gone. Hope is like that too, I think. Once you feel the spark of it, suddenly it haunts every image and who you was before, what you thought you was okay with, all that breaks open to leave you hunched in a tub surrounded by remnants of who you could've been. You left so exposed you can't never cover up quite the same again.

So when I was shoveling that sand and Jayden was going on about Emory and how much he wished she'd meet him in the dream he conjured, I started thinking about all the dreams I'd given over to those years with Tooth and how there wasn't no way I could keep moving forward if I was still tangled up in all the things I wished I could change, all those dreams now long taken by the wind. The whale needed to be buried. It all did.

"Y'all need to stand back now," I called to the twins. They protested, but I let them know I meant it and they took those tiny shovels up the sand hill and stood watching. I looked at Jayden. "We gotta push it in."

"Just us?"

"It's already halfway there." We'd dug the grave along the side of its body, so we could see a whole lot of its underbelly now.

"It's gotta be over five hundred pounds, we can't push it alone. Don't be like Emory, we can just call somebody to come get it—"

"No!" I wasn't being like Emory. I just ain't wanted the whale to get taken and chopped up and used as some kinda experiment when it shoulda got a proper burial. We all deserved that. "Just try, okay?"

Jayden made his way to the other side of the whale and I joined him, me by its head and him by its tail, and we counted down and pressed our whole weight into the whale and pushed. The tendons in my ankles felt ready to snap and I was still pushing out the same breath with every force I had but the whale didn't move. Not an inch.

We both stood. Luck called out, "Momma, it's not moving!"

"I know, baby," I called back. Then, again, beneath my breath, "I know."

We stayed silent for minutes and then Jayden clapped his hands together.

"We just gotta dig a hill for it to roll down."

"A hill?"

Jayden circled back to the grave and kneeled at the edge with his long shovel in hand. He scooped sand right beneath the whale and pushed it farther into the hole. I understood. If we removed enough sand beneath the whale, it'd slide right down into the grave. I joined him on the other edge. We reached, scooped, flung any sand we could access and just when I was starting to doubt the physics of it all, I felt the shovel pull away from me, the wood bar snapping as the whale's body pinned the metal part beneath it. Jayden got his shovel out in time, and we scrambled back from the grave, the ground beneath us vibrating, and then one reverberating thud sent chills up my body as the whale hit the bottom.

Lion called, "Earthquake!" Luck started lecturing him that it wasn't an earthquake 'cause earthquakes don't even happen here, it was just the whale. Jayden and I crawled to the edge of the grave and looked down. The whale had landed belly up, a heap of solid white, the shovel long gone, and that was that. It was resting at the bottom of its grave.

I must've strained a tricep pushing sand from the pile beside us back into the hole on top of the whale, heaving as we attempted to fill a crater the size of the truck bed and twice as deep. I let Luck and Lion help with their small shovels as long as they kept their bodies far from the hole and they was good about it.

After a few hours, we finished and the last shovelful of sand was patted onto where the hole once was, the ocean rushing to smooth out its past. The kids was hungry, so Jayden helped me build a small fire to roast ground beef topped with cheese for them. I collapsed on the sand, staring at where the orca had been and where now there was nothing but wet sand, and I think I started to cry.

At least I felt tears on top of my hands and Lion whispered to Jayden, "Why Momma cryin'?"

Jayden told them I was sad that the whale died but it wasn't that. I wasn't sad the whale died; I was sad it died alone. Somewhere out there was a mother circling the sea for a child who had taken its last breath and I just didn't think it was right to have to die lonely too. Jayden took the foil with the meat off the rack by the fire and put it on a plate with forks for the twins.

We all sat watching the smoke float up, silent, and then Jay started talking. "We gather here today, on this beach, to celebrate the life of this, uh, creature who has now returned home to God. May the Lord watch over it—"

"Whatchu doing?" I sniffed.

Jayden shrugged. "We gotta have a funeral, right?"

My brother reminded me in the moments I thought I'd lost all family that he was still here, looking at me, seeing me. I nodded.

"Okay. Um, well, what happened to the whale today is prob'ly the deepest shit that ever happened on this beach, if you think about it," he continued.

I turned to the fire, spitting flame and smoke into the air, adding heat to heat, and I started to think about the day Pops locked me out of the trailer, the rolling grief that sucked the air from me as I sobbed on the slab of artificial grass. My tears came quicker down my face and Luck hissed at Jay, "You made Momma cry harder."

"Don't worry, Lucky. Your momma just feeling shit. Nothing wrong with that." Jayden winked at me and I smiled, letting the tears leak into my mouth and coat my tongue. He kept going, "All of us got these moments, where big shit happens and everything changes, you know? We start tryna find a way back to what things was like before, but that's not how this works. Sometimes we can't go back. Sometimes we don't want to."

I looked to Luck and Lion, who had finished their food and found sticks to play with. They were trying to see how burnt their sticks could get before they crumbled.

"Death not a thing to be reversed, you know? It's what makes us rethink every step we 'bout to take while we still can. I'd like to believe that whale died so we could think about how we live."

I didn't know where his words came from or how they could fit so perfect. I thought he was gonna make up some bullshit about heaven, but this was so much more glorious and I saw an eyelash long as my fingernail resting on Lion's nose and I needed to grab it, so I took his chin in my hand, still wet from my tears, and delicately plucked the eyelash from his face, holding it up to the firelight, in front of his oval mouth, and I whispered, "Whatever you want, baby. Whatever you want."

And I knew I meant that, really meant that, so when he blew, when I felt his breath tickle my cheek, I also knew exactly what it meant for Pops to lock that door, for Momma to open a magazine in the doctor's waiting room and pretend I ain't existed, for them to look into my face and tell me to get out.

But I also knew exactly what it meant for my brother to be here, to exist in two lives at once: one where I was dead and one where I was alive as the laughter stuck in Luck's throat. Maybe some deaths gave us more life, or at least made all that was still living look even more miraculous.

Jayden said a couple more words and then he shouted, "Amen," and the twins repeated it. Emory showed up ready to feed her child not long after, even though she was two hours late for his feeding, but Jayden forgave her, like always, and she kissed him prob'ly 'cause she felt guilty, like always, and they left.

And that's how, after five years, I let my mind run back to the door of my parents' trailer, thinking only of eyelashes and how mine had shed and regrown prob'ly five times from the last time I left that place. That's what happens when you're young and alone and the people who are supposed to stay by you no matter what retract their promises with the same speed and echo as that whale hitting the bottom of its grave.

# ADELA

THE MOST IMPORTANT thing to remember when you're in the pool is that you are in control. The moment you forget you wield the water you weave through is the moment your neck begins to tip too far, your shoulders pulling away from the rest of you and pausing you at the end of each stroke, slowing you so even as you cup your hands and attempt to push the water back to propel the length of you forward, there is no way to fully make up for what you have lost. The moment you begin to worry you are not tall enough, your kick is weak, the current of the water is fighting you, it's already over.

I think that's how everything went wrong. I started to panic. At the bayou, Emory ruminated and ranted about regrets and miracles but never seemed to really say what she meant and then she rose abruptly and left me there, scratching at her fears lingering on me like dead skin cells, microscopic and prone to itch. She was already gone when I realized I forgot to ask for my sweatshirt back.

Bare and itching out by the bayou, I started to freak out too. Everything materialized and became real so fast, I didn't have time to think it all through with Emory's words sitting on my skin, so when I walked home, one arm folded across my torso, feeling all big, I should've expected that I would run into Chris. I'd lost sight of the end of the pool, become distracted by the wrinkle of my fingertips, and now it was all coming crashing down.

The more time I spent with Chris, the less I thought about how old he was or how old I was or how crusty his house was or how many roommates he had or that there was some other girl out there who his kids called mom. Most of the time, I was just worried about losing Chris, a trivial fear among the ruin my life was, but love was known to make you examine each speck of sand when there was a whole beach spread out and beckoning in front of you.

About a week ago, I popped. I'd spent the first twenty weeks of my pregnancy looking normal, maybe a little bloated, and then in one week I suddenly looked unmistakably pregnant. I'd been avoiding Chris since then. This made him mad, and I couldn't blame him for wanting the thing I'd promised, my body damp and open beneath his.

I'd been preparing to tell him I was pregnant next week, I really was, but then, about two blocks from Noni's house, I turned the corner by the school and there he was, shirt off, surfboard under his arm, and every opportunity for the truth to be mine to tell vanished.

I hugged my body tighter, pausing and facing him head-on so he couldn't see my profile, but I already knew he'd registered it. Chris's pupils eclipsed the brown in his eyes and his lip curled in a snarl that showed off his shark tooth and I stepped back, just one small step because he stared at me like I was the rodents he'd chase from his house when they crawled out the vents, but that step made it worse and Chris slammed his board down and charged forward, ripping both my wrists away from my body so I was standing there, uncovered.

I shook my head, begged him not to see. He'd touched me so many times before with the kind of gentleness that let me close my eyes and sink in, but this time was so different, and I could feel the ridges of his fingerprints pressing into my wrists and I was afraid.

"What is this?" he growled. "You having my baby and you ain't even told me?"

I knew this would've been the moment to confess, I knew any decent person would have, but I didn't want to see what would happen, how his grip could deepen, if he knew everything. He wouldn't understand that just because there was little truth in our beginnings didn't mean my love for him wasn't honest.

Besides, he was the one who assumed it was his. He chose not to see it, which might have meant he didn't want to know. And I didn't want to tell him. So when I should've said *It's not yours,* instead I shrugged and watched his lip uncurl and his fingers loosen their grip.

"I don't like lying. You know that." I did. But how could I tell him it was all I knew?

He released my wrists and massaged his beard. He'd shaved it and then let it grow out again and it was rough now, itchy when he kissed me. "Aight, then. We havin' a baby, I guess. God, Simone's finna kill me."

"Simone?" I whispered. My throat clogged like I was brimming with water and it would spill from me if I opened my mouth again. I already knew what he was going to say, but still I begged him with the blink of my eyes not to.

"My kids' mama."

Simone. His kids' mother. His kids. The twins. I wasn't sure how I'd missed it, except he'd had his kids at twenty-two and I assumed the woman would be older, but now I questioned how I hadn't put it all together before. Luck's stuffed koala tucked between his mattress and the wall, Simone's scent—piercing and firm as a forest floor—lingering in his car, all these things I thought were just coincidence come clear. And I couldn't speak. I couldn't tell him, or her, or anyone, because how could I destroy the only things I had here?

"How 'bout you come surf with me?" Chris picked up his board and nodded back toward the beach.

I came back to the clouds and his face and pulled a taut smile from my rigid skin, shook my head.

He stepped toward me again and leaned down, reached his hands around me and squeezed my ass, nipped at my neck with his teeth. I didn't have words but I knew I was going to cry and so I shook my head again and stepped away from him, throwing over my shoulder the only word I could get out, "Bye," and then I started to run.

I sprinted through the gravel roads of Padua until they turned to dust, under the thick gate of trees, and burst through the front door of Noni's house, tears flooding my eyes and settling in the creases of my neck. There Noni was, through the blur, sitting on the plastic-covered couch.

She stood and I was ready for her to assault me with questions like Dad, for me to shake my head and run downstairs to the basement, where I could sprawl out and sob without having to speak, but instead, Noni opened her arms wide and waited for me to step into them. And when I did, she sat us both down on the couch, crackling under our weight, and she let me lay in her lap, wiping away each tear just for another to follow.

◆ ◆ ◆

"When I was pregnant with your daddy, I was real old to have a baby. Back then, in these parts, old was twenty-five and I was twenty-eight when I had him, my first and only child. I married your grandfather thinking I was gonna have a whole clan of babies but then it took us six years of trying 'fore we got lucky with your daddy.

"I was happy, I mean I was gettin' ready to give up on having chil'ren, but let me tell you, that pregnancy was just awful, Delly, just awful. I felt like a fish flounderin' on the concrete, everybody just watchin' and laughin', talkin' 'bout how I wasn't suited to mother-hood, couldn't get pregnant to save my life, and then, when I did, I swelled up and couldn't stop vomiting. Had preeclampsia too and so I was on bed rest my whole third trimester, which sure didn't help us pay the bills, and all I could do was stay home and sleep, 'cept I couldn't get some shut-eye for the life of me. Worst time of my life was those ten months.

"I won't lie to you, Adela, I hated your granddaddy by the time your father was born. He'd spent my whole pregnancy complaining 'bout how I wasn't helpin' out none, even though you best believe I was still cookin' him biscuits for breakfast and sendin' him off to work with a sandwich I made with my bloated hands.

"I thought it'd get better after the baby was born, but it didn't. At least not with your granddaddy. He complained I didn't want to get down and dirty with him. He complained the baby cried too much. He complained I couldn't work my usual hours and then, when I left your daddy with my mama to go to work, he complained I didn't care enough about my baby."

I looked up at Noni, face all scrunched up and head shaking, her fingers still stroking my forehead. "I thought Grandpa was nice. Dad always said he was a good guy."

Noni hooted. "Ha! Your daddy barely spent five minutes with the man. He worked all through your daddy's childhood, said good mornin' to him at breakfast and good night to him at dinner, and then, when your daddy was sixteen, he dropped dead from some kidney stones 'cause he ain't listened when I told him to drink some water and then he ain't listened again when I told him to go to the doctor. I'm not tryin' to ruin your idea of your granddaddy for you, Delly, I'm just tellin' you all this 'cause you gotta understand how men gonna disappoint you. All of 'em. Every time. But you know who not gonna disappoint you? Your mama. Or, in your case, Adela, your noni."

I shrugged. "I think I found a man who won't disappoint me." After all, Chris wanted to be my baby's father so badly he didn't even stop to think the baby might not be his. If that wasn't love, I didn't know what was.

"Is that right?" Noni continued to stroke my forehead, trying to push the frizz back down. "Then why's my grandbaby comin' home cryin', hmm?"

"It's not him."

Her eyebrows crept up her face. "So you ain't just seen him?"

"I mean, I did. But I'm not crying because he disappointed me, I'm crying because . . . because it's too much. It's all too much and if I lose him, I have nothing, Noni. My parents won't even talk to me, my best friend at home isn't my best friend anymore, and my baby's dad is a guy who didn't even like me enough to text me back."

Noni smiled and hummed, "So it's *your* baby now, hmm?"

I'd never said it before. I'm not even sure I'd ever really thought of the baby as belonging to anybody. I'm not even sure I'd ever thought of the baby as a baby at all, not until then, because, until Emory called me to croon her worries to and then took my sweatshirt and I ran into Chris and he said we're having a baby, I'd never thought that the child would do anything but take away from my life, rip everything I had from me and leave me nothing.

But now I felt a part of me wonder if all I wanted could come at the hands of this child, that I wouldn't ever be lonely again, that Chris wouldn't leave and I wouldn't lose another best friend and I could have something that was really, truly mine. As long as I didn't tell Simone about Chris and I didn't tell Chris about Simone or the baby's real dad or anything. I could keep the two of them separate, make sure I was never around them at the same time. I could do it. I would have to.

I felt the tears coming again. "Yeah." I smiled. "I think she's mine."

And then I settled back into Noni's arms and cried some more because Noni was prepared to hold me through it all, because it was too much but, for the first time, I was sure all this too much was mine.

# EMORY

I GOT INTO COLLEGE. Not just one college, but damn near all of them, including Stanford, and I'd been gathering up all my acceptances to surprise Adela. But when I sat down across from her at the picnic table, something was wrong.

Adela's eyes were all swollen like a captive goldfish, like the ones I'd see in the pet store the next town over whenever I begged Pawpaw to take me as a kid. Something was different about her, had been for the last few weeks maybe, since the orca and the snake and the bayou. Something in those eyes, in the way her shoulders slouched.

I still thought about that orca every day, but I'd accepted that everyone else thought I was crazy for it. Same way they thought I was crazy for applying to colleges on the other side of the country. Same way they thought I was crazy for wanting to go to college at all. That was the way things always went for me. Everyone brushed me off, hoping I'd shut my mouth about the things that buzzed inside me like a swarm of moths in the harsh glow of a flashlight. I was used to a dark and sad world, so I concealed all my light inside me and dreamed about my orca and the life she'd lived on my own time.

I imagined my orca's ma circling the waters of Texas looking for her baby, calling out again and again. I imagined her wishing she'd followed her child or kept her close for a few more months, till she was ready to go off alone. And then I imagined my orca's ma continuing to swim with the pod, deciding she'd leave behind the child that didn't know better than to find her way back.

After all, don't most mothers turn the fault on their babies when the guilt's too much to bear? That's what mine did, and then she dropped me off at Grammy and Pawpaw's and never came back.

At the picnic table, I waved the orca from my mind and focused in on Adela. Before I could tell her about my good news, I had to make sure she was okay, because I loved her and that's what you did when you loved someone. Except I almost wish I hadn't, that I'd just kept my mind floating in the ocean with the orca's ma. I didn't, though.

At the table over lunch, Kai now old enough he was holding his head up all by himself, staring at the trees, I asked Adela a question I couldn't take back.

"What's wrong?"

She tilted her head. "What do you mean? Nothing's wrong."

"Yes, it is. Don't pretend with me, Adela. I know you."

It's true, I did. She was my best friend, after all. Even if I wanted more. Even if she wanted more. She was the best friend I'd ever had. Maybe the only real friend outside the Girls, and they didn't count 'cause they were family.

When I was eight, I thought I'd made my first real friend. At that point, my auntie and my cousins had moved up to Georgia to be closer to my uncle and we'd moved into their house on the inland side of the highway. I'd gotten used to the way Pawpaw put hot sauce on his pancakes in the morning, the tickle of Grammy's brush through my hair in the evenings, the boring church service I was forced to go to every Sunday.

I went to school like anybody else, but I wasn't used to playing with other kids who weren't my cousins, and I didn't know how to introduce myself to anybody, so I'd go up to people and ask if they wanted to be my friend and, to any five-year-old, that's an invitation for ridicule, so I mostly played alone. Then, 'cause I refused to write my name or some silly thing like that, my kindergarten teacher told Grammy it'd be best to hold me back for another year, so every year after that I was the oldest in my class and somehow that made the other kids wanna be my friend even less. But, in second grade, I met Sylvia.

Sylvia liked to play with the class pet, a turtle, just as much as I did, so we'd watch him and feed him side by side till, one day, I asked if Sylvia wanted to have a sleepover. I'd heard the other girls in my class talking about sleepovers and I wanted to give it a try. To my surprise, Sylvia said yes. Her ma and Grammy coordinated and the next Thursday, Grammy picked us both up from school and walked us back to my house.

Sylvia and me watched *Lilo & Stitch* on DVD and then, when it got dark, Pawpaw kicked us out of the living room for his episode of *Dateline.* But instead of going to sleep, me and Sylvia whispered to each other all our fantasies about being ballerinas and finding princes and getting pet pit bulls. Sylvia started to get sleepy, quiet, but I was wide-awake and I just didn't want the night to end, so I asked Sylvia if she wanted to see something and Sylvia said yes. I pulled down my underwear and lifted up my nightgown and put a finger into my privates and started moving it around.

"What are you doing?" Sylvia whispered. She looked confused.

I was just happy to be the one who knew more and so I helped Sylvia out and pulled her dress up.

"It feels good. Try it."

Sylvia copied me and slipped her finger inside herself.

"I don't like it," Sylvia said. "It's where the pee comes from."

"You're not doing it right," I insisted.

"Whatever. I'm going to sleep."

Sylvia pulled her underwear up, turned onto her stomach, and fell asleep within minutes. I just had to lay there, wondering why Sylvia didn't like it and if she was doing it wrong even though I wasn't really sure what "it" was, and I knew I wasn't supposed to talk about it anyway.

On Friday evening, the phone rang and Grammy swept into my

room, eyes frantic and twitching. She grabbed me up and slammed me into my time-out chair and started screaming about how Sylvia's mother called and I was dirty and I'd ruined the family name and now how was she ever gonna show herself at church again, huh? What was she supposed to say to Pawpaw? And even when I spent the rest of the night in my time-out chair sobbing, Grammy didn't take me into her lap and hold me like usual. She didn't apologize and ask me any questions.

In fact, she didn't talk to me at all that weekend. She set some food outside my bedroom door at each meal and then, on Monday morning, she took me outside the house and she pointed down the street.

"See up there? You take a right up there and then another right when you get to the stop sign. Come back the same way after school. And if Sylvia tries to talk to you, ignore her. Or even better, tell her she's lying." And then Grammy went back inside the house, locked the door, and she never walked me to school or back home again. I wasn't allowed to have sleepovers after that.

It wasn't like Grammy or Pawpaw were cruel. They were actually about the friendliest people in town, anyone would tell you, but they didn't mess around with any tomfoolery. It took me a couple of years to figure out that meant they liked a secret kept exactly where a secret was meant to go: the bottom of the ocean, where you couldn't find it even if you had a scuba mask and some flippers.

After Sylvia, I decided friendship was a risk not worth taking. I was sure that if anyone got too close to me, they might not want to be my friend at all. Adela was the first person to disprove that. As much as I loved her, wanted to run my hands along the ridges of her shoulders and feel her lips smeared in Vaseline, I also loved just being her friend. And as her friend, I couldn't ignore when something was wrong. Especially 'cause I was still waiting for her to tell me the truth. About her feelings for me. And every question I asked was secretly a hope it'd lead back to that.

At the picnic table, Adela looked over at Kai, reached her hand out and offered him her index finger to grasp, and she didn't even look at me when she said the next thing. "Remember when I said I was in love?"

My chest swelled up like Adela's eyes, so tight not even a whistle could find its way through my lungs. This might be it. I nodded, even though she wasn't looking at me.

"Well, the guy I'm in love with found out I was pregnant a few weeks ago and I—well, I let him think it was his. So nothing's wrong. Actually, everything's great, I'm just scared I made the wrong choice." Finally, she looked at me. "What do you think?"

I wasn't prepared to hear it. That's the worst part of it all: I actually thought she loved me. I'd never paused to think that maybe Adela only winked at me as her best friend. That she disappeared for more reasons than just communing with the water alone. That she might have someone else I knew nothing about.

Since the hurricane party, we spent our afternoons after school laid out on the beach or the floor of her grandma's living room listening to the old CDs her grandma kept around. We wheezed in fits of funny, watched reruns of TV shows Adela'd never even heard of before she came down here, told each other the kinds of things you tell your diary. I was the pages she could pour into, and I did the same for her. On Friday nights, sometimes I slept over, in her bed, knotted in the sheets. Wishing she'd come closer.

For months, I'd been so sure every tell and sign was meant for me. When she rolled over in the middle of the night and her knee touched my thigh. When she asked for help getting up the dunes and I pulled her with me, and she kept holding my hand even after we made it down to the road. When she talked about the feeling of love, vague but vibrant, and I thought she might just finally say she felt it all for me.

I tricked myself into seeing it all through a murky film, like the bayou's surface skimmed in dirt. Maybe that's how the baby orca got so lost, thinking the sound of a giant ship passing by was the call of her mother until she was too far to hear anything at all.

Unrequited love is like believing in fairies for a little too long, past the age it's acceptable. Sure, there's the eventual devastation that this thing you thought was real suddenly evaporated into nothing. But the worst part of it is the shame that you ever believed at all.

I choked on my own exhale. There Adela was, her finger in my son's hand, across a picnic table from me, asking for advice about a boy like she hadn't just destroyed me.

"Um, I don't know. Maybe you should ask someone else."

I couldn't stay there. I couldn't talk to her about this, not without crying, and if I cried then she'd start asking me what was wrong, and I'd have to confess that I believed in fairies and miracles and she had just crushed my faith between her molars on a Tuesday afternoon.

I stood up and grabbed Kai as he shrieked and tried to pull Adela's finger with us. I raced away before she could follow, before she could ask anything, 'cause I couldn't answer her, I wouldn't, and when I shut the front door of my house with us inside and called out for Pawpaw and Grammy and when no one responded, I let myself sob.

Kai, on my hip, put his whole hand in his mouth and sucked, looking around at our living room like he'd never seen it before and, to be honest, it felt like I hadn't either. Adela Woods had broken my heart, and nothing would ever return to the way it was before.

# SIMONE

EVERY MARCH, I braced myself like the rest of Padua for the dreaded stampede of spring breakers rolling into coastal Florida. They was a wild bunch, came to rave and roar, but at least they brought cash to do it with. The only season we all knew there'd be work and customers, ragers and tan lines. Really, it was the only time of year anybody thought much of anything about Padua Beach.

We weren't a hub or nothing, but a couple hundred college students stumbled onto our white beaches and settled in for a week or two or three every spring and the rest of us, the ones who'd been here since forever, resented them for their shrieking, their disregard of who and what we came from.

But they spent their money and so we smiled and welcomed them, like any good southern town would, while we gossiped about their willingness to pay twenty dollars for a drink and some fried oysters behind their backs in the secret pockets of town where none of them knew to holler.

This year, me and the Girls decided to get creative for spring break season: we decided to get rich. It was the beginning of spring, when warmth beckoned and all of us Girls gathered to spend the evenings and weekends together, without no more worries than any other mothers during flu season.

It was Adela's idea. The jungle juice. We was sitting by the dune lake, cooling down as the sun set, and I was the one who said we should go on out to the most popular beaches and try to make some money off the thirsty fools. I thought we could sell bottled water. It was Adela who shook her head. "There'll be plenty of other people with the same idea. You need something that sets you apart, a demand that isn't being met. It's the key to a thriving business."

"What do a bunch of wasted students want that they don't already have?" Emory asked. She was mad at Adela, had been for weeks. We could all tell, watched them sit nowhere near each other when before you couldn't find 'em apart. None of us knew why, though, and so we let them hurtle hurting words back and forth and continued about our days.

Adela shrugged. "More alcohol, of course. On the beach, where they don't have to go up to a bar or a store or anything. And something stronger than beer."

I shook my head. "We can't afford to buy none of that."

"Don't buy it, then. Make it."

That's when Emory shot up. "Jungle juice."

◆ ◆ ◆

The plan materialized quickly, just in time for the arrival of the spring breakers. We created schedules and divided up the tasks of who would get what when, and then, as we approached the first weekend, the jitters of all we'd poured into this plan keeping us frenzied in the night, everyone whose shift was scheduled for the second or third weekend begged to switch to the first one, and nobody wanted to trade.

Eventually, to quit all the quarreling, I said anybody who wanted to come that first weekend was welcome and so, on our first Friday selling jungle juice, all of us went together.

On Friday afternoon, I gathered the Girls, picked Emory and Adela up from school, and then we all swung by Crystal's for the tub, Walmart for the soda and juice, and finally the old liquor store half a mile from the dune lake.

When we pulled up at the beach and opened the truck doors, the familiar sound of unruly folks going wild on land that was not their own and would never hold the consequences of their spills and stumbles roared. Lion held my hand and looked up at me. "Why they yellin'?"

"'Cause they don't got no sense," I said.

"But I do," Lion said. "I'm not yellin'."

"That's right." He nodded once and, proud of hisself, walked ahead of me to follow his sister, the rest of the kids, April, Jamilah, Adela, and Tori. Emory, Crystal, and I climbed into the truck bed and poured gallon after gallon of liquid into the tub, stirring it with an old bat Jayden scrubbed the night before and loaned us.

He told me I had to give it back and it better not be broken, 'cause him and his son was gonna use that bat to play ball as soon as Kai could walk. Boys was so single-minded, so focused only on force and friction, never on the victory of a small boy learning to take a step, only on what he would step toward.

"It looks too brown," Emory said.

"You add enough color and anything gonna turn brown," I said. "Look at your son." I laughed and so did Crystal. Emory didn't.

"Add some more Fanta," Crystal said.

I grabbed the last bottle of Fanta and poured it into the tub. It blubbered and fizzed until the bottle was empty. Now the liquid had a red-orange undertone to the brown.

"Nothing's wrong with a little brown. Besides, they so crossed, they ain't even gonna notice what color it is," I said. "You got the cups?"

Emory nodded, holding the cases of red Solo cups.

"Y'all got the signs?" I called out to Luck and Lion. They held up the signs they'd each helped decorate, their little swirls and scribbles of cups beside the lettering Tori meticulously worked on for two hours: JUNGLE JUICE $8 PER CUP. CASH OR CASH APP ONLY.

"Let's go," Emory said, tightening the straps on the BabyBjörn carrier Jayden got her for Valentine's Day even though they still weren't together, the Solo cups in her hands. Luck and Lion stood behind the wagon that held the tub full of jungle juice and helped push it while Adela pulled the wagon from the front.

Dozens of sun-scarred white folks were scattered on the beach, making out, titties busting from their swimsuits, ocean salt turning their hair even thinner and straw-like. A small group played volleyball with a net they'd set up too close to the water and every time the tide crashed, it pulled their feet out from under them and they were body-slammed to the sand, cackling in a drunken daze.

"These boneheaded motherfuckers gonna eat this shit up," I said, low enough the kids wouldn't hear.

"Let's set up here," Tori said, pointing to a clear patch far enough from the water it wouldn't come close to touching us, but visible enough everybody would be able to see where we was.

I taped the signs to the front of the tub, Emory unwrapped the cups, and then we each took a seat on the sand beside the tub. I turned to Luck and Lion.

"Alright, y'all, you gonna help us out?"

They nodded, diligent.

"Go on over to whoever you can and ask them if they want a drink. Say your momma selling hooch right over here. And then I want you to point so they know where to go. You can even bring 'em over, but only if they seem like nice folks. Don't be messing with nobody shady, okay?"

"Yes, ma'am," they said, then spun around and marched off on their mission.

"You really think they're going to remember all that?" Adela asked.

"Course they will. They my kids."

And I was right. Luck and Lion went up to every single group on that beach and, one by one, brought them back to us. At first the slobbery drunks were all skeptical, asking about what was in the jungle juice and saying they just didn't wanna say no to the kids, but once they had a single taste of that stuff, they was hollering about it to anybody they could find, back to get a refill before the booze even hit their stomachs.

It only took us an hour and a half before we sold out. By the end we were charging ten dollars a cup, just 'cause we could, and all these people was paying for it. I thought none of 'em would have cash but turned out most of 'em got cash for all the drinks and games at the water park in Destin and they happily dished out all the change they had.

We started by stuffing it in our swimsuits, but then we had to switch to putting it in one of the empty Pepsi bottles we cut the head off of with my pocketknife. By the time we ran out of jungle juice, we'd made a couple hundred dollars and we was all shocked. We'd known they was desperate for something to drink, but Adela was right. Give 'em something they want but don't got, and they'll get themselves in a frenzy just to have it.

We huddled up and counted the money. If we kept going, weekend after weekend for the next month, we could walk out of this with a couple grand.

"How're we gonna split it?" Emory asked.

"We should split it evenly once we know how much we made," Tori said.

We agreed we'd leave the money in one place till the end of spring breaker season and then we'd divvy it up later. But, for now, someone had to keep it.

Every one of us volunteered, except Adela. We argued over who was the most responsible, the most frugal, had the least nosy roommates, and had earned the most trust. Adela stayed out of the arguments, used her toe to draw patterns in the sand.

"Why don't you wanna do it?" Jamilah asked.

Adela shrugged. "It doesn't matter to me. I don't even need a cut."

"What? Why?" I asked. Sure, she might not need it, but who didn't want some extra cash?

"If I want to buy something, I'll use my credit card."

"You have a credit card?" April gawked. "Are you in a bunch of debt?"

Adela laughed. "No, my parents pay it off every month. They say it's good for building credit. I haven't used it since I got here, though. My parents send my grandma money to take care of me and it's not like you have anywhere good to shop here anyway."

We all stared at her, even Emory. But none of us could ever, not even for a moment, fathom what Adela was saying. That she didn't want any extra money 'cause there wasn't nothing you could buy in this part of the world she couldn't already have.

"Adela should take it," I said. "The money."

"I just said I don't need it."

"No, Simone's right. Adela won't spend it, she don't really care about it, and she'll pay everybody their fair cut at the end of the month." Crystal agreed.

The other Girls looked disappointed, but even they nodded. It just made sense, after all. Adela would take each soda bottle full of money at the end of every weekend, setting aside enough for more ingredients, and then, once the spring breakers were gone, we would figure out how to split it and all get our share.

Before we started to pack up for the night, some of the Girls wanted to take a dip in the water. Jamilah started it but then Adela and Tori said they wanted to join and the kids who could talk all begged to go with. April hung back to nurse her son and Crystal returned to the truck to put Cece down, since she was getting fussy. It was just me left, sitting by our now-empty tub stained in orange-brown juice.

The beach was still swarmed. Scattered among all the young for-eigners come down from South Carolina, Texas, Arkansas, were newly retired old women from Padua dragging their great-grandbabies through strangers' burnt legs. An older guy stood under an umbrella in his swim trunks and a big fedora that he never took off, prob'ly 'cause he was embarrassed of the tan line rimming his bald scalp. Then, among the old locals and the spring breakers, were all the near and far bottle-blond moms.

One of them, the wife of the manager of the Alvin's Island water sports store farther up the highway, snickered to the women next to her through her gummy lip gloss about how maybe Johnny Boy Dive was the one who dug the crater on the other side of the beach all their kids were sliding into and climbing out of, with how we all knew Johnny loved to get deep inside someone. The ladies beside her all hooted.

And then, sitting a few feet to the left of me, were two women who looked familiar but I ain't known their names, just that they were locals and somebody's mom. They discussed what at first I was sure was a pyramid scheme for patterned leggings but now I was fair certain was about how horny they was. I started listening in.

The woman closest to me still had a hair bump, just couldn't let go of the early two thousands, and the other one had left her hair dye in so long her platinum blond was bordering on white, smoky eye a sickly purple that continued beyond the eye itself and all the way to the bridge of her nose.

The hair bump woman, who I was pretty sure worked as a nurse at the doctor's office I took Luck and Lion to, tugged at the ends of her hair. "I just want something more. I'm tired of all these people thinking they can take advantage of me, you know?"

"I know what you mean." The smoky eye lady smacked her lips and dug around in her bag till she found a cigarette and a lighter and once she'd had one good long drag of her cigarette, she gestured across the beach. "This could be it for us. Last month, when Tim asked me if we could take the risk, I wasn't too sure, but this . . . this could be good right here. What's a husband for if he can't support you, huh?

We been so strapped for cash, I been holdin' off on getting a Brazilian for months and I just can't keep the forest tamed no more, if you know what I mean."

The other one cackled. "Didn't you know, Carmen, all the young girls these days been letting their bits grow out? At least that's what the doctor told me about all the girls she's examining. Course, I sure hope none of them have any reason to be shaving nothing."

"I've seen it too," Carmen said after the smoke exited her lips, blowing back to me with the breeze. "At the Center, over half of 'em shedding hair all over the examination table. Now, I'm in the business of God, first and foremost, but if a girl's gonna give herself up like that, how's she going to turn around and not even keep things clean and tidy?"

When I first heard them talking, I felt the smallest prickle in my sternum, but I wasn't sure where it came from till the hair bump woman said the Center. Sure, she could've meant the community center or something, but I knew women like these two. I'd met a woman like Carmen before, at the Center, where women like Carmen go to feed off what someone like me didn't know until I knew.

I was fifteen when I went into the Center for the first and last time. You don't go to the Center unless you have a reason to and, by then, you're probably too late to know better than to not walk through those doors at all.

It was my second week without a place to sleep after Momma and Pops told me to go and I was still sneaking into Beach Row and crawling under Pops's old rowboat to sleep until just before the sun came up, when I would slip out, my whole backside covered in orange dust, my mouth sticky in dirty bayou water and my own sweat. I spent my days with Tooth, watching him work, crying in the bathroom at the bait shop when he was with a customer. All I wanted to do was fix the mess I'd made. Go back to how it had been.

So I walked to the Center, tucked away in a strip mall that also housed the Methodist church and an electronics supply company I'd never seen nobody go into. I'd passed by the Center a million times in my life, and it seemed like the perfect place to go when you didn't know what to do, when you found yourself in a situation like mine. I'd heard a girl could get the kind of operation I needed at this sort of place and the sign looked friendly: PADUA PREGNANCY RESOURCE CENTER, with a little blue heart around each *P*.

When I walked in, I approached the older lady at the front desk, and she looked up at me like I was the first person to willingly walk in that door all year.

"Hi, dear, how can I help you?" she drawled, and her gums showed crimson.

Her desk had a little jar full of lollipops in it and I'd been expecting condoms or something, so that made me feel a little better, that at the end of all this at least I'd get something sweet.

"I, um, I'd like to have the operation."

"The operation?" The woman's mouth purred but her eyes didn't move, not once.

I nodded, skittish. Afraid to name it.

The woman seemed to understand and smiled. "Let me take you back and Mrs. Harris will help you out, hmm?"

She stood from her chair, crucifix pendant tangled and heavy on her neck, and as she took me through the door, down the hallway, into the one box of a room where Scripture quotes lined the walls, my stomach felt the slippery mass of what I'd done and I started to laugh. I laughed like the old woman had made the funniest joke I ever heard and as she slipped out of the room to get Mrs. Harris, I saw her lips move, her Hail Mary.

Mrs. Harris was a God-fearing woman. That was the first thing she said to me when she sat down on a stool in front of me and took my hands, her skin so thin I was sure it could tear off like wet paper. I stopped laughing.

"As a God-fearing woman, it is my right and duty to tell you that despite the way you've sinned, in the eyes of God, it isn't too late to make the right choice and save yourself from damnation. If you murder this baby, then you and this child's sweet innocent soul will forever be doomed to an eternity in Hell. But, if you keep this baby, God will find it in his heart to forgive you." She let go of my hands. "Now, go on and lift up your shirt so we can meet your angel baby."

I didn't know what to do, didn't understand why we was talking about God when all I was thinking about was Pops's face as he opened the door to the trailer to let me back inside. I laid there, just staring up at the ceiling, where a portrait of this baby-faced white man holding a one-year-old Jesus was taped, and when I didn't lift my shirt up, Mrs. Harris did it for me, turning on a machine older than the guy swaddling baby Jesus. She squeezed gel on my abdomen and started moving the little tool around like in the movies.

I told myself not to look at the screen. I focused on the tremor in my chest, the tight ball caught in my throat like when I was a kid and forgot to chew my food, praying for God to make the clump of dry meat go down and find my stomach. I didn't wanna feel what was happening below my ribs, where Mrs. Harris was pushing hard on my stomach. I hadn't even thought much about how there was something in there and now I was staring up at baby Jesus and trying hard to swallow while a woman looked for a baby in my body.

A baby. It was sorta funny, until Mrs. Harris turned to the machine and fiddled with something, adjusting the sound on the sonogram, I think, and then the doppler caught a heartbeat and she turned the volume up until the sound filled the whole room like smoke.

And then one quick pounding of rain turned to a tumult of sound and Mrs. Harris beamed. "Looks like you've got twins!"

Then it wasn't so funny anymore. I swallowed and it made my chest burn.

I looked up at the screen, even though I told myself not to, but it didn't matter 'cause the screen was nothing but fuzz and gray and Mrs. Harris said, "Don't worry, these babies are just too small to look at yet. Wait a few weeks and you can come back, hmm?"

"But . . . but what about my operation?" I wanted the sound to stop. My thoughts couldn't penetrate the parade of little raindrops hitting the ground inside me, two torrential storms.

When Mrs. Harris turned the sonogram machine off, the sound still echoed inside me till her voice cut through it. "You don't need an operation. You need to remember what happens when you go against the Word of God."

She stood and went to a cabinet drawer, where she retrieved a stack of pamphlets and brought them back to me. One on fetal heartbeats and pain, another on saving marriages, another on the merits of baptism. I didn't know if I could even stand to touch them. I came in here thinking I was going to leave with no baby and a home to return to and now here I was with two babies and three pamphlets that threatened to ferment inside me and come up in my midnight bile.

"I don't want these," I whispered.

Mrs. Harris gritted her teeth into a smile and shoved them into my lap. "What you don't want is to kill these babies and find out ten years from now that the operation ruined your chances of having another one. What you don't want is to suffer the wrath of God when you destroy an innocent life. Are you that heartless, honey?"

"I didn't—I don't. I don't know."

Mrs. Harris patted my knee. "From one God-fearing woman to another, how about you go home, spend another few weeks thinking about the blessing of these babies born out of a sin so reprehensible, and then come back in a month and we can take another look. By then, these babies will have fingernails and everything!"

I left with a stomach still sticky with gel and, on my way out, the old lady with the bleeding gums offered me a lollipop. When I shook my head, she grinned and said, "Maybe next time. God bless you, sweetie."

But there wasn't a next time and they must've known this, looking at the untamed forest of my body, the wild lines growing on my hips.

Years later, during a cold winter with the twins, I was in the library reading a book about Florida and all it'd been, when I started crying right there on the floor in the stacks while my toddlers slept wrapped in blankets beside me 'cause I got to the section about our little part of Florida and it broke my heart.

West Florida had been split and swapped so many times, exchanged between all these countries and warred over the borders, only to be given up, left alone to wither where no folks ever thought of it again.

I was West Florida, tricked into thinking I was important, grown weary in the war of weeks and heartbeats, and then suddenly left on my own to rot.

By the time I would think to go back, Tooth had already convinced me to keep them. And even if I had returned to the Center, even if their sonogram had finally been able to see fetus instead of static fluid, they wouldn't have done nothing. And if somehow I'd gotten myself to Planned Parenthood instead, they would've told me I needed my parents to sign a form and there wasn't no world where my parents would've done that. So, in the end, I was the flapping sliver of Florida nobody knew what to do with, and my babies became my babies.

Carmen was not a doctor, but she understood enough to know no fifteen-year-old girl scared and burdened with time would be able to withstand the fallacy of that God-fearing room, little baby Jesus wrapped up in some saint's robes, a lollipop threatening to turn my Florida mouth red.

# ADELA

LYING DOESN'T MAKE you a liar. It's impossible never to lie, tangled in a moment when eyes are turned on you and you realize you don't want to feel as small as the pellet of truth inside you, so you make up some story about what time you went to bed, your dress size, how many people you'd slept with.

The problem is that lies demand to be followed by more lies, and once you're knotted inside them and forget which things you've told which people, you have no choice but to continue on and eventually, you realize the only person with whom you can be truthful, wholly and without second thought, is yourself.

I wasn't a liar. I was just trapped in the spindly circuit of my attempts to be so important to someone my truth would be enough.

But, with Chris, I was in too deep to reverse or confess. He couldn't know and, honestly, he didn't need to. Not about Simone and not about David. Sure, he might suspect something when the baby came out looking a little too light, but my mother's white, so that could be explained as genetics skipping a generation, and it's not like anybody in Florida besides Noni really knew for sure when I got pregnant or by whom. Except the Girls.

But Emory was mad at me for some reason and so I spent even less time with the rest of the Girls the past two months, and if Chris never knew I was part of them and they never knew he was the guy I talked about, then nobody would get hurt. Plus, Chris had made my choice about the baby easier and, ever since then, I'd felt complete relief.

Maybe lying was wrong, but sometimes it's the only way through, the only way to bridge the distance between one little life and another. Not exactly right, but reasonable. Necessary, even.

When I entered high school, I told everyone my dad was from the South of France. I didn't intend to lie, but it was a new school, my first private school, and everyone already knew each other from middle school. I was novel, suspicious, not worth knowing, and, making it worse, I was the only Black person not from the continent and definitely the only mixed one any of the other kids had ever gotten close enough to touch.

During the first week of my freshman year, at least a dozen people each day came up to me—at my desk in class, on the bleachers at the assembly, in the cafeteria nibbling on mushy apple slices—and before they even asked my name, they'd squint and whisper, "So . . . where are you from?"

Confused, I said, "Um, here. I'm from Indiana."

They shook their heads, giggled. "No, like, what are you? Where are you from, before that? Your parents."

"Oh."

I didn't know what to say. Sometimes I'd just blush and say, "All over." But they weren't satisfied with that. They'd frown and wander away, back to their groups, deciding I was not interesting enough to know. Once I figured out they were really asking how I got to be this specific composition of hair, skin, eyes, I started saying, "My mom's white and my dad's Black."

But even that didn't seem to do it for them. They'd slump at my answer, disappointed I couldn't be something more tantalizing, more fun to dissect. I had to tell them something else, something that would make them stay. I didn't have a choice.

It was the beginning of the second week of school when Lindsay came up to me. Lindsay with her wispy blond hair, with her purplish lips. I'd watched her with her friends before; she was on the track team, and they sometimes showered in our locker room. Lindsay was easy to spot: she was loud, adored, unapologetic, and worshipped for it. If you were loved by Lindsay, you were safe.

I was standing in front of the line of mirrors by the locker room sinks, desperately trying to untangle fairy knots from my hair, the rest of the girls from the swim team already gone, and Lindsay had just gotten out of the shower. She was pulling on her sweatpants under the deep blue glow of the windowless room lit by fluorescents, and the rest of her team was nowhere to be found. When her shirt was on, she turned and seemed to see me for the first time, even though I'd been standing by her the entire time.

She blinked her pale eyelashes at me. "You're new to town, right?"

I shook my head. "No, I went to Westlane, actually. Just new here."

Lindsay nodded slowly, then leaned closer to me. "Your eyes are so pretty."

I smiled. I got that compliment a lot, and it always felt vaguely backhanded, but it was somehow nicer coming from her. But then Lindsay cocked her head and I knew she was going to follow the compliment up with the question all the rest of them loved to ask. "So where are you from?"

I sighed. I started by pretending I didn't understand the real question, hoping she might be dissuaded and ask me something that actually had to do with me. "I live off Spring Road. My dad goes to the country club there."

"No, like, before that. Where's your dad from?"

It was Lindsay. I couldn't tell her my dad was just from a town in Florida that wasn't even on a map. I couldn't tell her sometimes when he watched football or got angry, his voice would turn wobbly and his accent would emerge, raging and southern. I couldn't have her look at me and think, *You don't belong*. So, instead, I told her the first thing I could think of.

"He's from the South of France. And my mom's from Wisconsin, but before that Ireland and a little bit of France too. My parents always say they would've met in this life or another."

I don't know why it's always been so easy for me to lie. It somersaults off my tongue and next thing I know, I've created something I can't take back and it's expanding. It spreads and multiplies until it has consumed everything, and I feel, for once, powerful.

Lindsay grinned. "I love France. My aunt has an apartment in Paris we stay at every summer. I even have my own room, chez moi. Maybe when you go see your family there, you can come visit."

"I'd love to. J'adore Paris."

Lindsay found me in the hall the next morning and pulled me with her, introducing me to her friends. "This is Adela. She's French." A chorus of girls cooed and asked me all kinds of questions, but I didn't have to answer because I was with Lindsay and Lindsay kept us moving, had no time for anyone to talk but her.

I was relieved just to have a friend, and since that friend was Lindsay, I quickly became friends with everyone else. Two days after I met Lindsay, I went to my counselor and switched from Spanish to French class and when anyone asked why I was in beginner's French, I would gawk at them and say, "Haven't you heard of assimilation?"

The word about the new girl who would soon be on the brochures at all the school's open houses spread quick. *She's French. I know, she doesn't look French, but I guess they have Africans in France too. I heard her family has a castle by the water. I heard she has dual citizenship. I heard she has a French boyfriend she sees in the summers.* By the time I entered my sophomore year, my teachers greeted me with bonjours.

Luckily, school wasn't close enough to my house to ever have my parents run into my friends' parents, and my friends happily invited me to their houses and never asked to come to mine. It was simple enough to keep my lives separate, and my lie gave me nothing but friendship and mystique. I was no longer just unusual, just mixed-up, just confused. I was exotic, foreign, special. Sometimes that's how I felt with Chris: the glowing center of his universe, different and all the more beautiful for it.

I arrived at the community pool in the middle of Chris's shift, just like every other Saturday afternoon. I hadn't swum in a few months, not in the pool, and I wasn't planning on it. I'd brought a book and my phone and a sun hat, so I was just going to sit by the edge of the pool watching Chris lifeguard until he closed and took me back to his place. But when I swung my bag onto my corner of cement, he was by my side in seconds.

He tried to lean in and kiss me, but I shoved him away.

"There are kids around," I said. The pool wasn't as crowded as it was in the summer, but there were still a dozen children and parents floating in it. I was worried one of them knew Noni or Simone or Emory, that word would travel rapid as gas flame in this town.

Chris kissed me anyway and I checked over his shoulder to make sure no one was looking before he pulled away, retrieving something bright red from each of his pockets.

"It's for you, girl," he said, shoving the cloth into my hands.

"What is it?"

"A swimsuit."

I unrolled each sliver of red cloth until I could see how it might pass for a swimsuit. Not any kind I'd ever worn, but I could see the red matched Chris's lifeguard shorts and the grin on his face made me want to like it.

"It looks a little . . . small," I said.

He shook his head. "Nah, baby, it's perfect. I know your size."

"But I'm, you know . . ." I whispered the next part. "Pregnant."

"Yeah, I know you got a belly. That's why I got you a bikini." His smile was faltering, and I knew I was pushing the edge of his kindness, that we were close to fighting like we did about his roommate's dirty briefs on the floor. And even though I'd fought before, even been pummeled by Simone, nothing was worse than Chris when his eyes looked like spilled oil, when I could feel that every tendon in him despised me.

"Thank you," I said.

I started to stuff the swimsuit into my bag when Chris coughed. "Whatchu doing? Go on and put it on."

"But I'm not swimming."

His lip quivered. "I just wanna see you in it. Besides, you ain't gotta hide nothin' from me no more, so how 'bout you go and put on the present I got you so you can swim for me?"

He loved to watch me swim and usually I loved to swim for him, but it was so exposing, being pregnant in the water, taking up all the empty space. Still, I wanted to do it for him. I wanted to make him happy.

I grabbed my bag and the red swimsuit and made my way to the changing room, where I waited for an old lady to be done showering before I stripped my clothes off and stepped into the swimsuit bottoms, twisted my arms around my back to tie the top. My breasts were overflowing from the triangle cloth, so I settled for just trying to get the fabric to cover the nipples. Even then, my nipples were bigger than whoever's the company had designed the bikini for, and I could see the edge of deep brown coming out the side.

Some people looked romantic pregnant. I'd seen some in real life and on TV too: women whose abdomens made a perfect globe, who walked barefoot because they were at one with the earth and not just because their feet had swollen and none of their shoes fit. Some girls looked like they were always meant to be the fertile ground a child flourished in. But I didn't.

I was at the very end of my second trimester and I looked and felt like a mess. No matter how much oil I slathered on my stomach, the skin refused to stretch gently. I had hemorrhoids on my ass and nosebleeds every morning that kept restaining my sheets a yellow brown. Even after Simone cured my nausea, every time I stood up I felt like I was going to fall or faint, the world going white.

I knew I didn't look like a pregnant goddess in that red swim-suit. But, still, I felt better about it all than I had since I took the pregnancy test and hid it in my locker. So when I walked out of the changing room and set my bag down on the cement again, I kept my chin raised and my eyes unfocused on the stares.

I was different than I used to be: I could tune it all out, forget about everyone but me, me and Chris. Sure, I didn't always tell the truth, but at least now my lies had meaning, purpose. They were so much more worth it than they had ever been before.

◆ ◆ ◆

My first big lie imploded on Lindsay's sixteenth birthday. It was a pool party and I even came early enough to help curl her hair and put it in a high ponytail so it wouldn't get too wet. She tried curling mine but it wouldn't work unless I straightened it too, and we didn't have time for that. Lindsay made me promise I'd let her straighten my hair another time, since she really wanted to see it, even though it was a waste of time when the next morning I'd be back in a swimming pool, all those hours sitting in a chair washed away.

Lindsay's sixteenth birthday party was a dream. Her parents hired a caterer and a party planner to set up the backyard so it was exactly the way Lindsay wanted it, and then they sat at a table on the back porch away from the pool and sipped margaritas, greeting Lindsay's friends and their parents as they came and went.

When Mom dropped me off, I convinced her not to come inside.

"Lindsay's parents don't like that many people in their house. It's a closed guest list," I said.

"Fine." Mom gripped tight to the steering wheel. "Your dad will come pick you up at five."

I climbed out of the car and Mom drove away.

It was just us girls in the pool. Lindsay's parents didn't let boys in the house, but she had plans to sneak out and meet her boyfriend at his older brother's apartment that night, so she was happy having just us, her friends, giggling and splashing in the pool. And if Lindsay was happy, so were we.

Lindsay loved making me show off my swimming to the other girls.

"Do that one where you go across the whole pool without taking a breath!" she called from her throne on the poolside lounger, rotating every ten minutes for an even tan. The other girls cheered until I took a breath and dove beneath the water, propelling forward headfirst, reemerging at the other end. They applauded.

"You're literally a mermaid, Dela," Lindsay called.

Friendship with girls is a strange beast. Before I met the Girls, the only friends I'd known were these: Lindsay, my swim club teammates, little girls I chased and followed just for a glance thrown my way. All I'd known was bared teeth disguised as a smile, wounds treated with an envy-fueled giggle, every girl hiding behind another, hiding behind herself.

True friendship was a stolen breath in a smog-filled sky, a thing to chase but rarely catch. We were all too scared of solitude to abandon the bonds that hinged on our own disregard, too scared of ourselves to risk being seen as what we were.

Before I met the Girls, I'd never considered there were people who would stand in front of me and see me for exactly what I was and somehow believe I was worth sitting beside. But I didn't know better back then. All I knew was that the sound of these girls cheering for me was enough to make me do another lap for them. And another. And another.

I was below the water, my ears buried under pressure and an indistinct echo of voices, when Dad must have shown up. If I'd been watching when he arrived, I would have pulled myself from the pool, intercepted him before Lindsay's parents even had the chance to introduce themselves, and pulled him back around Lindsay's house to wait in the car. But I was beneath the water and all I heard were a few extra rumbles of a bass voice as I mermaid-swam to the other side. When I emerged, no more than sixty seconds after Dad must have arrived, I wiped the water from my eyes and saw him there, seated at the table with Lindsay's parents, mid-conversation.

"Adela, is that your dad?" Jenny asked.

I climbed out of the pool, pulled my towel around my shoulders. "Yeah. He's early."

I walked quickly through the tanning girls and up to the porch as I heard Lindsay's mom say, "When we were on our honeymoon a million years ago, we went on a tour of James Baldwin's estate in Saint-Paul de Vence. Have you been? Of course you have, why am I even asking, Nice isn't even an hour away. Truly gorgeous. Historic."

Dad was sitting with a spine straight as a stick and nodding slowly, his mouth held tight. He turned to see me and even the speck of jaundice in his right eye looked angry.

"Dad, I thought you were going to wait outside," I said.

"And I thought it was time I introduced myself to my daughter's best friend's parents. Leslie and Tim were kind enough to offer me a drink and discuss the allure of France. My *hometown*." His eyes narrowed on me as he rose from his seat and reached his hand out to shake each of Lindsay's parents' hands. "Thank you for the drink. I promised my wife I'd get Adela home before dinner."

Dad didn't even look at me as he spit, "Adela, say your goodbyes."

I lowered my head and walked back to my lounge chair, where I gathered my things and said bye to Lindsay and the girls. Lindsay barely looked up as I left.

"Thank you for having me." I waved at Lindsay's parents. Dad was already by the door, still not looking me in the eyes. As I walked past him, he growled, "Get in the damn car, Adela," his accent flaring.

The moment the car doors slammed shut, I expected Dad to start yelling, but somehow the silence was worse. He began driving and it wasn't until we were halfway home that he spoke. He only said one thing, but it would never leave me, would resonate in the background of every conversation, every decision, every single time I introduced myself.

"You are only what you believe yourself to be. When you are ashamed, you become shameful. I won't let you make me look bad in front of these people, but I didn't raise a liar, Adela. I raised a winner. That is what I believe."

It was true. My father raised a winner. Every time I lied after that, I made sure it was in the pursuit of winning. I made sure what it said about me was what I believed. So when I decided not to tell Chris it wasn't his baby, I chose to believe the baby was his. I chose to believe this family I could have with him would make me a winner.

I was not ashamed, I was not shameful. I was deciding my own fate and doing what I needed to do to make it real. And when I put on that red bikini and walked out into the open air, I chose to believe I was beautiful, that I could swim, that I could be everything Chris wanted me to be.

◆ ◆ ◆

I dove into the water, into an empty space in the deep end, and didn't even feel embarrassed by the massive splash I created, the current that rippled out from where my body hit the water. Instead of swimming my faux laps, I did something I'm not sure I'd ever done before. I rotated and began floating on my back like I was preparing for the backstroke, but I never began the movement of the stroke. I just laid there, on the surface of the water, eyes closed, arms stretched out, belly up and growing cold in the open air, and for a moment, I felt really, truly free.

My ears were below the water and so I only heard Chris's muffled shout that the pool was closing before I felt his arms slip beneath my thighs and back, cradling me so when I lifted my head up and my body folded in on itself and collapsed into the water, he was still holding me.

I looked around, found the pool empty, found Chris looking at me like I was the wave he was determined to catch and ride to the end of its life stream.

"You know how special you is, Adela?"

I rested my cheek on his shoulder's bulge.

"So special," he whispered as he leaned in to kiss me, lips wet and chlorine fresh, and nothing felt better than his skin, than us beneath the water, than me weightless in his arms. "I want you, Adela."

"Not here," I said.

# EMORY

WALKING THROUGH THE marsh on the edge of the bayou with a stroller is ten times harder than doing it with just your own two feet. I wanted to kick the stroller into the mud and leave it there. I even thought about turning around, but then that made me think of the rats in the maze and regret and Adela. Which led me to think of the orca all alone, washed up on that beach.

I'd started going through articles and forums online about orcas, trying not to think about Adela, trying to fill my head with the simple logics of facts and studies. I read about one time, a couple years ago, when a mother orca carried her dead calf with her for seventeen days straight 'cause she couldn't find a way to let go of the life her baby was meant to live. I got that, prodding at my own heartache, wishing I could carry on the life me and Adela could've lived in my head.

There was no point in anything, now. All those college acceptances remained at the bottom of my email and I had no plans to fish them out. I had to get out of bed today because Jay demanded to see his son and it was Sunday, so I owed him, but now that I was outside, under the hot breath of the sun, I'd do just about anything to go back inside. Instead, I sludged through the weeds and mud, until I finally saw Jay there, sitting on a boulder shaped like a rubber duck.

I put the brakes on the stroller, pulled down the shade so Kai wouldn't burn as he slept, and I trudged up to Jay and fell into his arms.

He kissed me like I was a drinking fountain and he was a feverish child. He kissed me like I hadn't left him brokenhearted at the bottom of a ravine too many times. He kissed me like I was the fairy he knew he shouldn't believe in.

I'd be lying if I said this afternoon by the bayou was like in the beginning, 'cause the truth is you can never have those first moments back. The ripple of new breath as skin meets skin and a hand that's never held yours finds the dip of your waist. That kind of tingle is impossible to retrieve and that's prob'ly for the best. All that newness gets in the way of what's real about two people, two bodies intertwining. It was science. They called it the Coolidge effect, but I liked to think of it as a good excuse for getting as many fucks in as possible. Maybe that's why folks are always leaving each other for somebody else. It's not biological, sentimentality.

Even as I kissed Jay back, three feet from our sleeping son, inches from the water, I knew I didn't want him any more than I had the week before, that we were never supposed to be what I envisioned when I first met him.

I saw Jay for the first time in the school auditorium at a spirit rally no one wanted to be at. On any other day, I don't think I would've noticed him at all, but it wasn't a normal day. It was my seventeenth birthday and Pawpaw'd taken an extra shift at his new job, so he'd be working till midnight. Grammy'd bake me a cake, give me a new color of nail polish, and be in bed by eight o'clock like every other birthday.

I didn't tell any of the seaside girls about my birthday, not that they would've remembered or done anything but snuck me shooters during math. They didn't know, though, so I couldn't be mad that they all left school at lunch and I was there, sitting alone in the auditorium on my birthday, when I saw him.

Jay was a nice-looking guy but nothing special. Not built enough or loud enough to be sought-after, but he wasn't a virgin or anything either. And, on my birthday, when I looked over at him across the auditorium aisle, he smiled.

I knew everybody'd be pissed off if they knew I was trying to get with Jay. I could imagine Pawpaw's bloated red face unable to contain his fury if it got back to him that I was flirting with somebody like Jayden. I'm not saying I went after him 'cause I wanted to make Pawpaw mad, but it made me chase just a little harder.

I was on the hunt for Jay for two whole months before I caught him, like a spotted hyena on the prowl for a mate. For the last few weeks of school before summer vacation, I placed myself at the water fountain outside his algebra class after I figured out he always left ten minutes late. I learned where his family lived and changed my route walking home from school so that I could run into him.

School let out for the summer and I discovered Jay was working with a group of other guys on a construction site for a new addition to the hospital, so I found three reasons in one week to end up at the hospital, where I'd wander over to the construction site and find him in a hard hat, strike up a conversation about different types of wood.

In July, one of the seaside girls dragged me to a party in a vacant lot off the old post office and I only went 'cause she said everyone from school would be there, and I made sure she really meant *everyone*. There he was. Sipping from a plastic cup, talking to two African American girls whose eyes wandered around the parking lot the whole time. They didn't want him like I did.

I decided that night was my chance. When the seaside girl wasn't looking, I marched up to him, grabbed his hand, and led him off around the side of the old post office to the back. I was planning on just making my move there, but another couple was already fondling each other against the brick.

I saw an open window, though, and I told Jay to lift me up. He started protesting and talking about how he should get back to his friends, so I put his hands on my hips and told him to lift. Once I was inside, I snuck around to the back door and slipped him in, locking it again behind us.

Nobody had been in the old post office since they moved into the strip mall by the highway and we could hear all sorts of critters, but it didn't matter once we were alone, in the dark.

I touched him like he was already mine until he was. We didn't talk much that first time, not before, not after, but I told him to meet me back behind the post office tomorrow and he nodded before my sentence was over. He was hooked.

That summer, we fucked in the abandoned post office once a week, laid on the dusted floor, where he confessed his whole life to me like I was the church he prayed in. Somewhere around September, Christa and the baby had started to get to me and one day, in the post office, I asked Jay if he ever wanted kids.

"Yeah," he said. "Lots of 'em. Nothing like havin' somebody who loves you like that." That night, I stopped taking the pills I went behind Grammy's back to get when I was fourteen, just in case. It's not exactly like it was planned, I just wanted to leave it up to God or fate or something bigger than either of us.

By the time we finished the first semester of junior year, when we snuck out to fuck by the bayou at lunch, I was already pregnant. By the time I found out, I was already ready to be done with Jay. The thrill had washed away quick and unforgiving as drawings in the sand, and I would've broken up with him sooner if that pregnancy test hadn't come back dark pink.

Pawpaw said I shouldn't've been surprised. "You act like a whore, you gotta face the consequences of a whore," he screamed while Grammy sobbed and melted to the floor.

Maybe he was right, but I'm telling you, I really didn't think it was gonna happen, not that fast. Maybe I was being stupid, but I wasn't all that upset either, 'cause even though I wasn't crazy about Jay anymore, I kept remembering what he said, about nobody ever loving you the same as your baby, and I wanted that more than anything.

Now our son was alive and well, sleeping in his stroller as my spine dug into the lip of the boulder and Jay thrusted up like he always did, deep and to the left, the way I liked it, and he tried to kiss me as we fucked, but I turned my cheek to him. Kissing shouldn't be confused with sex. I didn't want him getting the idea that this was our second beginning. But I guess it was too late 'cause as he came, he whispered in my ear, "I love you, Emory. I love you so much."

I pulled my panties back up and tied my hair into a bun on top of my head. The roots nearly all dark brown. When Jay's forehead sweat slowed to still beads, he stood from the boulder and looked at me.

"Can I ask you something?"

I shrugged. Despite all my efforts, I was thinking of the orca and then, as though I couldn't think of one without the other, I was thinking of Adela.

"Why can't I come to your house?"

Jay never once asked me before why my pawpaw wouldn't let him inside. When I first told him, I was relieved the teen pregnancy seemed to be reason enough, but I guess he'd finally got tired of my explanation.

I looked away from him, out at the water, dark and shining. "You got me pregnant."

"Yeah, but I been thinkin' about it and it don't make sense." He stepped toward me, tried to find my eyes. "Your momma had you young too and your grandpa didn't tell your daddy he couldn't come inside his house."

"You don't know that. Besides, they were engaged."

"I do. I seen pictures of him and your momma taken at your kitchen table when your momma was pregnant. So tell me the real reason, Emmy. And I don't buy the marriage bullshit. Tell me why I'm not allowed in your house."

I looked at him. Hands chalky in dust from when he touched the ground for balance as he kneeled so his tongue could find my inner thighs. Eyes still glittering for me.

"It's not important," I whispered.

He came closer. "It is. 'Cause maybe if I was allowed in your house, then we could be a real family, same way we always talked about. You want a big house on the other side of the road? I'll build you one. And I won't never leave, you know that. You know that, right?"

"I know." Even when I wished he would. But I guessed it'd be better to just come out and tell him, since it wasn't like he was my man anyway. "I'm not racist or nothing, just so you know. Neither is my grammy or my pawpaw."

"Ahh," Jayden sighed, looking up at the sky. "I knew it."

"That I wasn't racist?"

"That your granddaddy don't like niggers."

"Oh, please, Jay, I told you he's not racist. And don't say that word around my son."

It was like Kai heard us, beginning to babble right then, and both me and Jay dashed toward the stroller to pick him up, but I got there first. Lifted the shade and took Kai into my arms. He'd grown so much in the last two weeks, his latest onesies pulling tight at the back of his neck, his wrists sprouting an extra roll.

Jay glared at me. "Why don't you just tell your granddaddy I'll pretend to be his footman if anybody comes knockin' and it'll all be good. I'll even use the back door whenever I come over."

"You don't need to be an asshole about it."

"You don't gotta be so pussy about it."

We stared at each other. His eyes hard, daring. My eyes prob'ly glossy and bloodshot from lost sleep. Our son in my arms, his little hand locked around the silver *K* necklace Jay bought me when Kai was born.

"Why do you even care?" I croaked.

And the way his gaze changed, the way he looked at me told me why. It was the way I looked at Adela across that picnic table when she told me she was in love with someone else.

"I miss you, Emmy. There's not a day I don't wanna spend with you and Kai and I know everything's been weird with us for a while now, but I just think . . . I just think we could be real good together, like in the beginning. So . . ."

He kneeled into the marsh grass and time sputtered and stopped. I wished it would reverse, knew I wanted to go back even before he did what he did. I thought he was gonna pull something from his pocket, but instead, he was fidgeting with a few long blades of marsh grass. Braiding it, like I taught him to braid my hair on the floor of the post office.

I wanted to tell him to stop, wanted to turn around and run through the mud like it was a track and I was a horse trained for escape. But I couldn't find words. I couldn't think about nothing but regret and Adela and the orca I couldn't save. Jay twisted and tied until the grass was one small golden ring and then he held it up to me, like an offering.

"Will you marry me?"

# SIMONE

OMMA USED TO set a glass of milk in front of each of her kids every morning and tell us to drink up so our bones didn't get weak and snap in half. When I was seven, I looked down at my cup of milk on the table that was also my bed and then down at my hands, arms, legs, before I settled my eyes back on Momma with a dimpled chin and a face full of betrayal.

"There's milk up in there? Inside my bones? I don't want milk up in there, Momma. Get it out!"

Momma laughed until her muscles seized, and she shook her head.

"No, child, ain't no milk inside your bones. It just make 'em stronger."

"That why they white? The milk make my bones strong and white?"

Momma laughed some more and then just shrugged and nodded. "Sure, baby. Sure do."

Every morning, I mixed Luck and Lion their own cups of milk from powder and they both drank it, rain or shine, even though Lion complained the whole time 'bout how he don't like the way it tasted. I just looked at him and said, *"You want your bones to snap right off?"* Most days, his eyes turned wide and wild as a scared cat as he gulped down the last swallows of his milk.

It's a horrifying thing to think you could crack so easily, but it's a worse fear to look at these little people you made with your own bone and marrow and know that there are more than two hundred ways they could break open, just inside those tiny little bodies. So I kept them drinking that milk, even when it was the last thing they wanted.

Lion was getting more stubborn the older he got, and pretty soon no threat of broken bones was gonna get him to drink his milk without a fight. Today he was straight-up refusing. Lion's full glass balanced in his hands while he sulked and kicked his feet.

"Just drink it and you won't even gotta think about it no more," I said.

"Nuh-uh. I don't like it, Momma. It's nasty."

"And I don't like my baby havin' brittle bones." His waterline was filling with tears and I didn't like to see my baby cry, even when what he cryin' about mighta been silly as a fish sobbin' 'bout swimming in some water. I set the spoon down and turned to Lion. "How 'bout I make it taste better, huh? I know what might make it real tasty . . ."

I went around to the side of the truck cab and opened the door, fumbled in the glove compartment for a little jar of honey stuck behind some old baby wipes, and brought it back to Lion. He lit up at the sight.

"We got honey?"

I nodded. "Fixed your sister's allergies right on up and I forgot all about it. If I put some in, you gon' drink that milk?"

He squinted at me. I squinted back.

"You gotta put lots in, okay?"

I smiled. "Lots. Promise."

I screwed the jar open and held it over his cup, the honey slowly drooping, viscous and thick, toward the jar's edge. As it plopped into the creamy center of the glass, I remembered what Momma always told me, after I finished my milk. *Now those bones gonna be as strong as you is. You feel it? You feel 'em growing?*

I stirred the honey till the milk glowed just a little bit golden, and Lion lifted it to his mouth and sipped, just enough so his tongue touched it, and then he tilted that glass back and gulped until there weren't no drops left.

Luck watched him and placed her bag of pebbles down, kicked her feet. "I want some, Momma. Can I get some?"

"You already had yours. You can have another tomorrow."

"With honey?"

"Until all that honey's gone." I took Lion's empty glass. "Don't that feel good? Now those bones gonna be strong as you is."

He smiled. "I'm strong as a gator." He lifted his lip and showed me that toothy little mouth.

"Is that right?" I looked down at the half-empty jar of honey and wondered if Momma still gave my sisters milk. Wondered if she still thought I was strong.

"Y'all wanna do something different today?" I asked them. They both perked up.

Luck gaped at me. "Like go to the zoo?"

Lion squeaked, "Or go on a plane?"

I shook my head. "How 'bout we go see your grandmama?"

• • •

Momma raised me right till she refused to raise me at all.

In the confines of our trailer, she wrapped her children in the sacred fabric of her hums, the tap of her wet spoon against the hot plate, and then the sizzle that told her it was hot enough to fry an egg. The squeak of the screen door opening and then the clap of pillows releasing dust into the outside before bed.

Some of the Girls had mothers who didn't know how to love them, who saw their children as an obstruction to their freedom. But my momma wanted us. My momma worked every day to love us with the tender touch of someone who spent every breath learning how to mother, choking down all the urges to burst and batter.

Even when she was tired and angry and didn't have time for any of us beyond making sure we was fed and ready for school, I didn't think she'd ever leave me out in the cold. That's why it hurt so much when she told me to go. I never saw it coming.

I drove the truck slow toward Beach Row, still unsure what I was driving into.

Luck was confused about what we was doing, asking all these questions like I had any answers.

"I thought we don't see no grandmama, 'cause you and Uncle JJ say she busy. She finish all her work?"

"I don't know. Maybe. Maybe she finished all her work."

I tried not to let my breath quiver, tried not to show them how scared I was as I pulled through the open gate of Beach Row and into the empty spot beside our trailer. Maybe no one was home.

I turned off the truck engine and looked at Luck and Lion with enough seriousness they both went quiet.

"Momma hasn't seen your grandmama in a long, long time, so I might be a lil' nervous and maybe I'll even cry, but nothing's wrong, okay? And if you scared or you wanna go, you just tell Momma and we'll go. How that sound?"

Lion's eyes grew big. "Grandmama's scary?"

"No, baby. She's nice. Real nice, like the lady at the gas station."

Lion's pupils shrunk again and he nodded. I took one more breath and opened the truck door.

Momma opened the door to the trailer before I got a chance to knock, must've seen me through the window. Must've watched as we climbed out the truck.

I got a better look at her now than I had at the doctor's office and I could tell she'd aged, but not in the way I always thought she would. Instead of sagging, her face grew taut at the cheeks and her eyelids were the only part of her that'd grown heavy. She looked like a mother, still, just not exactly like *my* mother.

I couldn't've imagined how it would feel standing in front of her, holding my babies' hands, facing her not as her daughter but as their mother. Two mothers, face-to-face. Two women, tired.

"Hi, Momma," I said.

She only looked at me for a moment before her eyes flitted to the twins and she took in each of them and, in turn, they looked her up and down before Luck said, "You got a big bottle of gas too, Grandmama?"

"Gas?" Momma frowned.

I laughed. "There's a gas station we go to east off the highway and the woman at the cash register lets them watch the gas get pumped down into the ground sometimes. She looks sorta like you."

"Oh," Momma said. That was it. She seemed nervous, haunted almost, till her head snapped up and she pulled the door all the way open, her hospitality overcoming all else even though I knew she was thinkin' bout whether or not to let me in, whether or not to say nothing to me at all. "Come in."

Luck led the pack, skipping up the steps and into the trailer. Lion kept one hand in mine as we climbed into the trailer.

"Let me just make the table up for y'all," Momma said. She hurried to throw the sheets off the bed, pulling the cushions up with it, and then she fumbled to get the tabletop to latch back in, so I stepped forward and balanced it.

"Still ain't fixed the latch, huh?" I laughed. Momma didn't respond, just pushed harder till it clicked. She pulled the leg down and the two of us picked the cushions back up from the floor and rearranged them, just like we used to, a dance we learned to do in the sixty seconds it took Jayden to go piss in the mornings.

"Go ahead and sit," Momma said.

Luck obliged, climbed onto one bench of the tiny booth, and I slid in next to her, Lion on my lap. Momma ran around to all the surfaces in the kitchenette and tried to move all the little trinkets from sight. She brought glasses of lemonade to the table, salt and pepper, spoons, a kitchen timer, an oven mitt, anything that had no home.

While she ran around, I was able to fully see the place. I couldn't believe how little it had changed. The beds on each end of the trailer remained unmade, clothes piled up at the foot of each, and beneath the table my feet rested on the bundle of bedding that would be remade when Momma converted the table back to what used to be my bed after we left.

Before my sisters was born, Jayden and me each got our own beds. I loved my bed, put stickers from old schoolbooks on the ceiling to stare at while I fell asleep and ripped the perfume pages from magazines and rubbed them all over my bedding so it smelled like alcoholic flowers.

Then my sisters came. The first couple years weren't bad, 'cause they slept in Momma and Pops's bed, but then they started walking and talking and next thing I knew Jayden and me had to share the other big bed so the twins could sleep on the little one that became our table in the mornings.

I hated sharing a bed with Jay, but not as much as I hated sharing a bed with my sisters after Jayden hit puberty and insisted he needed his space, as a man, and Pops backed him up. Now I imagined the twins slept in the little bed that sat on top of the table and Jay got the other big bed to hisself and it was one less thing to worry about, not having me there. A little more room for everyone to sleep easy.

Momma finally slid into the booth across from us, though she still wasn't looking me in my eyes.

"Your pops took the twins to youth group and I trust Jayden is off with your little friend somewhere."

Momma said it like she was answering a question I never asked.

"I don't know where Jayden is. I came to see you."

Luck fiddled with the timer on the table and then looked up at Momma. "Uncle JJ likes to work, like you. He prob'ly working."

"Yeah," I said, "prob'ly," even though I knew he was with Emory, since Sunday afternoons he always saw Kai. Luck's idea of things was easier, simpler.

"When your momma was a kid, she liked to help me cook and she'd be in charge of that timer." Momma pointed to the little thing in Luck's hand and smiled, stared out the small window, talked about me like I wasn't sat across from her. "Every day, she'd come home from school, wash her hands, and tell me it was time to cook. Except for one day when your momma came home so excited 'cause she said she was special."

"Special?" Lion whispered.

Momma nodded. "Thought she was magical or something, 'cause she had what she called her mark."

The mark was a constellation of deep brown, almost-black spots on my right ankle. I ain't noticed it till I was six years old and showed it to one of my friends at school and he said it was a special mark, that he had one that looked like an octopus on his butt. But no one else had nothing like mine, dark and wide. That's how I knew I was special.

When I got home that day, while Pops and Jayden were out fishing with a couple of Pops's friends, I whipped off my sock and shoe and twisted around to show Momma my mark. "Look, Momma. I think I might have real magic."

"Is that right?" Momma laughed but didn't look.

"No, look, Momma!"

Momma made a show of turning off the hot plate and finding a rag to put the dripping spoon on before she kneeled to look at my ankle. "How you know it's not just some dirt?" she asked.

"Pass me that." I pointed to the wet rag and she grabbed it, cussing as the spoon that had been resting on it fell to the floor. She picked up the spoon to wash it and I started scrubbing at my brown-black spots with the dirty rag, going at it so hard I felt like my skin was about to break open.

"See, Momma? It's still there."

Momma returned to the hot plate. "I see, baby. You right. Now you wanna help me stir this or what?"

Momma asked the twins if they was hungry and of course they

said yes. She'd gone on telling all sorts of stories, keeping herself talking so there wasn't room for me to say nothing at all. I was starting to squirm, wanted nothing more than to take Luck and Lion and go back to the life I'd made for myself, away from the time warp this trailer kindled. But I had come here of my own free will and my kids was hungry, always hungry.

"How 'bout I fry up some hush puppies, hmm?"

"That'll take too long, Momma. We really should be going if we not gonna talk—"

"I'm hungry," Luck said, the timer dinging, her rewinding it. "Lion too."

Lion didn't say nothing but he didn't object neither.

"You will sit there and you will wait while I feed these chil'ren some hush puppies and then you will leave and you won't never show up at my house without no warning again. You hear?"

I cowered. I might have my own kids, but she was still my momma. "Yes, ma'am."

She took the batter from the mini fridge and started heating a pot of oil on the hot plate.

"I'm sure you remember when your sisters was born and you insisted you be the first to hold them. I told you you was, even though me and your pops both held 'em after I gave birth. You was just happy to think you was first. Told everybody you knew that you was the first person to hold your sisters, before their own momma."

When you grown, you think a child believes all your lies. When you grown, you can't imagine they know the truth from the way your eyelashes flutter, the croak in your voice at the beginning of every false sentence.

But when you a kid, you know. Or at least, somewhere beneath all the layers of you that want to believe what the grown-ups saying, you can feel the lie in it all. Some kids, like Luck, know how to unbury all that and say, *Uh-uh, Momma, that's not right.*

But children like me, like Lion, we wanted so desperately to trust what those big people who loved us said that we disregarded that tingle of feeling, slimy as marrow in the bones. It's when the lie comes out that you realize you knew it all along. When finally I saw a picture of the day my sisters was born and on the bed where Momma gave birth, she was holding both twins close, their umbilical cords still uncut.

"You ever had hush puppies?" Momma asked Lion.

He shook his head.

"Yes, you have," I said. "On your birthday, when we go to the diner, remember? They the fried little balls."

Momma lifted the first batch from the oil and set it on paper towels. "It was always one of your momma's favorites."

I wished she'd talk to me. I wished she'd look at me. I wished she'd tell me she was happy to see me and she'd missed me all this time. I'd even take her yelling at me over this. Anything but this polite treatment, the way you'd talk to a guest in your home and not the child you birthed.

Momma placed a plate piled with hush puppies on the table, and Lion picked one up and dropped it.

"Hot," he whined.

Luck proceeded to puff up her cheeks and blow on each one till she was heaving.

"Careful, now, we don't want you passing out," I said. "I think this one's cool. And this one."

Luck and Lion each picked up a hush puppy, bringing it to their mouths.

Momma stayed standing. I placed Lion down next to Luck on the bench and stood too, getting close enough to Momma that the kids wouldn't hear nothing.

"Talk to me." She stared at the sink. I got closer to her. "I came here 'cause I miss you, Momma. I don't want no life where you ain't even know my kids' favorite foods, where you never even spoken their names. I want them to know you. I want you to know *me*, Momma."

Momma didn't move an inch, like she could statue herself out of witnessing me. The kids was making all kinds of noise, eating their food, but all I could hear was Momma's breath, all I could see was the way her eyelashes fanned. She didn't look at me as she spoke.

"If I wanted to know you, I woulda come and found you. If I wanted some part in your life, I woulda asked you to come home and see me. You seen me begging you to come here? I let you in 'cause I wasn't 'bout to make no fit in front of some chil'ren, but I won't stand by what you done. It ain't right. None of this . . . it ain't right."

Momma shook, her hands clutching the lip of the sink. I reached out and touched one of her hands and she snatched it away. I couldn't figure out how she'd sat here telling all kinds of stories about me as a kid and now she was saying she didn't even want to know me.

"It's been years. I'm a good mother. I don't need you to like the choices I made, but can't you at least forgive them?"

"Forgiveness is a gift only God can give you, baby. But me? I raised a child who shoulda known the difference between sugar and salt." Her words were spit hitting hot coals, sending steam up from the ground where she slung them.

Now I was thinking about all those stories Momma'd told, and I realized she'd never finished a single one. She left each one hanging in the before. Before it fell apart, before hot grease spilled down my shirt, before I saw my sisters' first photo, before she finally told me my mark was nothing special at all.

It was easy to look at Momma and remember her warm hands on my chest as she smoothed in Vicks VapoRub for the cough that wouldn't leave when I was nine; her church heels clacking down the hall of my middle school as she marched into the dean's office to argue my detention for selling homemade earrings out of my locker; her sweat-drenched nightshirt as she held me in a too-crowded bed on a too-hot night after a bad dream.

But maybe all the things I loved most about my momma were easiest to remember when all I wanted was to hug her, when the dream of an intact family was more enchanting than the truth of it all. And sometimes I wanted the lie. I wanted the easy story without its cold end.

The truth was, one day Momma got tired of me being special, tired of hearing me chant about my magic, and she turned to me from the stove and said, "You got a birthmark. It ain't magic. It ain't special. It won't scrub off 'cause it's just some mishap God made when you was growing inside me. That's it. A mistake."

She'd let me scrub my skin like a dirty dish, let me prance around Beach Row knocking on doors and claiming I might get my super-powers soon. When really, all along, she'd known the truth, that her child had a birthmark just like any other. And when she told the truth, she said the words that would crush me. *You're not special.*

Both my twins was born with identical birthmarks on differ-ent parts of their bodies. Luck, a bell below her collarbone. Lion, a slightly smaller bell above his right knee. I've memorized every dip on the bells, the exact shade of brown, whether you'd think they were right side up or upside down depending on the direction you looked.

When they discovered their marks and asked what they was, I said, "These are some of the only things in the world that's always gonna be just yours, unmistakably yours. And you know what that means? It means you special, 'cause you yourself and this your skin and every inch of it is precious."

Momma looked at me and I could see the disgust, with me, with herself, and beneath all the unresolved shame, I felt sad for her. She would never know a love as pure as the one I had for my babies, a love that began and ended the way oceans did: nowhere and everywhere, a thrashing constant.

Momma growled, "I did my job and maybe I failed, maybe I shoulda been harder on you, I admit that. I shouldn't've let you think that birthmark was magic for so long. But I won't make the same mistake, telling you just what you wanna hear, acceptin' your sins like they not dirty. Those chil'ren deserve a real mother. They deserve—"

At first I thought the scream was coming from my mouth, with my tears, but then I remembered where I was. I looked down at myself and saw grown hands, grown feet, and then I turned and saw my children. Luck was screaming. Luck was on the ground.

Splayed on the floor below the high-up bed, her right arm already swelling, the bottom of her forearm bent crooked, her head spilling blood. When Luck's eyes met mine, the screams ceased, but her mouth remained open, hung at the jaw like she couldn't believe where she was, her eyelashes spread open with drops of tears hanging from the ends.

She sat up, squeaked out, "Momma?" and then looked down at her arm, saw the swollen mass of limb in front of her, the puddle of blood where her head had been, and threw up soggy hush puppies all over the floor.

◆ ◆ ◆

If you chastising me for what I did and didn't do, you should know I was already punishing myself. I got Luck and Lion into the truck and to the hospital in less than ten minutes, both of them sobbing the entire time, but Luck's cries were silent, her tears simply streaming. Momma remained in the trailer, didn't offer to come with, even if I would've let her. None of what she said, none of what any of you might say, could mean nothing now, not until my baby was okay. Not until I could release this breath.

I pulled up outside the emergency room, stopped the car by the curb even though the curb was painted red, and hopped out. I opened the passenger-side door and picked Lion up, setting him on the ground, before carefully picking up Luck and holding her close to me.

"Lion, I need you to walk. Stay close to Momma and walk. Fast."

He blubbered but followed as I quickly made my way to the entrance, through the doors, to the nurse at the front station.

"My daughter fell," I said. "She needs to see a doctor. Now."

The woman looked up at me, at Luck in my arms, at Lion hiding behind my leg. "Name and birth date."

"Luck Turner. She's five, she was born on February—"

"Not the child's name. Yours."

"I'm not the one hurt, it's her. Her head's bleeding. Please, can y'all just call the doctor and—"

"Miss, the quicker you answer my questions, the quicker I can try to get your daughter seen."

She clicked on her keyboard and then told us to sit and wait.

"Wait? My daughter needs to see somebody. Now."

The nurse shrugged. "It's probably a sprain, maybe a small fracture. Head cuts bleed a lot. There's people ahead of her with much worse."

I looked to the waiting room, the green vinyl chairs, the dozens of people slumped in them, in all states of decay. I couldn't wait here. It would take forever. Then I remembered something Adela had said, in her basement, before I drank the tea. *If something goes wrong and we go to the hospital, tell them you have chest pain. They'll see you first. That's what my noni says.*

I turned back to the nurse. "She got chest pain. Right, Luck? Your chest hurt?" I looked at her with a stare only my child would understand.

Through her teeth chatter, her sweats, she nodded, but she still wasn't speaking.

The nurse glared, and stood. "Give me a minute, I'll check with the doctor."

Two minutes later, she returned. "The doctor will call you in a moment."

I nodded and took my babies to sit. Despite everything in me that didn't want to, I knew I had to call Tooth. He was Luck's daddy and at some point soon she was gonna look up at me and ask where he was. I wanted him to already be here so I didn't have to tell her, *He's coming, baby. He's coming.* So I picked up the phone and called him despite how much I wished we wouldn't never have to share the same room's stale air again.

# ADELA

CHRIS ALWAYS WANTED to fuck in public. Even after I told him the beach was a one-time thing, and we were hidden anyway, he kept trying to get me to do it in the ocean, by the pool, on the side of the road near his place behind an old detached car bumper.

I managed to get him somewhere a little more private, leading him with the promise of my lips, my love, my red bikini limp in his fingers. It worked better before he knew I was pregnant. Now he was always complaining about how I'd changed, and I had to convince him I hadn't, even though it was so obvious I had, the change taking up all the space between us.

My skin was still sticky and wet from the pool as I leaned down into Chris's lap. It had become a challenge to fuck in Chris's car, maneuvering around my belly like a ball passed hand to hand, so I decided to just suck him off quickly till we got back to his place and then I knew he'd touch me the way I liked, the way I needed.

I was fighting my gag reflex, trying to produce more saliva even though my mouth felt dry, when his phone rang. He always answered it, no matter who was calling or what we were doing, even though he knew I hated it, and I paused, removed my mouth from him, sat back into the passenger seat. He gestured for me to keep going and so I switched to my hand as he answered and said, "What's up?"

He tensed and swatted my hand from his dick, stuffed it back in his pants, and turned the key in the ignition.

"What's going on?" I mouthed.

He ignored me, spoke into the phone, "I'll be right there." He hung up and pressed hard on the gas, swerving out of the parking lot. Now he talked to me. "It's my kids. That was their mama. We gotta go."

His kids. Their mother.

"We can't," I blurted.

"What you mean? It's my kids."

I scrambled. "I just mean you should take me home first, so they don't meet me like this."

"We don't got time for that, Adela. My baby girl's in the hospital."

I know I should've been worried about Luck, and I was, but I just couldn't think about anything but what would happen if the Girls saw me in the passenger seat of Chris's car. I panicked as Chris sped from the pool, whipped through unpaved roads, and I knew I didn't have much time at all before we drove up to the hospital, where the twins would call to me, say *Adela!* like they knew me, and Chris would know I'd lied. Simone would do worse than just scratch and bruise me. At the end of this road, the lie I shouldn't have told would fall apart.

I started shaking my head, pulling my sweatshirt hood up over my face, sinking lower in the passenger seat.

"Why you being like this?" Chris swerved and then took a left into the parking lot of the hospital. Immediately, I saw Simone's red truck, parked haphazardly in front of the emergency room.

"I'll wait in the car," I said as he parked.

I could feel his eyes on me, his glare, but I refused to look him in the face.

"Whatchu talkin' about? It's too hot for you to wait in no damn car. This could take hours. C'mon. Simone and the kids won't hurt you or nothing. Just stay by me."

Chris opened his door and got out, but I stayed where I was. I couldn't go with him. I thought he would just give up and go inside without me, but instead he showed up at the passenger side and swung my door open. "Let's go," he said.

I shook my head. "I'll call my noni. She'll come pick me up."

"Like hell you will. I'm not about to have your grandmama thinkin' I left you in a hospital parking lot by yourself. C'mon, Adela. We goin' inside."

This time, Chris didn't wait for my response. He grabbed my wrist and pulled me up and out of the car with a force I didn't know he had.

"Stop!" I said, tugging back, leaning the full weight of my new belly away from him. "I'm not going in there."

He didn't even argue with me, just pulled harder, hissing, "Don't make a fucking scene," as he dragged me toward the sliding doors of the emergency room.

I was about to give in to him, was even going to start walking forward, when I remembered the whole reason I'd created this lie. The things that happen when a story collapses on itself. Dad's eyes never quite meeting mine again after Lindsay's sixteenth birthday. Mom's choked sob the night she found out I was pregnant.

If I walked in that door, I would have to witness the betrayal slashed through the middle of Simone's face and even if I didn't always like her or agree with the way she lived her life, I did not want to be the cause of her latest struggle, another reason for her to look at me with a snarl, take her nails and fill them with my skin cells.

I yanked my wrist back just before we reached the sliding doors. Chris fought, but I was harnessing every bit of strength I still had in my weakening muscles, and I could see him sweat, his bicep trembling, us in a tug-of-war with my hand.

"You. Gonna. Have. To. Meet. 'Em. At. Some. Point." Chris huffed with each breath, his neck veins lurching from his skin.

"Not. Today."

Just as I tugged free, the sliding doors opened. The mirrored glass gave way to the sight of a face I knew, braids blond as ever, stature solid and straight. She was looking around the waiting room and then her eyes rose and were on me, on Chris, back to me, and I knew it was all over.

# EMORY

**M**ARRY YOU?" Jayden couldn't be serious. We weren't even together.

It was a joke the bayou rattled at and I laughed with it. Giggled like Kai at the sound of my keys in the lock. I mean, he couldn't be for real. We were barely a unit at all, with him always gone to work and Pawpaw not letting him inside the house. We were a heterogeneous mixture, stuck in the same place without really being one. He couldn't possibly think I'd marry him.

"Just think about it. Me and you and Kai, we'd be together all the time and in a couple months I could maybe even get us a little place, somewhere near the water, and we could let Simone stay with us sometimes, when it rains and shit. Don't you want that?"

The bayou shone copper and I stopped laughing. I couldn't make sense of it, was about to cuss him out just for asking me a question so stupid, but then my phone pinged. Simone.

HELP. LUCK. HOSPITAL.

I turned my back to him and placed Kai in the stroller, started pushing it out of the marsh, knowing Jay would follow without me saying nothing at all.

"Where you going? Answer me!"

"It's your sister," I called over my shoulder. "She's at the hospital, she needs me, and so you're gonna drive me there and you're not gonna ask me again if I'll marry you till after I know Luck's okay."

Jay didn't resist, jogged ahead of Kai and me to open the truck door, and folded the mucky stroller into the truck bed as Kai and me slid into the cab bench. Kai was the only one who made noise as Jay drove. The only one whose breath could be heard wheezing over the truck engine. The only one who was not quietly thankful that Simone had texted, that there was a way out of this question that wasn't yes or no.

When we pulled into the hospital parking lot, I saw Simone's truck right outside the front doors and then Tooth's car, or at least I was pretty sure it was his, and I knew it was worse than I'd imagined.

"What the fuck's going on?" Jay breathed as he pulled in next to Tooth's car and we hopped out. I passed Kai to him and ran toward the entrance of the hospital, Jay following. Before I even got to ask the nurse where they were, I heard Simone's voice.

"Are you fucking with me?"

Simone's shout echoed down the hall, a marble sent rolling and growing with speed as I followed it toward rows of curtains containing so much sizzling pain. If I wasn't already swollen with worry for Luck, if I wasn't already sputtering over Jay's question, I would've been able to feel the resin of doom each footstep left behind as I walked toward Simone's howl and pretended I didn't feel what was coming.

There they were. Outside the last curtain. Simone's finger raised and whipping around. Tooth across from her with the same blank expression he always had, like his face muscles didn't work. And then, in the little triangle of them, someone else.

Wearing a hoodie and shorts, tan legs and a broad back, I knew it was Adela before she turned and I saw her stomach. I could spot her anywhere, anywhere at all. No matter how she attempted to cover her face with her hood and make herself small.

When you loved somebody, they were always gonna be the first one you saw in any room, the clearest blur in any crowd, the center of any photograph.

"Adela?" At first, she pretended she didn't see me. She looked at me and then looked away, back at Simone, as though I didn't know her eyes. As though I didn't dream of falling into the pit of them. "Why are all y'all here?"

If I wasn't still unwinding myself from the web of this day, I would've caught on quicker. All I knew for sure was Simone was in a fitful rage and something was very wrong. I was preparing myself to fix it, revive another orca, when Adela turned to me, Simone still staring at her like she'd just stolen the shirt off her back.

Adela met my eyes and kept them finally, and hers rapidly filled with hot tears. "I—I . . ." Her voice trailed into nothing, and Simone stepped forward, close enough to Adela I was starting to think another fight was about to go down, this time in the center of the hospital, two inches from the curtain that shielded so many strangers' wounds.

Simone rasped, "This high yellow hussy been fucking my babies' daddy this whole time. Riding in my car and then gettin' with him, pretendin' you ain't a two-faced ho, you and your stupid rich ass—"

"Whoa, whoa!" Tooth stepped between Simone and Adela and my body stirred and grew nauseous, while my mind resisted the plain truth of it and decided it couldn't understand. What was Simone talking about, Adela and her kids' daddy, Adela and . . .

Tooth held a hand up to Simone. "Back up now. What, y'all been friends or something?"

Adela burst into tears and my first instinct was still to grab her hand and lace it in mine. "I didn't . . . I don't . . ."

Simone started in again. "Like hell you ain't known. I let you near my kids, my friends, my entire fucking life, and you been lyin' and messin' around with this motherfucker?" Her eyes switched to Tooth and narrowed. "And you! I been nothing but good to you, I ain't even had to call you when Luck—"

"Ma'am?" We turned and the doctor was standing there, curtain pulled open, face stretched upward. I guess he'd been with Luck the whole time, or maybe just slipped into the curtained room at some point, but quickly more nurses were called to Luck's bedside, in a frenzy over her. I could see her right arm in a cast and a bandage around her head. "Whose child is this?"

"Mine," Simone and Tooth said. I could tell everything else disappeared for Simone in that moment, at the sight of the doctor's face scrunched like a fern's scaffolded leaves.

"I just took a look at your daughter's CT scan and there appears to be a fracture in her skull. The fracture itself isn't our current concern. It looks like there is a small hematoma, a bleed, and we may need to perform an emergency craniotomy if the bleed gets any larger. We need to take her back for more imaging. Since it's so small, we can't be sure until we complete an MRI. One of you is welcome to come back with her until the MRI begins, but then you will need to leave the room for the test itself."

None of us could make sense of it. You could feel that in the silent beats that followed, the group of us a family of deer paused in the moment they located the predator that had been stalking close the whole time, and I knew we were all wondering the same thing: how we could've been worried about something as pointless as reckless love when a child was in peril, laying in a bed a few feet away. Her brain bleeding.

"I'm goin' with her." Simone snapped out of the daze first, looked to Tooth. All the anger had fizzed from her face, replaced by undiluted fear. "Stay with Lion. Make sure he don't get too scared."

Lion was slumped in a chair by Luck's hospital bed, asleep through all the screaming in the way only children that small can sleep.

Simone followed the nurses from the room, pushing Luck's bed, sneakers squeaking across the vinyl floor. Luck herself just laid there in the bed, clammy and silent for the first time since I'd met her, and then the bed disappeared down the hall and the rest of us remembered everything that'd been said and stood there, staring at anything but each other.

Tooth was the first to move, slinking past the curtain and fully into Luck's room to take a seat beside Lion. Adela glanced down the hall, her pupils so dilated it made her hazel eyes look black as an owl's and I wanted her to look at me so bad, but she wouldn't. Her eyes bounced toward the nurses' desk, the fire alarm, and then settled on Tooth. Adela's eyes remained pinned on him, and my brain and body collided in one solid mass of understanding that gathered in the well of my throat.

Adela crying. Simone's sting and snarl. When it clicked, I felt the moment my heart split open. She wasn't here for Simone or for me. She was here for Tooth. And then it all made sense. Her weekends away, her pool friend, her revelation that she was in love with someone at the hurricane party. Her admission that that someone wasn't me at the picnic table. Adela loved Tooth. Not me. Him. The minute I knew the truth, I desperately wished to unknow it.

Adela stood there staring at Tooth, sniffling in her hoodie. *His* hoodie. "You—you're with him?" My voice fractured like cement bearing too much weight. Like Luck's skull.

She glanced back at me. "I'm sorry," she said.

I didn't know why she was apologizing. 'Cause I loved her? 'Cause she'd let me? 'Cause clearly she'd known about Simone but continued on with the man who'd hurt her or 'cause Adela hadn't cared enough to confess before she'd made us love her.

I didn't believe her. She wasn't sorry.

Pawpaw's words jumped out my mouth. I spit at her, "Don't piss on my leg and tell me it's rainin', Adela. Guilty's not the same thing as sorry."

Adela's tears quickened, a race to her mouth. Her voice crackled and she repeated, "I'm sorry."

Adela's head sunk to her chest, and I willed her to leave, to not force me to choke on the sight of her, but instead of walking down the hall, she glided away from me and into the hospital room, where I knew she was ready to stumble into Tooth's waiting arms. Before she did, she turned back to pull the curtain shut, and when she caught my eye, she grimaced. Like she was the wounded deer among us. The mint-green fabric fluttered closed behind her.

She was a coward. Or maybe she was just smarter than me. She'd made a choice to love somebody who could give her something, and I'd made the choice over and over again to love somebody who had nothing for me instead of the person who wanted nothing more than to give me everything.

It was just Jay and me left on the other side of the curtain, Kai still nuzzled in his arms, and when I twisted to look at my child's father, I saw something different in him than I had these past six months. I'd fucked up. Everybody said when I was pregnant, *That boy's gonna leave you soon as the baby's born*. But instead I left him. And yet here he was. Still here.

Jay's eyes had remained on me this whole time and they were creased in worry, ready to trample over himself to give me whatever I wanted, even if what I wanted wasn't something he could give me at all. He was gonna protect me. Not just me but the little one I loved. Kai's small body so delicate in Jay's arms.

Maybe I didn't understand what I was signing up for when I stopped taking the pill, when I gave birth and tried to pretend I could remain unchanged. But now I knew there was no going back, even if I wanted to. I was this child's mother and even though he'd never be as safe as the moment before he exited my body, I'd swim thousands of miles just for a chance to see his face clear and not swollen from sobs, his body smooth except for patches of dry scales I'd rub in lotion before bedtime.

One day he'd grow up and leave me. One day I'd send Kai to school or work or off in a car he was driving, and it would hurt like a snake shedding its own skin, knowing I couldn't shield him with the weapons I retrieved from the sharpest parts of my childhood. But, for now, that was my only job. My only dream. My only hope.

I'd rip myself open not to see my child hurt. For the first time,

I thought I might have it in me to love him selflessly. To give him a home where love was the wood and the carpets, the roof and the drain.

Now I knew what it looked like to see a child bandaged up and broken. To see a love dropped and shattered on the floor like all fragile things. My job wasn't to go to college or fall in love or swim in the ocean. It couldn't be. It was to coddle my child's soft skull. To keep the orca close so she would never wash up on the shore.

"Jay," I whispered.

Jayden looked at me, his eyebrows raised, his eyes milky with concern for his sister, his niece, me.

I leaned in closer to him so I was pressed into his chest and I knew even if he didn't understand how to love me, he understood how to love the person I created, how to keep him safe and, for once, this felt like enough. After watching the terror in Simone's eyes. After watching Adela walk away. This was all I could hope for.

"I'll do it," I whispered. "I'll marry you."

I could tell from the way he looked at me that he was shocked first, and then skeptical. I wrapped my hand around the back of his neck and pulled him close, kissed him like we were in the abandoned post office, and when I pulled away, I was sure that among all the things this day left broken, my little family would not be one of them.

# THIRD TRIMESTER

JUST WHEN WE *thought we'd extended to the limits of ourselves, our bodies find another way to expand. Time slows, the weight of our bodies pulling us from our center, makes us droop. Moving feels impossible, and still we walk. Breathing feels impossible, and still air swells in our lungs. You don't know what you're capable of until you surpass yourself, outgrow yourself, and still find your feet on the ground. Us Girls, we were years out from our first puberty and now caught in another spiral of growth, wishing we could be anywhere but trapped in the cage of ourselves.*

*For some of us, the terror is in the waiting. For others, it is in the dispossession of our own skin, how we turn raw and violet and breathless, our flesh gone translucent. We see the child that is growing inside us and we are not sure if we have enough in us to love it, to raise it. This foreign thing, this creature that has altered the axle of ourselves.*

*We pull our own dolls from boxes, missing eyes and crusted in night sweat. We ache for water to help us forget our own weight. We curdle with dreams of who is living inside us, what shape their skull will form on the way out. We nest. We uncover. We yearn.*

*In these sprawling weeks, we hope we have not built a bed too big for ourselves, hope it will not swallow. Pray on our own graves that whatever is made of us after it's all over is recognizable, that she will look across the river between us and wave, that her teeth will glitter in the water, her hands toughened and ready to cradle. Her. Us. As we become each other, we choke our fear and dive. Belly flop and watch the rest ripple.*

# SIMONE

I DIDN'T KNOW when I woke up that morning that it would be the worst day of my life. You never get no warning you're about to have your insides blown up like a balloon and then popped. Sure, maybe you sense something ain't right, hold your daughter closer to you in the middle of night, but you don't really know till you're pressed up against the edge of your worst nightmare and you see the trail hot and red in the distance. Until you feel your chest, your mouth. Burning.

My truck was gone. After my swollen throat faded to hot pink and the worst of the horror scraping my lungs went numb, I saw where it should've been. Standing right outside the hospital's sliding doors, looking out at a parking lot scattered with cars, I realized there wasn't no red in sight. At first I thought maybe I'd dumb forgot where it was I parked, so I wandered around the whole lot and still nothing.

Somebody took my truck, on the same day my baby's brain produced a bleed the size of her first tooth, and I couldn't do nothing about it. Somewhere in me I began to burn like the sides of my throat, black and blazing, as I hollered at those doctors to let me go and be with my baby. They didn't and they wouldn't and that's how I ended up an hour later out in the parking lot when I should've been stroking the sweaty lines of my baby's hand.

They might've been able to kick me out once, but they didn't get to say whether or not I came back, and after seeing my truck gone too, I wasn't about to roll over and let this town steal from me all the pellets of good I'd harvested from their rolling fields of rock-hard clay. I wiped my eyes of signs I'd ever been so destroyed, marched back into the hospital and down the hall, where I yanked the curtain open.

Everyone was gone.

Luck and the bed, Lion asleep in the chair, Adela, Tooth, Emory. Everything I had ever loved up and left me, all 'cause I put some honey in some milk and wanted my momma. What a goddamn thing, to be betrayed by everything you knew, all at once, like the sky itself turnin' on you. The only one left was Jayden. He stood up and looked at me like I was some disappeared woman who walked in the door after ten years missing.

"Where you been?" He pulled out his phone. "Emmy gone looking for you, I'll tell her you back."

"Where my kids?"

He sighed and motioned for me to sit. I wasn't about to sit while my kids was gone. I wasn't about to rest when everything had been taken.

"That motherfucker took my truck and my kids? I'll beat his ass when—"

"Simone. Stop." Jayden never called me Simone. I was Money to him. Always Money. "Nobody took your truck. They prob'ly towed it 'cause you parked in the red."

"Then where my kids at, Jayden?"

He pried his eyes from his phone and looked at me, and I could see he was harboring something in the soft gum of his cheek, swishing it around, and deciding whether or not to spit. "Luck's still getting her scan."

When they said I could go with her to the MRI, when they said *bleed*, I looked over at my daughter's face and saw, for the first time since she was born, the possibility of life not finding a wealth of fertile ground inside her to sprout from, and in a moment, it became impossible to care about none of the rest of it. Tooth. Adela. Momma. They all incinerated in the spell of fear that grasped me like a fishing line caught around skin, invisible and excruciating.

I held tight to Luck's hand as they wheeled her bed through the halls, into the elevator, up to the room where the MRI would take place. At first, they let me have a moment with her.

I whispered apologies in a grating hiccup of a mother decayed, I cried like my eyes were not my own but a drain through which sorrow spilled, I begged the nurses to let me stay with her, and when Luck's eyes blinked slow and then shut, I wailed. They told me she was tired, not dead. They told me it was time for me to leave the room. Then, when they dragged me out, they told me to leave the building.

I knew I did the one thing I wasn't never supposed to do: showed my panic. But when my child's life teetered on the edge of a boat I knew I'd sent rocking, I was not the good kind of mother.

I was the kind of mother who sobbed and scraped at strangers' necks just to keep my child with me. I was the kind of mother who forgot to hide her frenzy in a fold under her left breast. I erupted, I shrieked, I terrified my own daughter until I felt her hand go limp in mine and her head tilted away from me, not out of fatigue but terror, and still I grabbed to take it back, cried for her to look at me. And then my baby had to watch her momma go, nurses wrestling me out the door, so the last thing she saw of me was fear that would become her own.

Today, I was the kind of mother who wasn't even in the building while my baby's brain bled.

"Take a walk, ma'am."

I didn't walk. I ran. I ran till I saw water and then I ripped my shoes from my feet and let the sand blister. I let the sand burn till the shadow of my own legs shaded the sun and then I took one step forward and let it burn again.

Look what I'd done. It was foolish, stupid, childish. Bringing them to Momma. Looking away long enough for Luck to fall. Not seeing past skull and scalp to the spot of blood nesting itself in her brain and turning her sickly. I put my shoes on and walked back to the hospital, where I sobered outside the doors until the worst of the burn passed, and I saw the absence of the truck that was always there and suddenly wasn't.

Luck was still in her scan, and I was here, in this room, worried about a car.

I looked past Jayden to the chair where my boy had cocooned in sleep.

"And Lion?" I asked.

"Tooth took him home."

I scoffed. "Please, no he didn't." I started looking around the room. No way Tooth had taken Lion when he ain't never even shown up to take the twins to a goddamn doctor's appointment. I couldn't believe it. Somebody was lying to me 'bout my children and Jayden knew the truth, had it soiling in his mouth.

Jayden shook his head and blew from his cheeks. "I guess when a kid splits open they head like that and the parents out here screamin' at each other, well, the doctors gotta call DCF if they got any reason to think the kids might be in trouble. A caseworker showed up, talked to Tooth, said he was gonna go talk to Momma and then come back and interview you after. He recommended Tooth take Lion home."

When I was a kid, Jayden and I took turns hitting each other with pillows to see who'd fall over first. It was a toss-up the first dozen times we played, but then we figured out what would make the other one instantly crumple. I'd hit Jayden right in the groin and he'd be on the floor in seconds. He'd hit me in the stomach with enough force that all the air inside me came rushing out and all I could do was keel over.

There wasn't nothing like the feeling of losing all ability to gasp for breath, like your body just done forgot how to do it and for a minute you scrambling to remember, trying to get yourself to gulp down just a little air. And only at the last moment do you heave in a breath and all the worry exits your body and you left, on the floor, clutching your stomach.

Jayden told me another threat was coming for my family and I was suddenly breathless. I'd narrowly avoided DCF over the years. I found addresses to pretend was mine so the doctor and the government didn't worry none, found spots I could park without rangers calling nobody. I made sure we never came nowhere close enough to DCF to have them squint too hard at us, 'cause I was sure they wouldn't understand nothing about what they saw.

Tooth and I even had a plan. If they ever came asking questions, we'd say we all lived together, at Tooth's, and that sometimes we went camping in my truck, just in case the kids talked about it. But after the blowup with Adela, I wasn't sure he was gonna follow our plan. Maybe he wanted me gone, maybe he wanted to play good daddy with Adela instead.

"Sit," Jayden said. This time, I listened.

Jayden let me sit silent for a few minutes, let me listen to the clicks and beeps and whines of the hospital while I tried not to let myself unravel like I had before. I had one child with a fractured skull and another at home with a father who only wanted him when it was easy. I choked on my breath. I found it again. I sniffled and then, seconds later, I sobbed.

Jayden pulled me close. "It's okay, Money. You gon' be fine."

I shook my head, croaked and coughed. "Momma's gonna tell 'em I ain't fit to be no mother. You shoulda seen what she said to me. This everything she wanted, them comin' to her asking her to shit on me till they take away my kids. She gon' make sure they take 'em."

Jayden smoothed away my snot with his thumb and wiped it on his pants. "No, she not. I already called her."

"Nothing you can say gon' change her mind." I leaned back and my head hit the wall, hard. All I thought was *Luck's musta hit harder, to crack open like an eggshell.*

"What's Momma's worst fear?"

I shrugged. "The trailer catchin' fire."

"Nah, you know she'd get that insurance money and buy a new one." Jayden laughed dry. "She scared of bein' alone. She never been on her own. She married Pops when she was my age, had you, had me. We started growin' up, went to school, and what she do? Popped out some more kids so she had somebody to fill all that empty space. Lived up in that trailer not 'cause she couldn't've got a job and rented a house somewhere, but 'cause she liked all us so close together. Never has to hear herself think."

My whole life, Momma was always lecturing us, cleaning up after us, grounding us, cooking for us, doing whatever she could, but never still. Never silent.

"You sayin' she kicked me out 'cause she ain't needed me when she had y'all? You think y'all leave and she'll want me again?" A small piece of me hoped he'd say yes, say there was a world where Momma wanted me.

"I'm saying I called Momma up and told her I'd leave and take the twins and Pops with me, get us all a nice place with Emmy and Kai, if she ain't told DCF you done everything you coulda done and it wasn't your fault. Now, she wasn't happy with me, but I could tell she was scared. She won't say nothing against you."

The relief only let me gasp for one gulp of air before I was thrown under again. She would tell the caseworker that it wasn't my fault. Meaning, Jayden thought it was. They all prob'ly did. And, if I was being honest, they was right. That was the hardest thing to accept. That I'd turned away for the sole reason of nursing my own wound just to open up another one in my daughter. How selfish. How shameful. How—

Jayden took my hand in his and squeezed and it was like we was kids again, pulling each other back to the ground when we started floating skyward.

"I'm sorry," Jayden said, and his eyes were leaking water.

"For what?"

"For staying when they kicked you out. I never apologized for none of it. For them. For me. I'm sorry." Jayden smoothed the tears away with the back of his free palm.

"You a good mom, Money. You was young, shit was hard, but look what you did. You made something from nothing. Didn't have no village, so you built one. You fuck up, you tell your kids you sorry. You doing what every good parent does. You show up. It's about time somebody does that for you. You not on your own, Simone. We got cousins and aunties and uncles all over and you got me and the Girls and even Tooth, and you know I don't like him like that. We here."

The curtain flew open, and Jayden let my hand go, wiped away any sign of crying. The nurses wheeled Luck back in and the doctor followed close behind. Luck was awake again. I stumbled out of my chair and to her bedside and she tilted her bandaged head toward me and smiled. She looked so tired.

"She's coming out of the sedation now, but she'll probably be pretty tired with the medication. We've started her on antibiotics to reduce the risk of infection and we'll be monitoring her through the night." The doctor looked antsy to leave, like he was afraid of me.

"What about her brain bleeding?"

The doctor rubbed his lips together in a false smile. "The hematoma is still very small and we believe it should resolve on its own. We'll monitor and get more scans in the morning, but for now we just wait. Please let us know if any new symptoms appear. Loss of vision, hearing, speech, that kind of thing."

Loss of vision. Hearing. Speech. He said it as though it was nausea or fatigue, as though it wasn't the lenses my baby looked through to see her favorite color, the ears she used to listen to her favorite melody, the voice she wielded to call out her big bewitching thoughts and stun a whole circle of Girls. He didn't understand how precious she was. And then he left.

The nurses slowly filed out after the doctor and, next thing I knew, it was just us again. Me, Jayden, and my little girl. I kissed her fore-head over and over again, softly so it didn't shake her brain and make the bleed grow, and I whispered to her, "Momma loves you so much, baby. You had a big fall, but it gonna be okay. It's gonna be okay."

The caseworker came and left. He asked all the questions I expected he'd ask and I tried to smile, but not too much. Talk, but not too much. Exist, but not too much. He said he'd spoken to every-one he needed to and that he'd be in touch but saw no reason for immediate removal of the children. He said they each needed real beds at Tooth's house, though, and that he would be checking in with the doctor to ensure I brought Luck back for all follow-up appoint-ments.

When he exited the curtain, I felt my body remember how to breathe again. Drinking air like Lion guzzled that honey milk back before all this began, and, even though I wan't sure whether my lungs deserved to expand again, when I swallowed breath, it sung inside me and the air was so good. It was so good.

◆ ◆ ◆

Sleep was impossible. Even though I was exhausted, the hospital room was still bright with fluorescent light and I couldn't keep my eyes off the machines attached to Luck. Heart: still beating. Lungs: still full of oxygen.

Jayden went home, said he'd call Tooth in the morning and check up on Lion, and Luck fell asleep, but I couldn't make myself shut off. I didn't quite believe that Luck's bleed would stay small and keep shrinking, or that the caseworker wouldn't come back and say he changed his mind.

I had to be ready, just in case.

The possibility that I could really lose my children, to death or some man's determination that I wasn't good enough, felt as tangible as the saliva sticky in my mouth. Waves of grief rushed in like nausea.

I couldn't survive without my babies. And I couldn't survive knowing they was being raised by Tooth either, by a man whose face I still found myself shaking loose from my head every time a memory of the twins arrived with him on the sidelines.

It wasn't that Tooth was a bad father. It's that he didn't want all of what came with being their parent. He wanted photos with them on their first birthday, but he didn't want the taste of their bile in his mouth after their first stomach flu. He wanted to fuck their momma without worrying about why he wanted to fuck their momma. He wanted me only when I was young, when I was soft and unsure and believed he'd handle me like a fish sent back to sea.

God, I wished he could be the kind of father I didn't worry about leaving alone with them, and sometimes I told myself he was. When they were fed and happy and the three of them played a game of chase on the beach before Tooth inevitably left to surf, to go where his children couldn't, deep into the water. But that was not how you loved a child. That was how you let a child love you.

I didn't want to look tired when Luck or Lion looked into my face next. I didn't want them to stare at me and fear they had lost a mother to a worried spiral of skin. My eyes closed and I urged my body to sleep, to slip into unconscious just long enough for morning to come, just long enough for me to see Luck's specks of sweet brown freckles on the bridge of her nose.

I've made mistakes. You don't have to tell me, I already know. But here's the thing: there's not no parent that hasn't stung with the same hand they used to stroke their baby's head with. The difference between a mother who's forgivable and a mother who's not is whether she gives enough of a shit to try to redeem herself in the first place. Apologize and do different. And I would've given anything to be better for them.

For Lion to wake up in the middle of the night, climb on top of me, and whisper to me his dream of how me and him was on an airplane and Luck was flying the plane and all the clouds was under us. For him to ask me if we could go on a plane someday and for the worst thing to be the sorrow of my repeating *no* to the one thing he wanted.

I loved them kids like I was born for it, and I would give up all the purest air in the world just for a chance at getting to hold their small, dimpled hands every day. When I fell asleep, in that hospital, I thought of this. Their eyes. Their hopes. Us, together again.

# EMORY

YOU KNOW WHAT I resented? Everything. But especially peanut butter and jelly sandwiches. They were supposed to be easy to make but they were a bitch to get right. Everybody wanted 'em a different way. How was I supposed to know to cut the crusts off? More jelly than peanut butter. Strawberry or raspberry jam. It was impossible, and I was doing it alone.

Me in the kitchen while Jay and Kai laughed in the living room. I could see them, having a jolly time while I smeared sticky peanut butter on white bread and hoped I was doing it right.

Jay placed Kai's feet on the carpeted floor, held Kai's hands from his place perched on the side of the sofa, his movement making the cheap leather squeak. Kai shrieked, giggled as he held on to his father's hands, standing and bouncing at the knees. This was his new favorite thing, standing. I could see from the bubbles his mouth blew how badly he wanted to walk before he crawled.

"You could help out over here," I mumbled. Maybe I was being whiny, but Jay had shown up with Lion this morning without any warning and now he wasn't even gonna help me make him a peanut butter and jelly sandwich (without the bottom crust, but with the top crust, and lots of jelly but only if it's grape) or answer Lion's questions about his mother and sister?

It wasn't fair that Jay got to sit there, making our baby laugh, and I had to take all the moments when he was crying, when he crawled to the worst parts of the house and found pieces of years-old food to stick in his mouth. Though I guess if Pawpaw let Jay, he'd be here for all of it. But he didn't and he wasn't, so I was rightfully mad.

Jay rolled his eyes and stood, picking up Kai and making his way to the kitchen, where Lion sat at the table drinking apple juice, and instead of helping me with the food, Jay sat down at the table with Lion, bouncing Kai on his knee.

I closed up Lion's sandwich and cut it in half, brought him his plate.

Lion looked up at me, his brows knit, his eyes flooding. "Momma cuts it in four pieces."

I sighed, went back to the counter and grabbed the knife, brought it back. Sliced the bread again.

My hands were smeared in peanut butter and I went to the sink to wash them. I knew I had no right to be mad that Lion was here. That he was scared. That Simone didn't want my help yesterday. That Tooth was the one who'd called Jay this morning and asked him to watch Lion until Simone and Luck were out of the hospital. I couldn't say I would've done nothing different from Simone if it'd been me and at least Lion was safe with us, even if only for the next hour.

I sat down across from Jay. "You sure Tooth'll come get him by one?"

"That's what he said. Luck should be discharged by one and then he'll come grab Lion."

"Pawpaw comes home for lunch at two, so you gotta be gone by then. And when Tooth comes, you can handle that. I'm not talking to him."

"Why you not talking to him? I mean, I get why Money don't wanna talk to him, but why you?" Jay's voice dropped. "You ain't fucked him, right?"

"Don't cuss in front of them," I hissed.

Lion giggled. "Momma say bad words are okay if you don't say 'em to strangers."

"Or people at school, right?" Jay raised his eyebrows at Lion. "When y'all go to kindergarten next year, you not gonna be cussin' in front of the other kids or your teachers, huh? You don't want them puttin' you on the naughty kid list."

"There's a naughty list?" Lion asked.

"Oh yeah. It's how Santa makes his choices about presents." Jay turned back to me. "Emmy, you on the naughty list?"

"No, Jay, I'm not. I haven't done nothing with Tooth. I just don't like him."

I wished it came down to likes or dislikes. That would've made hating Tooth simpler, but really I'd never minded him. He didn't do nothing to me and I rarely saw him anyway, but now when I pictured him, all I thought of was Adela. How he was the one she loved, how she'd chosen him and betrayed Simone all in one swoop. How could I cordially pass his child off to him like he hadn't ruined the life I wanted? Like sitting here at this table with Jay, marsh grass braided on my finger, wasn't all his fault.

"If you say so." Jay shrugged.

"Whatever," I said, reaching my hands out for Kai. Jay passed him off and I left the room with him, went into my bedroom, where I could nurse Kai alone in the dark and let my tears go. Where I could be a bucket under a leaky roof without letting Jay dump himself into me and leave me feeling guilty for overflowing.

I replayed the fight between the three of them in the hospital in my head and tried to figure out who to be angry with. Adela, for not loving me. Tooth, for manipulating Adela into loving him. Simone, for not seeing it coming. All of them, for their lies, for their vanishing, for their disregard of me in any of it. I knew I didn't have no right to be the forefront of everyone's thoughts, but how could Simone not have sensed something and warned me? How could Adela not think to tell me sooner?

Maybe I'd never loved Adela. Maybe all this was fate leading me back to Jay. To stay in Padua Beach even if I never got to swim with sea otters. Maybe all this was one big reminder that the only thing that mattered was the kids. I looked down at Kai in the dark and whispered, "You, my little melon, are the only thing that matters."

• • •

Kai was just suckling for comfort, not drinking nothing, when I heard the door open and Pawpaw's bellow rattle through the house. I pulled my bra back up and sprinted to the living room, where Lion was sitting on the couch watching cartoons and Jay was sitting beside him, his phone on his lap. Pawpaw had a plastic bag of groceries from the Winn-Dixie that he'd dropped to the floor and his face was bloating redder by the second. I looked at my phone. It was 2:03. We'd lost track of time and Tooth still wasn't back to get Lion.

"Pawpaw, Jay and Lion were just leaving. They were supposed to go before you got home."

He looked from the couch to me, his eyelids spread so wide I could see the blood vessels leading back into his skull.

"So you decided it was okay to . . . to . . ." Pawpaw seemed to catch himself before his tongue tipped off a ledge and the strangest thing happened. My pawpaw, who normally lectured at me till the sun went down, straightened his spine and pursed his lips and spoke slowly. "You decided it was okay to come into my house and trek in all this *sand*? You know how hard your grammy works to keep this house clean?"

"Sand?"

I looked around the room, an ocean of brown carpet, and sure there were grains of sand sprinkled into the foundation of the rug that'd been there for as long as I had, but nothing more than normal.

"Yes, Emory, *sand*. You and your . . . friend . . . came into my house with your shoes on and got sand everywhere and now how am I supposed to enjoy my home on my only break from a long day at a job that pays me next to nothing? I use my whole check on you, slave away all day, and this is how you repay me? You wanna have a child young as you are? Fine. You wanna forgo the natural way of things and do it out of wedlock? I can't stop you. But you want to mess up the house I so graciously raised you in after your fool of a mother left you stranded? I won't have it, Emory. I just won't."

Somehow this was worse than if he just came out and said he hated Jay, that finding him and Lion on his couch made him writhe deep beneath his skin where his veins snaked. Worse than if he just looked me in the eyes and said, *I wish we'd never taken you in.* Or better, *I wish you'd never been born.* Instead, he couldn't even admit it, so how was I supposed to respond to his complaints about some sand?

"You want me to vacuum? Fine, buy a vacuum and I'll do it."

"I certainly won't be buying no two-hundred-dollar vacuum to clean up your mess. You gonna get down on your hands and knees and pick each speck off that floor till I can take my shoes off and sink my tired feet into my soft, clean carpet."

Something about that must've shocked Jay out of his stupor 'cause he stood, quick and unexpected.

"Sir, I'm sorry about the . . . the sand. I don't got a vacuum but I'm sure I could rent one out from somewhere and bring it. I've got a truck, you know, and a job over in Panama City. You ever been out there, sir?"

Pawpaw glared at Jay wicked and I gulped.

"I lived 'round here my whole life, course I been. I been up and down this coast more times than you can imagine. In fact, I been alive since before you could buy a vacuum on the internet, so don't go acting like you can teach me nothing. I know everything I need to know."

"I'm sorry, sir, that's not what I meant. I just wanted to fix the problem so Emmy doesn't have to clean more than she already does."

He'd said the wrong thing. We both knew he had, the moment he said it, but it was too late.

Pawpaw laughed. "Emory don't clean any more than I'm sure you do. In fact, she don't do much of nothing around here, hasn't since she arrived on my doorstep, her mother gettin' it in her head she could have all she wanted without no work, like she's better than the rest of us. Bet you think you're better too, huh? Can't stand people like you, walkin' all over people like me and gettin' excused for it, not even having to marry a girl after you knock her up, then tracking sand into *my* house. You got some nerve, boy."

Jay straightened, looked proud. "Actually, sir, I am marrying her. And I intend to clean the house and respect you and Emmy's grammy like you my own, I swear, and if you want me to get on my knees and clean, I—"

"Jayden, stop!" I yelled.

He'd said too much. He didn't know Pawpaw like I did. He didn't know that all he needed was a reason to rage.

Pawpaw's face was redder than I'd ever seen it, like all the blood in his body was pooling in his head, poisoning him. Kai was silent for the first time all day, like he understood what was about to happen, Lion unsure if he should listen to the old man who walked in the door or keep watching his cartoons, so he stayed huddled on the couch, his eyes flitting between the two.

Pawpaw's lips curled. His forehead wrinkled and then turned smooth. He looked at me, and I knew it was over. It'd been coming for a while, ever since Kai was born, ever since that hurricane, but now Pawpaw had reached his final straw, the moment when he decided Grammy couldn't protect me no more, that their sweet granddaughter couldn't be saved from the well of her sins. The moment his carefully crafted image of me rotted on the edges like a water-stained book.

"Married, is that right? Well, Emory, I guess it's about time you moved outta here and started living with your husband the way any young lady's got to." Pawpaw picked his grocery bag back up and grinned wildly at me, his face still bright red. "In fact, let's start now. How 'bout you go to your room and pack a bag and get goin' before the sun sets. I'll tell your grammy all about it and I'm sure she'll be just delighted to go to the wedding. Maybe she'll walk you down the aisle like your pecker of a daddy would've, if he hadn't turned out to be a real motherfucker. Hope you fare better than that, angel. You can write me a letter sometime and tell me how it's goin'. Send a picture of your wedding dress, why don't you?"

Pawpaw ushered me out of the living room, toward my bedroom, swatting like I was a possum that somehow got in the house.

"Oh, and here's a little wedding gift for you." He rummaged around in his grocery bag and pulled out a long stick of beef jerky, tossed it at me. It hit the floor in the door of my bedroom. He kept coming at me and I was scared he was gonna go get the broom and start hitting me till I packed a bag and left, so through my tear-washed eyes, I started throwing clothes in my backpack, pacifiers and onesies in my diaper bag, whatever I saw.

"Please, Pawpaw, don't do this," I whimpered as he tormented.

"Shee-iitt, might be a while 'fore I see you, so how 'bout a baby shower gift too, huh? I'm sure you'll have another one on the way in no time." He threw a sponge at my feet. Then a bag of corn chips. A jar of mayonnaise. A loaf of white bread. "You know, Emory, I always knew it'd come to this. From the moment you came to live with us, I knew you'd be gone 'fore you graduated. A girl who can't clean up no sand don't got no reason to be hanging around her pawpaw's house or working some mindless job like us. No, you always been so *progressive*, sweetheart, always doin' the new hip thing, marryin' a boy like that, havin' a baby that looks just like him. You always liked the monkeys at the zoo, remember? Just loved 'em. Ha! Look at you now."

I couldn't stand it anymore. I lifted the backpack and diaper bag over my shoulder and ran past Pawpaw into the living room, where Jay already had Lion in his arms, the door open. Lion burrowed into his neck but didn't cry. Or if he did, I couldn't hear it through my own sobs as I followed them out the door, turned around to see Pawpaw standing in the hallway, his face gone from red to near purple, and he didn't look like the pawpaw who tucked me in at night or the pawpaw who lost everything he had in one quick swoop but got right back up and found a way to make sure I never had a worry in my head. He looked feral, villainous, plain mean. Not like the man who raised me at all.

I slammed the door shut and fought not to look back.

# ADELA

I F I HAD KNOWN what was going to happen, with Simone, with the twins, with the collapse of all we were, I'm not sure I would've done it. Lied to Tooth, lied to Simone and the Girls. Believed I could be his family when he already had one.

But I didn't know before the hospital, I couldn't have. When I trained to be a junior lifeguard, they made us take first aid training and the whole thing was just one omission of information to get us not to panic, to do our job, to save a life. Sometimes you need to know what the aftermath looks like, though, because maybe if I had known, I would've been able to save us all the pain.

They don't tell you in first aid training about the way blood works, about the thump and swirl of red hot beneath the skin and what happens when it runs drought dry. They don't tell you this because nobody would ever intentionally cut off the blood supply of someone they love if they truly understood what they were doing, twisting the tourniquet so tight the limb went yellow.

If I had known I wasn't just cutting off Simone's blood supply to the gushing exit wound but also the blood in each of her toes, in the twitch that was our intertwined lives, then I would've thought about what would happen if she couldn't walk, if the pale numb seeped beyond Simone and into Chris and me and the twins.

But no one told me that my lie was going to lead to the severance between us in the hospital, to the social worker, that all that meant me and Chris in a house with a worried five-year-old who didn't trust the shake in my wrist as I tried spoon-feeding him applesauce and he laughed in my face.

After they took Luck away for her MRI, Chris asked me in the hospital parking lot to meet him at his place once the social worker left and help with Lion, and after all that had happened, I just wanted to be close to the one thing I still had, the person who didn't look at me with the scorn of a candle blown to smoke.

I didn't anticipate how the rims of his eyes would bulge as he shoved his kid toward me the moment I got to his house, said he had to make a call, and then didn't come out of the bathroom for an hour. And quickly, I realized I didn't want a life without Simone. I wanted what came before a lie erupted, not the aftermath of dried lava turned crisp black.

A life without Simone meant my boyfriend was edging on thirty and I was going to be the stepmother to two small children who made him want to run from sight. I assumed he'd be a good dad, and he was, sort of, but it was like he was waiting for me to lead and then he'd follow.

Chris came up behind me as I stirred mac and cheese at the stove and whispered in my ear, "It's just a day, Adela. Luck'll be outta the hospital in the morning and we'll get the whole thing figured out. We just gotta make it through the night. You and me, girl."

A night is long with a child too scared to sleep. Lion had questions. I flushed at each one and avoided answering because the only response I could think of to "Why's Momma not coming?" was *Me*. The social worker showed up because of Simone's screams and threats outside Luck's curtain in the hospital and the only reason she'd been screaming was me.

Before, I'd mined myself of guilt, believing it useless to feel remorse for things you couldn't know before you knew. But watching Lion blink at me in a dark room as he clutched his arms close, I realized I'd ruined their lives. These children's, Simone's. And maybe I'd even ruined mine.

The least I could do was stretch to the ends of myself so Simone's child wouldn't feel so scared. Lion wouldn't sleep in the bedroom because he said the mattress was too soft. He stood in the middle of the bedroom and refused to lay down, his face lit up in the dim of Chris's one lamp. Chris's roommates snored across the room.

"Fine," I said, kneeling in front of him, my belly pulling me forward. "You want to sleep on the floor? Go for it."

Lion's lip puffed out and I could see he was about to cry. I sighed. "I'm sorry, I didn't mean that. Where do you want to sleep? Anywhere you want."

He whispered, "The closet. With lots of pillows."

Lion didn't like the pillows with red pillowcases because they smelled funny. Lion sneezed every time he got near the leopard-print furry ones. Finally, I had to take all the pillows from the couch and Chris's bed and pile them along the floor of the walk-in closet, throwing Chris's clothes anywhere they'd fit, and when Lion finally laid down, he still looked so sad.

"I need a flashlight. But don't shut the door all the way."

I dug through every drawer in the kitchen looking for a flashlight, finding only used batteries, plastic wrappers, and cigarettes, and I was about to throw a fit when Chris entered the kitchen, asking what all the banging around was about.

"Lion needs a flashlight."

Chris turned on his heel, leading me to the hall closet, where a flashlight sat on the top shelf.

"Well, can I have it?" I held my hand out.

He laughed. "Jump for it."

I glared at him and, still, I jumped. I didn't reach it the first time, so I jumped again. On the third jump, I hit it and it rolled off the shelf and fell right on my big toe and I screeched "Fuck!" and snatched the flashlight from the floor, squeezing my throbbing toe as Chris laughed some more and said he was sorry and I shoved him and told him to sleep on the floor.

I shook my foot to try to free it from the blood rushing to my toe and hopped back toward the bedroom. I handed Lion the flashlight and silently begged this to be the last thing I had to do before I could finally lay down and massage the remorse inside me.

"Sleep, okay? Just until it's morning."

Lion squeaked. "And then we see Momma?"

I swallowed. "Yeah, I think so. Probably."

Lion nodded and turned around to stare at the closet ceiling. I slowly shut the closet door, leaving it cracked, and fell into Chris's bed across the room. Chris never came tiptoeing into the room carrying antiseptic cream or a Band-Aid, never tried kissing my eyelids and cupping his hand under my stomach. He stayed in the living room, where I could see the glitter of the TV screen from under the doorway.

I laid my head on the pillow-less mattress, the duvet in the closet with Lion so all I had were sheets, and I watched the yellow flashlight switch on through the crack in the door, Lion whispering to himself the way children do, in a rasp no quieter than his talking voice.

"It's okay. Luck just gettin' fixed up. And then I go see her when the sun out and Momma too and Momma will bring new Gold-fish, 'cause they so tasty. And then maybe she take us on an airplane, okay?" I pictured him nodding. "Okay," he repeated.

Lion whimpered and I could hear him move around, lay his little head onto a cushion, and tell himself stories of airplanes he'd never seen until finally he fell asleep. And even when the sun rose, the flashlight was still on.

◆ ◆ ◆

Chris wanted me to take care of Lion while he went to work this morning, but I told him I wouldn't. That if Simone found out about it, she'd be twice as angry as she already was, and when Chris left holding Lion's small hand to pass him off to Simone's brother, I immediately started sobbing. This could not be what motherhood was.

I tried reassembling the fantasy of our life together. Started sewing my baby a onesie by hand the way Noni taught me and finished the seams of some socks. Dreamed the baby would somehow come out looking like Chris, and cried myself to hiccups when I became sure Simone was going to lose her kids and I'd have to live with being the reason why. I ignored Noni's calls and changed my clothes twice, settled on wearing one of Chris's T-shirts, even though now it fit almost like it could be my own, barely covering the belly.

And then, just when I was sure I couldn't wait for Chris to come home anymore, I heard the door open. I heard him shake his boots off, heard him grunt. I took a deep breath and held it, counted the seconds like I did sometimes to make sure my lungs could still do what they once did. He opened the bedroom door and I let the breath go.

He was alone.

"You're back." I sat upright, the pillows behind me on the newly made bed. I'd hung each of his shirts up in the closet and folded his boxers in the drawers.

He smoothed his hands over his head and collapsed onto the bed, leaned up against the wall, pulled his shirt off.

"Never been happier to see you," he said.

It still got me. I kissed him slow, forgetting the night before, attributing it to a weak moment, all of us stressed and tired.

"What happened?" I laid on his chest and he caressed my back.

"Had to go get Simone's truck from the impound and bring it to her, but Luck's okay. She not allowed to run or nothing for a while, but she outta the hospital. And looks like they not gonna take the twins."

I paused. "They're not? How?" I'd already planned a life without her, where I'd destroyed her family and become a mother to three at once, and I wasn't sure how I felt, knowing it would go back to the way it was. Relieved, I guessed, but also so insignificant. So small.

"I told that social worker that there ain't no way I can be watchin' no kids all day while I work and if I had to answer another question about why there wasn't no milk in my fridge, I was gonna explode. Told him we all lived together and that I'd childproof the house and shit and that it was just a fucking fluke."

I stared at him. He rubbed crust from his eyes and yawned. He twisted my nipple through my shirt and I pushed him away. "Are you serious, Chris?"

He lifted his hands up like I'd accused him of something he hadn't done. "What? You told me you didn't wanna have 'em all day either."

"You told the social worker you were with Simone? And that you don't want to take care of your children? What about ours?"

I choked on the word and realized I'd started to forget this baby wasn't Chris's, that I was asking him to raise a child that wasn't his, even if he didn't know it. Still, what if he never found out, what if I gave up my everything and he still left me with this baby alone, didn't care enough to get off the couch and make the baby a bed out of pillows if that's what they needed.

"That's different. You take care of it during the day and I'm gonna buy you diapers and give y'all some good lovin' when I get home. What else you want? You think you gonna get much better from all them boys at your school?"

I shrugged, chewed on my inner cheek until it felt like ground meat. "I just, I thought we were going to be a family."

"What you think a family is? Reciprocity, Adela. I give you what you need and you give me what I need. Keep complainin' and you'll end up all shriveled up and alone like Simone."

I sat up, removed my hand from his chest, and reached for the closest thing I could find. My hand found the flashlight beside the bed and I whipped around and chucked it at Chris as hard as I could, but, of course, he caught it between his two palms.

I stood up, pulled my sweatpants on, and marched out of the room, out of his house, out of this life he'd constructed for us without ever asking me if that's what I wanted.

◆ ◆ ◆

When I first met Lindsay, in those beginning weeks of ninth grade, I was as sure she was going to be my best friend as I was she was going to toss me aside someday. She'd never met anyone like me, someone she could relate to like all the friends she'd had before, fawning over boys and trading secrets about past pains—lightly slicing her wrists a few times before deciding she was more emotionally evolved, watching the despair of her parents together but not in love—but who added something different, something special. A black fist against an off-white wall almost makes you believe it is the purest white you'd ever seen.

I didn't mind, though, because I was used to impermanence and the art of letting go, always chasing something new. It was part of what made me great. I was unattached. I was willing to soar from one end of a pool to the other and only care about those seconds it took me to glide.

Of course, what comes with having friends who you always suspect will dispose of you is having to remind yourself not to look like you care too much. Once you master the craft of pretending you have no stake in this life of yours or these people who disguise themselves with the face of loving you, you eventually start to believe you actually don't care at all.

In some ways, I think that's how I ended up in this mess. Pregnant. Alone. But on the day I left Chris's crying, for the second—or maybe sixth—time, I forgot not to care.

I'd reached the point of pregnancy where running caused a strange pulsing in my bladder, like a yo-yo, elastic and bouncing and heavy, so I tried not to run often, instead slowing myself down and swiftly walking the path to the beach.

When I got there and it was endless and empty, I turned around and kept walking. Sweated so much I removed Chris's shirt and threw it into a nearby tree so it dangled from a high-up branch, and then I walked on in my bra and sweatpants, through the mud ravine, losing my way and becoming tangled in overgrowth I was sure was rampant with snakes, until, finally, I arrived at the sound of them.

The Girls looked tender as a newly healed bone, sitting huddled together in the back of the truck, Simone in the center of them, Luck swaddled in her arms. Lion sat on Emory's lap to her left and April and Jamilah were gone, but the rest were there. I ran when I saw them, forgetting my bladder, my weight, because I had never been more relieved to see a full red truck.

"I went to the beach looking for you guys, I didn't know where you were. I'm so sorry, Simone, I really am, but I swear I didn't know Chris was yours when I first met him. I've had the worst day, I was just with Chris and he told me that he wasn't going to take care of the baby. I mean, he didn't say that, but he pretty much told me it wasn't his job and that I should be happy he wanted to stick around and I shouldn't push him to change a diaper because I should be grateful he was even willing to buy them. Can you believe that? I just feel like I'm all alone, and . . ." I slowed when I looked into Emory's face pried open and leaking disgust, Simone's blank stare, Crystal's sneer.

Emory spoke. "Get out of here, Adela."

"But . . . I said I was sorry." I wanted my shirt back, something to shield them from looking at my skin, my stomach. "I accepted your apology, why won't you accept mine?"

Simone wasn't angry like usual. Her voice was flatlined and coarse from crying, low and lucid. "I gave you a few bruises. You stole my children's father. And now, on the day I get my babies back, after the worst day of *my* life, you wanna come here whinin' 'cause you sad a man who's not even your baby's real daddy's not gonna take care of it? 'Cause you not special enough he'll change for you?" Simone shook her head. "I suggest you listen to the only person here who seems to care about you and go."

I wanted to look at Emory and see remorse, see change, but it was not there, not in the sun spots on her neck, not in the sprouting lines leading up to her hairline. She was done with me. So I did what I should have done before and tried not to care, went home and filled the bathtub Simone had bled into so many months ago.

I undressed and slipped into the water and I thought I was going to be okay, thought I had shaken the care from my skin and just had to wait for it to lift into a film floating at the top of the water, but when I looked down at myself, I saw what I was made of.

Full of soggy shame, a belly that would not submerge beneath the water and instead stuck out like a buoy. I tried splashing warm water over the dome of skin, over and over, but a moment later the water would slide off, leaving it dry and gasping for warm relief. A sliver of me that could not retain heat, that could not be hidden or cleaned, and would remain, for as long as I could see, impenetrable and cold.

# SIMONE

LION WANTED TO go on an airplane. Every time I told him no, it felt like swallowing a pebble and realizing once it went down that it wouldn't dissolve, that there was no amount of stomach acid that could handle something so solid. The pebbles piled one on top of the other until my stomach felt hard to the touch and I was throwing up twice a day even though I wasn't pregnant, just guilt-ridden and terrified.

It was Tuesday, four weeks after the hospital, and today was the day Luck's cast would come off. I was my mother's child even when I didn't want to be, and I caught myself with the same cutting voice every time the twins strayed from me. I made Luck cry yesterday after she climbed a tree one-handed and stayed up there for an hour, thought we was playing hide-and-seek and wouldn't clamber back down even after I started screaming out for her.

When I finally tilted my head up to the canopy of live oak branches my babies once found as fascinating as the concept of time and saw my little Luck crouched in the tree, I was already half-disintegrated. Once I got her close enough to reach and then finally on the ground, I grabbed her wrist like a ranger grabs his gun. Without thinking. She sobbed and only came to me for a hug after she realized mine were the only arms around.

I wanted to do better. I wanted this memory to be a blip on the highway of the childhood I'd created for them and, eventually,

they wouldn't even be able to see it. But I couldn't promise nothing. I couldn't promise plane rides or birthday cakes or Halloween
costumes. So instead, I raged before I reckoned. I slung words like a
jump rope and tripped over my own skin. I held Luck and Lion till
they begged me to let them go and, when I did, I fretted over scar
tissue from cuts I hadn't caused, 'cause what if I was the source of all
the ruin in our lives?

We all cope somehow and I didn't think my vices were any worse
than the next mother's. I stopped sleeping. I drank till I went dizzy
and I laughed more than I cried and hated myself for it. Most of all,
I had conversations with Tooth in my head even when I didn't say a
word to him in person.

I'd tell him I knew the only reason he argued with the social
worker to not separate the twins from me was 'cause he didn't wanna
admit he could only be their father in theory.

*I always been their favorite,* he'd say.

When you too young to know the moon is a constant loop, you
always wishing it was whole. Tell me a time they been as happy to see
you as they was to think you might be happy to see them. Tell me a
time you knew them well enough to know Luck's right eyelid will
fold so it looks half-shut when she really happy, that Lion will tell
you a story with *The End* signaling he's done if he cannot contain
his joy in his usual silence. Tell me a time you wanted more than our
outlines.

*You jealous. You always wanted me more than I wanted you and you
jealous they do too. You wish you could have me like that.*

Before I knew better, I wanted you. But I think I really wanted
you to want me but not do nothing about it, 'cause you looked at me
and you saw my mother's first child, saw the summer you fucked a
girl for the first time and I didn't know you yet, was still in the third
grade.

But instead you touched me like I was a woman and I was scared.
I was scared till I told myself I wanted you, that it was a miracle you

wanted me back, and I never did finish reading *All About Love,* 'cause I knew if I read it, I'd understand that wasn't what we had. And I couldn't face that. I was my mother's first child. I was still close enough to my first day of kindergarten, I remembered the color of my name tag.

*You got more excuses than anyone I ever met. How you gon' say you didn't love me? How you gon' look at our children and say I ain't loved you back? You selfish, Simone. You always got a problem with somebody.*

I'm selfish. I always got a problem with somebody. Somebody always got a problem with me. I wanted a truck for my kids and me to sleep in. I wanted a family who wanted me back. I wanted to love somebody who didn't grow disinterested when I aged, the cushion of my cheeks thinning, my body outgrowing my favorite Juicy skinny jeans.

Call it selfish. But I showed up at my momma's door to raise a white flag the color of honey milk and ended up worse for it. Took in another pregnant girl, who turned around and treated my family like it was a prize to be stolen from my grip. I been selfless and that's not no way to survive out here.

*You stupid for letting me go. You stubborn. Not fit for mothering. You seen Adela hold a child? You seen her tuck them into bed? She better than you ever was.*

In my head, Tooth was cruel. It was easier that way. I knew if I told him any of this, he would be soft, tell me he was hurting too, that if anyone was naive about us, it was him. He'd say whatever he had to say to get me to lean into him. But that is why I would never tell him. I knew better than to walk back into the fold of him.

◆ ◆ ◆

I had to make my children's dreams come true. I felt myself decomposing in the aftermath of the hospital, no light left to synthesize into another day worth trying. But if I didn't clip the dead leaves from my shell, I was only gonna spread my diseased parts to my children. And there wasn't no version of this life where I wasn't willing to turn myself inside out to give them everything.

Last night, while I watched them sleep, I came up with a plan. We'd go to the doctor in the morning and get Luck's cast off, the stitches on her scalp checked one last time, and then I was gonna take them to a plane. Maybe not one that would soar them to a landscape of snowcapped hills and peaking skyscrapers, but they at least deserved to see the airplanes that had journeyed far beyond them. I hoped that just watching those planes ascend into the sky till they disappeared from sight would begin to make up for all this. It had to.

I woke everyone up early. April and Crystal spent the past few nights with us 'cause April's Lola was visiting and didn't know she had a baby and her parents told her to go stay at her friends' place till Lola was gone, and Crystal and her sister kept going at it about who was responsible for unclogging the drain in their shared bathroom. As the sun rose and revealed the paleness of the sky, my future crystallized in the dim glimpse of light.

"Get up!" I shouted.

Crystal jolted, panicked, but April continued to sleep. "What? What's wrong?" Crystal'd already grabbed Cece and was pulling a shirt on over her bra.

"Y'all need to go," I said.

"Us too, Momma?" Lion asked, clutching Luck's free arm, awake and already cowering.

"Not you, baby." I poked April till she stirred. "Get up. I need y'all to go so I can take the twins somewhere, just us."

April was groggy but blinking open. "Oh. Okay," she croaked.

Slowly, they each packed their bags, gathered their children's loose pacifiers and lovies, and hopped down from the truck bed, kids held close.

Crystal yawned. "It still cool if I come back tonight? After my night class?"

I took a breath. "Actually, I was thinking the twins and I just need some time. Y'all can figure it out, right? Just for a few days? Maybe a week?"

"Oh. Yeah, course, we'll figure it out." Crystal and April looked at each other and I knew they was thinking, *What's Simone doing? Why she being all rude?* But I wasn't being rude. I was doing what needed to be done. I was choosing my children.

Once Crystal and April were gone, I told Luck and Lion we was gonna go to the doctor and then we was going on a trip. Lion burst into tears and asked if he had to go with Daddy and Adela again.

"No, baby, Momma's comin' with you. Don't you worry, I'll be there the whole time."

Luck pet the top of his head till he stopped crying. I made us all breakfast, gave them their glasses of milk, and then we piled into the truck cab.

The whole way to the hospital, Luck didn't say a word. I tried to get her to talk, asking her all kinds of questions 'bout what she wanted to do with her free arm and what her favorite drawing on her cast was, but she didn't say more than a word or two back. This is how she was every time we got in the car to go to the doctor's: silent, passive, gone from herself.

When we arrived at the doctor's office, I made sure the parking spot wasn't lined in red and held both of the twins' hands as we walked in, waited for the nurse to call us, finally got brought back into the little room where the last physical reminder of what happened would be removed.

The doctor knocked on the door and then entered. He smiled at Luck like she was an infant and not the astonishing child she was and she ain't smiled back. Lion hid behind me.

"Today's the day!" he said. "How are we feeling?" he asked me.

"I'm fine, but I'm not the one with the broken arm and the brain bleed, so you should really be askin' my daughter," I said.

His smile retreated, but he took my advice and turned to Luck.

"How does it feel? Fractured ulnas are no joke, missy, but you were lucky enough to heal so quick we could take this thing off you, huh?"

She shrugged. "I just wanna climb again. Momma say I can climb again when my cast off."

"That's right. Your head's healed so nice, you can run and climb all you want," the doctor said. He looked to me and added, "With appropriate adult supervision."

I sighed. "Can you please just take off her cast? We have places to be, don't we?"

Both twins nodded and I felt like we were one little pack again, charging through the line of trees together, on the hunt.

"Alrighty."

The doctor pulled out a corded handheld machine that looked like a tattoo gun from a drawer. He screwed a blade to the top and sat down on his spinning stool again, gliding right on back to Luck and me. He plugged the machine in and held it out so we could see.

"I'm going to use this to cut off your cast."

I put my hand up to stop him from bringing that thing any closer to my baby. "Wait, you not gonna put her to sleep or numb her or nothing?"

He laughed. "It won't hurt. The blade stops the moment it cuts through the cast."

"What if it don't? What if your blade thinks my daughter's skin's the same as the cast?"

He laughed harder. "I assure you the technology knows the difference, ma'am. If I used a regular knife I'd be far more likely to hurt her. It'll take about thirty seconds, alrighty?"

I looked at Luck. She was afraid, so I couldn't be. This was the mistake I'd made in the MRI room, letting her glimpse my fear split wide open and gushing from my chest. I couldn't make it again.

I smiled at her. "Trust the doctor, baby. He gonna fix you up and then we'll go on our adventure, okay?"

Luck nodded but I could tell she wasn't sure. I wasn't neither.

The doctor switched on the machine and the blade whirred. Lion shook behind me, Luck gripped her other hand on my knee hard enough to break skin. The blade floated down, closer and closer to her cast till it was touching it and the doctor was pulling this cutting machine down my daughter's arm, her eyes squeezed shut, my hands struggling not to reach out and snatch the machine from the doctor's fingers. And then it was done. The doctor switched the machine off, put it on a tray, and gently peeled the rest of the cast from Luck's arm till it was bare.

Where the cast had been, Luck's arm looked withered. It was lighter than the rest of her skin and scaly, but it also looked soft and wet. Like a newborn, after ten months soaking in fluid. Delicate and alien to the air, sort of bruised and misshapen.

Luck opened her eyes. Lion paused his shaking. The doctor touched her arm, asked a question or two, and rose with the same unnecessary enthusiasm he'd had when he entered the room, before whizzing right out again, leaving us alone.

"How's it feel, Lucky?" I asked.

"Broken." She burst into tears.

It took ten minutes of convincing before she'd move a finger, then her wrist, finally her whole hand and arm at once. It was brittle and tender and she winced, but once she saw it could move, her tears stopped and she started asking about the adventure, forgetting not to move her arm until her fingers were wiggling everywhere. I smiled.

"You'll see."

◆ ◆ ◆

We drove for an hour and Luck and Lion played I spy, 'cept they didn't understand that you had to pick something that'd stay in sight long enough for the other person to guess, so Luck kept picking highway signs and Lion kept guessing the sky till Luck declared she'd won and Lion started cryin' and whinin', "Momma, Luck cheatin'. She cheatin', Momma!"

I knew we was close when I started seeing planes. Just one at first, way high up, but pretty soon the planes were low to the ground and Lion spotted one and screamed so loud, my eardrum felt like it was 'bout to burst. Luck started listing all the places she knew planes went to.

"Hawaii and Utah and Disney. Sometimes they even land *in* the water, you know that? Like a boat!"

"In the water?" I asked.

"Mmm-hmm, and all the people get to swim to shore."

"That's only if the plane crashes, baby. Most of the time, the plane lands on the ground."

"No, that's not true, 'cause I seen it on the TV at the hospital and the nurse say it was real. For real." She nodded and pursed her lips like she hated to tell me I was wrong, and I choked back a smile. She was so sure. I worried I'd scared that out of her, when they was back with me and all she did was ask questions the whole first day, unsure of any answer. Unsure of the borders of her world.

I drove past the guard stationed at the entrance, smiling as he waved me by. I was worried everyone knew about me, that someone was circulating a flyer with my face on it saying "bad mother" and the caseworker'd come back to take my babies. I was haunted by the sight of his pen scratching on his clipboard. I still shivered at the absence of their skin touching mine when they rolled away in the truck at night. But I couldn't let my haunting reverberate through them, so I ignored my fears and drove on.

I parked the truck beside a green Jeep and helped the twins down till all their little feet was on the ground.

"Where we at, Momma? This an airport?" Lion asked.

"Not exactly, baby. This a museum."

The National Naval Aviation Museum in Pensacola was a place of legend.

I wasn't all that much of a fan of the military or the navy or any of 'em and I'd never in my life thought about venturing onto the naval base, but one thing I knew was that the navy had planes and my children wanted, more than anything, to see a plane.

"A museum? Like for art? I can draw them a picture and they can put it up so people can come look at it and go, 'Wow, that's so pretty and I wonder who made it,' and I'll say, 'Luck! Luck made it!'"

I laughed. "I like that idea. You can draw a picture when we get back in the truck, but right now we've got a museum to see. This a special museum, not an art one, not even a history one."

They bolted ahead of me, Luck dragging Lion with her strong arm, and Luck tried tugging on the door with her freshly mobile hand but it wouldn't budge, so Lion tried helping and still they couldn't open it. They both looked over their shoulders, up at me, and that sight's gotta be more profound than any museum painting ever could be, them looking at me like I got the key to the door, like I could do anything. I pressed the button that unlocked it and pulled.

Luck rushed forward into the room, but Lion stayed still. I gently touched his back and ushered him inside, toward the check-in desk, but still he walked slow, his eyes spread wide like a cat in the middle of the night, sure he'd miss something if he blinked too slow. Luck ran back to us and started talking about everything she saw.

"Look, Momma, you see the orange plane? You see over there they got statues of people but they not for real, they just statues, and you see the little plane? That one look like it made for me, huh?"

I turned from the check-in desk and leaned down to Luck and Lion. "Stay close enough I can see you, okay? You hear?"

"Yes, ma'am," Luck said. Lion nodded.

I smiled. "Go on, then."

I knew I'd done something right watching them fly into the room like that, the soles of their shoes still caked with mud, Luck's hair bobbles clacking together, even with the one patch of hair they'd shaved that was now slowly growing back. They was so small beside the big planes, their little selves not even tall enough to reach the wings, and watching the wrinkles in the back of Lion's head as he looked up at the propeller eased everything that had happened. They was still here. They could still look up at a plane and be mesmerized to silence.

I wiped a tear as Lion ran over and grabbed my hand with his clammy one. "Momma, you gotta see this one, over here. Luck say it's called a Tiger and I'm a Lion!"

I followed my son through the maze of planes to where my newly freed daughter was climbing up into a Blue Angels plane and, even if I had looked away at the one time that mattered, even if I had failed and failed again for that one day that broke us all, I knew I could put us back together.

I'd made something for them today that was gonna trickle through their veins for a lifetime, and when I looked down at my daughter's healing stitches on her pointy head as she talked, my son's dimpled cheeks as he gazed, I knew I'd done something right.

# EMORY

IN THE DESERT, there's a plant called the false rose of Jericho. It grows in places so dry and dusty it damn near kills itself so it doesn't have to think about where it might get its next drop of water. It shrivels up and tumbles in the wind, aimless.

I was rolling in the breeze, hoping the little drops of water I got when Kai giggled would be enough to keep me tethered, but it wasn't. I was drying up and it was getting harder and harder to pretend I wasn't.

The truth was, I didn't care a smidge about lace or chiffon. I didn't have half a horse's fucks to give about daffodils or sunflowers. Not a pot of gold or a barrel of wine could've made me worry about a church or a community center or an outdoor ceremony.

April was trying to convince me that a buffet's always the best idea and Jamilah was arguing with her that a plated meal's more classy, even the wedding magazine she stole from the gas station said so.

They both turned to me. "What do you think, Em?"

We'd been sitting at a booth in the McDonald's since noon, when I got out of school for lunch and beelined for anywhere but Adela. It was late afternoon now and I picked apart a french fry and held a piece on my finger for Kai to slurp up like a fish. A new wave of heat arrived without warning this week, sending us burrowing for shade like desert foxes, and the McDonald's was one of the only air-conditioned buildings to hole up and breathe in. Besides, Simone was gone for the day and so was the truck we all relied on.

I sighed. "I don't even know if I want a wedding. It's expensive."

"Please, girl, your man's got a real job, he can afford to rent out the church basement for two hours." Jamilah set her daughter down on the ground and let her hold on to her fingers as she walked. She was fourteen months now and she still wasn't walking and Jamilah'd gotten so worried, she trained her like she was some kind of athlete.

"You've seen how expensive a child is. His money goes to gas, food, and the garage we're renting from a lady at his church since Pawpaw kicked me out. I don't want nothing fussy, just a courthouse and maybe a little suit for Kai."

"You'd look so handsome in a suit, wouldn't you?" April cooed at Kai. He giggled and grabbed at a piece of her bangs. "I don't get it, you always loved shopping and doing your hair and stuff. Why wouldn't you want a big party where that's all you do?"

I shrugged. "Who wants a wedding no one will show up to?"

"I do," Jamilah said. "Can be just me and my Girls and my baby, but I'm taking my day."

It wasn't really my day to begin with. Jay was the one who wanted to decorate the church and hire a band instead of just using a playlist on my phone. He was the one who begged me to take a trip out to Macy's and look for real wedding bands. He'd been asking me for weeks when we were going to pick a color scheme, but I kept avoiding. The truth was, I didn't give a hoot. All I cared about was the little person in my hands and not letting him out of my sight in case he fell and they tried to do to me what they did to Simone.

"Do you know what's going on with Simone?" April asked. "It's been two weeks and she's still saying her and the twins need 'space.'"

"We spent the afternoon with them yesterday," Jamilah said.

April shook her head. "Yeah, but nobody's spent the night in weeks."

I shrugged. "She just heard that DCF closed her case. She's probably just being cautious." I stood from the table. "I should go. Jay's gonna get back soon and I told him I'd meet him by the school and we'd drive back to the garage together."

"At least think about the dress," April pleaded. "Short or long? Train? Bustle? Anything, Emory. You have to want something."

At some point or another you have to stop dreaming about things. You look around and realize where you are and, suddenly, the appeal of fluffy white clouds and satin dresses fades and you remember how much safer it is to not want nothing at all. The hospital room did that to me. Adela did that to me.

Then, when the social worker showed up, I looked down at Kai and realized how precious this was, getting to hold him, getting to love him. Anything else I wanted couldn't matter next to that. I'd made my bed. It wasn't plush or wide or warm, but it had sheets that covered the urine stains from the last person who wet the bed, and, regardless of everything else, it was mine.

I placed Kai into the BabyBjörn carrier and then slung his diaper bag over my shoulder.

"See y'all tomorrow morning for laundry," I said.

April tilted her head. "You're coming? But you have school."

I shrugged. "Doesn't matter much anymore. My grades are good enough to graduate even if I don't go back the rest of the year. We only have two weeks left anyway."

I waved behind me and headed into the thick outside, hotter than two squirrels humpin' in a sock, and I knew April and Jamilah were worried, but the truth was I didn't much care what happened after I graduated, so why work harder than I had to? A high school diploma was more than they had.

When I made it back to the school building, Jay was still an hour out, so I checked that Adela wasn't in sight and settled at a picnic table, deciding it was as good a time as any to paint my nails. I fed

Kai first and then I took out the only color I had on me, a salmon that didn't really go with my skin tone but was better than the old, chipped green I had on.

I scratched at the old paint till it came off in flakes and then laid my left hand on the table, working around Kai's body still strapped to mine, and delicately applied the first coat. It wasn't half bad either. I started thinking about how colors don't really look like what they're called and how salmon's not the color of salmon at all and if it was, I don't think nobody would wear it, kind of like peach or mustard. I was onto my second coat when I heard heels digging into dirt and looked up to the sight of Mrs. Simmons and a glare unlike any I'd seen since Pawpaw kicked me out the house.

"Miss Reid, gather your things and come with me."

"Sorry, ma'am, but I can't. If I move it'll smudge my nails and you see, I just painted 'em, so if we could do this tomorrow, I'd really appreciate it." I smiled, fanning out my nails so she could get a good look at them.

"I can't be sure you're gonna show up to school tomorrow, so I'm afraid it can't wait."

I pursed my lips. "Well, my fiancé's on his way and he's expecting me to be out here waiting for him, so I just don't know what to tell you, Mrs. Simmons."

Mrs. Simmons wanted to rip me a new one, I could tell. But she stayed composed, nodded at me, and lifted her skirt up so she could climb over the bench opposite me and sit down.

"Then I suppose I'll be joining y'all."

She was a tricky woman, that one. Just when I expected her to give up and go cry into all her years-old magazines, she grew a pair and did the unexpected.

"Fiancé, huh? I didn't realize you and Jayden were plannin' on gettin' married. That why you been skippin' class?"

"Jay?" I laughed. "Jay doesn't know where I've been. As far as he's concerned, I'm still gonna be valedictorian or whatever."

I started blowing on each of my nails to get them to dry faster, since I was pretty sure it was hot enough they might melt and clump if they didn't dry quick. Kai laughed as I blew and after I got through each finger, I'd blow right onto his forehead and send him into a giggle fit.

Mrs. Simmons rolled her wrists and I could tell she wanted to get up and go inside where she wouldn't have to worry about ticks finding her ankles beneath the picnic table.

"Then why, Emory? You're so close to graduating, all you gotta do is show up, but instead you're jeopardizing all your acceptances to these elite universities after I bent the rules to let you bring the child to class with you and all your teachers been real accommodating with your absences, but it's just gone too far. We can't help you if you decide you don't wanna help yourself. So what is it? Hmm?"

I stopped whistling at my fingers and looked at her.

Last week was supposed to be decision day, when all the colleges I'd gotten into demanded I give them a response, but apparently something went wrong with federal aid and now half the schools were emailing, saying I didn't have to commit until June. It didn't matter much either way since I wasn't going to any of them, but Mrs. Simmons seemed to still think I was.

"There're more important things than college, Mrs. Simmons."

I was ready for her retort, her scolding that I was being smart with her, but instead she said, "I agree." She leaned closer to me across the table. "But I remember the first week you came back to school when there wasn't nothing more important to you. Besides, of course, this child. But the two don't have to be mutually exclusive. Even I didn't think it was possible, but I've seen where you gettin' into. University of Miami, Washington, Michigan, Stanford, UC Santa Barbara."

"I'm not going." I couldn't look at her and say it, so I kept my eyes on my salmon nails as they hardened and began to reflect light.

Mrs. Simmons shook her head. "The best way to fail is not to try."

"Oh, please, you read that in one of your magazines?" I spit.

"My what?"

Mrs. Simmons was so righteous, coming to me saying I was giving up when I was fighting harder than I ever had to give my child a life I would've wanted if I was him. She had no right to judge me.

Mrs. Simmons sighed and composed herself again. "I've spoken with your teachers. Come to school on Friday, pick up your final exams, complete them and turn them in by the next Friday, and they'll honor your grades from the beginning of the semester. This is your chance, Miss Reid. Take it, and that gold sash is yours. Take it and head off to one of these colleges and prove to all the folks like me that you're bigger and better than we ever could've imagined. Take it."

She stood up, lifted her skirt, climbed over the bench, and smoothed her skirt again. "Alright, then. Congratulations on your engagement, Miss Reid." She nodded at me. "And I think your nails are cuter than a June bug."

With that, she smiled, turned, and marched her heels back through the mud and into the school building, leaving me with my salmon nails, a clever scolding, and Jay's horn blaring out across the clearing.

◆ ◆ ◆

Crystal's daughter was a biter. We all knew it, and when she wasn't biting us or our kids, it wasn't a problem. She only bit when she was upset or overwhelmed and so we yelped when she bit the way you'd train a puppy and worked on deep breathing, all of us wheezing in a breath together and humming as we released it. When that didn't work, Crystal moved Cece away from the group as soon as she saw that twitchy look of a toddler about to let herself loose on you.

Crystal was one of the more composed of us, didn't get ticked off easy like Simone or me—we got madder than a couple of wet hens more often than I think neither of us cared to admit. But not Crystal.

She didn't want people thinking of her like that, was always trying to make up for the life she'd lived and the life she'd made. It was beautiful, but it was also kind of sad.

Anyway, it was just me and Simone and the kids at the dune lake, our little group more distant than ever, when Crystal came up on us sobbing. We thought maybe Cece had bit her real hard, but Crystal was used to Cece's bites and we didn't see any blood on either of them, which was how we knew it had to be worse.

"What's wrong?" Simone hung up the towel she was washing on the clothesline and wove through it straight to Crystal. "You hurt?"

Crystal shook her head and Cece got close to her ma and kissed her cheek with a wide-open mouth, except she tasted the tears and she must've liked them 'cause then she started just sucking on Crystal's cheek. It made Crystal laugh for a moment before she put Cece on the ground and resumed her crying.

"It's not important." Crystal choked on her own words.

"Oh, please," I said. "Clearly it's got you in a fit."

Simone added, "Can't be sillier than Em callin' 'bout a dead whale at six in the morning."

I shot Simone a glare and then we waited for Crystal to gather herself and begin talking and when she did, I felt both me and Simone's anger curdle and boil up like milk on a too-hot burner.

Crystal was applying to all kinds of jobs, and she'd been spending time calling a career center to help coach her on how to prepare for interviews and format her résumé, real grown-up stuff like that. When she had interviews on the phone, she'd need a place to go do them while she was still watching Cece, and with Simone and the twins going on all kinds of trips in the truck, Crystal was left spending her days at the nearest park.

There were only two real parks in Padua. One had nothing but a rusty swing set and the other park had a whole play structure with a slide and everything. So everyone in Padua went to the park with the structure, which meant it was always crowded with kids and all kinds of different mothers and fathers and the occasional nanny too.

Two weeks before she came to us crying, Crystal'd been on the phone while she sat on the bench at the park and Cece was in the sandbox. Cece was only two and there were kids twice as big as her and babies half her size crawling and waddling and running all over the park while she sat in the sandbox pouring sand in and out of a plastic cup Crystal gave her. She was minding her own business and then somebody's four-year-old came up and grabbed the cup from Cece.

Cece did what anybody would've done and tried to take her cup back. But the four-year-old was bigger and stronger than her and Crystal was on the phone, so Cece did the only thing she knew how to: she bit. The kid shrieked and Crystal rushed over, but Cece was all fired up at that point and while Crystal tried to talk to the four-year-old's ma, Cece turned to the next closest child and bit them too. The sandbox was evacuated and Crystal left holding Cece close and walking her through her deep breaths.

Today Crystal had another interview, so she went back to the park with Cece. Cece'd got a good night's sleep and she was fed and happy, so Crystal wasn't worried about biting, 'specially 'cause Cece hadn't bit no one at all that week.

But when they showed up at the park, all the other mothers started whispering and some of them went up to their kids and said something, pointing to Cece. Crystal ignored it and unleashed Cece on the playground. Cece beelined for the sandbox, excited to dig. When Cece climbed into the sandbox, all the other kids climbed out, looking over at their mothers for approval.

Cece, not wanting to play alone, left the sandbox to go play on the structure, looking into the tunnel and waving to the two toddlers on the other side. The toddlers waved back, and they all started crawling into the tunnel to meet in the middle, but then their mothers ran up and yanked their toddlers back, taking them as far away from Cece as they could get. Crystal watched it happen, waiting for her call, and when her call came through, Cece had just been shunned from the swings too.

Crystal didn't know what to do but she knew you don't leave your child sobbing and looking around like a stray cat, so she told the interviewer she would need to reschedule, hung up, and raced over to Cece. She took Cece to get a frozen yogurt at McDonald's and then they came right here, to us, when Crystal started crying and wouldn't stop.

I turned to Simone, met her eyes. "Wanna drive or should we walk?"

Simone's voice was firm. "Let's walk. The towels still gotta dry."

The other Girls arrived within the hour. Strollers were unfolded. Children strapped to chests. Palms latched to one another. Shoes tied. All of us, except Adela of course, began our march to the park.

It wasn't that far but it was enough time to add heat to the boil and by the time it was in sight, all of us were prepared to do what had to be done in the name of the little girl who didn't know the power of her own jaws. We were ten years younger than most of the mothers, had backpacks and exposed midriffs and children clawing at our legs, and we knew we scared them. A whole coven of us stampeding toward them, Crystal and Cece at the back, the only ones cowering.

"Which ones did it?" I called back to Crystal.

"All of 'em."

All of 'em. We split up, pairs of us approaching each mother scrambling to pack up her diaper bag and get the kids home, most of 'em to the other side of the highway, but they weren't fast enough. These were the aunts, the sisters, the mothers of those seaside girls I used to think were my friends, and I thought this'd be the perfect opportunity to get back at all of them too.

I went up to a woman who I used to see at church when I was a kid, her fingers still disturbingly long as they now gripped a three-year-old's hand. Simone was beside me.

"Shame on you," I hissed.

"Excuse me?" The woman was trying to counter with the same husk, but I saw those long-ass fingers shake. "I didn't . . . you mean the biter? I'm not about to let my child catch rabies from somebody on a playground."

I spit on the ground at her feet. "Then why don't you just come out and say it to a mother's face instead of making your child do all the work for you?"

Simone was controlling herself in front of the twins, but I could feel the rasp of rage coming off her. "Don't be messing with nobody's kid."

"You threatening me?" The lady whipped her hair behind her shoulder.

I laughed. "You don't got ground to stand on. None of us forgot about what you did with Johnny in a public outhouse on a Thursday before sunset. In fact, Lisa Cobb got a photo, if I'm not mistaken, and Lisa was good friends with my ma back in the day, so I'm sure she'd be happy to share it. Your husband the one with the adult video addiction, huh? Bet he'd love something new to get off to."

The long-fingered lady snapped her mouth closed and dropped her child's hand. "Let's go, McKayleigh. We'll be spending our time at the other park from now on." She threw her bag over her shoulder and began stomping off, the confused child scampering after her.

By the time we got done talking to all of them, the park was empty. It remained that way the next time Crystal came by for an interview. The only people left were the ones who had heard the story of us Girls coming up, prepared to beat the asses of half the mothers in town, and decided they wanted to be on the right side of history. They took turns on the swing sets, and Cece happily raced all over the big playground, where no child feared her, taking her deep breaths and never biting again.

This was how us Girls reunited. In the defense of Cece's teeth.

# ADELA

E LOVES ME, Noni. What's the problem?"

"The problem is you too young to know nothing about love. And even if you did, today don't got nothing to do with love. It's about you and that baby."

Noni wrung her towel and swung it over her shoulder. She'd just gotten out of the shower and her robe was still on, the entirety of the hang in her left breast visible, and she was following me around the house as I packed my bag, went looking for my shoes.

A month ago, I would've been on Noni's side. A month ago, I wouldn't have even let Chris come to my sonogram. But then the Girls looked at me like I was a dead fish too rotten to even bother eating and I missed having someone's hand to hold. I missed Chris. We made up in the Waffle House parking lot and he kissed each of my temples, played with the small hoop of my earring, and promised to give us a good life. And I believed him.

I set my jaw. "Well, he loves me *and* the baby. It's just a doctor's appointment, why are you so upset?"

Noni followed close behind me as I exited the kitchen to the dining room. "Your daddy left you with me and I promised I'd take care of you. You think I can just let you go to a sonogram with some boy I don't know? You're thirty-eight weeks pregnant, Adela."

I found my slides under the coffee table and slipped them on. It was too hot for sweatpants and I was too big for my shorts, so I was wearing a huge dress I sewed myself last week. It looked like a tube, but at least I could feel the air coming up through it.

"Chris is a good guy and he's got a car and he'll bring me right home after. It saves you a trip to Tallahassee and it gives him a chance to see his baby. Don't you want that?"

Noni flung the towel on the floor. "He is not that child's daddy. He's some boy you picked up from Lord knows where and sure he's pretty, but the pretty boys are the most dangerous ones and everybody know it. Especially one way too old for you. What is he, twenty? Twenty-five? It's not normal for somebody like that to want a pregnant girl, Adela."

I stopped and looked back at her. "You don't think somebody could want me?"

Her glare eased up and her head tilted. "That ain't what I said and you know it. Just let me take you. I got myself smelling fresh and everything." She smoothed the edges escaping her wig cap.

Noni didn't think anyone could want me, looking like this. Smelling like chlorine and pickle juice. "You're not that different from Dad at all."

I slung my bag over my shoulder and hurried to the front door, slamming it in Noni's face behind me. By the time she got the screen door unlatched, I was already in the passenger seat of Chris's car, and before he could squeeze my thigh the way he always did, I was telling him to drive and we were off on the slow crawl of the highway, Padua passing us by before I even noticed the turn of pines to Spanish moss.

◆ ◆ ◆

Chris held my hand the whole time we sat in the waiting room, which ended up being an entire hour because I got the time wrong and made us arrive far too early. It didn't matter, though, because Chris wasn't mad. He loved me the way the Girls couldn't. Unconditionally, without pause.

I was pretty sure he loved me more than anyone else in the world ever had, more than any coach or friend or mindless crush. Even with all his faults, I knew that we were meant for each other and he was going to stand by me, the way anyone who really cared about me would. He would take care of me and our baby and that was enough, I'd decided. That would have to be enough.

When Chris glanced over, his eyes stayed stuck on me. That was what I reminded myself of when I forgave him: he might not want to be a parent who holds a screaming child or wakes up in the middle of the night, but he would love me, so I could do it. He would love me, look at me, adore me even when I was crusted with fatigue and soggy in breast milk. Wasn't that enough?

"Woods," a woman in scrubs called.

I pushed myself into a stand and held on to Chris's hand as we followed her through the door and down the hallway.

"Nice to see you again, Adela. I'm Melissa and I'll be your sonographer for the day. I know you make a long trip, and we try to schedule your appointment with your OB for the same day, but it might take an hour or so for me to get the results to her. Good news is, we've got a TV in the waiting room."

Melissa was the same sonographer as last time, her hair a new shade of burgundy, but her face still plump and young. She never judged me to my face and so I liked her.

Melissa made me step on the scale and I choked on the number. I'd never been so heavy before and I wasn't sure it was all the baby. What if this was my body now? What if Chris hadn't realized I could grow big and not deflate?

"Alright, Adela, you just sit down here and we'll take your blood pressure." I sat down in the plastic chair and she wrapped my arm in the band, squeezed the little balloon until my arm went numb. Just as I thought I couldn't stand it any longer, the band loosened, and I was free.

"Looks great. We'll get you all set up in the room now."

She led us farther down the hall and into an empty room. There were so many brochures, so many photos of small white babies and mothers with sparkling teeth.

I sat down on the examination table and Chris sat in the empty chair. Melissa began tapping at the computer and after verifying my name and birthday, she turned to Chris.

"It's nice to meet the father. How you feeling, Dad?"

I could tell this made Chris proud and I couldn't help feeling a sense of accomplishment too. I'd put together a whole family, someone my baby would call Dad.

"Ready to see babygirl," Chris said.

Melissa smiled. "Well, we're going to get Adela in a gown in just a minute and then we'll get to it, but we just need to go over some things first, mm-kay?"

Chris nodded.

Melissa turned to me. "Everything going okay in the pregnancy? Feeling movement? Any new symptoms?"

Chris cut in. "Yeah, we feelin' the baby. She kickin' like crazy."

I nodded. "I'm just worried because I've been getting these nosebleeds every night and then I wake up and I feel like my eyes are, like, swollen shut."

Melissa nodded, typing even as she stared at me. "The nosebleeds are very normal at this stage, just sit up, pinch your nose, lean forward, and let it pass. As for the swelling, you're what, thirty-eight weeks now? Some edema is very typical toward the end of pregnancy and as long as your blood pressure is looking good, we're not worried. I'll make a note to the OB and when you meet later, you can talk about some options for symptom management."

"Okay." I'd already forgotten what she said to do about the nosebleeds and I wished Noni was here to take notes. "I just really don't want to have to do bed rest and miss the last two weeks of school."

Melissa laughed. "You're the only teenager I've ever had who doesn't want a doctor's note saying they don't have to go to class.

Unfortunately, we can't exactly predict when your baby wants to make an appearance. Your OB can discuss induction with you if you'd like, as well as her colleague in Padua Beach, who will most likely be on call for the birth. For now, let's get you in this gown."

Melissa opened a drawer and pulled out a paper gown. I was up to the XL drawer and I hoped Chris didn't notice.

"I'll let you put that on and I'll be back in a few minutes."

Melissa shut the door behind her, and I stood, turned my back to Chris even though he'd seen me naked so many times before, and pulled my dress off. I tied the gown in the front and then sat back on the table, pulling the other paper sheet over my lap.

"You excited?" I asked him.

When I looked up, though, Chris's face was a labyrinth of lines and his eyes were a glossy prism. He looked like he was solving a math problem and getting all mixed-up.

"Chris?"

He snapped his head up. "Thirty-eight weeks," he said. "I ain't a genius or nothing, but thirty-eight weeks ago was almost two months before we got together. I heard of it being off a few weeks and all, but months? You don't mistake months."

I tried to stay calm, shrugged. "It happens. Maybe they got the wrong date."

Chris shook his head, looking everywhere but me. "I thought you was looking bigger than you should. I didn't wanna say nothing, but it ain't normal to not fit no clothes if you only seven months. You bigger than Simone was and she had twins up in there."

I wanted to hide behind a curtain the same spearmint green as the one in the hospital, but the paper gown was too small and my protruding belly button poked out and I was so exposed. "Stop, Chris." I couldn't hold back my tears for long.

"Me stop? You been lying to me for months. That's not my baby."

"No, she is. She's yours," I pleaded. "You promised."

Chris stood, twitching at the joints. "I promised I'd take care of my child. That ain't my child, ain't my problem. You can't be out here expecting me to raise somebody else's baby. Fuck that."

He paced to the other side of the room and kicked at the metal drawers till they dented. The ring echoed through the room and then a knock came on the door, Melissa walking in with her cheeks still raised like there was something to celebrate.

"Please, Chris," I begged. "She's yours in every way that matters."

"She ain't mine. I already got kids, real blood, Adela. You go be somebody else's skank-ass baby mama."

I tried to stand but I couldn't lift myself off the table without exposing everything. "Don't do this. You drove me here. Don't go."

He walked out like he didn't know me at all, like I was the ghost he ignored in the corner of a dark room, pushing Melissa into the wall on his way out. My whole body felt like it did during the blood pressure machine, squeezed so tight my skin tingled and I wasn't sure I could make it another moment. But it didn't release like the machine. It was a tight fist still clenched around me, and he was gone.

# SIMONE

ERE, IN PADUA, our sand's whiter than salt. Whiter than bone crushed to dust and softer too, and it's not 'cause the earth was made that way or 'cause there was some special rocks on the Emerald Coast or nothing that simple.

Warmth started it. Millions of years ago, the icy Appalachian Mountains teetering above us started to melt, causing all this frozen quartz hidden in the ice to tumble and chip and erode down silt mountains till those specks finally floated into a melted river and down into the Gulf. Over the next millions of years, that magnificent green ocean ground up all the quartz into pieces so small they only made sense together, as one impressive white beach bleached by the sea itself.

I like to think of sand like love. The thing that's true 'bout both of 'em is you only ever see them for what they look like when they're right in front of you. And isn't that sorta reckless? To only believe the thing in front of your face, not knowing nothing about where it came from.

I loved reckless once.

I took what was right in front of me 'cause it looked something like love and I didn't know different and that's what gets us sometimes. We think we're loving when, really, we're believing. We're choosing to believe the sand was always white 'cause when we sink our toes into it and the heat surrounds our feet like warm hands, it feels like it can only be God's hands. That there wasn't no way it wasn't created with the earth itself.

But real love—love that you see every glimpse of like knocking on the door of a glass room—shows all of itself before it materializes solid. Look close enough and you see your own face, your own hands leathery and creased. Step back and you see the whole world. The quartz tumbling down the mountain to make sand as white and soft as crushed bone.

When you young and chasing a life worth feeling, blind love is necessary. It keeps you from looking too close and finding out maybe it wasn't love at all but something that felt more important than love. Hope.

But I'm growing. I was growing when I sat inside that tub and made a choice when before there wasn't none to make, when I took my babies to see the planes, when I answered Adela's call.

The drive to Tallahassee felt short. It always does when the twins are with me, talking like they full grown till I almost forget they children.

I wasn't goin' there to save Adela or befriend her or tell her off. I went 'cause I knew things now she couldn't and she didn't have to believe me, but she deserved to love knowing more than I did, knowing more than maybe she wanted to, young as she was.

When I pulled up at her doctor's office, she was sitting on the curb in a strange rigid dress that was splattered at the front in what I knew could only be her tears. She didn't look at me when she climbed into the truck.

"One of you sit on her lap, okay?" I told the twins. Lion clambered onto Adela's legs and started bouncing on her knees.

"Do the game!" he said to her.

Adela didn't move or speak. She stared out the window through the narrow openings of her eyes.

"She not feeling well, baby," I told Lion. "How 'bout you and Luck go on and sleep now and I'll wake you when we home."

Luck protested for the both of them and I ain't argued 'cause I knew five miles down the road they'd both be slumped against me and Adela, past the point of fighting sleep. A car could do that to a child in ways nothing else could and during their younger years, I was so grateful to the truck for those hours of lulling my babies to sleep, I kissed its side before climbing up into it every night.

With the twins asleep, it was just Adela and me riding the shake of an endless flat highway back to Padua. I could feel she was trying not to cry beside me, could feel it through the seat and up into the creaks of her skeleton, where her jaw locked and refused to let go.

"You can cry," I said.

She laughed. "With you? We both know I can't."

I loosened my grip on the steering wheel, passed it into my left hand, and reached across Adela to open the glove compartment with my right hand. I handed her a semi-clean rag.

"Do it now so I don't have to feel you shaking next to me for the next three hours."

She sobbed so hard it turned into coughs, hacking up her hurt and waking Lion up. He patted her knee and went back to sleep slumped against her chest. Adela cried so hard I knew her throat throbbed, and then, when her cries faded, she pressed her chin down on Lion's head and wrapped her arms around him, the way I used to do when I was sad. He burrowed deeper into her chest. Adela's jaw went loose.

"He left me alone. Didn't even try to make sure I got home safe. What kind of guy leaves you alone hours from home when you're nine months pregnant?"

"One who wasn't never really there in the first place."

"I hate him."

I smiled, soft with the slippery past. "You'll go back. He'll call you, come askin' 'bout if you around, and you'll go back."

Adela shook her head. "He found out it's not his baby."

"You think he really gives a shit about that baby?"

"You don't understand. He was so happy when he found out I was pregnant."

I switched into the right lane and watched a motorcycle whip around and pass me by without another thought.

"I thought so too. But it ain't the baby that gives him a high, it's you. He thinks he got another piece of you and he feels big, important. His baby or not, the second it's born, he wasn't gonna care no more anyway. He'd play with the baby every once in a while, sure, but you, you the young thing no one else can have that he wants. And when he calls, and he will, you gon' answer."

"I won't," she squeaked.

"I don't blame you. But let's be honest now, Adela, 'cause all the lying only gets you sitting on a curb in a city you not from cryin' 'bout a man who thinks it's okay to fuck a child. This won't be the first or last time this week or month or year you push him away only to let him pull you into his tide again, seaweed wrapped around your ankle, always tugging, but this the first real time you found out it was possible to hate him, to return to your own water. After all that heavy, don't you feel like you could float? When he calls and you answer, you should remember that, Adela. 'Cause one day, maybe it'll mean more than the lure of his smile."

Adela leaned her head against her seat belt till it cut into the skin of her cheek. "Why did you even come? You don't owe me anything."

"Why did you even call me? We both know you coulda called your grandmama or a taxi or your parents. Somebody woulda come got you. But instead you called me."

She shrugged. "You weren't going to ask a million questions."

"That ain't it. You didn't want to call somebody whose opinion mattered. 'Cause then you couldn't justify why you'd go back with him. You know I'm right."

"That's not why."

"Then tell me."

"Maybe I called because you're the only one who knows him like I do. Maybe I wanted to hate him with somebody. I don't know why I called you, I just did. Just like I don't know why you answered."

I was so exhausted from lookin' at people look at me and seein' the same thing they always seen: metal bars on the trailer windows, my molars instead of my gums, a forest too menacing to wonder whether it might be hiding heavenly green. I grown tough in the face of chronic icy stares, made callus out of what was once chaste skin. I had to. That was all they saw of me anyway.

But I was tired, so tired, and for once, I wanted to drop the mask and return to the pure I must've been before I saw the looks. Before I saw all these people seein' me as only the pain they expected me to stir up within them.

I sighed. "I know you might not think so, Adela, but I'm not a bad person. For a long time, I've lived my life according to who I owe or who owes me, but it don't help you get nowhere. Sometimes it's the people that do something for you despite the fact they don't owe you nothing that changes everything."

I glanced over at Luck, whose head was now resting in the crease of my hip, and I could no longer find the missing patch of her hair in the rest of it. "Besides, we need to talk about Emory."

◆ ◆ ◆

They say it takes a village, but sometimes an extra hand or two is enough. I had to admit I missed what it was like to have another person hold one child while the other rested on me, and the twins trusted Adela. I hated it at first, but now I was starting to think I'd gotten it all wrong.

The Girls and me, calling when we needed to 'cause nobody else gave a shit about us, but never calling when we wanted. When was the last time I'd told them I loved them, played a game not for the prize?

"Emory thinks she has to marry him."

"Your brother?"

I nodded. "I love my brother and I know it'd make him happy, but she don't want that. Jay found all these letters, college acceptances, in the trash. She won't even hold on to the envelopes. It's not like I care if she goes to some university, but I don't think we can let her live a life she don't want."

"I can't change that. She won't talk to me."

"You right. She won't talk to you. She wants you to talk to her. Don't you get how much she loves you? You don't gotta love her back, you don't gotta step in and save her. Just make her think twice. Don't we all deserve to have a second chance at choosing the thing that'll choose us back? The real version of us, not the one we slip into when we think everybody watching, but who you is when it's just you and your babies and the moon. Don't you get that?"

Adela turned her whole head to me, so I could see the tip of each ear. "What about me? What about what I choose? You think I wanted to come here? I had everything I could've imagined, I had a life ready for me, and now I'm starting over and everyone I meet loves me until they don't.

"You think I wanted this baby? Emory wanted hers. She *chose* this. It's not my fault. I was going to choose something different, but they wouldn't let me. I was *sent* here, Simone. And just because I was too afraid to take some herbs and risk bleeding out like you doesn't mean I didn't try to have a choice. I used to have muscle that clung on to me tighter than a child ever could. I used to have friends who woke up at dawn and swam beside me in a pool bigger than your whole town. I used to have everything. I know you think it's so hard for you and Em because this was all you got, but can you imagine losing something even bigger? You don't know what I've sacrificed just being here. Why do I have to save you all too?"

Lion must not've liked her voice's rising growl. He grunted in his sleep, and I resisted the urge to match Adela's pitch, to flash my teeth and show her how they'd sharpened. But I remembered the hospital and the fallout of a snarl and sealed my lips before I spoke.

Suddenly, I was calm. "It's funny, you the only one who's ever tried comparing your life to ours. This whole town knows you different, Adela. Not 'cause your parents rich or 'cause you wear your hair out or 'cause you went to some fancy school and swam in a pool full of perfectly balanced chemicals. You different 'cause you look at us like we red tide that washed up in your sliver of ocean and now you can't swim without risking a rash. You judge us like we never had a thought about nothing but this town and you don't even bother knowing nothing about it.

"Padua Beach shouldn't even exist. We not on no map, nobody knows 'bout us but us, and every time folks pass by, they snicker at the way we live, the way we talk, the way we eat, but we keep us alive. We keep Padua goin' through generations of everybody else forgettin' we here, 'cause we know all these lonely, rotting parts are also bordered in the most green oaks you ever gonna see, ocean strips that beckon like a toddler's waiting hand, boats patched up and reinforced ten times over, but still resistant to sinking.

"We don't need you to be like us, but at least understand we not tryna be like you neither. Keep your baby. Or don't. Help Emory, or stay locked up in your grandmama's house till you give birth and get to go back to your slice of heaven. But don't judge us like you know us when you ain't even tried."

Adela went quiet. The twins had woken up and were staring between us, trying to understand what was going on but knowing better than to ask. Lion burrowed under Adela's arm and blinked.

Luck hiccuped. "I spy with my little eye something red."

Lion perked up. "It's the sunset, up there, I got it!"

She shook her head. "Nope."

"What is it, baby?"

"You, Momma. It's your mad face."

"My mad face? Momma's not mad. Adela and I just talkin'."

"No, Momma, you got the face you make when you talk to Daddy. You mad at Adela. But it's okay 'cause your mad face always go away when you talk to Adela, kinda like the sunset. Then you go back to your normal Momma face."

"What color is that?"

She giggled. "Brown, of course. Like Adela and Daddy and Uncle JJ. The only one who not brown is Emmy, but that's 'cause she pink. Not red. But not brown neither."

"Is that right?"

Lion nodded. "And Tori and Crystal and Milah brown, and April too, but she a different kinda brown 'cause she got straight hair and it grows out her head." He twisted and looked up at Adela. "Kai brown even though Emmy not. Dela, your baby gonna be brown too?"

Adela laughed, and I felt air in the truck again. Her jaw unlatched. "I don't know," she said. "We'll have to wait and see."

# EMORY

I T MIGHT BE hard to believe, but I liked church. Well, not church itself, but everything leading up to it. I'd been thinking about that a lot lately. Every Sunday, I went back to the patch of beach where the orca washed up. I thought at first it was 'cause I loved that orca, wanted to keep remembering her even if no one else did, but now I think I went 'cause I missed Grammy and Pawpaw and it was the only peaceful time of the week.

Reminded me of our good moments together. Pawpaw and me taking our slow walks to church. Grammy always left early to go hang around with the old ladies and help set things up, so it was just Pawpaw and me strolling through town, the sky still and neither of us talking. We held hands till I got too old, and then we held pinkies.

When I told them I was pregnant, we stopped our walks, stopped attending church at all. I never much liked our church itself. It was cold. We didn't sing. We didn't hum. We glanced around at each other and listened to the pastor until he made our cheeks turn pink. But now I missed it. Or at least I missed Sundays. Missed those walks, the only times I felt truly close to Pawpaw, the only times there was ever that much peace between us.

So now, when I needed a moment of open air, especially on Sundays but sometimes Wednesdays and Fridays too, I'd sneak out of the garage early, leave Kai with Jayden, and walk to the beach. Sometimes I'd hear Simone's truck roll up, but she knew better than to walk down the hill of sand to sit with me. Simone left me alone with the smooth beach, stripped of all signs the orca'd ever been here, and let me wallow.

I'd been a mother for nine months now. I'd watched his hair fall out and come back curled, watched him learn which fingers he liked to suck best, settling on the middle and ring fingers, watched him see his first tree, love his first auntie, hate the smell of beets and me right out the shower. I'd lost more hours of sleep than I could ever hope to regain. I'd wondered why anyone ever wanted to do this at all.

Still, I thanked God I could roll on the floor with him when he first started to commando crawl, and I wished for nothing but the smell of the nape of his neck after hours apart. It was a paradox, loving him, being his mother.

Sometimes I stared at him and was angry he didn't look much like me at all.

Sometimes I stared at him and was relieved he didn't look much like me at all.

I'd done it for nine months and I still wasn't sure I'd survive to the end of the year let alone the end of my lifetime. I'd heard about male lions who killed other lions' cubs when they took over a group, just for the chance at a fresh start, and sometimes I understood that.

There were moments I wanted to throw Kai across the room. Motherhood bred the cruelest of hate and still I loved everything about the me that made him, the me that held his neck in my palm every night and stayed despite his cries. The me that wanted so much for him. I loved that person almost as much as I hated the mother who resented the life he took from me.

Adela was easy to spot on a beach empty as a desert's freezing night. She waddled, clutching at the air like it'd catch her if she fell. I wished hope didn't bloom in my chest when I saw her, but it did. I desired. I loved. I tore an opening in my stomach where I thought she belonged and waited for her to fill it.

And when she made it down the beach to where I sat, struggled to find a way to sit without toppling over like a poorly constructed building, I was surprised to see her face wasn't a smattering of delusion like it normally was. She wasn't pretending. For the first time since I knew her, Adela might just tell me the truth.

"You never loved me." I meant it as a question till I said it and it wasn't one.

"Of course I do. You're my best friend," she whispered to me. At least it sounded like a whisper beside the roaring ocean.

"You know that's not what I mean."

"I know you're making a mistake."

If you've ever loved somebody and watched them tell you what you don't wanna hear, you know it'll make you spiteful in a way no stranger could. How could she question my choices when she'd chosen a man who wouldn't love her like she was a tree newly transplanted and prone to wilting?

I grabbed a fistful of sand and watched it slip from my hand back to the ground. "Go back to Tooth and stop pretending you know better. You don't even know if you want your own kid." I bruised her. I'd wanted to, till I did it, and then I wanted to take it back. "Sorry."

She ignored it even though I knew it hurt. "Don't act like you aren't conflicted too. I know you, Emory. You applied to schools you'd never even heard of just to prove you could get in and now you did and you're going to pass it all up to marry a guy you don't love?"

"I love him, okay? He's my child's father."

Adela rolled her eyes. "And you're your child's mother. Doesn't really help anybody to watch the two people Kai belongs to pretend they love each other until eventually it all falls apart and he realizes he is the reason his mom is so unhappy she doesn't even bother to brush her teeth anymore."

I ran my tongue over my teeth. They were fuzzy with plaque, and I tried to remember the last time I'd brushed them and couldn't.

"That's 'cause I got a baby to take care of, not 'cause I'm unhappy."

"Then tell me why you started dyeing your roots again when I met you and now they've gone back to brown. I like your brown hair, but you don't. You don't like yourself like this, Emory."

"So what?" I hissed. "Maybe it's not Jay or college or whatever that made me like this. Maybe it's you."

I was poison ivy bound to spread to anyone close enough to touch, but Adela didn't show any signs of itching.

"I know I hurt you. I know that. I just want you to think of yourself before you do something you can't take back. Or, if you can't think of yourself, think of Kai."

"I am." My voice cracked open like a glass in a porcelain sink. "I thought of myself so much I was gonna hurt him. I let Pawpaw look at him like he was infecting our family, I let myself forget he was more than just some stray cat I was forced to feed. I'm not gonna let him hurt like I did, growing up in a fractioned family. I won't do that to him."

Usually, Adela waited for me to stop crying. She'd wait patiently, sometimes for an hour, but she'd never console. Never touch. Never show her cards. It was part of what made me like her: she was an impossible mystery. But today she reached forward and placed her hand on the middle of my back, smoothed in circles, felt my tremor beneath her fingertips. Her hand felt different this way than when we held hands. It was firmer, more sure of itself.

Finally, she spoke. "That's not what makes a family good, Emory. You can't protect him from everything. You can't give him two parents with wedding rings on and expect that to fix it. It's your job to make peace with your mistakes. And then it's your job to try again. Buckle under the first time you get scared and how will you do this for the rest of your life? You're supposed to teach me, Em. Any day now, I'm going to feel hopeless and scared and unsure and you're supposed to show me what to do. You can't give up on yourself or you're just like every other mother who thinks she's choosing her baby when she's really choosing her own fear."

Back when I told Grammy about Matilda the snake, she gripped my wrists tight, made me look into her ghostly blue eyes, and whispered, "Don't you tell your pawpaw, Emory. He'd just about have a stroke, with all he's got goin' on. Just stay away from Ron and you'll be fine. Boys only do that when you tempt 'em."

I always told myself Grammy didn't mean to shut me up and make me curl in on myself. She was a woman who thought she was done rearing children and couldn't handle me making it any harder. But now I was thinking back, and Grammy was wrong for it. She did everything for herself and then said it was for the both of us 'cause that was easier than admitting she was in over her head.

"What if he hates me for it? In fifteen years, what if Kai decides I was just as bad as everyone thought I'd be and he leaves me and I'm all alone?"

Adela touched my cheek with her thumb. "Stop running from being alone, Emory. Sometimes alone is the best place to be." She smiled. "Besides, if he grows up to hate you, then you'll spend the rest of your life trying to do better. And that's more than most people can say."

Tears were still pooling in the canals of my face when Adela leaned in and kissed me. I'd never been kissed like that before. Like she didn't mean it, not really. She kissed me like someone waves goodbye, halfhearted and with the same urgency as a kettle inching toward a boil. She wanted me to know she was there, wanted me to feel her, by breath, by heat, but she didn't mean the kiss like I meant it when I kissed her in my daydreams. All of me falling into it, like a wave crashes.

She pulled away and smiled, patted her belly and told me the baby was kicking. I was embarrassed to have her see me want more but I couldn't wipe the desire from my face.

When she got up to leave, I didn't beg her to stay. She didn't ask if I wanted to come with her. She climbed back up the hill like she walked down, but this time, Adela used her hands too, clawing at the sand like a baby on all fours, her stomach low and scraping the ground beneath her.

When she was gone, I tasted the kiss. Adela always smelled like chlorine, even when she hadn't been in a pool, but beneath that, I could taste how Adela loved me. Like a new mother loves an older one, searching for something, relieved at their touch. Finding solace but never fire, because Adela did not love me the way I loved her. Like a girl loves another girl she saw across the sand, shoulders broad as a Florida sky, and found something she wanted beneath all the fatigue of need. And even though this devastated me, it did something else too. It shocked me awake.

# ADELA

SIMONE WAS RIGHT. He called a day later and I answered. He apologized and I was fragile enough to not care whether he meant it.

Simone, Emory, and the rest of the Girls didn't hate me as much as they had, but they didn't trust me either, and so I'd wander town, find them at the beach or the lake or rolled up in a parking lot laughing or dancing or talking, and I'd know from the squirms on their faces that I wasn't part of them, not really. They kept me at the outer ring of their family, where they could see and know me, but I would not know them, didn't belong to them, never would.

But I was a part of Chris. Chris still wanted me, even as he spat about the child that wasn't his whenever I asked him to put down the toilet seat or get me a glass of water. And then I'd be racing out the door screaming *never again* and he'd be calling after me to get the fuck out and only in the silence of the after, when Noni braided my hair back and then held my heavy cheek in her hand, would I remember Simone's words.

And then he'd call, and I'd answer, and we'd do it all again.

I returned from my thirty-nine week appointment and went over to his place. I tried not to upset him. I even let him take me from behind, the only way he liked it when I was big-bellied. After it was over, as I got dressed again, I heard him grunt. I twisted around to see him slumped on the mattress, glaring at my back.

He shook his head. "Why you always do that?"

"Do what?"

"Get dressed right after I fuck you, like you ain't even wanna be here. You do that with that other nigga? You let him come inside you like it's nothing too?"

I hated when he talked to me like that. It was dirty. It was crude.

"I told you, it was one time with him. And I wasn't pregnant and my bladder wasn't pulsing every time I moved and I didn't even love him like I love you, okay?" Despite myself, I leaned down to him and stroked his beard. "I love you."

He swatted my hand away. "How come he get you when you all sexy and trying and all you ever wear 'round me is joggers that don't even fit you no more?"

I shrunk back. "I thought you thought I was sexy."

He fizzed and shook. "How am I even s'posed to know, when I never seen you when you ain't all big?"

Criticism wasn't new to me. I'd been examined, weighed, whittled to the smallest imperfections that could increase the time of my free-style, the depth of my lung capacity. I did it to myself too, every time I faced the reflection that taunted me, I seethed at the sight of who I was.

But Chris was the one who was supposed to love what I didn't. Where I saw a droughted river, he was supposed to see a bubbling creek. Where I saw a spoiled swim penetrated by rainfall, he was supposed to see a chorus of water all colliding into one. Where I saw a ruined young girl, he was supposed to see a flourishing grown woman.

Tears spit from my eyes back onto him and, this time, I didn't scream at him or cling to myself, or silence my cries. This time I spoke clearly, like my voice was the drip of one well of water into another, resounding but steady.

"Never again, Chris."

He slung insults at my back as I wove through the hall and out his front door and I thought, for the first honest time, I would truly never come back.

◆ ◆ ◆

Every morning of the past few weeks of pregnancy was brutal. Waking up after only a few hours of restless sleep, to feel the full weight of me. The plumbing in the basement bathroom was broken and old sewage water came up anytime I turned on the faucet or shower, so now Noni and I were sharing the upstairs bathroom, and every morning I had to walk the flight of stairs before I'd even put my contacts in.

I was sleeping less and less, my back spasming, my eyes itching to open in the deep night, the baby punching me from the inside, and so I rose earlier and earlier until I was up before Noni even left for work most days. Today I sat up in bed until the sun rose to light the basement silver, and then threw the blankets off me. I clawed for the staircase banister, used it to guide myself up the stairs, and reached for the bathroom doorknob, pushing it open.

Noni yelped. I could see her blurry figure by the shower, standing on the bath mat, a blue towel wrapped around her. "Knock before you come up on a grown lady in the restroom," she panted, clutching her chest.

"Sorry, I just need my contacts." I felt for them on the vanity counter and breathed relief when they settled in my eyes and everything became clear again.

Noni had switched her towel out for her robe and was cleaning up the plaits on the side of her head before she placed her wig on for the day. I started to wash my face, a six-step process that used to take two minutes and now took twenty since my pregnancy breakouts began. Noni came up beside me and started to powder her face.

I watched her, the way she traced the lines of her skin, the way she still glowed after all her years, and then I saw myself again. I looked worn, swollen, unkempt, and it didn't seem to matter what makeup I put on or how I did my hair. Chris was right, I didn't look like I used to. I wasn't what I had promised him I'd be. For the first time since

I'd left his place yesterday, I was contemplating going back. Maybe it wasn't fair of me to be angry with him. Of course he was disappointed.

"Wipe that look off your face." Noni tsked.

"What look?"

"Disgust. Like something rottin' right in front of you. I don't see nothin' but life in that mirror."

Noni continued to put on her makeup, lining her lips, placing her wig, and I just stared. I didn't know if I could believe her. She had to see me and feel just an ounce of disgust too. They all must. But Noni was honest, if nothing else. She hadn't lied to me yet.

"Noni?"

"Hmm?"

"Do you think I'm pretty?"

Noni put her lipstick down, her mouth plum now. "Lord knows you're much more than that."

"But . . . you think people like me? The way I look, I mean."

I watched Noni find me in the mirror, her eyes slate as they dropped down to stare at mine through the glass.

"What you think someone liking how you look gonna get you? Far as I know, nobody liking how you look mean you loved or fed or got a roof over your head. Truth is, always gonna be somebody in this world who like how you look and somebody that don't and neither of 'em gonna change nothin' about who you is."

I shook my head. She was being nice, but that wasn't how it worked. "If people like how you look, then you're more likely to succeed. Have you ever seen an ugly millionaire?"

"You ever seen a happy one? I don't know where you got this idea that if you pretty and rich you gon' be successful, but I known a whole lotta people in my life, Adela, and success don't got nothin' to do with money."

"Dad says—"

Noni turned to look at me, not through our reflections but really, truly at me.

"Your daddy works for people that make they money off protecting companies full of folks so sad inside they go ripping off any poor soul they can find just so they can make a couple extra coins. And then they go on and hire somebody like your daddy to cover it up so they can make everybody forget they got holes bigger than they fists inside them and they not afraid of using those fists on their poor wives' faces just to get rid of all that emptiness. You listen to me now." Noni looked at us both in the mirror, four silver eyes in the sterile bathroom light.

"Beauty don't never got nothing to do with it. You think your great-great-grandmother got freed 'cause she pretty? No, she freed herself with her own two feet, a whole lot of luck, and the will to have something just a hair bit better for her babies, even if it meant living in the swamps of Florida. Beauty ain't nothin' but a scapegoat for some dollars. That's why they gotta say Black folk ain't beautiful, 'cause they worried then they gotta pay us. You know why I told your daddy he could send you to me?"

"So no one at home would know I was pregnant."

Noni tilted her head in the mirror. "That's why they asked to send you, that ain't why I said yes. I wanted you here 'cause I needed you to know where we came from. I wanted you to know this land, understand the way the earth in these parts works. Sand's not like nothing else in this world. It can't die. It can condense and blow away and erode, become unusable or inhospitable, but every grain and molecule of sand that's out there on the beach or in this backyard or in between your great-great-grandmother's toes still exists somewhere out here. Might be hidden or underwater or all the way in your daddy's old suitcase in Indiana, but it don't never disappear.

"Your parents real concerned 'bout what this child means, so is this town, this country even and don't get me wrong, I care 'bout what happens to that baby, but I wanna make something real clear to you, Adela. You can add new sand on top of the old sand and you can sew all kinds of new clothes for a child that don't exist yet and you can find some boy who wants to give you a life that sounds a little more acceptable, but none of that makes the old sand go away.

"And you can make yourself look any way you want to, but if you think it's gonna get the hurt inside you to disappear, you sure wrong. So if you asking me if I think you'd be prettier if you was skinny as a reed, you askin' the wrong person. I don't much care if you skinny or pretty, and don't you start thinking they the same thing, but I sure as hell always gonna think you prettiest when you breathing, when you fed and housed and happy."

Noni's foundation was striped in bare skin and the mirror suddenly looked dusty and ancient, like it had lived so many lives and shown so many people themselves and I was just another in its history, to be consumed and thrown back in my truest form. I wanted to turn to Noni and ask for a hug, but I wasn't sure what would rupture if I did.

"How do I be happy?" I whispered.

Noni turned back fully to the mirror and took her bottle of homemade perfume and spritzed it on her face, neck, wrists, rubbed it on each inch of visible skin, and then turned to me, spraying a cloud of it in front of my face. Eucalyptus and ocean water. She clicked her tongue as she did this and then sighed.

"Eat the sand. I don't mean you should go out to the beach and spoon sand into your mouth, though I'm sure it's full of all kinds of good things. I mean that if everybody always shoveling new sand to cover old shit that always gonna be there, then you best find a way to make that old shit really disappear. Can't nothing go away till you stare it in the face"—Noni pointed to herself in the mirror—"so you eat the sand and somewhere inside you, it'll make itself known and you'll reckon with what's been done and be able to do somethin' different when you shit it out."

I laughed, wiped my cheeks, and found the tears sparkling on my hand.

"Can I tell you something, Noni?"

"Course you can."

"I think I know what I want to do. With the baby."

When our eyes met in the mirror now, and then flitted to look at ourselves, I could see what she meant. Swollen and balmy, scarred and fatigued, when you peeled it all back these were the same eyes that looked into every face I'd ever loved, same hands that Kai and Luck and Lion reached for, same skin that had been pulled and pressed and pummeled by Simone and this world and, most of all, by me, and nothing I did or didn't do would change that.

Maybe the purest part of me couldn't be seen in the falsehood of a mirror or the glare of a man. I was all covered in sand and the one thing that's true about sand is it's a bitch to ever rid yourself of. Maybe I could eat it, but maybe all I needed to do was learn to live with my skin a chalky mess, my eyes a swollen truth, my body a changing thing.

"Tell me," Noni said. And I did.

That day, when Chris called to apologize again, I didn't answer. When he called ten times in one hour the next day, I turned my phone off. When he showed up at my door while Noni was at work, I listened to him knock and stopped every part of me that wanted to throw the door open. When he came back the next day, I did throw the door open. And then I saw his face and remembered every searing word he'd flung at me and slammed it shut again.

It was an undying fight, to remember he did not make me who I was, that I existed without him, but in the mornings, when I washed my face and stood in front of that mirror, I saw my skin start to dip and dimple and then I saw a smile, and it looked glorious on me. Not pretty. Not sexy. Not likable. It was more wild than that. It was what I saw in the Girls the first time I let myself love them: a fierce dedication to be what no one wanted them to be. Abundant. Knowing. Big.

# SIMONE

IF EMORY WAS gonna be stupid and get herself hitched, then we were at least gonna give her one last hurrah. Every woman deserves a bachelorette party that makes her wonder if she even wants to jump the broom at all.

It was prom weekend, so even more reason to take Emory somewhere far away. If she was gonna refuse to do things the rest of us wished we'd gotten the chance to do, swaying with somebody cross-eyed in a poorly lit auditorium with no bump standing between you and them, then she was gonna have herself a grown-up weekend. And what was more grown than a bachelorette?

At first, when we told Emory we wanted to do something fun on prom night if she wasn't gonna go, she said no. Resisted and resisted until finally she gave in after Adela went on begging up a mountain. Emory couldn't say no to Adela and we all knew it.

The bachelorette party was gonna be the first time we were all back together in months, everyone except the youngest Girls and the kids. We left the kids, all of them except Kai 'cause Jayden was happy to have more time with him, with April and Jamilah and one big tent set up by the dune lake for the night.

We drove for about two and a half hours, and I kept having to shout back to Adela and ask her if I was really going the right way. She'd peek at the directions on her phone, careful not to let none of the other Girls see, and then tell me, "Yep. Just keep going."

So I kept on. On and on and on, till finally Adela yelled, "Turn left up here," and I whipped left, sending them skidding in the truck bed.

I watched what had been open Florida, or maybe Georgia, or possibly even Alabama—there was no distinction out here—collide with rural thick bush and marsh, bayous and air that drenches, borders having no stake in this mess of land. There wasn't even no separation between truck and sky and body out here, driving beneath a sky ceiling in a tangle of trees.

I slowed down as the road beneath me became dirt and then, finally, Adela told me, "Stop, right over there."

The truck rolled into a clearing in the middle of the forest, and I could hear music faint and floating through the trees. I parked beside other cars, but there was no people, no clear path to where the music was coming from or what would be beyond the curtain of trees.

I hopped outta the front seat and even though I was starting to think this was a bad idea, starting to consume myself with thoughts of Luck and Lion at home with two fifteen-year-old girls who took every opportunity they had to make out, I couldn't let the other Girls see me panic. I clapped my hands together and held my hand out to Emory in the truck bed. She took it and hopped down.

"Where are we? If this is some weird forest prom, I'm not going any farther. I told you, I don't wanna go to prom—"

"It's not prom," Adela said. She was beaming, her and her full-term belly looking like she'd won an award. "It's . . ." Adela looked to me like it was our little secret. "Your bachelorette party!"

"What? No, I don't—"

Before Emory could protest, Crystal was placing a little plastic crown over Emory's grown-out roots, and Tori was shimmying a little red dress on over her tank top. Emory groaned but allowed us to fawn over her, all of us talking about how she was about to have the best night of her life and to not let us forget to give her our surprise, and then Adela was stuffing everyone's phones into her big old tote bag and we was pulling Emory through the forest curtain, in the direction Adela claimed we had to go.

I felt the solid ground morph to mud and weeds as we went deeper into the trees and the only thing that kept us knowing where we was going was the hollers ahead of us and the excitement Adela radiated.

The shack came into view suddenly and without warning. It looked like it was about to collapse from the roof, country people spilling out, the outcasted South swarming around the wooden structure.

I'd never seen nothing like it. At first, we thought maybe we could just find some kind of girls' club, but nothing seemed right when we looked it up, and then I remembered Pops's cousin Randall. Randall was a little funny, that's what Pops always said, and he used to go up farther south to some hidden bar where him and all the other funny people went.

I called him up and asked him where to go. Randall didn't wanna tell me, thought I was gonna rat it out or something, but then I explained to him I had a friend who needed to see that she could be the way she was and have some fun while doing it, and so he gave me the address and I sent it to Adela and she mapped out a way to get there. Still, I was pretty sure it was gonna be low-key, maybe even near empty, just a stereo and some sad barstools and a few folks who didn't have no place else to go.

But this was something else entirely.

The shack was in the middle of thick woods, adorned in dirt and lanterns, large amps releasing a raucous beat into the night, dozens of folks rubbing up on each other on the dance floor, girls grazing in the sweet soft napes of other girls, men twirling each other till they dizzied, all kinds of bodies moving wild, letting their sleeves flutter and fall, letting themselves dance.

By the time we reached the shack, folks was pushing drinks into our hands, strangers grabbing onto our waists to pull us through the front door or into the crowd.

I thought the heat was suffocating when I first got out the truck, but inside the shack it was so much worse. Someone handed me a cup before I could even see the face attached to the hand, and I took a sip. I'd never tasted nothing like it. The liquor took you over and compelled you to reenter the swamp and release your hips in winding circles among all the freed.

But before I could return to join the parade of dancers outside, Adela grabbed my hand and pulled me and Emory to a table in the corner, both Tori and Crystal already lost to the dance floor, and when we sat down, food arrived in seconds, all kinds of bone and meat, even though none of us had ordered and it wasn't clear if there was even a kitchen in the place. I smelled smoke, though, and knew whatever we was about to eat had been roasting all day, slow and hot over a handmade fire.

"What is this?" Emory asked, pointing to the food, to the whole place. She looked scared as a squirrel in the street.

I laughed, taking a bite of the food and then stuffing it in my mouth. "Why you gotta question it? Ain't gonna hurt you."

Emory whispered in a growl, "I thought this was my *bachelorette* party. Why would you bring me here?"

Adela rubbed her belly and smiled. "We wanted you to know it's okay, Emory." She lowered her voice. "I know I couldn't return your . . . feelings, but that doesn't mean someone else won't. Where I come from, there are plenty of people who—"

"I don't have feelings," Emory spit. "I have a son. And a man who wants to marry me at home and now I'm stuck in the middle of fucking nowhere at some dyke bar. Next time, kidnap April and Jamilah. Not me."

Emory stood up and stormed out of the shack. Adela and I sat facing each other, her face fallen, her spark gone.

"It's fine," I told her. "She just needs a little time."

Adela and I kept eating, avoiding any talk of Tooth, and eventually Crystal and Tori came inside, panting like they'd just exited a marathon of sweat, and we got brought a whole other foil platter of food. Eventually somebody came up asking us to pay and I was ready to dish out at least twenty bucks for all that food, but they said, "Pay what you can, honey," and so Adela reached into her big bag and pulled out forty dollars and handed it over.

Some folks came over and joined our table and even though they never told us their names or where they was from, we spent an hour talking and cackling about some crazy lady named Stella and how she shot a peacock and that's how the bar got started. Eventually, when the liquor's haze faded enough, I remembered why we was there. Emory.

I stood and wove through the shack, stepping out back to where the dance party was still raving. And that's when I saw her.

Emory was in the center of the crowd, where people chanted and clapped and writhed, and she was facing somebody with a knotted puff of orange hair, their noses nearly touching as they rolled in time with each other, in sync with some rhythm not coming from the speakers, and I watched Emory smile and lean forward and kiss the girl and I watched the girl kiss her back, wrap her hand around the back of Emory's neck, and pull her closer.

It wasn't that I was happy Emory was stepping out on my brother, but I was satisfied to know I was right. That if she married him, she would always be on the edge of finding her lips on another's, seeing a girl and filling to the brim with regret. And that wasn't good for neither of 'em.

Emory and the girl separated and she did that familiar thing I'd watch her do every time she stared too long at Adela: glance around at anybody who might've seen, just to be sure, and when her eyes found mine, they bowed in shame and she peeled apart from the girl and disappeared through the crowd in the other direction.

I ran into the crowd and pushed through, following in the direction Emory had gone, and when I came out the other side, I saw her blond hair disappear down a hill.

I followed the trickle of water and found Emory settled beneath a cluster of willows, the swamp only a few feet away, her knees to her chest. I climbed down to the spot beside Emory and sat, realizing too late that the ground was wet and muddy and now soaking the back of my shorts.

Then Emory turned to look at me, eyelashes clumping together with sweat or tears or both, her face crooked and red.

"It's okay, Em. Jayden might be hurt at first, but he gon' get over it once he realizes—"

"I'm not telling Jay about any of this. I'm marrying him in two weeks, Simone."

I scoffed. "You can't still marry him after this."

"Yes, I can. It's my bachelorette party, right? What happens at a bachelorette party stays at a bachelorette party."

She shook her head, not looking at me but down into the murky deep of the swamp, and I ain't never been so disappointed to call Emory my sister as I was when she sat there telling me she'd let my brother beg and burn and burrow all 'cause she couldn't accept that she didn't want him.

"I'll tell him," I said.

She looked up at me and I saw hate in her eyes. I could match it, though. I could make her cower and she knew it. "He won't care. He thinks two girls making out is hot. He told me."

Emory wasn't backing down. I thought about tackling her, about scratching at her skin till she agreed to break things off with Jayden, but then I remembered who Emory was. Despite all she tried to make people believe about her, she was always gonna be a fragile thing, someone who responded better to pity and apology than she ever did to the firm truth.

"Fine," I said. "I won't tell him. But I think you should."

We heard the slosh of footsteps in mud and turned to see Adela slowly making her way down toward us, leaning back to support the dragging weight of her belly.

"We've been looking for you guys," she said, huffing as she walked. I remembered the feeling of not enough space inside me to breathe and for a moment, I missed it.

"We was just talking," I said. "You have something you wanna tell Em?"

Adela looked at me, confused, and then remembered. She took the bag off her shoulder and reached out, passing it to me. I passed it to Emory.

"Open it."

Emory opened it, looked inside, and her forehead stretched and wiggled. "Why do you want me to have all y'all's phones?"

"No, not that," Adela said. "The envelope."

Emory reached into the bag and pulled out a thick envelope. She peeked inside and then quickly closed it, stuffing it back into the bag.

"What is this? Are you trying to pay me not to marry Jay?"

Adela shook her head. "No, no, that's not what it's for."

When Emory looked at Adela, there was still raw grief on her face. "What's it for, then?"

"You." Adela smiled again, happy with herself. "For whatever you want to do. We all agreed we wanted you to have options, so this is all the money from the jungle juice. We know you don't have much to fall back on since your grandparents kicked you out, so we thought maybe this would help. As a gift."

"A gift?"

She nodded. "Call it a graduation gift, even a wedding present. If that's what you want."

"But when you deciding what you want to do, I want you to remember what it felt like, up there." I nodded toward the shack and the sound of unhampered delight. "We don't get a lotta moments when we get to forget ourselves, shed every sullied idea of what we are, and just be. You young, Em. You can be alive, however you wanna be alive. You can float and dance and kiss whoever you want, as long as you keep your baby safe and happy. Marry Jayden if you want. But only if you woulda done that anyway, without all that's happened this year, without Adela or Kai or nothing else. Okay?"

Emory stared into the bag, into the swamp, into the sphere of Adela's stomach. "Okay."

# EMORY

**I** THOUGHT I WAS ready to break Jay's heart until I saw him standing there. I was sure it was what I wanted, and it wasn't the girl at the bar or the money or even the acceptance to the only program that could make me going to college possible. It was the orca. It was death taunting me like a cat playing with its food. At some point, you gotta face it or you're just gonna starve.

If my life as I knew it was ending, in some ways had already ended, then that meant I needed to decide how I buried myself. Hold a funeral for what could've been me and then decide what my afterlife would look like. I wanted to be buried deep, somewhere where the sand was mixed with emerald and my corpse would be colored green. I wanted an afterlife among the ocean, not washed up and half eaten by birds.

It was graduation day, a week after my bachelorette party. This day I'd waited for since before Kai was even a thought floating in my mind, and now here I was. Cap and gown and child. And it was also the day I had to break my child's father's heart.

I would've done it yesterday, but when Jay showed up on the beach looking for me, he had a ring. A real one, with a tiny diamond and everything, and staring at the shiny circle that was supposed to be mine, I just couldn't do it. Not in front of Simone. Not in the garage we shared with Kai sleeping right beside us.

I had to do it here, in the grass surrounding the picnic tables where I'd first officially met Adela, a hundred yards from the field where the stage was set up and the chairs were quickly filling. A stage that would be my ending and my beginning. Simone, Adela, and Kai were somewhere in the chairs facing the stage, waiting for me. But Jay was always two feet from where I was, always following me.

And now he was standing here, and I faltered. I wasn't sure how I could do it to him.

"How's my girl?" He was so happy. Always smiling since I'd said yes to him.

While my life collapsed, Jay was just happy to share a bed with me in a church lady's garage, where he spent our evenings together talking about the place we were gonna rent in the fall and how bad he wanted Kai to have his own room. I hated to wreck his dream like Adela'd wrecked mine. But then I remembered she'd also revived it, somehow talked me into doing what Mrs. Simmons said, going to my teachers. So if all that hurt she'd caused led to this, to what I really wanted, maybe hurting Jay was only gonna help him in the end.

"I need to talk to you."

He didn't register my tone as serious, still smiled and said, "What's up, Emmy? You want me to take a video of you up there?"

I shook my head. "Actually, I think you should go. Before it starts."

"What?" Finally, his smile wavered. "I make you nervous or something?"

"No, I just don't think you're gonna wanna stay after I tell you this." I inhaled, stared him directly in the eyes. "I don't wanna marry you, Jay."

The air swirled around us. People chattered at the picnic tables. Jay croaked a single word. "What?"

"I can't marry you." I tried to be blunt, make it easy to understand.

"I heard you. I just . . . why?"

I tried to think of a way to say it that'd hurt less, but every option felt frozen and heartless, so I decided to just tell him. "You don't make me forget it all. I love you, but I don't love you any way that lasts. It doesn't consume me. It doesn't comfort me. It's a small love, Jayden. A short one. And I don't want that."

I watched Jay's whole demeanor change, like a scared tortoise retreating to its shadowed cove. His arms crossed over his chest and his smile, which couldn't seem to catch up to his feelings quick enough, remained taut and tilted upward, even as his eyes rolled and then fell to the ground.

"So what, you're just gonna fuck around and find somebody who can buy you a million-dollar house and give you some pale-ass baby?"

"No." I took a breath. "I'm leaving. To go to college. In Seattle. I accepted my offer yesterday to the University of Washington. They have a program for students with kids and they're covering an apartment and childcare. They have whole groups just for whale-watching and there's more orcas out there than anywhere else in the country. I'm gonna study them. We'll be heading west a few weeks early so I can get a job and start saving. It'll be good for us."

Jay blinked at me and I watched him boil, take one step backward, shake his head, and step forward again. "No," he said.

"What?"

"I said no. You can't just take my son like that, not across the country. You don't wanna marry me? Fine. But I'm not gonna let you keep me from being my son's father. No, Emory."

His voice had never been this low, this firm, and so I think the words slipped out of my mouth before I'd even thought them through. "Okay. You can take him."

Now it was his turn to look at me with disbelief. "What?"

I nodded, growing more sure by the moment. "Kai can stay with you while I'm in school and then he can come out and be with me on my breaks, and during the summers I'll come home and stay with one of the Girls."

"You wanna just give him up like that?"

I shrugged. It hurt, but it also sounded like the only way. Almost selfless. "I want to make a life worth living. For him. For both of us." I knew in the back of my mind that leaving him would be a steady torture, but I also knew it made sense. I would study. Kai would be taken care of by somebody who loved him as much as I did, and I wouldn't scar him by resenting all he'd ripped from me. I could do this. If I'd survived these last nine months, I could do anything.

Jay nodded. "Okay. But you gotta know I'm done, Emory. Don't expect to come back to me changing your mind about us or nothing. I'm done."

And when he turned around and walked away, I knew it'd be the last time. Not 'cause he wouldn't take me back, I knew he would, but 'cause I wouldn't ask him to. This was a death that shouldn't be undone, no matter how easy it'd be to reverse and find him mine again. Kai deserved to have a mother that wouldn't do that to him. And some days I wasn't sure I could be that mother. But I would try, and when I failed, I would try again.

◆ ◆ ◆

I was number forty-three to have my name called in my seventy-six-person graduating class. I'd been waiting in line for an hour, as they cycled through names, looking out at the chairs and seeing all these people I'd known my entire life. Parents and uncles and great-grandmas who waved to me when I used to walk home from elementary school, who fixed the plumbing when Grammy and Pawpaw's pipes burst, who glared at me when I slept with their cousin's son.

It was a mind fuck to be from a place so small, so insular that you could never be anonymous, that you could have every seat at your high school graduation filled with someone who'd seen you, thought about you, applauded or despised you.

As Mrs. Simmons called my name, I felt a rush of home, the feeling of hot breath on cold skin, at the same time as I felt suffocated by the squeeze of this place. How my name itself was known and owned by so many in this town, it was impossible to hear it and think of myself.

"Emory Reid."

I walked, heel in front of heel, dress hem bouncing at my ankles, and I heard Adela's high-pitched squeal and Simone's howl above all else. Kai laughed and his giggle rang through all the noise. When I looked down and saw them there, it was an overwhelming pride that made my feet stop just before I reached out to shake the dean's hand and accept my diploma.

There they were. My proof I could do this. That there wasn't no limit or barrier that could hold me from my big life. That it was possible for me to be it all. Maybe the only reason all these people believed otherwise was 'cause they were so scared of who they'd been when they were my age, so young and afraid, that they couldn't imagine living a life that demanded so much of them and building something worth having in it when they were just starting to think of their little selves in a world this big.

But me, the Girls, us together, we knew more than that. We knew risk and failure and worry. We knew release and reckonings and all kinds of regret. But we also knew what it was to expand beyond what you believed of yourself. And on that stage, looking at Adela holding Kai and Simone taking pictures and all those faces of folks who'd judged me but would never understand, I knew I'd never unwish myself as Kai's mother.

Even as I wished I knew enough to know he couldn't fix me, even as I wished I could've been better for him nine months ago, realized all it required to be his mother, my biggest wish was to grow. Beside him, before him, because of him. And I hoped that all those stretchings would lead me to a life full of moments of alive. Moments like this one.

I turned back to Mrs. Simmons and shook her hand, took the diploma, thanked her sincerely for the first time all year, and right before I walked down the steps and back to my seat, I took one more look out, this time over the chairs, over the picnic tables, into the distance where I could see the ocean.

Right there past the school and the highway and the beach, the sea glistened, and I could've sworn, way in the distance beyond me, an orca soared from the water, flashed its black-and-white body, and disappeared again under the glittering turquoise, as if emerging just to watch me, on this day, transcend myself.

# ADELA

**D**AD ANSWERED THE phone and when he coughed up my name, I immediately felt tears wet my cheeks.

"Hi, Dad," I whispered.

"Is it over?" he asked.

Over. Done. Completed. Had I fulfilled my responsibility of birthing a human and giving them up, had I checked off my to-do list and booked my flight back home. Could I be his daughter again.

"No, it's not." And it never would be.

I'd been thinking lately about how, even if I did what Dad wanted me to and returned home without a baby, giving it up to some nice family who'd love it, I would never be able to simply resume the life I'd been living before, like these months were a black hole in the timeline of my life.

They'd changed me. I couldn't sit poolside next to Lindsay and listen to her complaints about her hair and the renovations on their kitchen and who she wanted to ask her to prom.

Even the way I swam had changed. Instead of diving straight and narrow, kicking with precision, and cutting the water with a rigid hand, I curved with the current. I smiled as I came up for air. I cherished every ripple of the water created from the gentle cup of my fingers.

"I spoke with your coach, and he thinks if you train hard this summer and get back to peak condition, you should be ready to compete nationally by next spring."

I still felt a jolt of drive every time I thought of this thing that had been my dream for so long, but I also felt the full weight of the sacrifices that would get me there. Sometimes a dream isn't worth the life you lose on the journey there. Sometimes a dream is not meant for waking hours.

"Dad, I need to tell you something." I choked on my own spit. I was sitting on my bed, the dress I planned to wear for Emory's graduation already on, Noni already in the kitchen upstairs, the soles of her feet making music above me. "I'm not coming back."

Dad was not the laughing type. Instead, he coughed once, twice, and then composed his question. "What do you mean, Adela?"

"I'm keeping my baby. And I'm staying with Noni and she's going to help me raise her, at least until I graduate."

I'd imagined saying this to him so many times and I knew if I let him talk before I was done, I'd lose all conviction.

"I understand if you and Mom aren't willing to help us out, with money or anything. I'm going to be teaching swimming lessons here in the evenings and I'm prepared to get another job if I need to. However, I would really appreciate your support because I . . . I know I'm giving up a lot, but I'd rather not give up my family too. But I need you to know that I will, if I have to. Because I found family here too, and if I have to lose you to love my daughter well, I will."

I heaved in a breath. I waited. The other end of the line remained static, Dad's breath barely audible, and then he coughed. Once, twice.

"Adela, I don't think you understand what it means to raise a child. You're too young—"

"I understand as much as anyone who hasn't raised one yet can. And what I don't understand, I can learn. I know you think it's a transgression to a good life, having a child young, but maybe this is exactly where I'm supposed to be. Just because it's not going to be easy doesn't mean it's the wrong choice. And even if it is, it's my choice to make."

"I'm sorry, Adela, but no. Your mother and I will come down to get you and bring you back. We are not going to let you destroy your entire future."

I'd expected him to say this. "You're welcome to come visit us. But you can't make me give up my baby and I don't think you want me raising her in your house."

Dad went silent, but I could hear his jaw clicking, could imagine his knee shaking, trying to come up with some way to tie me down.

"I don't know what to say, Adela. I think this is a massive misjudgment and your mother and I are very disappointed you haven't seemed to learn any better. We will be calling your grandmother immediately and we strongly encourage you to rethink your decision."

Dad had disappeared into his lawyer talk, speaking for him and Mom even though I knew she wasn't even there.

"Okay," I said. "Noni's expecting your call and, you should know, she supports my choice completely."

Dad grunted. "I should've sent you to that boarding school instead."

"Maybe. Or maybe I would've made the same decision anyway."

We sat on the phone with neither of us talking for minutes, and the sounds of Dad's familiar breath calmed me.

"I never told you sorry," I started. "For telling everyone you were from France. There's no reason you or me or anyone should have to hide this place or pretend it doesn't belong to us, that we don't belong to it."

Dad coughed. Three times. "We won't be withdrawing our support. Financially or otherwise."

It wasn't warm or kind or sweet, but it was his way to love me.

"I love you too, Dad." And before he could cough again, before he could argue or reverse or ruin it, I hung up. I looked in the mirror, belly forming a full cone it was so big, the dress draped over it. This was what Noni was talking about: I ate sand and it was so gritty.

◆ ◆ ◆

It didn't feel like what they always said contractions felt like. I'd been in prodromal labor for weeks now, that's what the doctor said, and all of those contractions took place in my pelvis, where I expected it to hurt, but when I was standing, clapping for Emory as she graced the stage and shook the dean's hand, I felt it in my back.

It was more of a throb than anything and it only lasted for a few seconds before it released. I assumed it was just another symptom that came with passing my due date, refusing to induce labor because I'd heard that made the contractions even worse. I was three days past forty weeks and the baby was so big now that my entire body drooped. I didn't think anything of the throbbing in my back, even after it returned, became just another part of my day's pains, and I never even said a word, not to Simone, not to Emory, not to any of the Girls.

I let the current of pain seize me and then pass and by the time I realized it was not just an ordinary part of pregnancy, it was too late.

# SIMONE

JOINTS. WHERE BONE meets bone and finds a way not to grind in the crunchy tissue that cradles it. Where despite all the hard masses that make us up and should rub us raw, instead we move, wiggle, bend.

I don't know another way to explain to you how we all ended up there, on the beach, a bonfire crackling and lighting up the babies' faces as they slept, beyond the miracle of joints: Adela next to Emory next to me. Crystal, apart from Tori, who was long gone with her boyfriend and her child to somewhere we couldn't see but we could feel. April beside Jamilah, now fifteen and sixteen, now not just kissing in the night but the daytime too. Vanessa, a new Girl, her stomach swelling with another, while her eldest slept on her chest, a ring gladly resting on her finger, where the rest of her skin pooled around it.

It was Emory's graduation bonfire and she was still in her gown, her cap disappeared, looking more relaxed than I'd seen her in a long time. Not obsessed, crazed, afraid but, instead, at peace.

"So what's the plan, Em?" I passed a cup of jungle juice to her. This one was watered down but I figured we might as well see what all the hype was about, celebrate all we was and all we'd done. "You gonna buy a house or something?"

Emory laughed. "Not at all. Actually, I was gonna tell you: the money's yours."

---

The Girls all quieted around the fire, listening in. "Whatchu talkin' about?"

"It's yours. I don't need it." Emory cocked her head just a little. "Most of it, at least. I spent part of it paying Mrs. Nichols to rent a room in her house this summer. But the rest is yours."

Adela cut in for the first time all evening. She'd been unusually quiet. "I don't get it. We gave that to *you*. You're supposed to use it to do something. Anything."

Emory shook her head. "I don't need it."

"So you giving up?" Crystal looked at Emory like she was dumb, sitting there in her graduation gown talkin' about giving away free money.

"Not at all." Emory took a breath in. "I'm leaving. To go to college in Seattle."

"Seattle?" Emory, leaving. I ain't known if I should be proud or devastated. "Then you definitely need the money. You gonna need to pay tuition and buy all your books and find somewhere to live 'cause ain't nobody gonna wanna be your dorm roommate with no baby."

Emory shook her head again. "I'm going alone. Jay and I agreed that Kai should stay here with Jay and come with me on breaks. The program I'm in is paying for all my housing and I got really good aid, so I'm good. We're good." She smiled down at Kai, who was now so big, his whole body spread across Emory's lap as he slept.

"You're leaving him?" Adela breathed. We all stared at her, bewildered.

"Just for now. Jay's better with babies anyway. It all came natural to him but I just need some time, to make me a better ma. Besides, Kai won't even remember this."

I knew he would. He'd feel it swim in him forever and part of me was so angry at Emory for being so selfish and the other part of me was so in awe of her for being so selfish and I think none of us knew what to say, so we all nodded.

April spoke next. "We can help Jay. And send you a lot of pictures."

Emory smiled and then looked back to me. "So I want you to take the money. There's two thousand left. You earned it, anyway, right?"

Emory looked to the other Girls and I watched as they all nodded, reluctantly, with just a twinge of the envy we all knew well. But eventually they was all smiling, nodding, the orange fire lighting them all golden.

"Okay," I said. "You don't gotta beg me, I'll take it."

I knew I had to tell them what I'd decided now. Two grand meant it could happen, really happen, and if I didn't say it out loud, I wasn't sure I'd ever go through with it. And I had to. I had to.

Jamilah's marshmallow caught on flame at the end of her stick and she blew on it till it was just a smoking black crisp. Then she bit into it and the white cream revealed itself again. She ate all the black off and when it was just the white in the center, she passed it to April, her elbow hinging and then straightening again.

This was the way we existed together: each of us an extension of the other, all of us full. But I also knew we could be this way on our own, that knowing each other at all was what made each movement smoother, easier, and we would be able to walk the same alone.

"I'm leaving too," I said.

All the Girls' heads whipped toward me, and I saw each one give me the same looks they'd just given Emory: curled lips, dipped eyebrows, a tear that sprung at the sound.

"What?" Emory breathed. Even though she'd just said she was gonna leave herself, she looked the most hurt, like she'd expected me to always be here when she returned. You prob'ly did too, 'cause how could you imagine that I could be something different than the way you always saw me?

Joints don't always stay the same. When you was as pregnant as Adela was, as we all had been, your joints started to loosen, move, stretch, and suddenly your lower back ached and you kept rolling your ankles. Maybe the joints would all tighten back up again or maybe you'd forever feel that gnawing in your hips, a spasm in your pelvis, from all those joints you relied on to not hurt making way for new life to exit and altering everything about you in the process.

"I love y'all, you know I do," I said, and I had to stop myself from tearing up, had to pause. I didn't cry, not after the hospital. There wasn't no separation that could ever hurt like that. "I just keep thinking, what's the point of the hurricane, that bathtub, Luck's accident, if I'm just gonna let this whole town dangle the promise of home over me without never letting me reach it? I want something that's mine. I don't want my kids growing up with Tooth always pushing and pulling with them too, or they gonna look at an ocean and see a fleeting wave instead of the whole sea. They gonna look at me and see somebody who shoulda done different."

"But you have us," April said.

Crystal whispered, "Where else you gonna go?"

"Anywhere. Everywhere." I smiled, looked down at Luck and Lion asleep on a blanket right beside me. "I'm gonna take 'em on a plane. A real one. And we'll find Girls like us wherever we go."

Somewhere in the hidden corners of each town, each city, each stretch of land, we existed. It wasn't some kind of phenomenon. Girls been having babies since the beginning of time and we was just another iteration of a country needing to find a reason to reckon.

We was just mothers figuring it out and even though every year I grew older I wished I knew what I known now when my babies was little, ain't that the fate of raising a human? Bones fuse and joints break down and rebuild and eyelashes grow and fall out and we are still the same body, a body capable of the miracle of creating another one.

The Girls was still asking questions and then sitting in silence when I heard Adela's teeth grind and when I looked over at her, she stared up at me beneath a layer of eyelash and I saw that familiar knowing that your body was about to break itself open. Here, on this day of ruptures, of joints loosening and bodies preparing to let go, a baby would be born.

# EMORY

I T WASN'T SUPPOSED to happen this fast. Right? I thought so but I didn't really remember much about my own labor, just that I went into the hospital thinking I was just getting weird floaters in my eyes and next thing I knew they were inducing me for preeclampsia, said there wasn't time for us to get to the hospital with the maternity ward in the next county over and so I was left in that ER bed, the hospital noisy with sick and hurting.

For me, all I felt was that frenzy, so I'd never experienced nothing like this. Adela deep in her animal state, a guttural roar echoing from a part of her further than eyes or ears could reach.

The children woke screaming, the children woke eyes wide. We all crowded around Adela, where her hands and knees touched sand warmed by the fire and I didn't know what to do. Simone did, though. Simone's hands pressed at Adela's low back and rocked with her. Simone called out for April's jacket, for Crystal to go get the flashlight from her truck, for me to go sit in front of Adela's face and talk to her.

Adela's face was dripping in sweat and her eyes were shut, but every time she started a new roar, her eyes flashed open and she looked up at me and I swear it was the same look a predator gets before they pounce, her teeth baring.

"What do I say?" I looked to Simone, but she was busy shining the flashlight under Adela's skirt and she just shouted, "Moan with her."

Moan with her? I wasn't the one giving birth. I didn't know why I needed to play animal with her and, I had to admit, I was kind of panicking. I'd only given birth nine months before, but it felt way longer, 'cept now I could almost feel the unending pressure that felt like it was about to rip my asshole apart. How scared I was to not know what would happen next. But I couldn't tell you if it took an hour or twenty, if it was one push or ten.

I never did what Adela was doing, never growled like an animal. Instead, I cried and asked for my grammy, even though she refused to come inside the hospital, insisted on waiting outside, just me and Jay left through the whole thing.

Adela was something else, though, like she was built for this pain, knew exactly what to do. I couldn't just leave her alone like that, so I did what Simone said. Adela's mouth curled open again and out came sound and so I joined her, grew louder as she did, until we were nearly screaming, and when Adela looked at me this time, I saw her eyes focus in on my mouth, like she was concentrating, using me as a conduit for her breath.

"You're doing this," I said. I hated when the nurses told me, "You can do this," as though I had any choice. I didn't want to do it, wouldn't've kept going if I was given a choice, but the reality was that I was doing it, that despite how much I believed I couldn't, I would. I did. Adela nodded, nodded, and even as the next contraction took hold of her, she didn't stop her nodding.

"You're doing this," I said. And she was.

# ADELA

WAS DOING IT. I knew I was, even as I didn't know how this could be happening, even as I felt everything in me rotate like swallowing pool water and knowing almost immediately it was going to churn inside you all day. But even as I felt it all change, felt my body drop into something feral and otherworldly, I didn't panic.

For some reason, none of my plans seemed to matter much at all as I rocked back and forth on my hands and knees in the sand, Emory in front of me, Simone behind me, her voice steady like this had been our intention all along, to birth my baby on the beach with no light but fire and a single flashlight.

Back before Padua Beach, I thought all I needed was a pool and just enough love to make me not feel so alone: a hand to hold, but not a soul to swallow; a friend to laugh with, but not another person to tangle with, intertwine, to welcome each other as food and friction. I thought I needed a body of water to cut through in the name of speed, but I didn't know all I needed was a body to feel float.

And yet, after a whole life of misdirection and craving only the surface of hopes and dreams, the moment I realized I was not only in labor but minutes from birth, I knew with such clarity that this, here on this beach, was where I was fated to be, the desire I hadn't known to dream.

The crashing of waves with my breath, these Girls who knew all the ugliest outlines of me but understood that there was something far more soft in the center, in this town where my noni raised my dad on salty air and miracles found in the booths of a tired McDonald's. This was where the child I once thought was a burden to me would be born: into an ocean of possibility, to a mother who had grown to truly, completely want her.

"Adela, I can see her hair," Simone said from behind me. I knew I was supposed to be on my back, that's what the doctor said, but I didn't want to. I felt right, belly hanging below me, scraping sand, my hands supporting me as I swayed. Simone spoke to me and I never imagined her voice would be such a comfort. "Don't push, okay? Not unless your body tells you to. All those doctors lyin' to you, trust me, if you just breathe, she'll come out and you not gonna need no stitches neither. Just breath, keep breathing."

I didn't have any time to question it, I just kept doing what I was doing, shutting my eyes and swaying, opening them at the next wave and using the circle of Emory's mouth as a mirror of my own as I groaned. I didn't mean to make all the noise, it just came out of me. And then Emory would take a breath in and I would breathe in with her, then out again. I felt the baby's head emerge. I felt her stretch me and then I felt her still at the neck.

"Perfect," Simone hummed. "She's so pretty. She's so so pretty."

I didn't care if she was pretty, though. I cared if she was happy and fed and breathing, I cared if she felt my skin and heard my voice and knew these Girls were the reason I had become her mother.

Another contraction came and I felt the full force of this one, felt it like a wave that scoops you up and throws you twenty feet farther into the water, forces you to beg for breath. My hands shook and buckled, I screamed, I felt Emory slip her hands under my arms and hold me up, a lifeguard pulling me from the water.

Simone yelled, "That's her shoulders! Wait, here she is, she's coming, pull her out!"

I reached down through my legs and my child tumbled out of me and right into my hands. All that pressure dissipated as I sat back on my heels, held her slippery body to me, heard nothing, nothing, nothing, rubbed her back, and then one squeaky cry. I looked down at her face and let a breath out.

"That's right," Simone said. "You did it. Just the placenta left."

I did it. My daughter's wrinkled purple face squirmed on my chest and I looked into her distraught self and knew I would do it all again just to meet her. My heart swelled and burst, broke and mended, all in those moments kneeling in the sand, introducing myself to my daughter for the first time.

"I'm your mommy. I'm your mommy," I whispered.

The Girls were quiet. The kids too. They let it be just me and my baby, me and my forever, as all those fantasies I'd had of David, Chris, a gold medal, faded to an overwhelming understanding that I could not fuck up and forget to love her well.

My daughter quieted and her lips touched my skin and she slowly crept closer and closer to my breast, looking for her life source, and I did not want to cover up how she came into this world with lies, cover up my fear of doing this all on my own with a man who was never going to show her care that was as soft as her fresh skin, cover up my young with decades of attempting to make up for an act that was not unholy, but wholly human.

Instead, I tasted salt and sand, as my daughter tasted her first lick of life and the only people in this world who knew exactly how sacred this was watched by the glow of fire, feeding on night sky and moon, and we all felt ourselves fill up, on who we were, who these nine months had made us, and I could feel that, in all the regrets we might have had, this—us, here—would never be one of them.

As though all singularly possessed, we each looked down at our babies' faces, dimpling and delicate and so new, and thought, *I wouldn't change a thing.* Because I was this child's mother, and all of me—sun and moon, sea and sky, body and bone—would forever stand in the wild truth that I could be mother and child and freed, all at once.

# ACKNOWLEDGMENTS

This book was a joy to write and I owe that in part to the incredible people who talked to me about it, about their own lives, about Florida, and dared to shift the way we think and speak about young motherhood, girlhood, and, ultimately, the task of living a liberated life in a world that seeks to confine us.

First of all, thank you to my brilliant editor, Diana Miller, who approaches every draft with thought, warmth, and a gentle hand. You have taught me to slow down and think deeply about the choices I make for these characters. It is an honor to be edited so deeply and diligently. To my agents, Lucy Carson and Molly Friedrich, thank you for being champions of this book from the very first chapter and approaching it with the ferocity and ambition you always do.

I'm writing this far before even the first meeting with the publicity and marketing team, so I am saddened to not be able to thank you all by name, but please know I am supremely grateful for the amount of emails, calls, and effort you put into introducing the Girls to the world. To whomever creates the cover art, I am sure it is gorgeous and I am always amazed by those who are able to produce image from words. To MacDowell, thank you for the time, space, and quiet to finish this book; there is simply nothing that can feed a writer more than those woods and the artists who commune inside them.

Carolina Ixta, with whom I sat in the same room writing much of this book, thank you for challenging me to work harder, reminding me of why I do this in the first place, and making me laugh when I want to cry. Shannon St. Aubin, you are a constant inspiration and have taught me what it is to mother with pure love and selflessness.

To all of the friends and family in my life, I am tremendously grateful to be seen by you and to share space with you whenever I get the chance. This work is impossible and unsustainable without that love. To the writers and artists who have given me a community to be nourished by—especially Cleyvis Natera, Nicole Dennis-Benn, Kearra Amaya Gopee, Cece Jordan, and Cava Menzies—thank you for your being and your work.

Most importantly, because this book doesn't exist without you, thank you to each of the girls and women who have been generous enough to allow me to hear your stories, learn from you, and, most of all, witness the love and care with which you mother. Both to the mothers in my life and the ones who have allowed me a window into theirs, it is a radical thing to raise children in a world that often refuses to respect the amount of work, intention, and resource it takes to parent with kindness and love for the little people we get to call ours. I am in awe of you and endlessly grateful for every lesson in not only parenting but girlhood and womanhood and the miracle that comes when we can find refuge in ourselves and each other.

Mo, to grow up with you has been a gift I will be thanking you for for the rest of my life, into motherhood and beyond. Thank you for every meal cooked so I could write this, every hour spent reading and rereading it, and, really, for being my person and my partner and my friend. I love you infinitely. And, lastly, to my future children— let this be a testament that I've been dreaming of you since forever. Know that you will be surrounded by a force of women who love you unapologetically, intentionally, and unconditionally, however and whenever you enter this world.

# A NOTE ABOUT THE AUTHOR

LEILA MOTTLEY is the author of the novel *Nightcrawling,* an Oprah's Book Club pick and a *New York Times* best-seller. *Nightcrawling* was a Best Book of the Year for *The New Yorker, The Washington Post,* the *Los Angeles Times,* the *San Francisco Chronicle, Time,* and NPR. The novel was a winner for First Work of Fiction at the California Book Awards, a finalist for the Lambda Literary Award and the Hurston/Wright Legacy Award, and longlisted for the Booker Prize and PEN/Hemingway Award for Debut Novel. She was born and raised in Oakland, where she continues to live.

# A NOTE ON THE TYPE

This book was set in Adobe Garamond. Designed for the Adobe Corporation by Robert Slimbach, the fonts are based on types first cut by Claude Garamond (ca. 1480–1561). Garamond was a pupil of Geoffroy Tory and is believed to have followed the Venetian models, although he introduced a number of important differences, and it is to him that we owe the letter we now know as "old style." He gave to his letters an elegance and feeling of movement that won him an immediate reputation and the patronage of Francis I of France.

Composed by North Market Street Graphics,
Lancaster, Pennsylvania

Printed and bound by Berryville Graphics,
Berryville, Virginia

Designed by Marisa Nakasone